G000058496

KILL AND RUN

A THORNY ROSE MYSTERY

BY
LAUREN CARR

KILL AND RUN

All Rights Reserved © 2015 by Lauren Carr

Published by Acorn Book Services

No part of this book may be reproduced or transmitted in any form or by any means, graphic, electronic, or mechanical, including photocopying, recording, taping, or by any information storage retrieval system without the written permission of the author.

For information call: 304-995-1295
or Email: writerlaurencarr@gmail.com

This book is a work of fiction. Names, characters, places, and incidents are products of the author's imagination or are used fictitiously. Any resemblance to actual events or locales or persons, living or dead, is entirely coincidental.

Designed by Acorn Book Services

Publication Managed by Acorn Book Services
www.acornbookservices.com
acornbookservices@gmail.com
304-995-1295

Cover designed by Todd Aune
Spokane, Washington
www.projetoonline.com
Cover Photo: LukaTBD@www.fotolia.com

ISBN-10: 0692477152
ISBN-13: 978-0692477151

Published in the United States of America

*To Beagle Bailey, Ziggy,
and (last but not least, by any means) Gnarly!*

My inspirations for the forty-five pound couch potato.

KILL AND RUN

A THORNY ROSE MYSTERY

CAST OF CHARACTERS

(in order of appearance)

Officer Nicholas (Nick) Gates: Pennsylvania State Trooper. Recently married.

Officer Reese Phillips: Pennsylvania State Trooper. Officer Nicholas Gates' training officer.

Cameron Gates: Homicide detective with the Pennsylvania State Police. Recently married Joshua Thornton. Her first husband was Nicholas Gates. She doesn't do weddings or funerals.

Joshua Thornton: Hancock County, West Virginia, Prosecuting Attorney. Commander in the United States Navy (retired). Father of five. Recently married to Cameron Gates.

Irving: Cameron's Maine Coon cat. All black with a white stripe from the top of his head to the very tip of his tail, he has the identical markings of a skunk. He doesn't spray, but he will give you plenty of attitude.

Murphy Thornton: Lieutenant in the United States Navy. Naval Academy graduate. Hand-picked by the Joint Chiefs of Staff to serve as a member of their elite team of Phantoms—Murphy is not your average navy officer. Joshua Thornton's son. Newly wed to Jessica Faraday.

Major Marshall Ford: Member of the Phantom team. Officer in the United States Marines.

Major Seth Monroe: Murphy's training officer in the Phantoms. Officer in the United States Marines.

Tawkeel Said: Member of the Phantom team. With help from American soldiers, his family escaped out of Iraq. He now works for the CIA.

CO: Stands for Commanding Officer. Top Secret/Need to Know classification of the Phantoms prevents Murphy from knowing her actual name. For this reason, he calls her CO (See-O).

Jessica Faraday: Murphy Thornton's lovely bride. Her inheritance from her late grandmother Robin Spencer thrust her into high society.

Spencer/Candi: Jessica Faraday's Shetland sheepdog. With her blue eyes and long bluish fur, she is a blue merle. She has a long way to go in training. Jessica calls her Spencer. Murphy calls her Candi. She answers to Candi.

Newman: Murphy's mixed breed dog. A forty-five pound couch potato, Newman won't bite—unless you try to change the channel on his television.

Tracy Thornton: Joshua Thornton's grown daughter. Her wedding is in one month.

Donny Thornton: Joshua Thornton's seventeen year old son.

Admiral: The Thornton's huge dog—Great Dane-Irish Wolfhound mix.

Special Agent Peter Sanders: An FBI agent who delivers surprising news about Nick's death.

Special Agent Dylan Horrigan: FBI agent. Agent Sander's partner.

Sal Bertonelli: A professional hit man. Has done a lot of work for the Russian mob and the drug cartels.

Special Agent Boris Hamilton: Deputy Chief of the Naval Criminal Investigation Staff, where Murphy serves as military liaison between the civilian staff and the military.

Hillary Koch: Chief of the Naval Criminal Investigation Staff, stationed at the Pentagon. Murphy calls her 'Crotch" due to her unpleasant personality.

Special Agent Susan Archer: Agent with Naval Criminal Investigation Staff.

Wendy: Hillary Koch's administrative assistant.

Special Agent Perry Latimore: Agent with Naval Criminal Investigative Service. Susan Archer's partner.

Admiral Clarence Patterson: Deputy Chairman for the Joint Chiefs of Staff. Navy's Chief of Staff.

Lieutenant Bernard Wu: Homicide detective with the Loudon County Sheriff's Department.

Donna Crenshaw: Murder victim. Petty officer with United States Navy. Single mother to Isadora (Izzy) Crenshaw.

Francine Baxter: Murder victim. Professor at George Mason University. Former army officer. Homeowner of townhouse where crime took place.

Colleen Davis: Murder victim. Unmarried. Elementary school teacher and an authorized Cozy Cook dealer.

Maureen Clark: Murder victim. Housewife with young son (Tommy Clark).

Hannah Price: Murder victim. Engineer. She and her husband own an engineering firm.

Colonel Lincoln Clark: Maureen Clark's husband. Colonel in the United States Army.

Isadora (Izzy) Crenshaw: Donna Crenshaw's thirteen year old daughter. After her mother's death, she has no one.

Tristan Faraday: Jessica Faraday's brother. In his third year of college at George Washington University, he's studying natural science. He's an intellectual and proud of it.

Monique: Tristan Faraday's pet tarantula. She's approximately the size of a luncheon plate—which is big.

Sarah Thornton: Murphy's sister and Joshua Thornton's younger daughter. She's a second year cadet at the Naval Academy.

Natalie Patterson: Admiral Patterson's wife. She is the president of the Naval Officers' Spouses Club.

General Sebastian Graham: Four-star general—hero during the Gulf War. Third generation West Point graduate. He's on a very short list for Chief of Staff of the United States Army.

Paige Graham: General Sebastian Graham's devoted wife. President of the Army Officers' Spouses Club and chair of dozens of clubs and organizations.

Bernie: CO's body guard and chauffeur.

Cecilia Crenshaw: Donna Crenshaw's sister. Specialist in the United States Army. Murder victim.

Dolly Scanlon: General Sebastian Graham's personal assistant—in more ways than one.

General Maxine Raleigh, USAF: Five-star general in the United States Air Force. Chair of the Joint Chiefs of Staff.

Our character is what we do when we think no one is looking.

H. Jackson Brown, Jr., American Author

PROLOGUE

Thirteen Years Ago
Friday, January 24: 10:25 pm
Pennsylvania Turnpike—Roadside Stop West of Pittsburgh

"Man, it's colder than a witch's tit." Pennsylvania trooper Reese Phillips shivered while bringing the steaming hot, freshly-brewed coffee to his lips.

With a grin that stretched across his face, Officer Nicholas Gates asked, "Where do you come up with phrases like that, Phillips? Do you make them up?"

The middle-aged officer looked the young trooper up and down. With the fresh face of a college heart-throb, Nick Gates was little more than a rookie.

"Don't tell me you never heard that one, Gates," Officer Phillips grumbled. "You're killing me."

Chuckling, the two men made their way to the cashier to pay for their coffees.

"Half hour more and I'll be checking out to go home and climb into bed with Rufus." Officer Phillips shot a wicked glance over his shoulder at his trainee. "Wipe that grin off your face, Gates. My hound dog may not be as pretty as your sweet bride, but he doesn't complain when I snore either."

"Neither does Cameron," Officer Gates replied.

"She's never heard my snoring."

"I'm referring to mine," the young officer laughed.

"She will. They all do." Officer Phillips handed the cashier a five dollar bill. "This one's on me, Gates. Next will be your turn."

Officer Gates slipped his money back into his wallet and picked up the coffee he had set down on the counter in order to pay. "Hey, Phillips, do you still have that contact with the FBI?"

Officer Phillips had to think a moment while they strolled toward the door that led out into the sub-zero temperature. "Do you mean Hatfield? He used to be with the Pennsylvania state police and then joined the FBI."

"He works in Quantico now, right?"

Bracing themselves for the blast of icy air, they pushed open the doors and stepped outside.

"Yes," Officer Phillips said, "Why? You looking to move on already?"

"I was wondering if he'd be able to look through their national database for a missing person."

Too cold to continue talking, the two men ran in opposite directions for their cruisers.

"I'll have his number for you tomorrow," Phillips yelled above the howling wind.

With a wave of his hand to acknowledge that he heard him, Officer Gates climbed into his cruiser. On the other side of the parking lot, Officer Phillips spotted a sedan speeding past the rest stop at top speed. Before the older man could react, Officer Gates turned on his flashing lights and gave chase.

"Yeah," Officer Phillips sighed while enjoying the warmth of his hot coffee in the comfort of his patrol car. "Leave it to the young ones."

A pair of headlights bathed the compartment of his patrol car with its high beams. A black truck followed Gates' cruiser out onto the turnpike.

Officer Nicholas Gates checked the time on the dash-board clock while calling in to dispatch the description and tag numbers of the speeding sedan. Ten twenty-eight in the evening. Another half hour and he'd be heading home to curl up in a warm bed with the love of his life.

A recent graduate of the police academy, Cameron was on her way to joining the state police. They were the perfect pair. Life was grand.

Bracing himself against the cold wind and the speeding cars on the turnpike, Nick opened the door and stepped out of the cruiser. Keeping a close eye on the sedan, he approached the driver's side window. The young woman behind the steering wheel had the window down and was waiting for him. As he approached, he could hear muffled sobs.

He shone his flashlight into the darkened car. "Your license and registration please." The flashlight beam caught the tears in her eyes. "Are you okay, ma'am?"

"No." She handed her driver's license and registration to him. "My father is going to kill me."

"I'm sure it's not that bad." Nick checked over the documentation. She was sixteen years old. "I clocked you at t hirteen miles over the speed limit."

"Because my curfew is eleven o'clock. I was out at the mall by the airport with my friends. Now, not only am I going to miss curfew, but I'm going to have my first speeding ticket, too." She hiccupped.

She could have been faking. She could have been using her pretty face to charm him out of a speeding ticket. She probably was. Nick considered how long it would take to write up the ticket. It was freezing and he really wanted to get home.

Nick handed the documentation to her. "Tonight's your lucky night."

Her mouth dropped open. "Really?"

"I'm letting you off with a warning. You need to slow down. Better to get home late and safe than to not get home at all," he said. "Do you understand?"

She nodded her head vigorously. "Oh," she gushed, "you are the sweetest cop I ever met. I could kiss you!"

The last thing she saw was his brilliant smile filling his handsome face seconds before the black truck speeding down the turnpike swerved off the road to plow down Officer Nicholas Gates.

CHAPTER ONE

Present Day
Rock Springs Boulevard, Chester, West Virginia

His hands felt warm on her flesh. His breath was hot and heavy on her neck. Arching her back to press her body against his, Cameron prayed that this moment, this instant, the euphoria of being so connected to the man she loved could be frozen in time so that it would last forever.

Her breathing quickened and deepened. Her head spinning with ecstasy, she dug her fingers into his flesh. Tightening his grip around her waist, he pulled her hips ever closer into him. "Come with me, babe!" he breathed in a husky voice into her hair.

Breathless, all she could do was hold on tight. Their bodies rose and fell in sync. Lovingly rubbing his back—still hot with passion—Cameron recalled how they had been in sync since the first instant they met.

Exhausted, he collapsed onto her.

"I love you," she whispered into his ear.

Rising up, he gazed into her face. "Love you, too, babe."

The moonlight shining through the glass doors leading out onto the verandah shone on his blond hair. A wide grin filled his boyish face.

Cameron felt as if the breath had been sucked out of her body with one glance into his brown eyes.

Nick! No! But you're dead! Unable to form the words—her mouth hung open.

Fear filling every fiber of her being, she glanced across the bed to where Joshua, her husband was sound asleep.

No, this isn't happening! Unable to speak, she tried to push him away.

He grasped her by the arms and held her still. His eyes met hers. Even in the dark, she could see them clearly. They weren't filled with malevolence or hurt or even betrayal at her moving on to a new life with another man.

Insistence. Conviction. That was what she saw.

"You're not finished with me yet, babe."

"No!" Cameron sprang up straight in the bed.

With a screech, Irving, her twenty-five pound Maine Coon cat leapt from the bed where he had been curled up against his mistress's legs to the dresser where he growled at the sudden interruption to his sleep.

Joshua Thornton sat up an instant after her. "Cam!" He grabbed her arm.

Thinking she was still trapped in the nightmare with her late husband, she swung around to fight off the ghost with a slap to the face.

Seeing her hysteria, Joshua ducked in time so the slap flew over his head. "Cam! It's me! Josh!" He tried to reach for her but she was out of the bed. "Wake up!"

His voice broke through her terror.

Heaving deep breaths, she gazed at her husband of a year, reaching out for her. The dim light of the bedroom caught on his silver hair falling in layered waves to his neck and his closely trimmed auburn beard and mustache. She could see the blue hue of his eyes pleading for her to wake up.

"Josh," she said in a hushed voice.

With a sigh of relief, he held out his hand to her. "That's right, darling. Come back to bed."

She welcomed the warmth of his touch when he grasped her fingers. When she climbed back into the bed, he enveloped her against his firm chest and caressed her head. She welcomed the sound of his heart beating against her ear.

"Want to tell me about your dream?" he asked into her hair.

"No." She rubbed her face against his bare chest. "Promise me that nothing bad will ever happen to you—that things will always be like they are now—at this moment."

Joshua tightened his arms around her. He took a whiff of her cinnamon colored hair. "You know I can't promise that."

"Lie to me." She brushed his chest with her fingertips. "Isn't that the first thing they teach you in law school?"

"You're rotten."

They chuckled together in the darkness, then fell back into silence.

"Promise me, Josh," she whispered.

"I promise that I won't let anything bad happen to me," he said, "Things will never change between us. They will always be like they are right now—this very second."

With a deep sigh, she drifted off to sleep.

Seeing that things had calmed down, Irving leapt back onto the bed and proceeded to knead the covers to remake his bed before beginning the arduous process of smoothing his long hair back into place. Joshua thought, not for the first time, how much Irving's markings resembled a skunk.

"Who invited you?" Joshua asked the cat in a whisper.

"Sshh," Cameron replied, clinging to him tighter. In an effort to be as close to him as possible, she wrapped her legs around his.

As if in response to him, Irving turned around to aim his rear in Joshua's direction before hitching his butt with his long black and white tail up high in the air and laying down on Cameron's side of the bed.

Joshua read it as a feline version of mooning him.

No respect.

The Mall on Washington, DC: Sunrise

The Nation's Capital doesn't wait for the sun. In the early hours, shortly before the moon relinquished the day to the sun, hordes of commuters were already migrating into and around the city in cars, SUVs, carpool vans, and buses.

Underground, the metro subway trains were packed with sleepy-eyed passengers quietly gearing up for their day. Trying to catch one more minute of solitude, the fares on the blue line abruptly woke up and moved out of the way when a muscle-bound, bald man in camouflaged pants crashed through the connecting door and plowed through passengers blocking his path down the middle of the train. With very little space to escape, some passengers grumbled and cursed until the door slid open again.

A young man with dark hair dressed in black slacks and a black t-shirt that hugged his lean, firm muscles hurdled a row of briefcases. Strapped around his hips was a gun holster packing a Sig Sauer DAK pistol. "Stop! Federal Agent!"

"Smithsonian Station," the speaker overhead announced.

Seemingly more interested in getting to work than stopping a suspected felon, the passengers stood up and moved to the doors—blocking the agent's pursuit of his quarry.

Craning his neck and dodging the passengers in his way, he searched the faces and forms moving between him and the end of the car where he saw the shiny top of a bald head waiting at the exit.

"Stop!" the young man screamed. "You're under arrest." In seconds, the doors would open to allow his target to escape out into the station packed with commuters. Unable to make it down the center aisle, he attempted to climb over the seats in a vain effort to capture him before the doors opened.

The train screeched to a halt.

The agent grabbed the overhead hand rail to catch himself. When his feet, encased in combat boots, slipped, he dropped into a seat filled with an overweight woman, who didn't welcome his company.

"How rude!" She shoved him to the floor before whacking him with her heavy purse.

The doors flew open.

Even while he was carried away by the mob out the doors, the agent didn't lose sight of the bald man. When the subway train doors slammed shut, their eyes met out on the platform. The two men stood forty feet from each other with the sea of commuters swarming around them.

With a cocky grin, the bald-headed man winked at his pursuer before whirling around and racing up the escalator—shoving people out of his way to make it to the top.

"Halt! You're under arrest!" the young man in black was right on his heels. At the top of the stairs, the bald man yanked a crate of fresh newspapers over to send that day's news scattering down the escalator. Some of the pages caught in the wind created by the speeding trains to fly like paper airplanes through the metro stop.

At a dead run, the suspect in camouflage pants took off across the grass in the direction of the Museum of Natural History.

His pursuer easily hurdled the stacks of newspapers. Keeping his target in sight, he sprinted across the grass until they hit the tree-lined street where the bald man disappeared behind a bus. Crossing the street, the young man caught a glimpse of his target ducking into an alley-way behind the museum—half a block away.

"Got you, you cretin!" Pumping his legs as hard as he could, he ran for the alley. Stopping at the corner, he extracted his gun from the holster.

Ready to fire, he turned the corner to see the bald-man waiting halfway down the length of the alley. The culprit was not alone. He shielded his body with a shrieking woman clad from head to toe in a burka. As he pressed the barrel of his gun against her temple, the woman hysterically babbled in a foreign language.

Though he could not understand the words, the young man understood the tone. She was pleading for him to not let her die.

"Put down the gun!" His gun aimed at his target, the young man moved steadily toward them.

"One step closer and I'll kill her!"

"And then I'll kill you. The only way this is going to end well is if you let her go. Then we can talk about this."

"No talk," he replied. "All you westerners do is lie."

"So you want to kill us infidels," the slender young man said. "I get that. But she's one of yours, why take her with you?"

"She's just a worthless woman," the bald-headed man said with a sneer. "I really don't care if she lives or dies." He chuckled. "But you care—because you're weak just like all you infidels."

With only her eyes visible, the woman shrieked and babbled.

"Throw down your gun or she dies!"

Releasing his grip on the gun, the young man tossed the gun to the ground.

The bald man laughed. "Kick it to me."

Holding both of his hands up, the young man shrugged his shoulders and kicked the gun to him.

The bald man took his eyes off the agent in black to see where the gun landed. In that instant, when he had dropped his guard a hair, the young man pounced.

Doing a shoulder-roll to drop below the gunman's line of fire, the young man burst to his feet directly in front of the gunman. Grabbing the weapon, he jerked it away from the woman's head. The gunman, too stunned to react, could only blink at the surprise attack.

Spinning on his heels, the man in black shoved the woman out of the way before wresting the weapon out of the gunman's grip and twisted the now-empty hand behind the bald man's back. He gave a quick kick to the back of the gunman's knee before bringing his own knee up to press into the assailant's spine.

Shocked by the impact, the gunman fell forward. Keeping his knee in contact with the gunman's spine, the young man locked the gunman's arm firmly behind his back.

It happened so fast that the gunman was face down in the alley before he knew what was happening.

"You're under arrest!" the agent announced to his captive. Over his shoulder, he called to the woman. "Are you okay?"

The hostage's answer started with the click of a gun.

Before he could react, the young man in black felt a barrage of bullets hit him in the back. He collapsed on top of his target.

"Get off of me, Thornton." Pushing the agent over onto his back, the bald man, Major Marshall Ford climbed up onto his knees.

"Damn," Thornton breathed.

"Lieutenant Murphy Thornton, what did you do wrong?" the deep voice of Major Seth Monroe came from the other side of the alley.

Rubbing the wet red paint that now soaked the back of his shirt to make it cling to him, Murphy groaned while climbing up to his feet. "I dropped my guard towards the hostage. I assumed she was an innocent bystander."

"You didn't even look closely enough at her to see that she was a *he*," Major Monroe said with a laugh.

When the major stepped aside, Murphy saw that the hostage had dropped the burka to reveal that he was in reality a slightly built young man who appeared to be of Middle-Eastern descent. Murphy recognized him from seeing him in the corridors at the Pentagon. Unlike Murphy, Major Monroe, and Major Marshall Ford, he was most certainly a civilian.

"You know Farsi?" Murphy asked him.

"Tawkeel Said was born in Iraq," Major Monroe said. "He's fluent in practically every language in the Middle East. Tawkeel, this is Lieutenant Murphy Thornton."

Moving his semi-automatic rifle, configured to carry paint balls instead of real bullets, to his other hand, Tawkeel offered his hand for Murphy to shake. "I think we met."

With a quizzical expression, Murphy shook his hand. "No, I don't think so. I've seen you around the Pentagon. State Department?"

"CIA." Tawkeel helped pull him to his feet. "I could have sworn we met someplace before. I'm sorry I had to shoot you in the back."

"Did you have to fire so many shots?" Murphy felt the paint from the paintballs seeping down his back to his underwear. He tried to loosen his shirt from his back. "That close? I'm going to have welts on my back for days."

"Better for you to remember not to let your guard down," Major Monroe said.

"The whole purpose of this training exercise is to learn," Tawkeel said. "If I was an extremist, I would have unloaded the whole clip and then doused your body in gasoline and set you on fire."

Murphy recognized the cold hard glare in Tawkeel's eyes. He was talking from first-hand experience.

"Tawkeel's father was a contractor who worked behind the scenes to help the American military during the Gulf War," the major explained.

"And he was in Iraq?" Murphy turned to Tawkeel. "Your father was one brave man. If he had been caught helping us, he would have been killed on the spot."

"Tawkeel's family formed friendships with some of the Americans and eventually converted to Christianity," the major said.

"Which sealed our family's fate for execution," Tawkeel said. "My mother's parents poisoned her during a family dinner. My father begged her not to visit them, but she insisted—she trusted them. As soon as he found out that she was dead, Father hurried my brothers and sisters and me out of our home with only the clothes on our backs. We hid in caves in the desert for two days and nights until some of Father's American friends in the military were able to slip into the country and get us out one step ahead of the death squad hunting for us. I was only eight years old, but I still remember everything about that like it was yesterday. Those Americans, three men and two women, risked their lives to save us." With a slight bow, he concluded, "For that, I am eternally grateful to this country."

"The operation was done off the grid," Major Monroe whispered to Murphy. "After being brought to the United States, Tawkeel's father helped to bring down Saddam Hussein. Tawkeel himself has been immensely valuable to the CIA, not to mention our team, in gathering intel from inside the country. Knowing the languages and customs and how they operate, he's managed to give us a leg up in our operations."

"I'm glad you're on our side." Murphy accepted Tawkeel's offer of a towel to wipe off the red paint from his clothes and back.

"You're lucky," the silver haired major turned his attention to Murphy. "You got shot up with paint. Seven weeks ago, three marines got cut in half by a machine gun when they dropped their guard around who they thought was a harmless woman in a burka. *He* was really an ISIS soldier."

"Understood, sir," Murphy replied. "Won't happen again, sir." He pulled his shirt off over his head to clean up the paint dripping down his back.

"Better not." Taking the towel from him, the major directed him to turn around while he wiped down his back. "You're too valuable to the Phantoms to lose due to a newbie mistake." With a glance up and down the alley, he ordered Tawkeel and Major Ford, "We need to get this cleaned up before the tourists start nosing around. I'll be contacting you about the next training mission."

Cleaned up as much as possible for the time being, Murphy put his shirt back on and picked up the gun he had dropped. He was wiping the dirt from the alley off it. Before holstering his weapon, he felt the major's hand clasp his shoulder.

"That was a very impressive move you made with the shoulder roll to catch Ford off guard," the major said in a low voice. "I had read in your file that you know gymnastics, but I've never seen an agent who put it to use in the field."

"Just a little something extra that I like to keep in my arsenal, sir," Murphy said.

"That and your sixth-degree black belt in mixed martial arts." The major looked the young navy officer up and down.

Two years out of the Naval Academy, Lieutenant Murphy Thornton was still green in many ways. For him, youth was not only an advantage, but also a disadvantage. While he still had a lot to learn, he had a fire in his belly when it came to pride in serving his country—a fire that had gone out for many people in Washington—including some at the very top ranks of government. What Murphy lacked in age and experience, he more than made up for in a quick wit, integrity, skill, natural talent, and passion to protect his country and her people. That was what put Lieutenant Murphy Thornton on track to becoming one of the Phantoms' top agents.

Aware of the morning sun rising in the sky, Murphy waited patiently for Major Monroe, the ranking officer and leader of the nighttime training exercise, to dismiss him. Instead of doing so, the marine officer asked, "How are things going at your current assignment as military liaison with criminal investigations, Lieutenant?"

"Fine, sir," Murphy replied, before adding, "Anxious to get back out in the field, sir. I know that's not your decision, but if you can pass that onto my CO, I would greatly appreciate it."

The older man furrowed his silver eyebrows. "But you just got married ... how long ago?"

Murphy said. "Celebrated our four month anniversary last week, sir. We moved into our new house that same weekend."

"I heard," the major said. "National Harbor."

"Brownstown with a view of the Washington Monument from our rooftop."

"I'd expect you to want to be home with your lovely young bride every night." One of the major's eyebrows arched.

"I do," Murphy said with a sigh.

"Is anything wrong, Lieutenant?"

"No, sir," Murphy said while shifting from one foot to the other. "I guess ... I'm just not meant to be cooped up behind a desk, sir."

"Like father, like son," the major grumbled. "Well, no need to worry. With your talent and abilities, you won't be cooped up for long. Just be patient."

"I will, sir." Murphy cast a glance to his cell phone to check the time. "If I may, sir, I need to go home to clean up and check into the office. We have a ten o'clock briefing and my supervisor in criminal investigations doesn't like it when I'm late."

"You did tell her that you were in training this morning, didn't you?"

"Yes, sir." Murphy gritted his teeth in order to not reveal his supervisor's reaction to that news.

For a long moment, the two men held each other's gaze. The set of the young man's firm jaw seemed to say what he did not want to express in words. "You are excused then, Lieutenant."

The sunny spring day, with the breeze off the Potomac River, tempted Murphy to take the day off to spend lazing along the river bank across the street from their new home with his "lovely bride" as the major had referred to her.

Murphy would be the last to argue with that assessment.

With her lush raven hair and violet eyes, Jessica Faraday was every man's fantasy—most of all his. Four months earlier,

Murphy was ready to propose thirty seconds after meeting the daughter of multi-millionaire Mac Faraday. Less than forty-eight hours later, she was his wife.

Some days, Murphy didn't feel like his feet had touched ground yet—except when he was sitting behind his desk in the Pentagon where he had been assigned as the military liaison to the Naval Criminal Investigative Service.

It was true, if his CO sent him back out into the field for an assignment, it would mean time away from Jessica. But there were some days when he looked out the window and ached to escape—especially when his supervisor was eyeballing him with her beady, dark eyes.

After turning off National Harbor Boulevard, Murphy eased his motorcycle into the townhouse development and rolled it down the hill to where their end unit brownstone rested along a grassy area in the corner. They were a short walk across a footbridge from the Potomac River.

As soon as he came into view of the two-car garage, Murphy pressed the button on the remote to open the door. Without stopping, he coasted the motorcycle into the garage and turned to park it next to his black SUV, a shiny GMC Yukon that Jessica had given him for a wedding present. Jessica's purple Ferrari took up the second car space.

After taking off his motorcycle helmet, Murphy opened the door leading into the recreation room to find Spencer, Jessica's sheltie, a blue merle, waiting on the other side. Murphy called her Candi, which annoyed Jessica—especially when the dog answered to Candi, while refusing to respond to the name Jessica had given her—Spencer.

Her blue eyes wide, the year-old dog was squirming with excitement. Her fluffy blue tail wagged so hard that it looked like it was going to fly off her butt. Placing his finger to his lips, Murphy gestured for her to remain silent before bending over to pat her on the head. Pawing the floor, Spencer looked like she was about to burst with joy.

Finally, Murphy held out his arms. Squirming with delight, Spencer leapt up into his arms to lick his face. "Is your mother still in bed?" he whispered to her. Spencer stopped licking to look into his face. Her blue eyes were filled with question.

After setting the dog down, Murphy sat on the arm of the sofa bed—still filled with half-unpacked moving boxes—to take off his boots and socks. "Where's your mommy?"

Spencer's ears perked up, though the very tops remained flopped over. She cocked her head at him.

"Mommy?"

When she uttered the start of a yap, he shook his head while making a shushing noise. "Take me to Mommy."

Spencer raced around the assortment of moving boxes that littered the recreation room before running up the stairs. While following her up the stairs to the living room, Murphy pulled his shirt off over his head.

On the main level, instead of taking the next set of stairs to the third floor, Spencer first detoured across the living room. Sailing from one side of a faded, overstuffed chair to the other, the dog hit the floor, made a U-turn back to the stairs, and bounded up to the master suite on the floor above.

Curled up in the overstuffed chair, Newman, Murphy's forty-five pound black and white mongrel—who resembled a cross between a Bassett hound and a half dozen other breeds—lifted his head at the sudden interruption to his morning nap. Upon seeing Murphy, he let out a deep sigh and tapped the television remote with his front paw.

On his way up to the next level, Murphy heard the television station switch from the Cartoon Network to a cable news channel.

The third level contained two bedrooms. One was the guest bedroom, behind a closed door on the left. The door at the end of the small hallway on the right was ajar.

Squirming with excitement, Spencer silently waited outside the door for Murphy to catch up.

Peering through the crack of the door, Murphy saw that she was sound asleep. She had promised to remain awake all night—waiting for his return.

Knew she couldn't do it.

Patting his thigh with his hand, Murphy gestured for Spencer to heel when he pressed open the door to ease through. Gazing up at him with adoration, the sheltie entered the room in step with him.

At the foot of the bed, Spencer raised her front paws as if to jump up onto the bed. Murphy held up his hand in a stop signal. With a stern expression, he gestured at the window seat that looked out toward the river.

Spencer's ears fell back in disappointment, Murphy bent over to pat her on the head and scratch her ears. His touch alone was enough to restore her happiness. With a bounce in her step, she jumped up onto the cushioned seat and laid down.

Murphy snuck over to his side of the bed. In silence, he watched his bride's chest rise and fall with each breath. Her long, dark eyelashes brushed across the top of her cheeks, which were flushed from the warmth generated by the comforter.

How he missed her during their nights apart.

He unbuttoned his black pants and eased the zipper down. Careful to suppress the rustle of the material against his skin, he slid his pants down over his thighs before allowing them to pool at his feet. Slipping his underwear down over his hips to join his pants on the floor, he stepped out of his clothes and slid under the covers.

The heat of her body beckoned him to slide across the king-sized bed to press his firm body against hers. Placing his hand on her bare hip, he gently kissed her shoulder.

Without opening her eyes, she said "My husband is going to be home any minute."

"Guess this means it'll have to be a quickie." He brushed her hair back to expose an ear. After kissing it, he whispered, "That's okay. I've got a ten o'clock meeting anyway."

With a wicked grin, she rolled over to pin him down by the shoulders. Under the covers, she pressed one of her thighs against his erection. Arching an eyebrow over one of her sensuous violet eyes, Jessica said, "I don't do quickies."

CHAPTER TWO

Rock Springs Boulevard, Chester, West Virginia

"Cameron's not up yet?" Holding a plate of hash browns and Eggs Benedict, Tracy Thornton looked at the empty kitchen chair on her father's left as if to ascertain that she was correct about Cameron not sitting in it.

Without looking up, Joshua Thornton continued scrolling through the news on his computer tablet. "She didn't sleep well last night so I didn't wake her up."

"She's not working on a case, is she?" Tracy slapped her seventeen year-old brother Donny's hand when he tried to take the plate of food she had meant for her stepmother. "I was hoping that she'd go to the bridal shop with me and Belle to pick out dresses for the wedding." After setting the plate in front of Cameron's chair, she dropped into the seat on her father's other side. "I know Cameron's not my mother, but as your wife, she is pretty much the mother of the bride. Hunter's mom has picked out a lovely dress. It's teal blue and Cameron likes blue."

The corner of Joshua's mouth curled up. "Have you ever seen Cameron wear teal?"

"She doesn't like to wear any colors that aren't found in nature," Donny said around a mouthful of the Eggs Benedict and hash browns he stole by sliding the plate down the table to his seat.

Shooting a chastising glare in her brother's direction, Tracy asked Joshua, "Cameron is coming to the wedding, isn't she? She said—"

"She said she'd *try.*" Joshua laid his hand on top of hers. "Honey, put yourself in her place. You and Hunter are having this lavish wedding. You've been planning it for a year. I can see that you love Hunter with all your heart. He's the love of your life."

Happy tears came to Tracy's lovely blue eyes.

"Now," Joshua continued gently. "Imagine four months after that wedding, you end up back in that same church, with all of those same people for Hunter's funeral."

"Dad ..."

"She's making an effort," Joshua said. "She hasn't said no, and that's a big step for her."

"Dad, the wedding is a month away," Tracy said. "I need a commitment of yes or no." With a pout, she crossed her arms. "Frankly, I don't see why she can't just get over it. She got over her first husband enough to marry you. What's with this garbage about not doing weddings? You two had a wedding—or so I heard since I wasn't invited."

Clenching his teeth, Joshua dropped the tablet he was reading down onto the table.

"I was there," Donny said before eating another forkful of the eggs.

Tracy shot a glare in her brother's direction.

"That wasn't a wedding," Joshua said. "We eloped. There's a big difference between a lavish ceremony with gowns and tuxes and flowers and hundreds of guests and rolling out of bed, putting on your pants and running over to the church to get hitched before lunch."

"Then going to Cricksters for ice cream," Donny said. "I texted you the picture of their wedding sundae. It was huge." He held out his hands to illustrate the size.

"Yes," she bit out. "I got your text, Donny."

Joshua folded his arms across his chest. "If anyone needs to get over anything, you need to get over our eloping."

"What is everyone going to think if my new stepmother doesn't come to my wedding?" Tracy asked. "This is as much about our family as it is about me and my wedding."

"I thought it was Hunter's wedding, too," Donny said.

This time, Tracy added a snarl to the glare she shot across the table to Donny.

Patting Tracy's hand, Joshua said, "She knows how important this is to you."

"Murphy and Jessica have already RSVP'd," Tracy said. "I can't wait to meet Jessica."

"*You* didn't go to *their* wedding," Donny said around a mouthful of hash browns. "Murphy's not holding that against you. You were the only one of us kids not there."

"Your sister Sarah made it to Deep Creek Lake from the Naval Academy to be maid of honor," Joshua said. "J.J. rushed there from Penn State to be Murphy's best man—"

"J.J. is Murphy's twin," Tracy said. "There was no way he'd miss Murphy's wedding."

"J.J. even brought a date," Donny said with a chuckle. "The only one of us five kids who didn't show was you."

The sound of the front doorbell prompted Admiral, the Thornton's Irish wolfhound and Great Dane mix to jump to his enormous feet with a deep bark and gallop for the door. The ruckus woke up Irving where he was asleep on a windowsill, who joined the welcoming committee.

"Like I could get to Maryland from New York on New Year's Eve with twelve hours' notice." Tracy turned in her chair to counter Donny's quip. Seeing that he had finished off the stolen breakfast, she said, "Dad, do you see what he did? Donny ate the breakfast I made for Cameron."

"You snooze, you lose." Joshua got up from the table to answer the door.

In the foyer, he peered through the frosted, cut glass in the door. Two men in suits were taking in the view from the wrap-around porch of the three-story, stone house. The porch provided a view of the rolling front yard which ended at the corner of Fifth Street.

When Joshua opened the door a crack, the two men turned around. "May I help you?" He kept one hand on the door while holding his dog back. While Admiral was basically a coward, his huge size was enough to intimidate strangers.

"Are you Joshua Thornton?" the older of the two gentlemen asked. They both displayed their badges designating them as agents with the Federal Bureau of Investigation.

"Yes." Allowing Admiral to stroll out onto the porch, Joshua reached out to take both badges in hand and examine them. After determining they were authentic, he handed them back. "What is this about?"

"We'd like to speak to your wife," said the older agent.

"She's—"

Behind him, Cameron interrupted his response. "Who is it, Josh?"

"The FBI, dear. They want to talk to you." Stepping back, Joshua allowed them into the foyer.

Dressed in faded jeans and a light v-necked sweater, Cameron came down the stairs. "What'd I do now?"

The older agent reached out his hand to shake hers. "I'm Special Agent Peter Sanders. This is my partner, Special Agent

Dylan Horrigan." He glanced around the two-story foyer. "Is there some place we can talk?"

"What about?" Joshua asked.

"This is a matter concerning your wife," Special Agent Horrigan replied.

"Anything you want to discuss with me, you can discuss in front of my husband," Cameron said.

"This has to do with your first husband," Agent Sanders said. "Pennsylvania State Trooper Nicolas Gates."

Cameron grasped Joshua's hand and squeezed it. He took her hand into both of his. "We can talk in my study."

As if to lead the way, Irving trotted ahead of them into the study. Spotting the cat for the first time, Special Agent Horrigan stopped. "Is that—"

"He's a cat," Joshua said.

"Then he's not going to spray me," the agent sighed.

"But he will give you plenty of bad attitude."

In Joshua's study, Irving jumped up into Cameron's lap as soon as she sat on the sofa. After closing the door, Joshua took the seat next to her and clasped her hand.

She opened the conversation by saying, "I would ask if you came to tell me that you found the driver who ran Nick down, but hit and runs aren't federal cases—even if a state police officer is killed. So what is this about?"

Special Agent Sanders leaned forward in his seat across from her. "Actually, we're here to tell you that we have the man who ran your late husband down in custody."

Shooting Joshua a weak smile, Cameron sighed.

Joshua squeezed her shoulders and kissed her forehead.

Fighting back tears, Cameron swallowed. "I knew that one day—eventually, we'd get him."

"I'm afraid it's not that simple," the senior agent said.

"Something told me it wasn't," Joshua said. "Like she asked, what interest would the FBI have in a simple hit and run?"

"It wasn't a simple hit and run," Agent Horrigan said. "It was a paid hit with your husband Nicolas Gates as the target."

Cameron's head shot up. "Why? Who would pay to have Nick killed?"

"We were hoping you could tell us," Special Agent Horrigan said.

"How did you come by that information?" Joshua asked.

Agent Sanders explained, "Last week, we arrested Sal Bertonelli, a professional hit man with a list of assassinations going back over twenty years. This guy was good. He mostly worked for the Russian mob. He's also done some important hits for major drug cartels. He's turned government witness in exchange for immunity. He's testifying against the top echelon of organized crime in the country."

"Part of the bargain was for him to give us a list of murders for pay that he has committed," Agent Horrigan said. "Pennsylvania State Trooper Nick Gates was on that list."

Cameron stared at one of them and then the other. When she found her voice, she asked, "Why would the Russian mob or a drug cartel want to kill Nick?"

"We were hoping you could tell us that," Agent Sanders replied.

"What does Bertonelli say?" Joshua asked.

"He never asked any questions," Agent Horrigan said. "That's why he was so popular with the mob. He just took the orders and collected his pay. He was ordered to make Trooper Gates' murder look like an accident. He was tailing him and saw him pull over a car for speeding—ripe for a hit and run."

"Was your husband working any cases involving organized crime or major drug dealers?" Agent Sanders asked Cameron.

"No," she blurted out. "He was a patrolman. Yes, he wanted to work up to detective, but he wasn't working any cases on his own. He …" Speechless, she turned to Joshua.

Seeing tears in her eyes, Joshua rubbed her back and told the agents in a quiet tone. "As you can tell, this is a big shock for my wife. Can you leave your card with us—"

"I want to talk to him," Cameron said in a surprisingly strong voice.

"I'm afraid—" Agent Sanders started to say.

"He killed my husband," Cameron said. "He and whoever hired him took away someone who was very dear to me. That night, my life changed forever. It was never the same from the very second that bastard ran down Nick. I have the right to a face to face with him to find out the name of the monster who ordered him to kill my husband and why."

"We have him in protective custody in Washington, D.C.," Agent Sanders argued.

"Both the Russian mob and the drug cartels have already put out contracts on him," Agent Horrigan said.

"I'm going to Washington," Cameron said.

"You're awfully dressed up for unpacking and doing laundry," Murphy noted when he went into the kitchen to find Jessica dressed in a pale violet suit with matching four-inch heels and hat. The fitted suit was cinched tightly with a belt to flatter her slender curves and small waist. The skirt was short enough to provide an impressive view of her long legs, which Murphy took in with a grin while she poured coffee into a mug. His green tea was steeping in a United States Naval Academy mug on the counter next to the coffeemaker.

41

"I'm taking a friend to the Four Seasons for lunch." She turned around to offer him the tea. With a sigh, she mused at him in his stark white uniform with four rows of ribbons over his left breast. *Man, I love a man in uniform … especially this one.*

"A friend?" Murphy took a cautious sip of the tea. "Are you seeing Amy?" As soon as he asked, he shook his own head at the suggestion. "She works across from the White House. Four Seasons is too far away for her to make it on her lunch hour."

"Not only that, but Amy's working on a huge project right now," she said. "But I made her promise to make time for lunch next week." She cleared her throat. "Speaking of Amy …"

Narrowing his eyes into blue slits, Murphy set down the mug to brace himself. "Remember what I said last time."

"Then we need to think of an excuse because it's only a matter of time before Amy suggests another double date," Jessica said.

"Why do we need to think of an excuse?" Murphy yanked open the refrigerator door and took out a bowl of strawberries. He slammed the bowl down onto the counter with such force that Spencer, who had been sitting next to Jessica's feet, jumped up with her tail between her legs. "Why can't we just say no?"

"Because Amy is my best friend," Jessica explained at his elbow while he ate one berry after another from the bowl. "How can I tell her that you can't stand her husband?"

"It isn't that I can't stand him." Murphy examined a dark spot on a rather large berry to determine if he wanted to eat it as is, or cut out the spot before doing so. "Okay, I guess I can't stand him. I can't have any respect for a man who mooches off women." He decided to toss it down the garbage disposal.

"He's an author," she said while fighting the grin working its way to her lips.

Laughing, Murphy pointed his index finger at her while clutching a strawberry in the palm of his hand. "You can't even say that with a straight face."

She burst out laughing.

"Don't you have to *write* a book before you can call yourself an *author?*" he asked.

"He's working on it."

"How long has he been working on this book?" While they were talking, Murphy held up a strawberry for her. Like an obedient child waiting for her medicine, she opened her mouth and he tossed the fruit in. "Between his YouTube blog where he rants about whatever happens to be on his tiny mind that day—which is usually some computer game— hanging out at the Irish Pub with his other writer wannabe friends, and spending his wife's money, he doesn't have time to work on a book. He's too busy *playing* author. The guy is at least ten years older than I am. Has he ever had a full time job?"

"No," she said around the strawberry in her mouth before chewing and swallowing it. "Amy told me about a year ago that he started this book his second year of college. I assume he was nineteen then."

"If he's ten years older than I am ..." Berry poised to pop into his mouth, Murphy paused to calculate in his head. "We're talking over a decade ... for him to write one book ... without having to juggle employment or housework—since they have a housekeeper and they have no kids, so he isn't bothered with any of that—the guy's a leech living off his wife's money." He tossed the strawberry into his mouth.

"Amy's one of my best friends, Murphy." Jessica wrapped her arms around his waist and gazed up into his eyes. "Sure, she's married to a pretentious leech, but *she's* the sweetest—"

"I have no problem with Amy." Murphy backed away from her and returned the bowl of berries to the refrigerator. "I'm glad she's your friend and I encourage you to spend time with her, but don't ask me to get up close and personal with her deadbeat husband." He slammed the refrigerator door shut. "I don't expect you to run for president of the Navy Officers' Spouses Club. I didn't even ask you to join."

Jessica folded her arms across her chest. "I wanted to join because I'm proud to be your wife. I'm proud to be married to a navy officer and I want to share in it. I've been learning a lot from the other wives about what I've gotten myself into."

"We're talking about apples and oranges," he said. "You *want* to learn about the navy and get buddy-buddy with the other navy wives. I've learned all I care to about Dean and I'm not going to spend any of our evenings out with him." When she opened her mouth to respond, he held up his hand to signal a stop. "I told you the last time we went out with them, no more double dates with Amy and Dean. I understand you want us to have a friend couple to do double dates with. As half of this couple, I have fifty percent of the vote on who that couple is going to be. It's not Amy and *Dean*. End of discussion."

Noting the time on the clock on the stove, he grabbed her by the shoulder. "I have to go." He kissed her on the lips. "I love you."

"Love you, too," she said with a pout.

He lifted her head up by the chin and peered into her violet eyes. "Are we good?"

"We were never not good."

"I love you, Buttercup." He gave her a quick kiss on the cheek while snatching his hat from the counter. "I've got a meeting at ten o'clock and Crotch is a bitch when anyone is late—especially when that anyone is me."

44

"One day, you're going to call her Crotch to her face and get into big trouble."

Murphy chuckled. "I get into trouble with her just waking up in the morning." He gave her another kiss on the cheek.

"Why does Koch hate you so much?" she asked his retreating form as he headed for the stairs down to the garage.

"You can't make everyone love you." He paused on the stairs to blow her a kiss before tucking his hat under his arm. "Love you, Buttercup. Text me when you get home."

Stopping at the top of the stairs that Murphy had just run down, Spencer sat and whined as if to call him back.

"Guess I'm going to have to tell Amy that Murphy is working on a big project and doesn't have time for going out," Jessica muttered over her coffee mug. She noticed that he had been in such a hurry to leave that he didn't even ask who she was meeting for lunch. "And I had such a good lie ready to hand him."

Checking the time on the clock, she went to the kitchen window to look down to the street. She could hear the low rumble of the garage door closing. Outside, she saw Murphy stop out on the street. Shifting the black Yukon into gear, he turned the corner and headed out to join the mid-morning commuters going off into Washington.

"He doesn't suspect a thing," she told Spencer who joined her at the window. The young dog wasn't tall enough to look out, so she opted for staring up at her master's face.

Giggling, Jessica snatched up her handbag and raced down the stairs to her purple Ferrari.

CHAPTER THREE

"Thornton, you must have nerves of steel to be sitting two feet from that box of donuts without batting an eyelash." After taking a Boston cream-filled donut from the box in the middle of the conference table, Special Agent Boris Hamilton, the deputy chief of the Naval Criminal Investigation Staff, sat down in the chair next to Murphy at the head of the table. Several files were stacked up in front of Murphy and, next to the files, he had a notepad and tablet. In contrast, Boris had a single file, notepad, pen, and big mug of coffee.

"That's because they're filled with refined sugar," Hillary Koch said while stepping up to her chair at the other end of the table. The staff chief, who Murphy called Crotch, added in a mocking tone, "and sugar *kills*." As if to make a statement of her opinion, she snatched a donut covered in chocolate and took a big bite out of it while eying Murphy.

Showing no emotion, Murphy raised his eyes up to meet hers.

With a smug grin, she turned around. With one hand on her broad hip, she sashayed back to her seat. Almost as tall as Murphy, who was six-feet, two inches, Hillary Koch was a large woman—not obese, but very much overweight—which added to her intimidating persona.

One of the requirements for each member of the staff—tasked with investigating crimes involving members of the navy or marines and their families, as well as navy contractors—was to be physically fit. How else could they run down a fleeing suspect on foot? In the three and a half months that Murphy had been assigned as the military liaison, the middle man between the civilian staff and the military, he had never heard of Hillary doing anything to break a sweat.

Murphy often wondered how Hillary Koch managed to pass the annual physical in order to remain chief of their unit, which consisted of three dozen men and women. Despite being in his late fifties, even Deputy Chief Hamilton would start the day in the athletic room working out on the weight machine or running on the treadmill.

"I've often thought of becoming a vegetarian." Special Agent Susan Archer came in to take a seat toward Murphy's end of the table. Only a couple years older than Murphy, she wasn't in any need of a special diet. Like the majority of those on the staff, Susan came from a military background. She had served in the infantry in the marines and completed two tours in the Middle East. She wore her long dark hair in a ponytail gathered low on the back of her neck. "But it takes a wealth of discipline to turn your back on goodies like these." She picked a glazed donut from the box. "Plus, I don't think I could say good-bye to Red Robin."

"Is Jessica a vegetarian, too?" Wendy, Chief Koch's administrative assistant, sauntered up to the box containing the morning meeting treat. A buxom blonde whose appearance met every requirement listed for the stereotypical air-head ditz from days gone-by, Wendy took her time bending over to provide Murphy with a view down her low cut blouse while selecting a chocolate covered donut.

"No," Murphy replied, "Jessie's not."

"Neither is Murphy," Koch said in a tone so harsh that one would have thought Murphy was a suspect caught in a lie. "He eats fish. That's meat. Therefore, he is not a *vegetarian*."

"No, I am a pescatarian." Murphy nodded his head in agreement. "I do eat fish. I don't eat any other meat, alcohol, caffeine—" he pointed with his pen at Koch's oversized coffee mug at the end of the table, "refined sugar, dairy, or processed food—it's also known as clean eating."

"How does your wife cook for you?" Wendy asked from where she had taken a seat against the wall across from Chief Hillary Koch.

"She's an *heiress*," Koch interjected with a juvenile roll of her eyes before Murphy could respond. "She doesn't *cook*."

"Yes, she does," Murphy interjected. "Jessie's a very good cook."

Wendy asked, "Doesn't your maid—"

"We don't have a maid," Murphy said. "Jessica has never had a maid and neither does anyone else in her family. Not all rich people have servants following them around." He chuckled. "Believe it or not, there are actual billionaires living very private, normal lives, who don't own mansions with servants or drive fancy sports cars."

Silence fell over the conference room while Hillary Koch shot a deadly glare in Murphy's direction. He responded to the glare with a steely gaze of his own.

"Let's get this meeting rolling." Hillary Koch slapped open her notepad. "Item one on the agenda ..."

The meeting went on with each team of agents reporting on the status of their open cases. In Murphy's role of liaison, he would take note of what information the agents would need from what naval departments, if any, in order to complete their investigations. While each agent did have security clearance, in some cases, they would not have enough clearance for the information needed. This would be where Murphy stepped in. If the agent was deemed not to have "need to know," then he would take over the investigation himself.

So far, he hadn't.

They had only completed one of the cases on the agenda, which Agent Susan Archer and her partner, Special Agent Perry Latimore had closed the day before, when the conference doors flew open. Two secret service agents stepped inside and held the door open.

A naval officer in a lieutenant's uniform stepped through the doorway and stood at attention. "Attention! All navy military personnel fall in for inspection from Vice Chairman Joint Chief of Staff, Admiral Clarence Patterson!"

Everyone in the conference room jumped to their feet.

Murphy almost spilled his tea jumping out from behind the table for inspection. Since everyone else in the room was civilian, they were not expected to stand up to the scrutiny of the highest-ranking naval officer in the country. Though most of them, out of respect and habit from their former military backgrounds, did stand at attention as if they expected to be inspected as well.

As the only military officer in the room, Murphy stepped over to the side of the room and stood up rod straight with his arms and hands locked at his sides.

Admiral Clarence Patterson stepped into the room. The tall, African-American had a muscular build and gray at his temples that gave him a distinguished appearance above and beyond his uniform, which was covered with ribbons and medals.

Holding a folder under his arm, the lieutenant accompanying the admiral introduced him to Hillary Koch and her deputy before they turned to where Murphy stood at attention—waiting to be inspected.

With a keen professional eye, the admiral looked Murphy up and down. The corners of his lips curled with satisfaction. "Lieutenant Murphy Thornton, I've been hearing a lot about you." His voice was a low, smooth octave.

Murphy swallowed. "Good, I hope, sir."

"Very good, I assure you."

Out of his peripheral vision, Murphy caught sight of someone in lilac coming into the conference room. Still at attention, he was unable to turn his head to see if it was who he thought it was.

"Lieutenant Murphy Thornton," Admiral Patterson raised his voice, "it is an honor for me to bestow on you today this military award of distinction and honor for your acts of heroism, bravery, and leadership this past winter in leading an impromptu team of marines and state, county, and local police, not to mention civilians," he cast a glance over his shoulder at the witnesses in the room, "in order to thwart a terrorist bombing attack, save the life of a major from the United States Marines, and identify and capture a group of domestic terrorists."

The lieutenant handed the admiral a bronze star hanging from a red, white, and blue ribbon. "For this, I am honored to present to you, Lieutenant Murphy Thornton, the Bronze Star."

Murphy felt his body trembling with excitement while the admiral pinned the star onto his chest, directly under his rows of ribbons. In a low voice, the admiral whispered to him. "You have done the Phantoms proud, Lieutenant Thornton. Your country is lucky to have you on our team."

Behind the admiral, Boris Hamilton clapped his hands. Within seconds everyone else in the room joined in. With a wide grin on his face, Admiral Patterson handed a certificate to Murphy and shook his hand. Then, stepping back, he saluted Murphy.

"At ease, Lieutenant."

Finally, Murphy was allowed to break into a wide grin. The admiral stepped aside and gestured toward the door. "Okay, you can kiss him now."

Jessica rushed through the secret service detail guarding the Vice Chairman of the Joint Chiefs of Staff and threw her arms around Murphy's shoulders. Before he could object, she planted a kiss right on his lips.

"I guess that friend you're having lunch with is me," he told her.

Her eyes filled with tears of pride, she nodded her head. "I have reservations to celebrate."

Admiral Patterson leaned in to tell Murphy. "Your wife is a complete delight. We had a charming conversation on the way up in the executive elevator about how you two met."

"You told the admiral about that?" Murphy didn't know whether to be horrified or intrigued.

The lieutenant who was assisting the admiral whispered into his ear. With a shake of Murphy's hand, the admiral congratulated him once again and made his way out of the conference room.

What had previously been a meeting quickly dissolved into a party with the agents on the staff wanting to get a close look at the Bronze Star now displayed on Murphy's chest, and to meet his wife.

"Murphy," Boris shook his hand, "you are one humble guy. All that stuff that the admiral said you did? I never knew. You never told us that."

"It was a classified mission," Murphy explained.

On the other side of the conference room, he was aware of Hillary Koch hanging back, with a bitter frown on her face. She had her arms folded tightly across her chest.

"Did he say domestic terrorism?" Susan asked. "That means it happened here in the United States, but I don't recall seeing on the news anything like that going down." She turned to her partner Perry. "Did you ever see anything like that on the news?"

Perry was confirming that he hadn't while Jessica laid her hand on Murphy's elbow.

"What about that lunch?" With pride, she fingered the star hanging on his breast pocket. "I know it's early, but I was hoping you could take a couple of hours leave to celebrate." With a naughty grin, she winked at him.

Abruptly, Hillary provided Murphy with the answer to Jessica's invitation. "Thornton, come here. I need to talk to you." The tone of her voice made the hair on the back of Murphy's neck stand up on end.

Wading through the agents, who sensed by Koch's tone that she was not calling him over to bestow her congratulations, Murphy made his way to the staff chief.

"Yes, Crotch—" In response to her glare, he corrected himself, "I meant Koch."

"Sure you did," she muttered.

Murphy noticed her eying the shiny addition to his chest. She had to refrain from touching it. To do so would be to acknowledge his achievement, and she would be damned if she did that. Instead, she grasped her cell phone with both hands.

"The Virginia State Police have what appears to be a home invasion in Reston. Five women murdered in a town house. One of the victims is a petty officer from the Navy Yard."

Wondering why she was telling him this, Murphy cocked his head at her. It was the duty of her staff to investigate criminal cases involving military or civilian navy personnel. He was only the liaison.

Koch planted her hands on her hips. "Since this petty officer appeared to be in the wrong place at the wrong time, we need someone to go to the scene, scope it out, and then allow the local police to take the lead."

"Why are you sending me?"

"Because this award ceremony of yours has set us back. This meeting is going to have to go through lunch," she said. "I need the rest of my staff here. This multiple murder was most likely a robbery or one—"

"Was it our petty officer's home?"

"No," Koch said. "If she was just collateral damage from another crime, then it's not our case. But we have to send someone out there to go through the motions of a pissing contest with the state police and then let them take it. Just make sure they know to keep us in the loop on the investigation." She smirked. "I'm sure a super man like you can handle that, Thornton." She glanced over at Jessica who was standing a couple of feet away. "Sorry to ruin your date."

Stepping around Murphy, Koch clapped her hands. "Okay, boys and girls, the show is over. We need to get back to work."

Jessica murmured into his shoulder, "What a—"

Murphy's mouth clamped over hers to stifle the rest of her protest. Caught off guard, she stumbled on her high heels to fall into his arms, which he wrapped around her tightly while whispering with a husky voice into her ear, "Smile. Don't give her the satisfaction of seeing that she's ruined anything."

Seemingly oblivious to the mouths of the agents hanging open at the abrupt display, Murphy gathered his folders and tablet from where he had been sitting before the admiral interrupted the meeting.

Jessica smiled broadly and grasped his elbow with both hands. "Are you going to show me your office?"

Taking note of her visitor's badge, which meant that she needed to be escorted at all times by someone with security clearance, Murphy took her out of the conference room and down the corridor to his office located next to the staff chief.

Admiring their wedding picture displayed on the book-case behind Murphy's desk, Jessica asked in a casual tone, "Why does Koch hate you so much? Based on the tension I picked up from her, it is more than a simple personal-ity clash. Did she make a pass at you and you turned her down?" She shot a naughty grin to his back, which he didn't notice. Instead, he was taking his gun and holster out of his desk drawer and snapping it on.

"I'm the last man she'd make a pass at," Murphy said. "I'm too WASP for her taste."

"WASP?" She slipped onto the corner of his desk and crossed her long legs.

"White Anglo Saxon Protestant," he replied. "Don't tell me you never heard that term before."

"But she's—"

"Caucasian," Murphy finished. "And she loves men of ev-ery different color—except white."

"How do you know that?"

"Because she brags about it," he said. "Her sex life is com-mon knowledge. In the four months that I've been here, she's slept with six men. She said at the last breakfast meeting that she's been averaging one and a half men a month."

"And none of them are Caucasian?" Jessica asked with a tilt of her head and an arched eyebrow.

"Three African-Americans, two Mexicans, and one Native American. I've noticed a definite pattern in her behavior."

"Any of them in the military?"

"No," Murphy said with mock disgust. "She hates the military and she despises every suspect and victim her staff investigates."

"That sounds like a conflict of interest to me," she said. "Why—"

"I have no idea," he said. "It makes me wonder if that's why the Joint Chiefs assigned me here—to investigate her." He muttered under his breath, "They put me here for some reason. Wish they'd give me more direction."

"Didn't you tell me that she was former navy?" she asked. "Did she retire?"

"Left," Murphy said with a shrug of his shoulders. "I know there's a story there, but no one I've spoken to knows it. She's clearly bitter toward the military, the government—"

"And white men," Jessica said. "Murphy, no wonder Koch hates you. You're the personification of everything that she blames for ruining her life."

"You're making quite a leap there, aren't you, Dr. Faraday?" Murphy asked.

Jessica grinned. She was still in the process of applying to Georgetown University Medical School for her doctorate in psychiatry. She ticked off on her fingers. "You're a successful, handsome, white, male, military officer serving your country." She sighed. "I wouldn't be surprised if there was a white male she blamed for drumming her out of the military."

"We don't know if she was drummed out."

"I saw her when the admiral pinned that Bronze Star on your chest," Jessica said. "She about dislocated her jaw gnashing her teeth with fury and envy. She was drummed out."

"Well," Murphy told her in a low voice, "whatever Crotch's story is, I need to get along with her."

"She's not your commanding officer," she replied.

"She's my supervisor," Murphy said. "Since CO is not on site and doesn't see me on a daily basis, Crotch sends a regular evaluation report on my performance to her and makes a recommendation about promotion or reassignment. She could very well keep me from getting promoted or get me reassigned to a hell hole someplace."

"CO loves you," Jessica whispered to him. "She recommended you for this Bronze Star. I'm sure that if Koch bad-mouthed you, your CO wouldn't believe a word of it." She grinned. "I'm predicting that in twenty years, you'll be the youngest admiral to make the Joint Chiefs of Staff. Everyone will forget all about General Sebastian Graham."

Impressed, Murphy smiled. "So the lady does keep up on the news."

For the past week, the news media had been covering the announcement that the army's chief of staff, General Steve Johnston, was retiring. The president had nominated General Sebastian Graham. A four-star general, the commander of United States Central Command Center was a hero from the Gulf War, who had risen quickly through the ranks. A graduate of West Point, the media had been painting General Graham as a charismatic man who had a talent for making all the right friends in the right places, which explained how he had gotten on the fast track to be in the running for Joint Chiefs of Staff before the age of fifty.

"Admiral Patterson told me that General Graham is basically a shoe-in for the Joint Chiefs of Staff." With a naughty grin, she revealed, "I heard a rumor this past weekend at the naval officers' wives tea that he was supposed to be quite a ladies' man. His wife is on the board of practically every major charity in the country—"

Murphy was skeptical. "That's what they always say when an attractive man gets on the fast track anywhere."

"I don't think General Graham is all that attractive, do you?"

"Buttercup, I don't think any man is attractive."

Pressing her long, elegant index finger against his chest, she narrowed her eyes until they were violet slits framed in lush long eyelashes. "You were the one who called him attractive, Honey Buns."

"Because that's what the news is saying," Murphy said while moving in closer. He could feel her long fingernail pressing through his uniform to his breast. "According to the news, all the ladies on Capitol Hill have been panting about this young general who practically won the Gulf War single-handed."

"Forget it." Grabbing him around the neck, Jessica pulled him in to kiss his lips. After releasing him, she held him close to admire his blue eyes. She could feel his breath on her face as she told him mouth to mouth. "Don't let the hell bitch rain on your big day. I'll change the reservations to dinner." A devilish grin came to her lips. "We both have something else to celebrate."

Murphy searched his mind for what she meant. Unable to comprehend what she was talking about, he asked, "What?"

Cocking an eyebrow, she lowered her eyes. "It's a surprise."

"Tell me."

"No." She giggled.

Grabbing her around the waist and lifting her up off the desk, he held her tight. "I have ways of making you talk," he whispered into her ear.

"Is it true that the Pentagon has security cameras *everywhere?*"

Reminded of where they were, Murphy released her. Playfully, she kissed him on the neck before saying in a low voice. "You're going to love it, darling."

CHAPTER FOUR

Rock Springs Boulevard, Chester, West Virginia

Joshua Thornton wasn't surprised when he stepped out of his study to hear Cameron running down the stairs. She wore her holstered service weapon on her belt. "Where are you going?"

"Where do you think I'm going?" she replied. "To follow up the only lead I have. Someone hired a hitman to take Nick out. There had to be a reason. I know it wasn't personal. So it had to be professional. If it had to do with his job as a patrolman, then his supervising officer must have some idea who would want Nick dead." She kissed Joshua quickly on the lips. "I'm going to see Reese Phillips. He's retired and living up in Ashtabula."

Joshua grasped her arm when she tried to hurry out the door. "I'm coming with you."

"You've got to be in court this afternoon," she objected.

"I'll get a continuance for a couple of days," he said. "I'll tell the judge that we have a family emergency. This is more important."

"Josh …"

"Cameron," Joshua gripped her by the shoulders, "don't forget, I lost my first wife suddenly. One minute, she was there and the next she was dead—gone. Now, Valerie died of natural causes. If now, after all of these years, I found out that someone had engineered ripping her out of my family's life …" He swallowed. "I'm trying to tell you that I completely understand what you're going through and I fully intend to be by your side every step of the way."

Cameron brushed her hand across his cheek. "I love you, Joshua Thornton." She reached up to kiss him tenderly on the lips. "You just better not slow me down."

"Have I failed to keep up with you yet?"

"There's always a first time."

Reese Phillips had retired to a lake-side cabin in Ashtabula, Ohio. He had a fishing boat and two hound dogs to keep him company. Upon their arrival, and after introductions had been made, Cameron allowed a minimal amount of time for pleasantries before recounting the FBI visit.

"Why would someone want to kill a nice guy like Nick?" the retired state trooper asked when Cameron gave him the news about Nick's death not being an accident. Reese stared out over the still water of the lake with his beer bottle stopped half-way to his mouth to ponder the revelation.

"I'm asking the same question," Cameron said.

"Did Nick have issues with anyone in the department?" Joshua asked.

"No," Reese said with certainty. "Besides, you said this was a hitman who worked for the Russian mob?"

"He also did work for a major drug cartel," Cameron said.

"Highly trained professional from what the agents told us," Joshua said.

"No one in our department was connected to anyone like that," Reese said.

"What about drugs?" Joshua asked.

"We've had our drug problems in these parts, but Nick had no part of any of that," Reese said. "Nick wasn't with us long enough to make enemies."

Agreeing, Cameron sat back in the comfortable, old deck chair.

After a long moment, Joshua broke the silence. "So the motive was not personal, and it wasn't a coworker who ordered the hit. Could Nick have given someone a ticket who took it too personally—maybe a DUI or an accident—"

"Jane Doe," Reese said with a snap of his fingers. "That was the case that really got under his skin."

"Jane Doe?" Cameron replied.

"Don't you remember her, Cam?" Reese asked. "It was only—had to be less than two weeks before Nick got killed. One night, Nick was patrolling the turnpike out by Somerset and he finds this woman on the side of the road. She had been thrown from a speeding vehicle or jumped out. The medical examiner said her injuries weren't consistent with the impact of being hit by a car. Nick said she was alive when he found her, but she never gave him her name. He said she kept saying 'She's safe' over and over. She died in his arms before the EMTs got there. It really got to him."

"Was she ever identified?" Joshua asked.

"No," Cameron answered. "She had no purse or ID, nothing to identify her. I had forgotten all about that. That did hit Nick really hard. He believed that someone had abducted her, and that she jumped out of a moving car to save her life. She had a family. He knew it and wanted to let them know what happened to her."

Reese told them, "We checked the missing persons reports in the tri-state area and Ohio Valley, but she didn't match any of those reports. He even went on television."

"I remember now." Cameron turned to Joshua. *America's Most Wanted.* He went on national TV and showed her picture asking for someone to identify her."

Reese nodded his head in agreement. "The last thing Nick mentioned to me that night was to ask about a contact I have in the FBI. I have no doubt but that he was going to ask him to check the national database."

Pressing her fingertips to her temples, Cameron was shaking her head. "It's all coming back to me now. How could I have forgotten that case? Nick wanted to know who the 'she' was that Jane Doe kept talking about. I remember him saying how awful it was that this poor woman—who had to have someone, someone she obviously cared about—died alone on the cold, dark freeway."

Joshua asked Reese, "Was Nick working on anything else?"

The retired patrolman shook his head. "Only regular traffic stops, a few DUIs and some accident reports."

"Maybe someone did know who Jane Doe was," Joshua said, "and Nick was killed because he got too close to finding out."

It wasn't until after Murphy had walked Jessica to her purple Ferrari in the visitor's parking lot and she dropped him off at his SUV in general parking, that he became seriously curious about what Jessica's surprise was—one that would make both of them happy.

After merging his SUV into traffic on George Washington Parkway, Murphy was able to relax and examine the clues.

He had noticed that she had been a bit secretive in the last month. Before moving into the brownstone, she would close the lid to her laptop when he entered the room where they were living in his small apartment. Murphy had dismissed it as her needing her space. If he was insecure, he'd think she had gone back to one of her former boyfriends.

Jessica was through with the debutante lifestyle she had adopted after her massive inheritance from her grandmother—world-famous mystery author Robin Spencer. Jessica was returning to school, but that was no surprise. She was applying to the medical school at Georgetown University. Granted, it would be fifteen months before she could start, if she was accepted, but Jessica swore that she intended to keep busy before going back to college.

So what's her surprise? Something for both of us to celebrate?

Seeing an SUV passing him with a baby car seat in the back, Murphy felt his jaw drop.

No! Could she—

A horn jerked him out of his thoughts when Murphy's SUV eased over into the next lane. Easing the steering wheel to return to his own lane, Murphy swallowed. *Am I ready for that?* He wiped the beads of sweat from his brow.

Newman is still adjusting to Candi and her puppy antics. How's he going to adjust to a baby crying over his television programs, touching his remote with slimy fingers, or worse, sitting in his chair? He'll never forgive me. I wonder if dogs can file lawsuits.

Forcing the thought from his mind, Murphy gunned the engine to hurry to Reston. He needed something challenging to take his mind off the feeling that a major change was coming to his and Jessica's newlywed lifestyle .

CHAPTER FIVE

The townhouse was in an older, middle class neighborhood in Reston, a half hour outside of Washington. Practically the whole street was blocked off by local and state police. As Murphy approached the barricade in his SUV, he held up his navy identification and agent's badge for the officer to see through the driver's side window. The Fairfax County sheriff's deputy stopped the vehicle to examine Murphy's credentials.

After explaining that he had been sent by the Naval Criminal Investigation Staff, Murphy took back his badge and identification. "We were told one of the victims is a navy petty officer. I've been sent to survey the situation."

Telling Murphy that he would radio the detective in charge, the sheriff deputy waved for him to pull over next to a state police cruiser. By the time Murphy placed his hat on his head and climbed out of the SUV, the deputy called over for him to go into the townhouse, where the lead detective would be waiting. Tucking a computer tablet for crime-scene notes under his arm, Murphy strode down the narrow sidewalk. The small townhouse was nestled in the middle of a collection of four townhouses that were easily half the size of his and Jessica's brownstone. Some had small gardens with spring flowers in the postage stamp sized front yards. Most were bare. The townhouse in the middle with the police officer guarding the front door had a neat, splendidly tended garden made up of peonies that lined the front stoop. Murphy climbed the steep steps up to the door.

With a curt nod, the police officer acknowledged the naval officer while opening the door for him. "You will find the lieutenant inside, sir."

"Thank you, officer." Removing his hat from his head and tucking it under his arm, Murphy stepped inside to a cozy split foyer. To his left, the steps descended to the lower level where the garage was located. To the right, they went up to a small hallway. At the top of the stairs, he could see an open doorway to the kitchen.

A detective of Asian descent, in a suit that appeared a full size too big for his slightly built frame, was waiting at the top of the steps. "Since when does NCIS send uniformed military officers?"

"They felt this case deserved the best," Murphy replied with a crooked grin.

His response got a chuckle from the detective, who offered Murphy his hand to shake. "I thought they deleted a sense of humor out of you guys. Maybe that's just the civilians." While shaking hands, he introduced himself as Lieutenant Bernard Wu.

Making a mental note of Wu's comment, Murphy asked in a casual tone, "They must be a lot of fun at parties."

"Hamilton isn't so bad once you get him out of earshot of Koch," Wu said in a low voice while glancing to see if anyone was listening. "She scares the hell out of everyone—not just in NCIS."

Returning to the reason for Murphy's visit, Wu jerked his head in the direction of the dining room located next to the kitchen. On the other side was a sunken living room. "Five victims. It's pretty bad." He handed Murphy a pair of evidence gloves to slip on.

"Sounds like it." Murphy followed the detective into the dining room where a woman was sprawled out on the floor in a giant pool of blood. A woman's purse rested on the floor with its contents scattered all around the room as if spilled during the struggle for her life.

This victim did not go down easy.

The shelves in a cheap curio cabinet against the wall were shattered where the victim ... or maybe the killer ... had crashed into the unit during the battle to the death. Two dining room chairs were overturned. An empty punch bowl rested in the middle of the table, which was covered in spilt punch and shattered punch glasses.

The wall was covered with blood spray.

"They were found this morning when two of the women's husbands reported their wives missing," the police lieutenant said. "Both victims had told their husbands that they were going to a Cozy Chef party and didn't come home. We pinged their cell phones which showed us that they were here. The police arrived to investigate about the same time that the homeowner's assistant arrived to check on her because she didn't show up at work. She's a professor at George Mason University and missed her classes this morning." He pointed down at the woman in the pool of blood. "This one is yours."

Murphy squatted down next to the body. On the floor under the table, he saw a forty-five caliber semi-automatic with an evidence catalog number next to it. "Have your people processed this gun yet?"

"Yes," Wu said. "We haven't run the registration number yet, though. It's been photographed."

"Then can I examine it?"

"You're asking?"

"Yes," Murphy said. "Until I say otherwise, this is your scene. You're in charge."

He heard a "humph" before Lieutenant Wu replied, "An officer *and* a gentleman. Go ahead."

Murphy crawled under the table to retrieve the gun and check the magazine.

"The victim's name is Donna Crenshaw," the detective reported while Murphy examined the weapon under the table. "Petty officer at the Navy Yard. She has a concealed carry permit and a forty-five caliber semi-automatic Smith and Wesson registered in her name."

"It's a Smith and Wesson. Could be hers. Three rounds missing from the mag." He sniffed the gun. "Recently fired." Crawling back out from under the table, Murphy noticed three bullet holes in the wall under the staircase leading up to the next level. "Assuming those bullet holes were made by this gun, she got off three shots before the killer took her out." He carefully placed the gun back where he had found it.

Next to one of the overturned chairs, Murphy saw a smart phone. It also had a catalogue number next to it. "I assume your people processed this cell phone, too?"

"It belongs to your victim."

Murphy turned on the phone to see a series of texts and missed calls listed. A number of the missed calls came from someone named "Izzy." The picture showed a young girl with curly ash blonde hair and big light brown eyes. One of the texts read, "Mom, where R U? I'm worried."

Murphy cursed under his breath before continuing to the next text conversation listed. *She's someone's mother.*

Someone from an unidentified cell phone number had texted:

> *Mtg set 4 7pm tomorrow. Pls come. Important.*
> *We need U if we R 2 stop him.*

Donna's response, sent at 7:12 the night before:

Running late. Accident has Route 7 @ standstill. B there ASAP. Count me in.

The reply back, sent at 7:27 pm:

No problem. We're waiting for you. Front door is open. Just let yourself in.

Murphy made a note of the responding text's phone number on his tablet. "Do you have all of the victim's cell phones and numbers?"

"Still cataloging them," Wu asked. "Why?"

"Our petty officer was running late last night," Murphy said. "Accident on the beltway held her up."

"Who wasn't held up last night?" Wu replied.

A fuel truck had overturned on the Capital Beltway in Northern Virginia in the midst of rush hour, closing the freeway down in both directions. With commuters taking alternate routes, traffic in and around Washington had screeched to a crawl.

Murphy told the detective, "Someone had texted Crenshaw at 7:27 that they were waiting for her."

Lieutenant Wu took the phone and checked the numbers in his notes.

Murphy glanced at the background report that the human services department of the navy had forwarded to his tablet. Donna Crenshaw was in the navy for thirteen years, after transferring from the United States Army where she had been a corporal.

She was lying face up on the blood soaked carpet. Murphy counted two gunshot wounds in her face, one in her shoulder, another in her stomach, and one in the chest.

"Someone really wanted her dead." Cocking his head, Murphy studied her face through the blood. She did not appear to wear much makeup, if any. Her cinnamon colored hair was streaked with gray and trimmed short. Checking her background on his tablet, Murphy read that she was thirty-four years old. While her small build would make her appear younger, he could see by the picture in her personnel file that her face looked worn. "Only thirty-four." He scrolled through the record on his tablet for the listing of her family members. "Why would someone want you dead, Donna? Who were you trying to stop and why?" He saw that she had never been married, but had a daughter.

Where RU? I'm worried.

Reading the age of the daughter, Murphy cringed. Thirteen years old. "Oh, God," he breathed before swallowing hard. "Poor girl." Glancing again at her face on the cell phone, he swallowed again. He remembered all too well his own mother's sudden death when he was only sixteen years old. He knew intimately the pain this young girl was going to experience.

"Has anyone contacted Crenshaw's daughter?" Murphy stood up to ask the police lieutenant.

"We sent a patrol unit to the school to pick her up and take her to the police department," Wu replied from the living room.

"Has she been told about her mother yet?"

"Our counselor will tell her once I get back to the station," Wu said.

Shaking his head, Murphy stared down at the bullet-riddled body of the woman at his feet.

"Preliminary from the ME says she died between eight and nine last night," Lieutenant WU said, "after the other party guests. They died between seven and eight last night."

Murphy turned to look over the railing that ran the width of the room to mark off the dining room from the drop down living room. Three women were sprawled in different positions around the small living room. One, who appeared to be in her late thirties to early forties, was in front of the sofa. Another woman, who could have been in her early to mid-thirties, was next to the chair. A petite-built young woman, who could not have been thirty, looked like she was crawling to the door leading out to the deck when she breathed her last breath. A cloth bag rested next to the sofa, the image of a big, white chef's hat emblazoned on the side, with the name "Cozy Cook" written in red letters across the hat.

Unlike Donna, none of them had been shot.

"Were they poisoned?" Murphy asked.

"Looks like it," Wu said. "We won't know for certain until after the tox screens."

"Whoever it was waited for my petty officer after they were dead," Murphy said.

"*Your* petty officer?" Wu arched one of his eyebrows. One side of his thin lips curled upwards.

"*My* petty officer," Murphy replied. "Tell me about the homeowner."

"According to the phone number listed for that last text, it was sent from her phone. Francine Baxter." Lieutenant Wu pointed to the floor above them. "She's up in the master bedroom with two GSWs. One in the chest, the other to the head. She died between five-thirty and six-thirty."

"She died about an hour before these three women," Murphy gestured at the women in the living room, "and two hours before Crenshaw?"

Wu nodded. "There's no way she sent that text to Crenshaw."

"That means the killer spent at least two hours in this house," Murphy said, "waiting for Donna Crenshaw. When she texted that she was running late, the killer replied, telling her to let herself in so that he or she could kill her."

Wu shrugged his shoulders. "If you do the math."

Murphy referred to Donna's Crenshaw's cell phone that he found he still held in his hand. "The meeting was at seven."

"Party," Lieutenant Wu corrected him. "Two of our victims told their husbands that they were going to a Cozy Cook party." He pointed at the bag with the chef's hat displayed on the front.

"Do you see any food put out?" Murphy asked.

Lieutenant Wu's narrow eyes grew wide.

"Have you ever been to a Cozy Cook party?" Murphy asked with a smile.

"Have you?"

"No, but my mother used to host them," Murphy said. "The sales lady comes to the house and cooks up all this food and lays out a whole bunch of stuff to sell to the guests." With a sweep of his arm, he pointed out, "There's no food or cooking stuff laid out. Your victims lied to their husbands. These women came here for a meeting."

He held up Donna Crenshaw's cell phone. "The day before the meeting, someone texted Donna saying that they needed her to put a stop to someone. She was important to the purpose of the meeting and that's why the killer hung out here for two hours and killed all of these woman—in order to kill *my* petty officer."

"Are you telling me that the navy is taking the lead in this case?" Lieutenant Wu asked with a sigh heavy with resignation.

"All evidence indicates my navy petty officer was not collateral damage," Murphy said. "She was targeted. Since the motive may have to do with national security or be classified, I have no—"

With an impatient shake of his head, Wu raised his hand and interrupted, "I don't have all day. Do you really want this case?"

"Yes, I really want this case." Murphy opened the camera application on his tablet and snapped a picture of Donna Crenshaw's body. "You need to show me everything you've got."

Lieutenant Wu chuckled. "I like you, Lieutenant Thornton. You've got guts. That's why I'm going to give you some advice."

"What type of advice?"

"They give you a ballistics vest with that bright, white uniform of yours?"

"Not with the uniform," Murphy said, "but I have one."

"Wear it when you tell Koch."

Murphy was cruising down Route 7 toward the concrete metropolis of Tyson's Corners when the barrage of signage leading up to the mall reminded him that he had not eaten lunch. His breakfast had consisted of a power smoothie. With the time approaching two o'clock, his stomach growled.

The early afternoon traffic was still congested with workers who filled the surrounding office buildings returning from their midday meals. Bracing himself, Murphy flipped on his left turn signal and checked over his shoulder before easing in to the upcoming left turn lane to get onto the access road to the galleria's parking lot. The hybrid behind him slowed down to allow Murphy's black SUV to cross over.

Murphy was halfway into the lane when a horn blasted behind him. With a jump, he checked his rearview mirror to see if he had accidentally cut someone off. Behind him, he saw a man with a bad toupee in a white Corvette convertible flip off a woman with maroon-colored hair in a green Volkswagen turbo. She had jumped across two lanes to cut off the Corvette.

Glad not to be her.

Murphy turned his SUV into the parking lot. Without bothering to circle the lanes near the entrance in search of an empty spot, he instead traveled to the empty lanes furthest away. It was his habit to grab whatever exercise he could and enjoy the trot in the mild, spring weather.

As a Phantom, he was still honing his observational skills. *Always look around. Be aware of your surroundings. Who is nearby?*

Kicking himself, he remembered how easily he had let his guard down during the exercise to allow Tawkeel Said to shoot him. The burka made him assume the hostage was a woman, therefore, she was worthless according to the ISIS culture— therefore, she was not a threat to him … or so Murphy had assumed. *What happens when you assume? You make an ass of you and me.*

Like Tawkeel and Major Monroe had said, that's the point of training exercises. *If I had been in the field, I'd be dead now, my body mutilated and dumped somewhere, and Jessie would be a widow. You need to keep aware, Thornton. Never let your guard down.*

Instead of looking down at his feet, Murphy made a point of making a sweep of the parking lot to take in every person rushing in and out of the galleria entrance. He noticed the maroon-haired woman leaning against her Volkswagen while texting on her phone. Among the horde of customers hurrying to get back to their desks in time, the woman's relaxed demeanor was out of place. Between her stance, and her hair color that bordered on reddish purple, she was hard for Murphy to not notice.

Must not have a job to run back to.

Taking note that her casual texting in such a place and time was "suspicious," he made an exercise of noting the license plate of the green Volkswagen. It was personalized, easy to remember: ANTIWAR

In the diverse region of the Washington, D.C. metropolitan area, Murphy never had difficulty finding an eating spot that met his dietary requirements.

On the first level of the galleria, near Macy's, Murphy found that Sweetgreen satisfied him with an Umami grain bowl, which was vegetarian, organic, and fast.

Grabbing his bottled water, he turned around to almost body slam the woman staring at the menu from behind him. "Excuse me," Murphy blurted out before recognizing her as the young maroon-haired woman texting next to the green Volkswagen with the ANTIWAR license plate. The same one who had cut off the Corvette while changing lanes to fall in behind him. Now, here she was in the same restaurant as he was.

Her fair face turned pale. Her mouth dropped open. "Ex-excuse me!" she said with a gasp.

"I can help the next customer in line," the cashier behind the counter announced.

Instead of stepping forward to place her order, she continued to stare at Murphy with wide green eyes. An impatient young man in khaki slacks brushed past her to step up to the counter to place his order.

"Can I help you?" Murphy finally asked her.

Spinning on her heels, she turned and fled from the restaurant. Unsure if he should follow her or not, Murphy watched her disappear among the throng of mall customers.

Maybe she was hoping that I was single and just followed me to get up the nerve to hit on me, Murphy thought with a coy grin until he became aware of a hand lightly touching his arm. A young woman in a business suit and pumps smiled

broadly at him. "You are certainly welcome to help me …
anytime … day or *night.*"

CHAPTER SIX

"How are you doing?" Joshua took his hand off the steering wheel and reached across to rub Cameron's leg.

Ever since they had left Ashtabula, she had been staring straight ahead. Her brown eyes, specked with green, were directed unblinking and unseeing through the windshield. She was in deep thought—lost in the past—once again grieving the loss of her first husband.

This is what it feels like to reopen an old wound—make it bleed all over again.

After a silence—long enough to make Joshua think she hadn't heard him, she responded in a soft voice. "I can't believe I forgot all about Jane Doe. That death really got to Nick. I remember it ... vaguely ... but I can't remember anything specific about the case. . . only him telling me that she kept saying, 'She's safe.' He held her while she died—grateful that she, whoever *she* was, was safe. That'd get to anyone."

Joshua said, "When we get back home, call your chief and ask for a copy of the report on the case. I'm sure once you see it, everything Nick told you will come back. We don't know for certain that her death is connected to Nick's murder."

"Maybe she was a mob boss's mistress who knew too much." Her forehead creased with frustration, Cameron turned to him. "It's not like me to forget things. Why didn't I jump on that when Nick was murdered? I let him down. All these years—"

"*Everyone* assumed it was a hit and run accident by a drunk driver," Joshua said.

"Nick was upset about her," she said. "How she died. That no one claimed her body. She had bruises around her wrists, proving that she had been tied up and, obviously, she was so desperate that she jumped out of a moving vehicle on the turnpike. She had to know that was going to kill her. Nick didn't want her buried alone without her family knowing what had happened to her. It was important to him. How could I have not followed up on that? How could I have forgotten?"

Attempting to comfort her as best he could while keeping the SUV on the road, Joshua squeezed her hand. "When Valerie died, our pastor's wife told me that it would take a full year, if not two, to start healing from the loss," he said. "Both she and her husband advised me not to make the decision to leave the navy and uproot my kids from their home in Oakland, California, to come back to Chester. She told me to wait a full six months before making any major decisions. I didn't listen. I knew I was hurting, but I *thought* I was strong enough and smart enough and had it together enough to know what I was doing."

"Are you saying you made a mistake?"

"Looking back ..." Keeping his eyes on the road, Joshua shrugged his shoulders. "One of the things I needed to do in preparation for moving was to get a law office to set up my private practice. This was before I decided to run for prosecuting attorney. Well, my grandfather had owned an office building in East Liverpool, Ohio. He had left the property to my grandmother, and I assumed it was left to me when she passed about five years before Valerie died. My great-uncle, Tad's father, had been the executor of my grandmother's estate and, in the midst of my hurting over losing Valerie, I called my cousin Tad, since his father had passed away since settling the estate. I wanted to know about renovating space in that building for my office."

Confused, Cameron studied his profile. "What does this—"

"The building was gone." Joshua plunged on. "Tad claimed that I had instructed his father to sell it and set up a college fund for my kids with the money from the sale. I swore I hadn't. Not being the executor, Tad could only go by what his dad had told him. He insisted that his dad didn't lie. I said his father had robbed me. Of course, Tad didn't take that lying down. We got into a big fight and didn't speak to each other for two months." He held up two fingers to show her.

Knowing the close relationship between the two cousins—Dr. Tad MacMillan even lived next door to them, Cameron was surprised to learn that they had once fought so severely that they didn't speak for months.

Joshua went on, "Eventually, Tad called to apologize and offered an olive branch. I accepted it because I did miss him. We never spoke of it again—until a couple of years ago, when Tad was buying the house next door." He glanced over at her. "Now here's the kicker. To this day, I have no memory of any of that. Not the argument, asking about that building, accusing Tad's dad of being a thief—none of it. I remember plain and clear authorizing him to sell the building, but I still have no memory of fighting with Tad and not talking to him."

"Because …"

"Now," Joshua said, "when I think back to that period, the first fifteen months after Valerie died, leaving the navy, the move, the renovation of our house where my grandmother had raised me—all of that—I remember it like being in a fog. I even solved two major murder cases and was elected county prosecutor and I barely remember any of it."

"Your memory was clouded with grief," she said. "It's the way I remember my journey into alcoholism. I thought it was all the booze that my brain had soaked up."

"Maybe that played a part in it for you," Joshua said. "I wasn't thinking right because I was in so much pain."

Her eyes narrowed, she cocked her head at him. "What would you have done differently if you had to do it all over again?"

Joshua shrugged. "Things turned out good. My kids turned out better than okay."

"You were lucky," she said. "I didn't turn out so well."

He shot her a grin. "You turned out fine."

"I practically ruined my police career," she said. "If I hadn't bottomed out when I did and gotten help, I could have died."

"But you came back like a champ," Joshua said. "You got help, sobered up, and now you're one of Pennsylvania's finest."

She squeezed his hand. "And I was able to love again … both of us were."

"That, too."

Worry crossed her face. "I wonder if I can make it through all this again."

"Sure you will," Joshua said. "Because this time, you aren't going through it alone." He shot her a smile.

Reassured, she brushed his hand across her lips, kissing his fingers softly.

As Lieutenant Wu had predicted, Hillary Koch blew her top when she learned from NCIS's medical examiner that the bodies of five women were being transported to the navy's morgue on orders of Lieutenant Murphy Thornton.

During Murphy's short time assigned to the staff, Hillary Koch had made no attempt to hide her dislike for the navy officer with snide remarks or agitated facial expressions—not the least of which included juvenile eye rolls—about or even directed right at his "precious" United States Navy. Every attempt she made to bait him into a debate went without so much as a nibble. After months of her lust for blood going without satisfaction, she was itching for battle. All she needed was an excuse.

The news from the medical examiner gave her that excuse.

As soon as Murphy stepped through the security door leading into the NCIS staff, Hillary initiated her ambush from the doorway of her office.

After letting loose with a long string of swear words, which included her favorite obscenity—the f-word, or variations and synonyms of it—with an occasional upping of the ante by preceding it with "mother"—inserted at every possible interjection, she arrived to the catalyst for her fit:

"Who the hell do you think you are, Lieutenant Thornton, taking on a multiple murder case involving five women—four who aren't connected to the navy or marines?"

As if the cursing that had preceded her outburst was not enough to communicate her fury, she let loose with another stream of profanity.

Usually, when such battles broke out, the agents would scurry for cover, not wanting to further humiliate Hillary Koch's latest victim with an audience to the annihilation. This time, the intensity and the one on the receiving end—the navy's golden boy of the hour—made it just too juicy to ignore sneaking a peek.

Without uttering a word in his defense, Murphy sauntered across the outer office to where Hillary Koch stood with her hands on her expansive hips. Between her blazing temper and extensive use of oxygen in her fit, her doughy face was red. Her nostrils flared.

Wordlessly, he regarded her. While every agent, clerk, and assistant held his or her breath, he studied her unattractive face with his blue eyes. Finally, he responded in a voice so low and smooth that it melted in the mouth of every woman on the staff. "As flattered as I am that you want to have sex with me—it ain't gonna happen."

Knocking over her soft drink, Wendy jumped up from behind her desk and scrambled for paper towels to mop up the mess.

Bursting into laughter, Special Agent Susan Archer covered her mouth and ducked into her cubicle.

Hillary Koch's eyes bugged.

"I mean," Murphy continued with surprising calm, "a woman as well educated as yourself should know that the definition for the f-word is sexual intercourse. Clearly, you must know it *very* well since you've directed it and variations of it at me twenty-four times since I entered the office less than one minute ago."

Her mouth dropped open.

The corners of his lips curling, Murphy winked at her. "I'm sure you heard of Sigmund Freud and his hypothesis about the human subconscious. The 'Freudian slip.' Obviously, you've gotten so hot and heavy for my body that you couldn't stand it anymore and had to scream all the way across this office your intention to have sex with me."

Hillary's chest was heaving.

"Unfortunately for you," he said, "one,—" he held up his left hand to show off his wedding band. "I'm married. Two," The grin on his face dropped, "I'd rather spend an evening being water boarded by ISIS than touch you."

Seemingly oblivious to the audience, Murphy moved in closer to Hillary Koch. "As far as the case goes, when you get a grip and are ready to discuss it like an adult, I'll be in a meeting with Deputy Chief Hamilton and agents Archer and Latimore."

Over his shoulder, Murphy gestured at Boris Hamilton and the two agents. "My office in five minutes. We have the murders of five women to solve."

To Hillary Koch's surprise, her deputy chief and the two agents didn't wait. They immediately fell in behind Murphy.

"You have no authority!" she screamed.

"Oh yes, I do." His back to her, Murphy grinned at her anger. "My CO is waiting for your call to report this conversation, at which time she'll confirm her approval of my taking the lead in this case."

He paused at his office door to shoot another smile, framed by his deep dimples. If she liked him, she would have found it charming. Instead, she found it annoying.

"I highly recommend you think through what you're going to say before you call her," he said. "If you accuse *her* of having sex with *her* mother, she'll make a special trip out here to the Pentagon to kick your butt, which I have no doubt that she can do."

After they filed into the office, Boris Hamilton closed the door—shutting her out.

Her eyes wide, Hillary Koch turned from the closed office door to where her assistant Wendy stood motionless with fear at her desk. She clutched an armload of dripping paper towels to her bosom.

Hillary stormed into her office and slammed the door so hard, the picture of the President of the United States hanging on the wall outside dropped to the floor with a crash.

With her tablet perched in her lap, Cameron sat in the living room window seat to study Jane Doe's case file on the Pennsylvania State Police's secure online database. Irving was stretched out across a sunray beaming through the window.

Since the victim in Nick Gates' case was an unidentified Jane Doe, Cameron had to first obtain the case file number from her lieutenant at the homicide division of the Pennsylvania State Police. Only then could she use her remote login to find the case details online. As she had suspected, since Nick's death, no one had made any further attempt to identify Jane Doe or find out how she had ended up on the Pennsylvania Turnpike.

The only picture of the young woman in the case file was a head shot of her body in the morgue. Through the bluish cast to her face, Cameron could see that she had high cheekbones and a delicate straight nose. Her long, curly, ash-blonde hair fell past her shoulders. She had a slender build. In life, she would have been an attractive, even pretty, woman.

Cameron moved on to the medical examiner's report on cause of death. It listed multiple broken bones—including a broken back. Her lungs had been punctured by broken ribs, and she had a ruptured spleen. The cause of death was massive internal bleeding. In the medical examiner's notes, he said her injuries were not consistent with being hit by a car but, rather, he speculated she had jumped or been thrown from a vehicle moving at a high rate of speed. Bruising around her wrists and ankles, indicating that she had been bound, caused Nick to conclude that she had been kidnapped and jumped from her abductor's vehicle on the turnpike in an effort to escape.

But no one came forward to claim her—even after Nick went on national television to plea for information.

Cameron continued reading through the medical examiner's notes. To her surprise, she found that he noted that Jane Doe had an extended uterus, indicating that she had recently given birth, within two weeks of her death.

That's right. Cameron recalled Nick mentioning that. *She was someone's mother. Where is her baby?* The thought of someone kidnapping Jane Doe to steal her baby crossed Cameron's mind. *Could the baby be the "she" that Jane Doe was talking about when she died in Nick's arms? Had to be. But then, she claimed "she's safe." Maybe she wasn't stolen after all, but the kidnapper wanted to steal her.*

Shaking her head in a vain attempt to sort the possibilities, Cameron returned to the case file. She needed to find out where Nick had left off in the investigation before his death. They had checked for her fingerprints in AFIS, the national police fingerprint database, but found no match. The police had released her picture to the media throughout the Ohio Valley, but no one came forward to identify her.

Cameron recalled how nervous her late husband had been when a national crime-stopper show had interviewed him to profile the case. It was his first and only introduction to the media. While they received some tips, none panned out.

Then Nick was killed and the case went cold.

Keeping in mind that thirteen years had passed since Jane Doe's tragic death, Cameron checked the medical examiner's report to see if they had kept samples of her DNA. Over a decade earlier, the national DNA database index system was still in its infancy.

Cameron picked up her cell phone to call her supervisor when she saw Joshua leaning in the doorway, with one ankle crossed over the other. He had his arms folded across his chest.

"How's it going, handsome?" she asked.

"How's it going with you? Find anything new about Jane Doe?" He sat down across from her. While the window seat was spacious, it was a cozy fit. He placed her feet in his lap and massaged them.

Displaced, Irving launched himself out of the window seat. After hitting the floor, he shook himself, and smoothed his fur. Shooting a glare with his emerald eyes in Joshua's direction, he sauntered out of the room.

"Jane Doe had a baby less than two weeks before she died," Cameron told him. "*That* was what really got to Nick. He didn't want some kid growing up thinking that his mother had taken off and abandoned him ... or her."

"Any sign of sexual assault around the time of death?" Joshua asked her.

"None," she replied. "The medical examiner took samples of her DNA, but I see no record of it being put in the national DNA index. Possibly, if she had been abducted or reported missing from someplace where they did put samples of her DNA in that database, we could get a hit now."

"If," Joshua pointed out.

"It's worth a shot." She pressed the button to turn on her phone.

"We still don't know if the hit made on Nick has to do with this Jane Doe," Joshua reminded her.

"I know that, hon," she replied. "But it's the only lead we have until I get to talk to Sal Bertonelli."

"You do realize that it is unlikely that the FBI will allow you anywhere near Sal Bertonelli," Joshua said. "He's a very important witness against some of the top people in organized crime, who have already put out contracts on him. The feds aren't going to risk their case to—"

"Find out why they wanted to kill a lowly state trooper," she finished with a healthy dose of bitterness in her tone.

"Nicolas Gates' murder case is important," he said.

"But not as important as the big wheels in organized crime."

"Cam," Joshua said in a gentle tone, "I understand completely how you feel, but as a prosecutor—"

"Lawyer."

In spite of the derogatory tone in her snap, he chuckled, "Lawyer. When it comes to justice, sometimes, we have to choose our battles. Maybe this hit against Nick will be what the feds need to bring down the mob or the drug cartels. It's been known to happen. But, when you consider the evil that these people deal in, the multitudes of lives that they have ruined—drugs, prostitution, dealing in illegal arms—"

Cameron practically jumped to her feet. She reacted so quickly, that the heel of one of her feet hit Joshua in the groin. After uttering a gasp, he asked, "What did I say?"

"Prostitution," she said. "The ME puts Jane Doe's age at late teens to early twenties. She was pretty and had ligatures on her wrists and ankles."

"Possibly, she was abducted to be forced into prostitution," Joshua said.

"Got pregnant—"

"If she got pregnant they would have forced an abortion on her and then put her back to work," Joshua said.

"She was white," Cameron said. "White babies bring in a lot of money. They could have decided to let her have the baby, sold it on the black market, and then put her back to work. By that point, she probably thought jumping out of a speeding car would be better than going back to work."

Joshua sighed. "We have a lot of theories but nothing concrete."

"That's why I need to talk to Sal Bertonelli."

"I made some phone calls," he said. "I tried to call in a few markers that some friends in the FBI owe me."

A wide grin filled her face. "And …"

"I'm not promising you anything," he said. "I just want you to understand that if I can't get you in to see him, it's not because the government doesn't value the life of a patrolman over bringing down major hitters in organized crime or drug dealers. It's just that Sal Bertonelli is such a valuable asset in achieving an indictment against these so-called people that they don't want to risk it."

"I do understand," she said. "And it is because bringing down these guys has such a high priority that Nick's murder can become so low on their list that they can completely forget about it." She tapped her keyboard. "The only way we are going to find out who ordered Nick to be killed is if we investigate it ourselves."

Joshua opened his mouth to respond only to be cut off by the chimes of her cell phone. After checking the caller ID, she grinned. "Washington, D.C. Maybe they got an answer."

"Be nice," he ordered.

"I'm always nice."

"Until you hear the word 'no.'"

With hope in her voice, Cameron brought the phone to her ear. "Hello …"

"It seems your husband has some juice," Special Agent Peter Sanders of the FBI replied to her greeting.

Sitting up, Cameron grabbed Joshua's hand and shot him a smile. "What kind of juice?" Her voice oozed with innocence.

"You're getting in to see Sal Bertonelli," the federal agent said. "It will be only one meeting in Washington, D.C. Ten minutes—not one minute more. The U.S. Marshal's office will set up the meeting. You're going to have to understand, in order for this to go down, to keep our witness safe, we can't prearrange the time and place. All I can tell you is to be in Washington, D.C., by the day after tomorrow and be ready to meet with Bertonelli when we call."

"I'll be there."

After disconnecting the call, Cameron threw her arms around Joshua with a squeal, holding him tight while kissing him fully on the lips. "You did it! Your markers came in. We're going to get to question Bertonelli." She gazed into his eyes. "You really do understand what this means to me."

Joshua brushed his thumb across her cheek. "It's important to you. That makes it important to me." He sighed. "I wish I could go with you."

Her smile faded. "I want you to go."

"I can't," Joshua said. "The judge on the Franklin case won't give us any more continuances. I have to be in court and ready to go. If not, he'll declare a mistrial and I can't risk that."

Tears of anger seeped into her eyes. "Once again, Nick's murder—"

"Don't even go there, Cam." He cupped her chin in his hand and held her gaze. "I called in a lot of favors to get you face time with Bertonelli. Even if I can't be there in person, I'm keeping my promise. You aren't going to do this alone."

"Josh, I am a trained homicide detective—"

"I'm not going to let you go charging into Washington like a female wrecking ball." Joshua stood up. "You'll not only ruin any chance of getting justice for Nick, but you'll also blow the feds case against the cartels and Russians out of the water. There's too much at stake on both sides. So I'm sending in someone skilled in the art of diplomacy to accompany you."

With her glaring at his back, he left the room to make another phone call.

CHAPTER SEVEN

Hearing the impact of a vase hitting the other side of the wall in Murphy's office and shattering to the floor, Special Agents Perry Latimore, Susan Archer, and Deputy Chief Boris Hamilton exchanged smirks. They heard Hillary's voice uttering a curse directed either at Murphy or his commanding officer.

"You'd think the Pentagon would have thicker walls," Perry said.

Bringing up the information that he had collected on his tablet and connecting it to the smart white board filling the side wall of his office, Murphy showed no indication that he heard the crash coming from Hillary Koch's office. "She just got off the phone with my CO," Murphy said while keeping his eyes on the tablet. "Today's a quiet day." He rose up from behind his desk. "You should have heard her the day she found out one of her boyfriends was going back to his wife." He lowered the light for them to see the information from his tablet on the screen.

Images of five victims with their names and ages listed below them filled the computer screen. With a laser pointer, Murphy ticked off the names and basic information on each one. "Donna Crenshaw was a petty officer at the Navy Yard. She worked in supply. She was single, thirty-four years old—leaves behind a thirteen year old daughter."

"Divorced?" Susan asked.

"Never married according to her personnel record," Murphy said. "We'll want to look into if the father was involved in the child's life to eliminate the motive being a custody issue."

"Where's the daughter now?" Susan asked.

"She should be at the police department," Murphy said. "I'm going to go question her after we're done here."

"I'll go with you," Susan said.

"That won't be necessary," Murphy said. "I can handle it."

"Protocol calls for female witnesses, especially minors, to have a female agent be present at all times during questioning," Deputy Chief Boris Hamilton said. "That means Archer has to go."

"Then I guess you're going with me, Archer," Murphy said.

"Are any of the other four victims connected with the navy?" Boris asked with a stern expression on his weathered face. "Their husbands …"

"Crenshaw's the only one," Murphy said.

Rising from his seat, the deputy chief scanned the images of the women and their ages.

Donna Crenshaw was thirty-four years old. Estimated time of death was seven-thirty to eight-thirty. Shot five times.

A widow, Francine Baxter, the homeowner, was fifty-seven years old. Killed between five-thirty and six-thirty. Shot twice. Once in the back. Second to the head.

Seemingly poisoned, Colleen Davis, age twenty-eight years old. Unmarried, she was an elementary school teacher and was an authorized Cozy Cook dealer. Thirty-two year old Maureen Clark was a housewife with one young son. Her husband, Colonel Lincoln Clark, was in charge of the Third Infantry Division when they invaded Iraq.

"An army colonel?" Perry asked.

"Colonel Clark is twenty-years older than his wife," Murphy confirmed. "They've been married for nine years."

The fifth victim was forty year old Hannah Price, an engineer. She and her husband, also an engineer, had been married for close to twenty years and had two teenaged children.

"Age-wise and profession, they're all over the map," the deputy chief said.

Perry started to say, "If the petty officer was just collateral damage—in the wrong place at the wrong time—"

"The killer spent at least two hours in the house waiting for Crenshaw and then shot her five times," Murphy said. "Plus, she had texted the host that she was running late. The killer replied that they were waiting for her—"

"How do you know it was the killer who replied?" Perry asked.

"Do you use shorthand when you text or do you spell out every word?" Murphy brought up a screen shot of Donna Crenshaw's cell phone with the text stream displayed:

Mtg set 4 7pm tomorrow. Pls come. Important. We need U if we R 2 stop him.

Running late. Accident has Route 7 @ standstill. B there ASAP. Count me in.

No problem. We're waiting for you. Front door is open. Just let yourself in.

Using the laser pointer to run under the first text word for word, Murphy explained, "The first text came from the host of the party, Francine Baxter, on the day before the meeting. Notice that she uses text shorthand. 'Meeting' is shortened to m-t-g. Instead of spelling out 'for' she uses the number four. 'Please' is abbreviated. The next text was from Crenshaw to

Baxter after seven o'clock. The medical examiner says Baxter died between five-thirty and six-thirty."

"So Baxter was already dead when Crenshaw texted that she was going to be late," Boris said with a nod of his head.

"And the killer replied," Murphy said, "telling her to come right on in—they were waiting … to kill her. If Crenshaw wasn't the target, why did the killer reply for her to come in, and then wait to put five bullets into her to make sure she was dead?"

"The killer wanted Crenshaw dead," Boris said. "She was the target."

Susan said in a breathy voice, "And he killed four other women to get to her? You'd think there would have been an easier way—less bloodshed."

"I'm suspecting he wanted all of them dead," Murphy said. "Did you read the text that Baxter had sent to Crenshaw? Clark and Price both told their husbands that they were going to a Cozy Cook Party. That was a cover story. Baxter texted Crenshaw that it was a meeting to plan to stop someone."

"They were all targets," Boris said.

"But they needed Crenshaw in order to stop him, whoever he is," Murphy said. "The answer lies with her and since she's navy, that makes it our case."

"Our prime suspect is going to be this 'he' they were planning to stop," Boris said. "I'll go talk to Crenshaw's boss at the Navy Yard." He turned to Special Agent Perry Latimore, who was already on his feet.

"I'll go search Crenshaw's house and take a look at her computer," the agent said.

Feeling his cell phone vibrate on his hip, Murphy checked the caller ID, which read "Dad." "I need to take this," he said.

Having a number of investigations under their belts, the team was already coordinating the investigation without him.

"I'm going with Lieutenant Thornton to talk to the victim's daughter," Susan said. "If we're lucky, the daughter may have something useful for us."

"We need to schedule interviews with the families of all of the victims," Boris was saying when Murphy stepped out into the hallway and made his way to the break room. "Latimore and I will divvy those up."

Murphy brought the cell phone to his ear. "Hey, Dad, what's up?"

"How're things going?" Joshua asked in a forced upbeat tone.

Murphy turned into the doorway of the break room to find Hillary Koch attacking a bag of potato chips that refused to be opened. Uttering a loud obscenity, she tore it open with a vengeance to send chips flying in every direction and raining down to the floor.

"Great." Murphy spun on his heels to head halfway down the corridor to his office and leaned up against the wall. "What's going on there?"

"Cameron is coming out to Washington tomorrow," Joshua said. "The feds uncovered evidence that Nick, her late husband, was a contracted hit. They've agreed to let her question the killer. I can't come with her because I've got this case and—"

"She can stay with us," Murphy interjected with a grin. "No problem. She'll be our first official house guest. And I'll go with her when she goes to question this slime bucket. Don't worry, Dad, we'll take care of Cameron."

"Call Jessica and—"

"Jessica won't mind," Murphy said. "She loves Cameron."

"Murphy," Joshua replied, "do you have a comfortable bed in your guest room?"

"Why? Does Cameron have a bad back?"

"No," Joshua said with a laugh, "I meant for you."

"What do you mean?" Murphy turned away when he saw Hillary come out of the break room. When her eyes met his, they narrowed into falsely lashed slits. Clutching a big bowl filled with potato chips to her chest, she rushed past him.

"You haven't been married for very long," Joshua said, "and clearly you have a lot to learn."

"Dad, I grew up in a house filled with brothers and sisters. I got along fine with Tracy and Sarah … most of the time."

"Sisters are different from wives," Joshua said. "Jessica is your *wife*. She is your *partner* in life. She is not above you, but you aren't above her either. That house is your home—both of yours. Rule number one for a happy marriage, don't invite people to come stay with you—especially your in-laws—without first checking with your spouse. Cameron is Jessica's mother-in-law. I love Cameron with all my heart, but I'll be the first to admit—she is not the easiest person to live with."

Joshua sighed. "I had to learn that lesson the hard way. Your mother and I were married only two months when I invited one of my navy buddies to some stay with us after his wife kicked him out. Your mother was pregnant with you and J.J., and having morning sickness, and we didn't have a guest room in our one bedroom apartment. Let's just say my next investment after that was in a very comfortable sofa."

The mention of his mother's pregnancy with him and his twin brother reminded Murphy of Jessica's mention of a surprise. "That's right. Mom got pregnant right away after you two were married."

"Your mother was happiest when she was pregnant." Joshua concluded his fatherly advice with an order. "Call Jessica and check to make sure it's okay for Cameron to come stay with you and that you can get off to go meet this hit man with her, and *then* call me back."

Click.

"Newman, I hate you." Hoisting the forty-five pound mongrel over her shoulder in order to dig her keys out of the stylish purse hanging from her shoulder, Jessica felt around the doorknob for the keyhole in order to unlock the door. The bulk of the hound in her arms was blocking her view. Finally, she was able to unlock, open the door, and shoulder her way inside. Upon their entrance, Spencer, yapping all the way, bounced across the living room to the entranceway and jumped up on them.

In her high-heeled sandals, Jessica fought to remain upright in order to gently deposit the dog and enter the passcode in their security box next to the door. She had only seconds to input the code before the security company sent over a unit to check on the house. She was in the middle of typing it in when the cell phone in her purse rang with the opening bars of "When I Fall in Love" by Celine Dion and Clive Griffin.

Murphy!

After completing the passcode, she dove into the purse to find the phone.

Meanwhile, Spencer was rejoicing at the playmate who had dropped from the sky. Snarling and snapping, Newman galloped into the living room for his chair with Spencer yipping and yapping at his heels.

"Hey, Buttercup!" Murphy greeted Jessica's breathless answer.

"I hate your dog," she gasped out.

"What did Newman do now?"

"I took him for a walk down to the river."

"Newman hates walks," Murphy said.

"I know!" Jessica dropped onto the sofa and removed her sandals to shake out a stone. "We got down to the river and he'd had enough. He sat down and refused to walk back. I tried dragging him on the leash, but it was like trying to drag a

forty-five pound bag of rocks. I ended up carrying his fat butt all the way back home. Do you know how steep that hill is?"

"Are you all right?" Murphy's tone was filled with concern. "You didn't hurt yourself, did you? Is everything okay?"

"I'm fine," she growled.

"Well, don't take Newman out for any more walks," Murphy ordered. "I'll walk him from now on."

"But you're not always here when he needs to go and he needs exercise, even if he doesn't like it," she said. "I never heard of a dog who waited until the commercial breaks to go to the bathroom and rushed back inside before they were over." After uttering a deep sigh, she smoothed her hair and asked, "How's your day?"

"Fine," he replied. "I'm investigating my first official murder case."

"Great," she said with a grin.

"Five women."

"That's terrible." Her enthusiasm faded.

"Three of them had children." Murphy noticed Susan waiting for him by Wendy's desk. "I'll tell you about it at dinner. Reason for my call—Cameron is coming out to Washington. Tomorrow. Seems the feds caught the guy who killed her late husband, Nick, and it was a paid hit. She's coming out to meet with them to get the low-down. Is it okay if she stays with us?"

Jessica voice was filled with glee. "Our first house guest."

"Then you're okay with it?"

"Totally! I'll go fix up one of the guest rooms right now. Hey, dinner at Four Seasons at seven o'clock. This has been a really big day. I can't wait to give you my news."

"Neither can I." In anticipation of news about expanding their small family, Murphy couldn't keep the smile out of his voice. "I love you, Buttercup."

"I love you more, Honey Buns."

As soon as Murphy disconnected the call, his cell phone was vibrating again with the caller ID reading "Wu." When he answered the call, the homicide detective sounded unhappy to pass on his news. "Isadora Crenshaw is gone."

"What do you mean gone?"

"Children's services took her before I got back to the station." The detective was as disgusted by the news as Murphy. "She has no family. No father—"

"She has to have a father!" Murphy said.

"Not in the picture. No family. Children's services was here to pick up another kid on another case. They didn't want to come back to pick her up so they took her. Since she's thirteen, they're taking her to a group home because they don't have a family able to take her."

"No!" Murphy yelled. "She just lost her mother. If she has no one then being locked up with a bunch of juvies will traumatize her even more."

"You're telling me," Wu said. "I'm texting you the address now. Good luck."

"I have a confession to make," Susan said after they had climbed into Murphy's SUV and merged onto the expressway to take them toward Rosslyn, Virginia.

"Are you sure you don't want to wait for a lawyer?" Murphy asked with a grin.

"I don't think that'll be necessary," she replied. "But I think you should know since you're bringing me along to interview this child who has just lost her mother … I mean, thinking that because I'm a woman that I'm all maternal and would know just what to say and all that."

"Out with it, Archer." Murphy glanced across the front seat in her direction.

"I'm not good with kids," the agent said. "I can take down felons and unruly, drunken, lecherous sailors and even terrorists, but kids eat me alive."

Murphy chuckled. "I don't believe that."

"Believe it," she said without humor. "Contrary to popular belief that all women are born with maternal genes and a deep, instinctive yearning to have babies and know instantly how to raise one, I got none of that stuff. I never babysat. My uterus never aches at the sight of a baby. Nada. So, if you think that I'm going to look at Isadora Crenshaw and know instantly what to say to her to make her give us all the answers about this case, I can tell you right now—ain't gonna happen."

"That's okay," Murphy said. "I come from a family with five kids. I've been babysitting since I was ten years old. We'll be fine."

"Good," she replied. "I guess coming from a big family, you and Jessica are planning to have a bunch of kids."

Saying nothing, Murphy smiled.

CHAPTER EIGHT

Murphy and Susan found Isadora Crenshaw at a group home down the freeway from Washington, D.C. The home for juveniles was a big old house in what had once been a middle-class section of Rosslyn. With the shift in economy during the past decade, those who had managed to move up the economic ladder had moved out of the area. With the influx of poorly paid, as well as illegal, immigrants, the once proud middle-class homes were now in dire need of new roofs, siding, and yard work. Simply picking up toys and bicycles from the front yards would have improved the rundown appearance of the community.

After parking his SUV on the street, Murphy spotted some teenaged boys making a drug deal two doors down from the group home. "Nice neighborhood," he muttered with sarcasm to Susan.

"Most nice neighborhoods have home owner associations that don't allow group homes for kids without families," Susan explained.

As Murphy climbed the steps to the front door, two teenaged boys ran outside, leaving the front door open. The smell of spaghetti sauce simmering and the sound of an argument floated to them from the rear of the house.

"Sounds like someone is calling for help." Murphy unclipped the holster on his gun.

While making his way down the hallway leading to the back of the house, they heard the stern voice of an older woman saying, "As long as you're living under this roof, young lady, we have rules against violence!"

"She started it!" The girl's voice was filled with both fright and anger.

"I didn't do anything!" another girl said before adding in a tearful tone, "Mrs. Peale, why is she telling lies about me?"

At the end of the hallway, Murphy and Susan eased the swinging door open to view the kitchen. Sitting on a bar stool in the corner of the country kitchen was a teenaged girl with thick blonde hair with tight curls and big red-rimmed eyes. With her arms folded across her chest, she glared at a seemingly older girl being tended for a bloody nose at the table. "Tell her the truth!" the girl with the curly hair ordered.

"Shut up!" the injured girl shot back before wrapping her arms around the plump older woman in a worn apron administering to her. "She scares me, Mrs. Peale."

Since his marriage to Jessica Faraday, Murphy had received a crash course in fashion and the high price of style. The bleeding girl's high-heeled sandals were a designer name that cost more than the monthly allowance Mrs. Peale received to support the children she took in.

"She's lying! Can't you see that?" the girl in the corner said. In faded blue jeans and a Hard Rock Café t-shirt that had also seen better times, she resembled a cinematic ragamuffin.

Caressing the injured girl's shoulder, Mrs. Peale pointed a finger at the girl in the corner. "You shut your mouth, you little troublemaker!" Then, she turned back to the girl at the table. "It's okay, Kate, she's not going to hurt you anymore."

"She broke my nose ... for no reason!" Throwing her arms around Mrs. Peale, Kate sobbed. "Can't you send her to juvie?"

Behind Mrs. Peale, Murphy cocked his head, observing that—while Kate cried hysterically—no tears came from her eyes. Glancing back at Susan, he saw that she noticed the same thing.

The girl on the stool used the back of her hand to wipe the tears from her eyes. "She took my iPad and said that if I didn't let her keep it that she and her friends here were going to beat me—"

"Why is she telling these lies about me?" Kate wailed.

"She's jealous," Mrs. Peale soothed.

"Jealous? Of what?" the girl on the stool yelled. "She's a whack-job!"

Her fat flabby arm raised up, Mrs. Peale whirled around.

Seeing the woman coming toward her, the girl let out a shriek and covered her head with both arms while jumping off the stool and backing away.

Mrs. Peal took a step toward the girl only to have Murphy grab her by the wrist and whirl her back to face him. The pressure of his thumb in the palm of her hand instantly dropped her to her plump knees.

Kate jumped out of her chair and headed for the doorway to find Susan blocking it. The stern glare in the agent's eyes sent the girl back to her seat.

Murphy's voice was low and menacing. "You lay one hand on that girl and I'll have this place shut down and your butt tossed in jail for child abuse."

Writhing from the discomfort of the pressure Murphy was still applying to her hand, Mrs. Peale gasped out, "Who the hell are you?"

Susan opened her jacket to reveal her badge and gun. "Naval Criminal Investigative Services. I'm Special Agent Susan Archer. This is Lieutenant Murphy Thornton."

"We're here to see Isadora Crenshaw." Murphy released Mrs. Peale's hand. "We're investigating her mother's murder."

Rubbing her hand, Mrs. Peale gestured at the girl on the stool. "That's the little troublemaker." Slowly, she climbed up to her feet. "She's been here less than two hours and already attacked one of the girls."

Murphy went over to the girl on the stool, who was watching them with wide frightened eyes. "Hello, Isadora. I'm Murphy Thornton." When he held out his hand to her, she backed away as if she feared he would force her to her knees the same way he had Mrs. Peale. "It's okay. I'm not going to hurt you, and I'm not going to let anyone else hurt you either."

After a long silence, during which she looked Murphy up and down, taking in his white uniform and the ribbons and medals on his chest, she said in a soft voice, "I hate the name Isadora. Call me Izzy."

"Isadora," Kate shot in her direction in a mocking tone. Her smirk dropped when Murphy turned around to fire off a glare. The fury that sparked from his eyes was enough to make her back up in her chair.

Kate's retreat caused the corners of Murphy's lips to curl. When he turned back to Izzy, he saw that the corners of her lips curled as well, even while her eyes were moist with tears. With a shuddered sigh, she took his hand.

He escorted her out of the corner. "Izzy, you're coming with us. Get your things." He shot a glance in Kate's direction. "And don't forget your iPad."

"You can't just take her!" Mrs. Peale said.

After handing Izzy off to Susan, Murphy brought his face close to hers. "I can respect that." He took his phone from the case on his belt and pressed a speed dial button. "My commanding officer will call a federal judge to get a warrant for us to take Izzy into protective custody as a material witness in her mother's murder." He sat down at the table across from Kate. "And … while we're waiting for that warrant, Kate and I will have a nice conversation about this protection racket that she's been running while living under your roof, Mrs. Peale."

Kate's pretty green eyes grew big.

Bringing the phone to his ear, Murphy winked at the girl. "Nice shoes, Kate."

On Pennsylvania Avenue, Jessica Faraday restrained herself from checking the time on the cell resting next to her clutch bag on the table top. It was way after seven o'clock and she was alone at the table for two at the Four Seasons. She had reserved a table next to the windows that provided an excellent night view of Washington, D.C., in all its dazzling glory.

She was alone—only her and her purple martini.

Murphy was late.

Suck it up, Buttercup. You married a hunk who is passionate about doing whatever it takes to make things right. The gold of her wedding band caught in the glow of the candle's flame. She wrapped her fingers—tipped with elegantly painted fingernails sporting hand-painted violets—around the stem of her martini glass and took a sip. *If it means being late for your celebratory dinner, so be it. This is only the first of probably a long line of missed dates.*

Her violet eyes lit up at the sight of the handsome man in his white uniform rounding the corner with the host. When he flashed his charming grin, complete with dimples in both cheeks, her heart skipped a beat. Catching her breath, she wet her lips and smoothed her raven hair. *Geez, Jessie, this isn't your first date.*

As they neared the table, Jessica noticed that Murphy was not alone. While he had his hat tucked under one arm, his right hand clasped that of a slender girl with a head full of ash blonde curls and the saddest red eyes one could imagine. Her tiny frame and face made her light brown eyes appear that much bigger.

As they grew closer, the maître d', a short, jolly man by the name of Francesco, was telling Murphy in a thick Italian accent that they would move them to a bigger table.

"Thank you very much." Murphy slipped some money to the host. He flashed an apologetic grin in Jessica's direction. "I'm sorry we're so much trouble."

"No trouble at all, sir." Francesco flashed a smile at the sad young girl. He then directed them to a table for four in the middle of the restaurant, away from the windows that Jessica had requested. "Suitable for you, Mr. Murphy?"

Placing his hand on Jessica's shoulder, Murphy kissed her quickly on the ear before whispering, "I'll explain."

Seeing the girl's tear stained face, Jessica cut him off. "No need." Grabbing her purse, cell phone and martini, she told the host, "The table is excellent. Thank you so much, Francesco." She saw Murphy sigh with relief.

"Anything for you, Miss Jessica." With a grin, Francesco dropped the linen napkin into Jessica's lap.

"This is Izzy Crenshaw," Murphy introduced the girl while holding her chair for her. "Izzy, this is my wife, Jessica."

Wordlessly, Izzy looked Jessica up and down. In her colorful soft dress, long bare legs, and high-heeled shoes, Jessica was a complete contrast from the girl clad in jeans and a faded Hard Rock Café t-shirt.

"Izzy is in my protective custody." Murphy took a seat between them.

"You're protecting her from what?" Jessica asked while Francesco offered her the wine menu. The maître d' had learned from their many dinners at the restaurant that Jessica would order the wine for herself, while Murphy drank only water with lemon.

"Right now, the system," Murphy said. "You should have seen the place they put her. She has no family—"

"You have no family?" Jessica asked the girl.

"That is so very sad," Making a "task-tsk" noise with his tongue, Francesco shook his head. Signaled by the snap of the host's fingers, the server hurried over with three menus for them.

"Mom used to have a sister," Izzy said to Murphy. "She died before I was born. Mom told me that I was just as headstrong as she was." Her voice trailed off.

Jessica and Murphy exchanged heartfelt glances.

"I'll have water and a plate of lemon wedges," Murphy requested from the server before asking Izzy in an upbeat tone, "What would you like, Izzy? You can get anything you want."

Seeing the girl's sad expression, the server said, "Even if it's not on the menu. Our chef is world famous. He can cook you anything. You name it."

Izzy stared at the menu without opening it. "I'm not hungry."

"Have you had dinner yet?" Spotting a dessert cart being wheeled past the table, Jessica asked the server, "Do you have your delicious chocolate lava cake and a scoop of ice cream?" He rushed to the kitchen to check on the item.

"It's okay, honey," Murphy told Izzy, "I wasn't hungry for the longest time when my mother passed away. When you're ready to eat, then you'll eat."

"She has to keep her strength up," Jessica said. "We can't take her home and put her to bed without dinner."

"She's in mourning," Murphy reminded her.

"Which is why we need to feed her," Jessica said. "Chocolate makes everything better. It won't solve the problem or take away the hurt, but it does soften the sting of the pain."

"Bull," he replied. "That's nothing more than an old wive's rationalization for endorsing gluttony. Grief is no excuse to pack yourself full of processed dairy products and refined sugar."

"One little lava cake for one dinner isn't going to kill her," Jessica said.

They both observed Izzy staring at her water glass seemingly without seeing it. She didn't appear to have any interest in the outcome of their discussion.

"What happens when she crashes?" Murphy asked Jessica. "She downs a tube of chocolate chip cookie dough and begins the cycle over again. Before she'll know it, she'll be a depressed obese diabetic with heart disease."

"It's *cake*," Jessica said, "not heroin."

The server arrived to announce that the chef would be glad to prepare the lava cake with a scoop of ice cream. "Would you like me to put in the order for the young lady?"

In unison, Jessica answered "yes" while Murphy said a resolute "no." A glare from Jessica prompted Murphy to back down. With a roll of his eyes and a shrug of his shoulders, he gave in and the server hurried off to put in the order for the lava cake.

For the first time since Murphy had met her, a hint of a smile crossed Izzy's face. With the tilt of his head, he caught Jessica's attention to point out the small breakthrough in the young girl.

At the sight of the young girl's sadness easing slightly, Murphy was reminded of the surprise that Jessica had promised. Reaching across the table to caress her fingers with his, his eyes met hers. A soft, reassuring smile came to her lips.

Unable to wait any longer to learn her surprise, Murphy excused them both for a moment, took Jessica by the hand, and led her to the lounge. Making sure he kept Izzy, his responsibility, in his line of sight, he pulled Jessica close and kissed her long and hard on the mouth.

When she came up for air, Jessica breathed, "What was that for?"

"For being understanding about Izzy." He gazed into her face. "You reminded me of what made me fall in love with you so fast."

"I thought it was my body that made you fall hard for me." She winked up at him.

For the first time, he noticed that she had changed into a soft pink and blue silk dress that hugged every curve of her body. Holding her against him, he caught an eyeful down the plunging neckline. "That, too." He grinned. "So, are you going to keep me in suspense any longer? What's your surprise?"

"Do you really want to know?" she demurred.

"I've been thinking about it all afternoon." In anticipation, he chewed his bottom lip. To his surprise, she opened her clutch bag and pulled out her wallet. Yanking a card out, she handed it to him. "It came in today's mail."

Murphy was so caught off guard that he could barely read the heading across the top of the laminated identification card. "What?"

"My license," she explained. "I'm now a licensed private investigator."

"You're a … PI." Disappointment seeped through his chest. He shoved the card back into her hand and whirled around. Anger taking hold, he turned back to her. "When did you become a PI? Why did you become a PI?"

"Because it's going to be over a year before I can start medical school," she explained. "After what happened in Deep Creek Lake, I thought I have the knowledge and natural talent that I could maybe work some cases—it will be a great way to observe and study the human psyche in the field. All of my friends have jobs or are married and have kids or are going to school—and I am not the type of woman to sit around all day and watch television with Newman or go shopping. I mean, a woman can only have so many pairs of shoes. So I decided to take a course online and then I took the test and I passed with a perfect score." She cocked her head at him. "What's your problem anyway?"

Humiliated by the error of his deduction, Murphy sighed. It wasn't her fault that he had jumped to the wrong conclusion and got his hopes up. "I thought it was something else."

"What did you think it was?" Studying the expression on his face, she narrowed her eyes to violet slits. When he didn't respond, she uttered a scoff. "What were you thinking?"

"You said your news would make *us both* happy," Murphy reminded her. "Why would I be happy about you becoming a private eye, spying on cheating husbands and running background checks?"

"I thought you would be happy that I wasn't lying around watching movies and getting fat or going out and buying another dozen pairs of pumps," she said. "You look like I just asked you for a divorce or told you that I was sleeping with another man. What did you think my news was going to be?"

"That we were pregnant," Murphy confessed in a low voice.

Jessica's eyes grew wide. With a small gasp, she stepped backwards while clutching her bosom.

Seeing her shock, Murphy stuttered out an explanation, "I know we use birth control, but it isn't a hundred percent."

"Murphy," she said, "we've only just gotten married. Did you really *want* to start a family this soon?"

"No," he said, "but when I started thinking that was your surprise, I warmed up to the idea real fast. My parents had only been married ten months when J.J. and I came along."

Stunned by her expression, he added, "You do want to have children, don't you?"

"Yes, but not right now," she said. "We have a lot of adjustments to make. Plus, we can't ignore the fact that we still have to get to know a lot of things about each other. I admit we were wild and crazy to get married as fast as we did—but then, to throw a baby into the mix immediately, that's just plain insane."

"Yes, it is."

"I'm glad to see we agree about that."

Letting out a deep breath, Jessica brushed past him to return to the table, but not before Murphy caught her by the arm. "So when are we going to have children?"

"Not today," she replied through gritted teeth. Yanking her arm free, she hurried back to the table.

"I'm ready when you are," he told her departing figure.

At the table, Jessica ordered another martini. This one was a double.

CHAPTER NINE

Wrapped up in *Dancing with the Stars*, Newman didn't notice the two-legged visitor to his home when his owners returned. He did hear the kitchen cupboard door and smelled the dog biscuit jar open, at which point he sat up and peered around the back of his chair in the direction of the kitchen with his floppy ears at attention.

Across the foyer and around the corner from the dining room, Murphy could feel Newman's eyes ordering his master to bring his biscuit to him. Heaven forbid the couch potato miss Karina Schmirnoff doing the tango.

Spencer wolfed down her biscuit in only one bite before turning her attention to Izzy, who knelt down to the floor to admire the sheltie while petting her soft blue fur. "She's got pretty eyes. I never saw a blue dog with blue eyes before."

"That's what makes her special." Jessica turned to Murphy who had returned to the kitchen after giving Newman his treat. "Why is it that when I come home alone, Spencer barks her head off, but she doesn't bark at you?"

"She didn't bark just now when we came in," Murphy said.

"But you were with me," Jessica pointed out, "and I noticed that she doesn't bark at you when you come home from work."

His eyes wide, Murphy shrugged his shoulders with a broad gesture. "I don't know. Ask Candi."

"Her name is Spencer," Jessica said.

"What should I call her?" Izzy asked.

Jessica answered, "Spencer," at the same time that Murphy said, "She answers to Candi."

"I'll call her Blue." Izzy brought her face close to Spencer's snout and kissed it. "Do you like that name, Blue?"

After uttering a yap, Spencer licked Izzy on the lips and nose.

"It's going to take all of Candi's two IQ points just to figure out what her name is." Murphy picked up the suitcase that he had left on the floor while retrieving the treats for the dogs. "Izzy, would you like me to show you up to your room?"

Remembering that she had fixed up the guest room across from the master suite for Cameron, Jessica uttered a squawk that caused Murphy to pause. "Cameron is coming tomorrow. I was going to put her—"

"Who's Cameron?" Izzy asked.

"She's my stepmother," Murphy answered before telling Jessica. "Izzy is my responsibility. I would feel more comfortable if she was on the same floor with us."

"How many floors does this house have?" Izzy asked.

"Four." With a sigh, Jessica agreed to fix up the guest room on the top floor, in the loft, for Cameron the next morning.

In the living room, Izzy stopped and took in the luxurious space of the brownstone. "Wow." Her mouth hung in awe. "This room alone is bigger than our house. I didn't know the navy paid so well."

"They don't." Murphy shot a grin over his shoulder. "I married very well."

"And don't you forget it." Jessica fell in behind them.

Spencer scurried to keep pace with Izzy.

The classic leather furniture still had the new smell, except for the old overstuffed chair from Murphy's previous apartment. The black and white hound with the short legs and floppy ears eyed the curly haired girl. On the flat-screen television hanging on the wall across from the dog, a couple in sequined outfits were dancing the tango.

"That's Newman," Jessica told her in a low voice. "He doesn't bite unless you change the channel when he's watching one of his programs."

Upstairs, Murphy placed Izzy's suitcase on a luggage stand in the closet. Children's services had stopped at the Crenshaw house on the way to the group home to pack a few things into an overnight bag. "I'll be going to your house tomorrow, Izzy," he told her. "If you find that you've forgotten or want anything, let me know and I'll get it for you."

Opening the door to the bathroom, Izzy's mouth dropped. Spotting the sunken tub with jets, she uttered a gasp. "Is that a Jacuzzi? Is that my bathroom?" She turned to them. "The bathroom at the other place smelled funny."

"As long as you're staying here, that will be your bathroom." As soon as she said the words, Jessica caught Murphy's eye from the other side of the queen-sized bed.

Wordlessly, they asked the same question. *How long is Izzy staying with us? Certainly not indefinitely.* By removing her from the group home, Murphy had saved her from a horrible place but, clearly, it was only temporary. Eventually, she would have to go back to children's services who would put her into the foster care system. With no living relative, she would be available for adoption. Unfortunately, the odds of a teenager being adopted by a good family were not good. She would most likely end up back in the same situation that Murphy had rescued her from.

Izzy unzipped the suitcase and retrieved a framed picture, which rested on top of the few things that she had packed. She held out the picture to Jessica. "Is it okay if I put this on the stand next to my bed?"

Jessica took the picture from her. It was of two young women, both in army dress uniforms, standing with their arms around each other. One had auburn hair pulled back into a bun secured low on her neck. She wore the private first class insignia on her sleeve. Murphy recognized her as Donna Crenshaw, Izzy's mother. Several inches shorter than Donna, the second woman, who wore her curly blonde hair pulled back into a French braid, had the insignia designating her as an army specialist.

"That's my mom and her sister." Izzy wiped her nose with the back of her hand. "This picture was taken on the day my mom graduated from army boot camp."

"Your mother used to be in the army?" Jessica asked.

"Then she switched to the navy," Izzy said.

"They were both very pretty."

"Mom tells me ..." Izzy choked before correcting herself, "told me ... that I have Cecelia's smile."

"Are you interested in going into the army like your mother and aunt?"

To Murphy's surprise, Izzy shook her head vehemently. "Mom said no way in hell would she ever let me join the army."

Before he could respond, Murphy's cell phone vibrated on his hip. Checking the caller ID, he saw that it was Boris Hamilton.

Not wanting to discuss the case within Izzy's ear shot, Murphy stepped out of the bedroom. Escorting Spencer down the hall to the master bedroom, he answered the call. "Hey, Boris, what's up?"

"Archer told me that you already have your first house guest," the deputy chief said with a smile in his voice.

"Did she tell you about the place they had sent her?" Murphy replied.

Boris said, "Doesn't surprise me one bit."

Even though Murphy closed the door to the master suite, Spencer sat at attention staring at the door cutting her off from the visitor down the hall.

"Between her, Latimore, and me, we managed to visit the families of the other four victims," Boris said. "Plus, I talked to Lieutenant Wu about his preliminary interviews and we discovered something extremely strange about this get together that our victims had last night."

"I already knew something was up with that party." Sitting on the bed, Murphy slipped his shoes off. "Two of the victims told their husbands that they were going to a Cozy Cook party. But there were no samples set out at the crime scene."

"Good catch, Lieutenant," Boris said. "My wife, Claire seems to have one of those parties every month. The sales lady comes out way ahead of the guests to make a mess of the kitchen. They stuff all of our friends with food, clean out their wallets, and then Claire gets a bunch of fancy kitchen stuff that she'll never use."

"Sounds like my mom." Murphy swallowed to conceal the note of sadness edging into his voice.

"But there's more," Boris said. "Murphy, none of these victims knew each other."

"What?" Murphy sat up. "What do you mean they didn't know each other? They were all in Francine Baxter's house. She had to know them. She texted Crenshaw to invite her to the meeting. Maybe they didn't know *each other*, but they had to know Baxter."

"If the victims knew Baxter, then their families didn't know about it," Boris said. "No one knows what any of the victims were doing at Baxter's place, and each family we talked to claimed they never heard of Francine Baxter."

Putting Boris on speaker phone, Murphy brought up the pictures of the victims on his tablet.

As if he sensed what Murphy was doing, Boris asked, "Have you talked to Crenshaw's daughter about her mother yet?"

"I don't want to push her," Murphy said, "but I'll go ask her about the other victims now." After confirming that they would meet the next morning to go over what evidence they had, Murphy went out into the hall and knocked on the guest bedroom door.

"Come in," Jessica called out.

Murphy found that Izzy had changed into a pair of gray pajamas and climbed into bed. Jessica was putting Izzy's clothes in the dresser drawers.

"Will I be going to school tomorrow?" Izzy asked. "I've got a math test and Mom wouldn't want me to miss it."

"We'll be talking to your teachers," Murphy explained. "I'm sure they'll understand if you miss a few days." He eased down onto the bed next to Izzy and brought up the pictures of the other murder victims.

While zipping the empty suitcase shut, Jessica watched him with concern etched on her face. Her dark eyebrows were furrowed.

Avoiding his wife's probing eyes, Murphy said in a soft voice, "Izzy, I know this is difficult for you, but, if we are to catch whoever it was who took your mother away from you, we do need to talk about what happened last night. Did your mother tell you where she was going?"

"She was going to a business meeting," Izzy said. "She brought home a pizza and was running late, so she didn't have time to eat it. She said she would heat it up when she got home, and then she left."

"Did she tell you what this meeting was about?" Murphy asked.

Izzy shook her head. "She said it was important though."

Murphy glanced down at the tablet he held in his hand. "Izzy, I'm going to show you some pictures—"

"Murphy," Jessica said in a sharp tone while Izzy sucked in a deep breath.

"No, these aren't bad pictures," Murphy told her. "They're driver's license pictures of people. Tell me if you recognize any of them?" Careful not to give her the names while he scrolled through each picture, holding them up for Izzy to see the image, the girl shook her head with each one.

After showing her the last one, Murphy sighed. "Okay, how about their names? Did your mother ever mention the name Francine Baxter?"

Again, Izzy shook her head.

"How about Colleen Davis?"

"No," Izzy responded.

"Maureen Clark?"

Izzy shook her head.

"Hannah Price," Murphy asked. "Did your mother—"

"No," Izzy said with a shake of her head. "Who are they?"

"They were with your mother when she was killed," Murphy said as gently as he could. "We believe whoever killed her, murdered them, too."

"All of them?" Tears filled Izzy's eyes. "How many ..." She tried to count but the names were all jumbled in her head.

"Five," Murphy murmured.

"Why?" she blubbered.

Jessica sat on the bed and hugged her.

"We're trying to figure that out," Murphy said.

Choking on her tears, Izzy demanded to know, "Why? Why would someone do that to my mom and all these other people? How could someone be so mean?"

Bursting into tears, Izzy let out a wail. It was as if the lid that the girl had used to seal in her emotions had been blown off to release her sorrow, fear, and anger all at once.

Unprepared for the outburst, Murphy jumped back from the bed. At the same time, Jessica rocked the distraught girl in her arms. Not to be left out, Spencer scurried in and jumped up onto the bed to offer her comfort as well.

"I think you're done for now," Jessica told Murphy in a soft voice, "Can you leave us alone? I'll talk to her."

Feeling like a monster for causing the outburst with his questions, Murphy left the room and silently closed the door. In the hallway, he could hear Jessica offering words of comfort in an effort to ease the child's pain, which he knew from his own experience would not be going away soon.

CHAPTER TEN

The next morning, Jessica woke up to the smell of bacon cooking and Spencer kissing her nose with her soft tongue. The pup's doggie breath quickly overtaking the bacon smell, she rolled over to escape the foul odor. Not to be rejected, Spencer hopped over her to demand attention.

"Spencer, why don't you go tell Murphy to take you for a run."

No sooner were the words out of her mouth when the alarm clock sounded, which was all the reason Spencer needed to up the ante with barked orders for her to get out of bed. Swatting the alarm, Jessica rolled over to discover that her husband's side of the bed was empty. She wasn't surprised.

Murphy was an early riser. During the week, he would get up at five o'clock to spend an hour working out in the gym or running five miles. Then, he would go to the roof for yoga, finishing off with meditation during the rising of the sun.

After several weeks, Jessica had finally gotten in sync with her husband's routine so that she would get up in time to have his herbal tea and protein smoothie waiting for him when he came down from the rooftop. While he started his day with exercise, meditation, green tea and protein; she

117

would wake up to coffee with an exotic creamer and sugar substitute, and a chocolate Pop-Tart.

Taking in another whiff of the bacon, Jessica concluded that Murphy must have taken a break from his regular routine to cook breakfast for Izzy. While the possibility of a big hot breakfast intrigued her, she was more interested in a few more hours of sleep. It was one o'clock in the morning before Jessica had managed to console Izzy to sleep.

Finally, lured by the scent of biscuits baking in the oven, Jessica jumped out of the bed and shrugged into her bathrobe.

It would be rude for me to stay in bed while Murphy is cooking breakfast for our guest. Besides, it's only right that I check to see how Izzy is feeling this morning.

Jessica went out into the hallway to find Izzy coming up the stairs from the living room. She was clad in the same Hard Rock Café t-shirt and a pair of baggy khaki shorts that accentuated her skinny legs and bony knees. Her curly mop bounced to the rhythm of her gallop.

"Good morning, Princess Jasmine," Izzy said before jogging up the next flight of stairs.

"Princess Jasmine? Why are you calling me Princess Jasmine?"

Izzy stopped with a foot in midair. Spinning around, she cocked her head at Jessica, who was still rubbing the sleep out of her eyes and tucking a stray lock of her raven hair behind her ear.

How can this child be so wide awake when the sun is only now starting to come up?

"Cause you look like Princess Jasmine," Izzy said.

"Huh?" When another thick lock fell into her face, Jessica finger-combed her hair straight back. She was surprised and glad to see a grin come to Izzy's face.

"Hasn't anyone ever told you? With your dark hair and pretty eyes? You look like Princess Jasmine from the movie *Aladdin*."

Flattered, Jessica was speechless.

A small grin came to Izzy's lips. Her cheeks turned pink. "Thank you for staying up with me all night. You must think I'm a real whack-job losing it the way I did lose it."

Jessica took Izzy into a warm hug. "You just lost your mother. I'd think you were a whack-job if you didn't."

Wanting to take part in the hug, Spencer planted her front paws on Izzy's leg and let out a yap. "Good morning, Blue!" Izzy knelt to give the sheltie a big hug before heading up the next flight of stairs.

"Did Murphy make you breakfast?" Jessica asked.

"No," Izzy called from the top of the stairs. "Monique's dad did."

"Tristan?" Jessica blurted out.

"I didn't catch *his* name." Izzy was out of sight. "He let me pet Monique while I ate breakfast. She crawled up my arm and curled up on my shoulder."

Jessica heard the door leading to the rooftop terrace bang shut. Izzy was now on the roof to interrupt Murphy's meditation. Anticipating Murphy's reaction to learning that her brother had brought Monique for a visit, a slow grin crossed Jessica's face.

The rooftop terrace was lined in stone. Four foot tall planters lined the walls to provide privacy from the brownstone next door and other prying eyes. Stone benches ran along the walls and planters. One corner of the terrace sported a six-person hot tub, which was covered with a leather top.

French doors opened to lead inside to a sitting area and the stairs leading down to the floors below. The second guest room was on the other side of the sitting area.

Murphy had been introduced to clean eating, yoga, and meditation by his martial arts coach while he was at the Naval Academy. A Christian, Murphy figured that if his coach could greet his Buddhist god in the morning with prayer, then why should he not greet his?

What started out as an exercise in discipline to hone his body and martial arts skills, also sharpened his mind and deepened his spiritual faith. He never felt more in tune than on those days that he felt the first rays of the new day's sun on his face. In the far corner of the terrace, Murphy was able to catch the morning sun rising in the east.

"How do you do that?" Izzy's sharp voice pierced through Murphy's peaceful aura like a dagger.

Moist with sweat from his workout in the rec room on the ground level, Murphy was standing on his head, with this body as straight as a board. It was an exercise in complete focus and concentration—which Izzy had just shattered.

Opening one blue eye in the direction from which the piercing came, Murphy regarded the bony ankles of the girl who was staring at him with her head cocked to one side.

Gracefully, Murphy lowered his feet behind him. One vertebrae at a time until his feet reached the floor. From a backbend, he stood up.

"Man, you sure are flexible." The awe in Izzy's voice betrayed that she was impressed.

Before Murphy could respond, Izzy uttered a gasp upon seeing the view of the Washington Monument and other tourist attractions—all from the comfort of their terrace.

Murphy joined her at the stone wall. "Some view, huh?" He closed his eyes to fill his lungs with the morning air. Slowly, he let it out. Opening his eyes, he spotted a green car parked along the road across from their brownstone.

A green Volkswagen.

Leaning over the wall, he peered down to see if he could catch sight of the driver. At the same time, she rose up in the driver's seat. While Murphy could not see her face, the maroon hair was unmistakable.

Now that is not a coincidence. Okay, lady, what's your problem?

"Is Jessie up?" Murphy asked her while studying the green car and its driver.

"Yeah." Izzy plopped down into a chair at the table on the terrace. "Why do you do that?"

"Do what?" Stepping back from the wall, Murphy took a long drink from his water bottle.

Discovering that the chairs around the table spun, Izzy whirled around in the chair while asking her questions. "Meditate? Get up real early in the morning and stand on your head and all that stuff? Why? I mean … your wife is rich and you live in this big house and I saw that Ferrari that she drives. She's obviously crazy about you. Why do you work and knock yourself out like that?"

"I don't consider it knocking myself out," he answered, eying the green car down below. "I consider it a blessing to have my time alone to talk to God in the morning. I look forward to it. It makes me feel connected to Him and better able to handle what life throws at me."

"Like catching my mom's killer?" Stopping in her seat, she looked straight at Murphy, daring him to answer.

He turned from where he was watching the red head watching his home. "Your mother and you are at the top of my prayer list."

The dare in her glare evaporated. They regarded each other in silence. Finally, she asked him in a soft voice, "You prayed to God for me?"

"Yes," Murphy said, "I pray for everyone I love—everyday."

Unable to respond, she shrugged while gazing down at her feet. Murphy touched her hand. Prying her stare from her feet, her big moist eyes met his. "What's going to happen to me?"

Murphy searched his mind for an answer to her question. In the silence, he remembered asking that same question himself, the morning after his mother died. While he was seeking comfort and assurance, he also wanted the truth. *You're going to be okay isn't going to cut it.*

"I don't know what's going to happen to you," Murphy replied in a soft voice. "But I do know this … Whatever happens, you aren't going to be alone."

"I'm already alone," she replied.

Glancing around the deck, Murphy spread out his arms and turned around in a complete circle. "Hel-lo! What am I? Chopped liver? There's another person here in case you haven't noticed." He flashed her a broad grin—dimples and all. "No, Curly Top, you're not alone and you won't be."

"I'm not a baby," Izzy said. "Yeah, right now, I'm here with you and Princess Jasmine, but as soon as things settle down, and you catch Mom's killer, or the case goes cold and you move on to rescuing other people, then I'm going to have to go someplace else. Some social worker will swoop in and take me to another place that smells bad like where you found me yesterday, and you and Princess Jasmine will go on with your fancy-dancy lives and forget all about me."

"I don't operate that way," Murphy said.

"Do you and the princess want to adopt me and let me live here forever?"

Murphy wanted to say yes. Not so much because he wanted to adopt a teenaged girl, but because he wanted to prove to her that she was wrong about him and Jessica abandoning her as soon as the case was closed or worse, had gone cold.

It's just not realistic, Murph. You can't go around adopting every lost kid. The brownstone isn't big enough for everyone.

"Guess that proves my point," Izzy broke through his thoughts. "I'm alone."

Murphy said, "Just because we can't adopt you doesn't mean that we don't care about you, or that we won't do everything in our power to make sure you don't end up in the system and alone. We'll be here for you whenever you need anything."

He pulled a chair around and sat down next to her. "Maybe if we can find your father, he—"

"I don't have a father," she said in a firm tone. "I already told that detective and the social worker that."

"Everyone has a father," Murphy said. "Just because he hasn't been a part of your life up until now doesn't mean that he wouldn't be willing to step in if he knew what had happened to your mother. He could even be a suspect. What do you know about him? Do you know his name?"

Izzy turned to Murphy. A cold glare came to her eyes before she replied, "He was a rapist and Mom wouldn't tell me his name."

Murphy swallowed. "Your mother was raped?"

Izzy slowly nodded her head. "She only told me a couple of years ago because I kept asking her to tell me about him. She said he raped her and he got away with it."

"He wasn't caught?"

Izzy shrugged her shoulders while shaking her head. "Mom didn't tell me the whole story. All she said was that he was one of those people who doesn't have to follow the rules." A spark of fury came to her eyes.

"I don't believe that," Murphy said.

"She said he was never arrested or charged or anything," Izzy said, "because he was—"

"There aren't two different set of laws," Murphy said, "one for the rich and a different set for the rest of us. Unfortunately, there are people responsible for enforcing those laws who are too weak to stand up to those who think they are above the law. If your mother knew who raped her, then it wasn't the system who failed her and you, it was the cowards in the system who allowed themselves to be intimidated into letting him get away with it."

"So what are you saying?" Izzy asked. "Are you going to find my daddy and put him in jail? Like I want to go live with my daddy the rapist? Still doesn't solve my problem."

"No, that won't solve your problem." Murphy leaned in close to her and grinned. "You're my friend, and I make it a point to never let my friends down."

Izzy met his gaze. A weak smile came to her lips.

"You're going to be okay, Izzy. I'm not going to let anything bad happen to you … I promise."

"Tristan, what are you doing cooking breakfast in my kitchen instead of yours?" Jessica charged into the kitchen so abruptly that her brother jumped from where he was buttering toast.

The slice flew off the counter and dropped into Spencer's waiting mouth. With a joyful bounce in her step, Spencer raced into the living room to show off her prize to Newman.

"My kitchen is too wet to cook in." Pushing his dark framed eyeglasses up onto his nose with the back of his hand, Tristan took another slice of bread out of the pack, dropped it into the toaster, and pushed down the lever. "Murphy doesn't eat bread, does he?"

"Only organic whole wheat and not very often," Jessica said. "He's not a fan of carbs."

With the butter knife, Tristan pointed at the blender containing a green frothy drink. "I made a kale protein smoothie for him."

She started to ask where her brother had found the recipe for Murphy's breakfast smoothie until she'd noticing Tristan's tablet resting upright on the counter with the webpage of a healthy recipe site displayed.

"It's got all kinds of green disgusting stuff in it," Tristan said. "Murphy will love it."

Tristan was a third year undergraduate student at George Washington University with a double major in natural science and computer engineering. With a tall, lanky build and dark framed eye glasses, Tristan Faraday resembled the computer geek he was, of which he was quite proud.

"What do you mean your kitchen is too wet to cook in?" Jessica peered into the aquarium resting on their dining room table. "It's true. You did bring *her*."

"I guess you didn't see the news this morning." Tristan opened the oven door. "When did you and Murphy decide to adopt?"

"We didn't." While peering into the aquarium, Jessica shuddered when she saw the huge, black, hairy tarantula looking straight at her. "Why can't you have a more normal pet—like a pit bull?"

"You have to walk pit bulls." Tristan plopped a warm plate filled with scrambled eggs, hash browns, and two slices of bacon onto the table—at the opposite end from Monique. "Here you go, sis." He kissed her on the cheek. "Now you can't say I never did anything for you. Who's the kid I fed a little bit ago?"

Uttering a low bark, Newman came into the dining room and stomped his big feet at the end of his short legs. At the same moment, the slice of toast popped up from the toaster. Tristan took the toast and tossed it to the dog as if it was a Frisbee. Instead of jumping to catch it, Newman watched it fly over his head. Once it hit the floor, he picked it up and returned to the living room to resume watching the morning business and financial news.

Tristan dropped another slice of bread into the toaster and pushed down on the handle. "Toast is on the way, sis."

Jessica asked, "Are you telling me you fed breakfast to someone without asking who she was and what she was doing in our home?"

Tristan came out of the kitchen with a mug of coffee, which he placed in front of Jessica. He also placed the cream and sugar next to it. "Maybe she thought I was the cook. I came out of the kitchen and caught her trying to take Monique out of the aquarium."

"Izzy was trying to take your tarantula out of the tank?" Jessica stopped with her fork in mid-air.

"She wanted to pet her," Tristan said. "You'd be surprised what a chick magnet that arachnid is. So, I took Monique out and introduced them. Monique took right to the kid. She crawled up her arm and chilled out on her shoulder while this kid ate her breakfast. She must have good vibes. Monique likes her and," he lowered his voice, "Monique doesn't like just anyone."

"Izzy obviously loves animals and they seem to love her." After blowing into the hot mug, Jessica took a sip of the hot coffee.

"What's she doing here?"

"Her mother was murdered yesterday," she said in a solemn tone. "Murphy is working the case."

"Oh." Tristan hung his head while Jessica concentrated on moving the food around on her plate.

"If I had known about her mother, I would have let her have the second pack of chocolate pop tarts."

"You gave her my pop tarts?" Jessica said

"You can buy more. My biscuits are burning."

While her brother rushed into the kitchen, she called after him, "What happened to your townhouse?"

"There was a water main break in Georgetown during the night," Tristan said. "Flooded two whole city blocks. Guess which brownstone bore the brunt of it."

"Yours?"

"The whole lower floor is under a foot and a half of water," Tristan said. "By the time they drain it, I'm probably going to have to replace drywall and the hardwood floors—the first floor is going to need to be completely renovated."

"What about your roommates?" Jessica asked.

"They both went back home to their folks." With a wide coaxing grin, he wrapped his arms around Jessica. "Of course, since Dad lives in Deep Creek Lake, the only place I could go …"

"Of course you can stay here." Jessica returned the hug. "But I'm not so sure about Monique."

"I can't leave her alone at the townhouse," Tristan said.

"Murphy hates Monique," Jessica said. "He hates bugs."

"His sister loves Monique." Tristan eased down into the chair next to her.

"Sarah is not like her brother," Jessica said. "Just like you're into spiders and crawly things and I'm into high heels to stomp on those crawly things, Murphy and Sarah are two different people."

Tristan cleared his throat. "Speaking of Sarah …" Staring down the length of the table at the aquarium, he fell silent.

Jessica dropped her fork. "What about Sarah?"

"Well, you know she and I have been texting and skyping and … stuff." He cleared his throat.

"I knew you two had become friends." Jessica's brows practically met in the middle of her forehead. "'Don't tell me it's more than that." She gasped. "Are you two sleeping together?"

"No," he replied sharply. "But if I play my cards right …"

"Cards right?" Losing her appetite, she shoved the half-filled plate away. "How long has this been going on between you two?"

"Uh … how long have you and Murphy been married?" He cocked his head at her. "I thought you'd be happy that I was finally dating again."

"Sarah is Murphy's little sister," Jessica said. "Think about it, Tristan. Murphy and I are married. One day, we're going to have children.—"

"Are you—" His eyes dropped to her stomach.

Clutching her flat tummy, she glared. "No!"

"Then why are you talking about having kids?"

"Because one day we will!" With a grimace, she plunged on. "My point is—our two families are joined together with Murphy and me in the middle. Our dads are friends. Dad had selected Josh to be a groomsman at his wedding. If you have a fling with Sarah and things don't work out, you two can't just walk away and never see each other again. When Murphy and I have family gatherings here then people are going to be feeling awkward with each other." She sighed. "If you really love Sarah, then go for it. You have my blessing. You'll have Murphy's, too. But, if this is just a pair of hormones calling to each other—then I suggest you go take a cold shower and walk away before it's too late."

Tristan's face fell with disappointment. "Problem is," he said, "it may already be too late. I feel really good about how things are going with her, and Sarah was planning to come out next weekend. We were going to hook up."

Jessica was out of her seat. "Here?"

"No, at my place, which is now under a foot of water," Tristan said. "I was hoping you and Murphy would go away for the weekend so that—"

"No!"

"No what?" Murphy asked upon entering the dining room. He had his towel slung around his shoulders. Upon spotting the aquarium with the huge, hairy, tarantula, he pointed and yelled, "No, no, no, and hell no!"

"That's exactly what I was saying no to Tristan about," Jessica recovered to explain.

"I like Monique." Izzy pulled up a chair and peered with wide eyes into the tank. "Can I hold her again?"

"Don't even think about it," Murphy ordered Tristan before he could answer.

"Tristan's townhouse got flooded in a water line break, and he's asked if he and Monique could stay here," Jessica said.

"Where?" Murphy asked.

"You have two guestrooms," Tristan pointed out.

"But Izzy is staying in the one and Cameron is going to be in the guestroom off the loft," Murphy said.

"Cameron?" Tristan's eyes grew wide. "Cameron as in your stepmother, married to your father, Cameron?"

With a quizzical expression on his face, Murphy replied, "If she wasn't married to my father, she wouldn't be my stepmother."

"She'll be here this afternoon," Jessica said. "Tristan, the sofa in the rec room pulls out into a queen sized bed. You can stay down there until Cameron leaves. It should only be a few days."

"Is your dad coming to visit too?" Tristan asked Murphy in a voice that was one full pitch higher than normal.

"No, he's got a big court case, and Tracy has him up to his armpits in her wedding." Murphy asked. "Why?" He chuckled. "Are you afraid of my dad?"

"He carries a grenade launcher in the back of his SUV," Tristan said.

"Your dad carries a grenade launcher in the back of his SUV?" Izzy's eyes were wide.

"He only uses it when he has to," Murphy replied with a shrug of his shoulders.

"What does he do?" Izzy asked.

"He's a lawyer," Jessica giggled.

"Must be some bad-ass lawyer," Izzy muttered before turning her attention back to Monique. "I wish I had a tarantula. If she has babies can I have one?"

"She's not going to have babies," Tristan said.

"Thank God," Murphy replied.

"Why not?" Izzy asked. "You should get her a boyfriend. She probably gets lonely in that tank all by herself."

"Spiders don't get lonely," Murphy said.

"How do you know?" Izzy asked him.

"Yeah," Jessica giggled. "You're not a spider."

With a wink, Murphy told his wife, "I'll explain it to you later ... upstairs."

Tristan whispered to her, "I thought you already knew about the birds and the bees."

"But Mom never told me about spiders," she replied in a low voice.

"Can we get back on topic?" Murphy asked.

"What were we talking about?" Jessica asked with a smile.

"About getting Monique a boyfriend," Izzy said.

"No," Murphy said.

"You were about to say that Monique can stay," Tristan said.

"Not exactly." Murphy gestured for him to follow him into the living room.

Watching them leave the dining room, Izzy pried the lid up from the top of the tank and peered down at Monique, who was resting on top of an artificial log.

"Don't touch that spider," Murphy called to her from the living room. "Drop that lid now."

Jumping back from the tank, Izzy allowed the lid to drop back down.

In the living room, Newman raised his head from where he was resting it between his two front paws while watching *People's Court*. A woman was suing her ex-boyfriend for a seven hundred dollar unpaid loan. Gloating over what she considered to be a great catch, his current girlfriend—the plaintiff's former best friend—claimed the lawsuit was nothing more than a vengeful act by a woman scorned. "She's just jealous because I have a man and she don't!" the girlfriend claimed with a cocky swagger, while her deadbeat boyfriend beamed with pride over being the prize sought by the two squabbling women.

With a groan, Newman slapped the remote with his paw. The channel switched to a profile of Bassett Hounds on Animal Planet.

"How does he do that?" Tristan asked Murphy, who was peering out the window onto the street.

"He's self-taught," Murphy replied. "Hey, I need you to hack into the DMV for me to check out a license plate."

"I don't *hack*," Tristan said. "I *access* secure websites without *proper* authorization."

"Then I need for you to access the DMV database to check out a Virginia license plate for me."

"You work at the Pentagon," Tristan said. "Don't you know people who can do that legally for you? Who are you wanting to check out?"

"A woman who has been tailing me." Murphy stepped back to allow Tristan to look out the window at the green Volkswagen still parked across the street.

"She's not very good at it," Tristan said. "Green car and purple hair. Obviously not a professional."

"No, she's not," Murphy said. "But she's been following me since yesterday afternoon. Before I bring my team in on it, I want to know if she has any connection to our case or is just a nut who has a thing for men in uniforms. That's why I want you to run a check on her license plate."

"I'll do it on one condition."

Murphy turned from the window to Tristan. "Seriously?"

"She'll stay in the tank."

"Promise?"

"Promise." Tristan took his smart phone from his pocket. "What's the license plate number?"

"Virginia plate. A-N-T-I-W-A-R."

"Anti-war?" Tristan asked.

Murphy nodded his head.

"And you're a military officer." Tristan shook his head. "I already have a bad feeling about this."

"Honey, you need to eat breakfast before you hit the road!" Joshua called up the back staircase to where Cameron was packing her suitcase.

"Do I smell pancakes?" Donny raced down the stairs so fast that if Joshua had not stepped out of the way, the tall muscular teenager would have body slammed him.

Resigned that Cameron was not coming straight down, Joshua offered the plate he had made up for his wife to Donny. Snatching the plate, the teenager grabbed his cell phone from his pocket and went downstairs to the family room.

"Where are you going?" Joshua demanded.

Whatever Donny answered, it was fast and mumbled. Joshua failed to catch it. When he heard the television turn on downstairs, he concluded that Donny was in search of some sports scores. With another batch of pancakes finished on the griddle, he made up his plate and went around the counter to set it at the head of the kitchen table.

When he turned around to return to the griddle, he felt a pair of emerald green eyes glaring up at him. Without turning around, Joshua knew who had him in his sights. Irving sat at attention in the kitchen doorway, his green eyes narrowed to slits.

The latest on the list of offenses that Joshua had perpetrated on the twenty-five pound skunk cat—the night before, Joshua had locked Irving out of the master bedroom while spending one last evening making love to his wife before she left town. Afterward, they had both fallen asleep—forgetting to open the door to allow Irving inside to curl up next to "his girl."

When Joshua had gotten up that morning, and opened the door, Irving was waiting in the doorway—his green eyes boring straight up at him.

Joshua didn't speak cat, but he still got Irving's message.

This means war.

"Hey, Josh," Cameron called from the floor above, "is my cell phone down there?"

"It's charging in the study."

Opting to cook her pancakes after Cameron had finished packing, Joshua turned off the griddle and went into the study to check on her phone's battery. Seeing that it was fully charged, he unplugged it. He was halfway down the hallway to the kitchen when he heard an unpleasant and familiar noise—deep and guttural—from the kitchen. Even before he hit the doorway, he knew who had made the noise and what it meant. The only question was where Irving had deposited the hairball.

In the kitchen, Joshua rounded the corner to see Irving on the table. He swore he saw a smirk on the great cat's face before he hopped down off the table, scurried across the floor, and scurried out the doggie door to the back porch and back yard.

His jaw clenched, Joshua stepped up to the table to find that Irving hadn't jumped up onto the table in order to steal his rival's breakfast but, rather, to fire his first shot in the latest round of skirmishes in the ongoing war between husband and cat.

Irving's shot hit its target dead on—the giant slimy hairball hit Joshua's pancakes dead center.

Trotting down the stairs, Cameron announced, "Well, I think I finally have everything packed."

Shooting a glare in the direction of the back door through which Irving had escaped, Joshua said, "Not quite, my dear. You have one more thing to pack."

CHAPTER ELEVEN

"This is nothing like what I expected the Pentagon to look like inside." Her light brown eyes looked even bigger while Izzy turned completely around to take in the intimidating atmosphere of the Pentagon corridors. Taking her by the hand, Murphy escorted her up the stairs and down one corridor after another. Everywhere she looked, there were military personnel and other government employees, all rushing here and there. Like Murphy, many were dressed in military uniforms ornamented with rows upon rows of ribbons and medals on their chests. A few seemed to stretch from their shoulder down beneath their breasts. Others were in civilian clothes.

After Murphy had signed Izzy in, the security guard handed her a red visitor's badge sporting a big red V, which she clipped to the collar of her button down shirt.

In the midst of rush hour, a crowd quickly gathered around them to wait for the elevator. When the doors opened, they were swept onto the car to ascend to the upper floors.

Deputy Chief Boris Hamilton was filling his coffee cup while contemplating a plate of brownies when Murphy escorted Izzy through the double doors into the staff office.

135

Spying the visitor, the staff took note to cover up items in their inboxes with sheets of blue cardboard and turn over reports in the middle of their desks.

After Murphy introduced him to Izzy, Boris stuck out his hand to shake hers. "I heard a lot about you." While clasping her hand, he patted it with the other. "We are so sorry for your loss. I assure you that we're going to do everything we can to find who took your mother from you."

"Thank you," she replied in a quiet voice.

Spotting her eying the plate of brownies, Boris offered her one. "And we have sodas in the fridge if you want some."

"Did you eat any fruit or vegetables today, Izzy?" Murphy turned around from where he was going to his office to ask her.

"Sure," she said. "This morning for breakfast I had two servings of vegetables."

Folding his arms across his chest, Murphy directed his steely gaze at her. "Jessie told me you ate her chocolate pop tarts for breakfast."

"Which was two servings of vegetables," she replied with a straight face. "Chocolate is derived from cacao beans. Beans are a vegetable. Sugar is derived from either sugar cane or sugar beets. Both are plants, which places them in the vegetable category. Thus, chocolate is a vegetable and I had two—" she held up two fingers for him to count, "chocolate pop tarts that are made up of chocolate and sugar."

"I like this kid!" With a hearty laugh, Boris held out the plate of brownies for her. "According to the health department, you should have four servings of vegetables a day. So I suggest you take two more, my lady, and then you will have made your daily quota."

"It's my father's curse," Murphy muttered on the way into his office.

"Are you talking to me?" Susan startled him while he was still trying to figure out how to combat Izzy's argument about the chocolate.

"Chocolate is not a vegetable," he said forcibly.

"She's thirteen years old," Susan said. "Were you as disciplined as you are now when you were thirteen?"

"I was a hellion when I was thirteen," Murphy said with a chuckle. "Would you believe I really was the evil twin? My twin, J.J., was perfect—still is."

"What happened?" she asked.

Murphy grew silent. "My mother died of a massive heart attack."

"I'm so sorry … I didn't know," she replied in a quiet voice.

"She wasn't even forty," Murphy said. "She had an undetected heart defect. She worked out four times a week and ate right, but …" His voice trailed off.

"So you totally identify with what Izzy's going through," Susan said.

"Overnight, everything changed. My dad was left alone with five kids. He couldn't do it all by himself. My brothers and sisters needed me to put away my childhood toys and grow up." He looked out through his office door. "Just like she'll end up having to do."

"That's rough on any kid," she said. "At least you had your father and brothers and sisters. She has no one."

"Yeah," Murphy said in a soft voice. "She deserves to know who killed her mother and why."

"Is that Crenshaw's daughter attacking the brownies out there?" Special Agent Perry Latimore stepped into Murphy's office to ask.

Murphy stepped into the doorway to call over in the direction of the coffeemaker. "No more brownies."

"But I've been really good on my diet." Wendy whirled around from where she was helping herself.

"I wasn't talking to you," Murphy looked around for Izzy. "Does that mean—"

"Yes, you can have a brownie, Wendy. Where's Izzy?"

"Who?"

"Curly-topped teenager with an oversized sweet tooth."

"She's over here," Boris called to him from the break room. Behind him, Izzy clutched a brownie in one hand and her iPad in the other. "I'm uploading a game on her iPad for her to play while we have our meeting."

"I'm going to be on leave tomorrow," Murphy announced after Boris joined Susan and Perry in his office and he closed the door. The group took seats around his small round conference table. "My stepmother is coming into town today and we'll have some personal family business to take care of. But I will have my cell phone with me. Feel free to call me if you uncover anything significant."

"What about Izzy?" Boris asked.

"Jessica will take care of her." Murphy turned to Perry. "Was there anything on Baxter's laptop?"

"Wiped clean." Perry shook his head before he allowed the corners of his lips to curl. "But we won't be needing her laptop. Baxter used an off sight remote backup service that not only backed up everything on her laptop, but had an up-to-date mirror image of it. We're getting a warrant now for all of the files."

"Excellent," Murphy said.

"Not only that, but we may have found a possible link between all of the women at the Baxter place," Boris said. "We're still digging but …"

"What did you find out?" Murphy asked.

"Francine Baxter, the homeowner," Boris said, "was a professor teaching human resource management at George

Mason University. According to her background, she got an honorable discharge from the United States Army after more than fifteen years as an adjunct human resources officer. She had made it all the way to major."

"Five more years and she could have retired with a pension," Murphy said.

"Exactly," Boris said.

"Donna Crenshaw used to be army," Murphy said. "Enlisted. She switched services from the army to navy. According to something Izzy said, I picked up less than pleasant circumstances behind the switch."

"She wasn't the only one with a connection to the army," Susan said. "Hannah Price is an engineer. She and her husband worked for the Army Corp of Engineers. About sixteen years ago, they left to start their own engineering firm which does a lot of work on contract with the army."

"Three out of five …" Murphy said. "Maureen Clark was married to Colonel Lincoln Clark—"

"Serves on the National Security Council Staff as director for Strategic Capabilities Policy," Boris said with a nod of his head.

"That makes it four out of five."

Perry was scouring his laptop. "Not directly."

"My mother was a navy officer's wife," Murphy said. "If they want to, they can be as involved in the military as their spouses—especially if they join the officers' wives club. How about the Cozy Cook dealer?"

"Colleen Davis' day job is teaching elementary school," Boris said. "At first glance, we didn't see a connection. Once we dug deeper. . ."

"What is it?"

"Colleen Davis was an army brat," Boris said. "She was never in the military, but her father was. He was Lieutenant General George Davis."

"My father knew him," Murphy muttered before he could stop himself. "Died in a helicopter crash—when was that?"

"Almost ten years ago," Perry read from his tablet. "He and five other officers plus the pilot were killed when the helicopter blew up and went down into the Everglades about five minutes after takeoff at Camp Blanding in Florida."

Boris sadly shook his head. "Everyone agreed that he was on the fast track to joint chiefs. Helluva guy."

"Colleen Davis was his daughter," Murphy confirmed in a soft tone, "and now she's been murdered. What about her mother?"

"She died when Colleen was just a young girl," Boris said. "She was very close to her father."

Standing up, Murphy went to the smart board where he had posted pictures of each of the women along with a listing of their names, ages, and how they had died. "Five women murdered. Each of them directly or indirectly connected to the United States Army."

Susan slowly shook her head. "It could be a coincidence. I mean, this is Washington. We have military and government people all over the place. You walk down the street and throw a pebble and what are the odds that you aren't going to hit someone connected to the army in some way?"

His phone buzzed to indicate a text from the medical examiner. He had completed his autopsies of the victims. After reading the message, he saw Boris checking his phone. With a nod of his head, the deputy chief acknowledged that he had received the word.

All eyes in the office fell on Murphy.

Susan has a point. Here in Washington, what are the odds? We could be reading too much into the connection—

Murphy whirled around so fast that he startled them. "There's something else they all have in common. They're *women.*"

Boris, Susan, and Perry exchanged glances.

Seeing their puzzlement, Murphy rushed over to the table. "Baxter sent a text to Donna Crenshaw telling her that they needed her in order to *stop him.*" He slammed his hand down on the table. "Him! A man!" He turned back around to review the board. "And five out of five of these victims are women." He turned back to the team. "What if they were all raped by the same man? They're his victims—coming together to formulate a plan to stop a sexual predator."

Susan and Perry turned to Boris, who cleared his throat before asking, "Where did you—"

"Donna Crenshaw was a rape victim," Murphy said. "Izzy told me this morning. That's why she has no father in the picture. Her mother told her that she was raped and her attacker got away with it. Suppose—"

"Did you find that in your background check on Crenshaw?" Boris interrupted to ask Perry who was already tapping the keyboard to his tablet in search of the information.

The agent was shaking his head. "I saw nothing in her background about filing a sexual—"

"Hannah Price filed a police report with the Washington, D.C., police back sixteen years ago claiming that she was raped," Susan interrupted Perry. With a grin, she looked up at Murphy. "I knew I read it somewhere that one of these women was raped."

"What happened in that rape case?" Murphy asked. "Was anyone charged?"

Susan took her time reading the incident report on her screen before relaying the information. "She had gone to a party at the Executive Office Building. Her husband was working on a project in Central America. The party was hosted by some military big wigs and contractors connected to a project she had managed. The last thing she remembered was talking to a group of army officers. The next thing she knew, she was waking up naked in a hotel room in Arlington near the airport."

"Was anyone charged?" Murphy asked her. "Did she name her attacker?"

"According to the tox screen, she had been slipped a roofie," Susan said. "No viable DNA was collected. They found spermicide and latex, consistent with a condom. The police started an investigation, but then she withdrew the charges and the investigation was dropped."

"She was raped," Murphy said. "I can't believe the investigation was dropped just because—"

"I can," Boris said. "It was a party at the Executive Office Building. Major movers and shakers not just here in Washington, but in the world. These people know just the right pressure points to make the police and victim back off."

"According to the time line," Susan said, "Hannah Price and her husband left the Army Corps of Engineers the next year to start their own engineering firm, which has been receiving some major military contracts."

"She and her husband were bought off," Murphy said. "She either knew or found out who raped her and he had enough juice to reward her silence with government contracts."

"Most likely," Boris said.

Perry was shaking his head. "I'm finding no record of Donna Crenshaw filing any incident report about being raped … or any of our other victims. I think that's a dead end, Murphy."

"Not necessarily," Susan said. "I think Murphy may be on to something."

"If Hannah Price was being paid off, then why would she be at a meeting to expose the guy?" Perry asked.

"Because she decided after sixteen years to do the right thing," Susan said. "Maybe sixteen years ago she thought she was the only one. Maybe then she rationalized that her dignity and pride could be bought and paid for. But, after discovering that her lack of action allowed this predator to continue preying on women, she decided it was time to step up and join the cause with other victims to stop him."

"I'm not finding any record of any of these other victims being raped," Perry said.

"Maybe you're looking in the wrong place," Boris said. "This is the army—the military. It's its own world. Just like the navy—they like to keep things in-house."

Agreeing, Murphy turned to his team. "Right now, these are the only leads we have. We have no choice but to follow them." He slipped his cell phone from its case. "I'll contact the army to request the military files on each of these victims— including the case file on General Davis' helicopter crash. Maybe these murders are connected to that crash. Who knows?"

Bringing his cell phone to his ear, he stepped out of the office. "I'm going to need a bunch of records from the army."

"Yep, U look like Princess Jasmine."

After reading her best friend's text in response to the selfie Jessica had taken and sent for her opinion, Jessica hit the call button on her phone.

While waiting for the call to connect, she took in her image in her dressing room mirror. The white strapless top with matching tapered pants did resemble the ensemble of the fairy tale Arabian princess. Her raven mane falling to brush her golden tanned shoulders completed the look. She topped it off with a wide teal belt around her waist, matching four-inch pumps and topaz bracelet, necklace, and dangling earrings.

"Good morning, Princess Jasmine," Amy laughed when she answered.

"Is that a good or bad thing?" Jessica asked her closest friend from college.

Amy was one of only a half dozen of Jessica's friends who had moved to the Washington, D.C., area after graduating from the College of William and Mary. Both her father and mother were high-level executives with the federal government.

While not gorgeous or flashy, Amy was pretty and generous to a fault, which was what made her a target for her freeloader husband. They were one of those couples that made everyone say, "She could do better."

"Well, Princess Jasmine is Disney's most *fully developed* character," Amy giggled.

"Okay, I'll keep this outfit in mind for our Halloween party." A grin came to Jessica's lips. Bending over at the waist to provide a scenic view down the top, she blew a kiss toward her imaginary prince. "Get Murphy to wear one of those Arabian knight costumes—"

"Oh, I can see him now," Amy said breathlessly. "Chiseled chest and all."

"Hey, Aladdin, want to go for a ride on my magic carpet?" Naughty thoughts coming to her mind, Jessica winked in the mirror while envisioning the scene. "Now I'm getting ideas for our Fantasy Friday night."

Amy snapped her out of her dream. "I thought you were dressing for your mother-in-law."

Jessica went over to the clothes rack to study her massive collection of blouses, skirts, and dresses. "That's right."

"Why are you worried about dressing up for Cameron," Amy said. "We met her when you and Murphy got married. She's totally cool. I can tell you what she'll be wearing. Skinny jeans and a tank top with flat shoes. Don't worry about impressing her. Throw on a maxi skirt and discount sandals, if you have any, and you'll be good to go."

Jessica smiled to hear her friend's suggestion at the precise moment she was removing a long skirt from the rack. "You're right."

"I know I'm right," Amy said. "I have to go. I've got a luncheon meeting in ten minutes. Hey, how about if we go out this Friday? One of Dean's author friends told him that David Baldacci and his wife are regulars at 1789. Maybe if we start eating there—"

Jessica uttered a gasp.

Hearing it on the other end of the line, Amy asked, "What's wrong?"

"Nothing," Jessica choked out. "I'm just not sure how long Cameron will be here and Tristan is staying with us— things are pretty hectic right now, Amy. I'll have to let you know."

The doorbell saved her.

"She must be early," Jessica said. "Gotta go!"

Hurrying out of the dressing room, Jessica checked the time on the clock to see that it was only ten minutes before noon. *No way can that be Cameron. The drive from West Virginia is at least five and a half hours.*

The doorbell rang again to send Spencer racing out of the dressing room, across the master suite, and down the stairs— sounding the alarm the whole way in high pitched barks.

Taking one last glance in the mirror, Jessica groaned. *I guess today I'm Princess Jasmine.*

In the foyer, she peered through the cut-glass front door. Waiting on the doorstep, two women were admiring the view of the Potomac River and Alexandria on the other side. Older, in their forties, both were dressed in stunning clothes befitting their roles as military officers' wives.

Recognizing the African-American of the two, Jessica punched in the code to deactivate the security system, snatched up Spencer, who was poised to shoot outside at the first opportunity, and opened the door. "Mrs. Patterson, what a surprise! I didn't know you knew where we lived."

"Jessica, call me Natalie, please." The wife of the navy's chief of staff stepped inside to greet her with a kiss on the cheek. "I have friends in all the right places. Paige and I were going to lunch at the marina and I remembered you saying at the last meeting about you and Murphy moving here. So, I made a few phone calls to get the address. Why don't you join us for lunch?"

Squirming to greet the visitors, Spencer reached out a paw to the blonde in a red pantsuit with low-heeled pumps.

While the blonde ignored Spencer, Natalie accepted her paw. "This must be Spencer." Scratching her behind the ears, she whispered to Jessica, "She's gorgeous. Beautiful home. The view from the rooftop must be to die for."

A former beauty queen, Natalie Patterson was the personification of elegance. In her late forties, she was still as gorgeous as she had been the day she was crowned Miss New York, which was the same night she had met Clarence Patterson, one of the judges. She won his vote in more ways than one. At the last navy officer wives club meeting, Natalie revealed that she and the admiral were planning a second honeymoon to Naples to celebrate their twenty-fifth wedding anniversary.

As gracious as Natalie was, Jessica felt like she was being inspected by the way her friend strolled through the dining room and circled around to the living room—taking her time to check out every wall hanging and the view from the window along the way.

"Have you met Paige Graham?" Natalie finally stopped petting and cooing at Spencer to ask their host. "General Sebastian Graham's wife."

"No, I haven't had the pleasure." Recognizing the name of the wife of the general topping the list for position of army's chief of staff, Jessica stepped into the living room where Paige was eying the out-of-place, worn, overstuffed chair among the new leather furniture. Sitting up, Newman was returning her penetrating gaze.

"That's Newman," Jessica said. "You might want to step aside. You're blocking his view." Gently taking her by the arm, she tugged Paige over to the sofa.

With a clear view of the television, Newman laid down to resume watching the Bloomberg Business report. The DOW was up. NASDAQ was down.

"It's nice to meet you, Mrs. Graham." After setting Spencer down on the sofa, Jessica shook her hand.

"Jessica Faraday and Lieutenant Murphy Thornton are newlyweds," Natalie told her friend. "Her husband was awarded the Bronze Star yesterday for breaking up a domestic terrorist ring and rescuing a marine officer who had been kidnapped by terrorists."

Jessica noticed the stocky blonde eying her while she shook her hand. A smug grin came to the older woman's face while she appraised the young officer's wife boldly clad in a fitted white jumpsuit. Her eyes dropped from Jessica's face to her abundant bosom flaunted in the strapless top. Arching an eyebrow, she cocked her head before releasing Jessica's hand.

With the wordless gesture, Jessica's psychological analysis of Paige Graham was completed.

As leader of the army officers' wives club, Paige Graham inadvertently wielded the power to bless or doom the careers of young officers who worked beneath her husband. By her approval, a wife and her family would be included to private social events held by the spouses in the inner circle, which provided ample networking opportunity for an officer's name to become known among the top brass for consideration when it came to promotions or coveted assignments. This woman's rejection could make the wife and her family, and as a result her husband, an outsider. Depending on the influence that the club's leader had over her husband, the rejected wife's spouse's career could be stalled or even worse, he could end up with unfavorable or dangerous assignments.

As the spouse of an army general who had spent close to the last thirty years racing on the fast track—now on the brink of being the highest ranking post in the United States Army, Paige Graham embraced the power that came with being in such a social position.

The arched eyebrow, smirk, and silence would have caused most young officers' wives to stutter out an excuse before running to their bedroom to change into something more modest.

Jessica Faraday was not most young officers' wives. "Cocktail before lunch, ladies?" With a wave of her hand, she sashayed toward the kitchen. "We have a fully stocked bar. Pick your poison."

"I like the way you think, Jessica." Natalie fell in behind Spencer to follow their host. "How about a pitcher of margaritas?" After perching on a bar stool at the breakfast bar, she urged Paige to take the seat next to her while Jessica went to work on the pitcher of drinks.

"This brownstone reminds me of Sebastian and my first house," Paige said. "I was so young then. To think now about how nervous I was—twenty-three, just graduated from Yale, and married to an actual war hero. To those on the outside looking in, I should have had the world by its tail, but I was scared as hell."

"All wives are nervous when they marry a military officer," Natalie said. "Many don't realize until after the wedding that they haven't just married a man, but they've married into the military." She turned to Paige. "I would have thought it would have been easier for you. Sebastian came from a long line of army officers. He was third generation West Point. I'm sure his mother—"

"His mother gave me squat," Paige said in a blunt tone that brought shock to Natalie's face.

Jessica pressed the power button on the blender to whip up their margaritas. While the whirl of the mix filled the kitchen and their ears, she studied Paige's reflection in the glass front of the microwave. Likewise, Paige was watching her.

"I'm sorry," Natalie muttered.

"No need to be sorry," Paige said. "It wasn't your fault."

Jessica took three margarita glasses from the cabinet and the salt plate in which to dip the rims. After powering off the blender, she detached the pitcher and turned back to the breakfast bar.

With the blender silenced, Paige resumed. "I remember the very first time I met Mrs. Graham—"

"Your mother-in-law," Jessica confirmed while dipping the rims of the margarita glasses in the salt.

"She was Mrs. Graham to me," Paige said. "Even a full year after we'd gotten married, the bitch refused to let me call her anything but Mrs. Graham."

"That's ..." Jessica searched for the right words, "not nice." She poured the drinks into the glasses and handed them to her guests.

Paige sipped her drink and smacked her lips before continuing. "The first time I met her, Sebastian took me to his parents' summer place in Martha's Vineyard for the weekend. His father at that time was a four-star general, just like my Sebastian is now." With a smug grin, she added, "Only he never made army's chief of staff."

"Making four stars is nothing to sneeze at," Jessica pointed out.

"That's very true," Natalie said.

"When Sebastian introduced me to *Mrs. Graham ...*" Paige pronounced her mother-in-law's in a mocking tone. "She looked me up and down over the top of her glasses. She asked if my family was in any way connected to the Capone family in Connecticut. I told her that we weren't. She then said, 'But you're attending Yale,' to which I said that I was but on an academic scholarship. No way in hell could my father, a foreman working on the docks in New Jersey, have afforded to send me to Yale without a scholarship. That was when one side of her ugly red lips kicked up and she said to Sebastian, 'Are you telling me that her family has no money?'"

Paige sighed while picking up her margarita. "That was the last time I was ever invited to Martha's Vineyard. Even after Sebastian and I were married. He was invited, but not me." She gulped down a swallow of her drink. After smacking her lips, she said, "They didn't even come to our wedding."

Not knowing quite what to say, Jessica glanced at Natalie who seemed to be equally shocked. After clearing her throat, the admiral's wife said, "But you joined the army officers' wives club—"

"And fought tooth and nail to be accepted," Paige said. "But I wasn't because that bitch was their leader. After all, her husband was a four-star general. Even though Sebastian was awarded the Medal of Honor for saving his whole team in Kuwait, as long as Mrs. Graham blackballed me, I was out. I wasn't accepted until after they'd died." A smirk crossed her lips. "Then I became queen."

"They both died?" Jessica asked.

Paige ran her finger around the rim of her margarita glass. "Their lovely summer house in Martha's Vineyard burnt down to the ground one night—with them inside." Sticking her finger into her mouth, she licked off the salt. "It was such a tragedy. General Graham had flown fighter planes in Vietnam and survived both a plane and a helicopter crash—only to be burnt alive with his snooty wife." Eying Jessica over the top of her margarita, she took a sip of her drink. "Such a tragedy."

"I'm sorry to hear that," Jessica said in a low voice.

"The world is full of tragedies," Paige went on. "Like just the other day, the wife of a member on Sebastian's staff was murdered in Reston."

"Was she one of those five women killed?" Natalie asked.

"At a Cozy Cook party of all things," Paige said. "Maureen Clark. Her husband is Colonel Lincoln Clark. He has served under Sebastian for over twenty years. They have a little boy—five years old."

"Terrible," Natalie said.

"It is terrible," Jessica agreed.

"Maureen used to be very active with the army officers' wives club." Paige held out her glass to Jessica to refill. "Beautiful. Charming. Everyone loved her. But then, during her husband's last tour overseas, the stress of managing a family on her own got to her. She hasn't been too active the last few years—not since she had Tommy."

"That's too bad," Natalie said. "The main goal of the officers' wives club is to offer support to each other while our spouses are away. It can be extremely stressful having your husband stationed overseas and not knowing what's happening to him, or what they're doing, or if they're ever coming back. Probably if she had reached out instead of withdrawing—"

"I tried to talk to her," Paige said. "But I'm afraid I didn't become aware of her problem until it was too late."

"Why do you think it was too late?" Jessica asked.

"Unfortunately, Maureen became paranoid," Paige said. "She started imagining things."

"What kind of things?" Jessica asked.

"Would you believe she started making up all kind of conspiracy theories?" Laughing, Paige placed her hand on her chest. "Why would the army be out to get her? She was just an army wife."

"Someone did murder her," Jessica said. "I think that kind of confirms that someone was out to get her."

"Did she tell you what made her come to believe someone was out to get her?" Natalie asked.

"Not specifically," Paige said. "My husband can be a very charming man. He's attractive. You can't be married to such a man—" With a laugh, she gestured at Jessica. "I've seen your husband, so you know exactly what I'm talking about."

"You've seen Murphy?"

"Meet and greets and other functions around the Pentagon and Washington." With a wicked grin, Paige said, "He's hard to miss." She turned serious. "The fact is, when you're married to men as handsome and charming and charismatic as ours, there are disturbed women who will confuse fantasy with reality."

Jessica suspected Paige Graham had heard about her husband's strong reputation for cheating. Here she was rationalizing that he was the victim of his charm, rather than the perpetrator taking full advantage of it to chase every willing skirt. Fully aware of the social power of the general's wife, Jessica was unsure of how much further to allow this conversation to go.

Does she even know that Murphy is the investigator of Maureen Clark's murder? If she is, she has to know that I need to give this information about Maureen Clark being disturbed to Murphy.

Natalie saved Jessica the trouble. "Are you saying that Maureen Clark was involved with Sebastian?"

"No," Paige said firmly. "She *thought* she was involved with Sebastian. Big difference. She misinterpreted some things he had said to her or a touch on her arm. She wanted to reciprocate and made a pass at him. When he rejected her advances, she was embarrassed and tried to cause trouble by lying about everything that happened."

Holding up her hands, Jessica shook her head. "I think I need to make you aware that Murphy is investigating Maureen Clark's murder. All this stuff you're telling me, I would need to pass on to him to help him with his case."

Paige Graham's mouth dropped open. Her eyes grew big. She dropped her margarita glass down onto the bar. "Seriously? Why would a navy lieutenant be investigating the murder of an army officer's wife?"

"One of the victims was a naval petty officer," Jessica said. "Evidence indicated that she was targeted so the navy took the case."

Blinking, Paige turned to Natalie. "Did you know this?"

Natalie shook her head.

"Where is Murphy in this investigation?" Paige asked.

"I don't know," Jessica said. "He doesn't discuss his work with me."

"Well, needless to say," Paige said, "many of the wives in the club are very nervous about this. If there's anything that you can tell us, or that Murphy can tell you that you could pass on for me to offer—"

"It's an active investigation," Jessica said.

"It can be off the record."

"No, Murphy can't tell me anything," Jessica said in a firm tone. "I'm sure you understand. How much can Sebastian tell you about his work?"

Paige's eyes grew dark.

Slipping her hand over to grasp Paige's wrist, Natalie said, "Jessica just said that the naval petty officer was the target. Considering that Mrs. Clark was an army officer's wife, I think it is safe to assume that there was no connection between these two women. You could tell the wives in the club that sadly, most likely, Mrs. Clark's murder was a matter of being in the wrong place at the wrong time." She offered a reassuring smile at both Jessica and Paige.

After a long silence, in which Jessica and Paige regarded each other, the older woman finally forced a smile on her face. "Sounds good to me."

"Me too," Jessica replied.

After slapping her cell phone down on the counter, Paige dug into her handbag for a business card.

Draining the last of her margarita, Natalie set down her glass. "How about if we go to the marina for lunch?"

"Oh my, I'm afraid I can't join you ladies," Paige announced while checking the screen of her cell phone. "I forgot all about a meeting with the literacy council. I'm afraid I'll have to ask for a rain check." After slipping off the bar stool, she slapped a business card on the counter. "Jessica, please be a dear and do keep me informed about your husband's investigation—"

"But—" Jessica tried to argue.

"As a favor from one officer's wife to another," Paige said while rushing to the door. "We all have to stick together." With a slam of the door, she was gone.

A long silence stretched between the two remaining women. With the arch of an eyebrow, Jessica cocked her head at the admiral's wife.

"Paige Graham is an organizational whiz. Would you believe she chairs no less than five non-profit organizations?"

Shifting her weight to her other high-heel, Jessica arched the opposing eyebrow at her.

Shoving the empty margarita glass in her host's direction, Natalie asked, "How about another round for the road?"

CHAPTER TWELVE

Walter Reed Hospital: Morgue

Unlike the average person, Murphy Thornton was familiar with morgues and what happens during an autopsy. His second cousin, Dr. Tad MacMillan served as the medical examiner for Hancock County in his hometown of Chester, West Virginia. That being the case, Murphy had tagged along with his father to visit Tad at the morgue on more than one occasion.

In his fifties, Dr. Tad MacMillan was still a handsome, distinguished man who had earned the reputation of being a ladies man—until he married in his late forties. Before settling down with a wife and baby, he rode motorcycles and lived simply in an apartment over a garage, even though he was the doctor to most of the citizens of his small town.

Therefore, when Boris introduced him to Dr. Walter Reed, the military's medical examiner, Murphy's shock was due to preconceived impressions left by his second cousin about what M.E.'s were like.

Connecting the name of the medical examiner to the hospital where they stood, Murphy looked down at the stooped over, gray-haired man who peered up at him from over his bifocals.

After a beat, the medical examiner replied to Murphy's unspoken question, "No relation."

"Huh?" Murphy uttered.

"To the Walter Reed this hospital is named after," the old man said while peering up into Murphy's face. "I'm no relation. Total coincidence. Though, it could be the higher ups' sense of humor that they gave me the job."

When Dr. Walter Reed stood up on his toes to examine his face more closely, Murphy backed up a step.

"Did Boris say your name was Thornton?" Dr. Reed asked.

"Yes," Murphy said, "Lieutenant Murphy Thornton."

"Thornton?" Dr. Reed murmured while cocking his head to and fro. Magnified by the thick lenses of his eyeglasses, his eyes blinked repeatedly while he studied Murphy's face.

Struck with a thought, Murphy opened his mouth at the same time Dr. Reed asked, "Was your father in the navy? JAG!"

"Joshua Thornton." Murphy nodded his head with a grin. "Commander Joshua Thornton."

With a crippled finger, Dr. Reed tapped Murphy on the chest. He smiled so broadly that his face wrinkled up into a maze of smile lines. "I knew your father. From West Virginia."

"That's right."

"You're the spittin' image of him." With a chuckle, he turned to Boris. "There's no basis for denying paternity here. Jury would take one look and know which tree this nut fell from."

Boris joined in the old man's laughter while Murphy's cheeks turned pink. Embarrassed wasn't the word to describe his feelings. He was proud when compared to his father, whose reputation was long remembered in the navy.

"Brilliant man," Dr. Reed said while nodding his head up and down. "Are you a chip off the old block?"

"I hope so."

"We'll see." With a wave of his hand, he gestured for them to follow him out of his office into the morgue, where he had five gurneys filled with bodies covered with white sheets.

Several inches shorter than Murphy and Boris, Dr. Reed moved with the speed and grace of a giant turtle. His stooped back gave him the appearance of one standing upright on its hind legs.

Anxious to find out if the doctor had learned anything during the autopsies, Murphy had to rein in his impatience, while following the medical examiner to the first gurney. There he picked up a clipboard that hung from a hook on the side of the metal table.

"Donna Crenshaw," the medical examiner read. "Shot five times. Forty-five caliber slugs. They broke up upon impact. No useful parts for ballistics comparisons, I'm sorry to say."

"Were the bullets hollow-point?" Murphy asked.

"Not just hollow-point," the doctor replied. "Hollow-cavity. From looking at the bits that I removed from Ms. Crenshaw, the hollow dominated the volume of the bullet to cause extreme expansion or fragmentation upon impact."

"Not the average twenty-two that a lady would carry for protection against a carjacker," Boris said.

"More like a pro looking to make sure his target didn't survive," Murphy said.

Dr. Reed tottered around to the next gurney. "Same type of bullets were used on Francine Baxter. None of the fragments were whole enough for a ballistic comparison, but the way the bullets broke up, in my professional opinion, they were the same type. Most likely the same weapon was used."

Murphy moved around to the last three gurneys. "But the killer poisoned these three?"

"Sodium Monofluoroacetate," Dr. Reed stated in a tone devoid of emotion. "Colorless, odorless and tasteless poison used to kill rats and coyotes. All three ingested enough to kill a grizzly bear."

"There was a punch bowl at the scene," Murphy said.

"Could have been in that," Dr. Reed said. "The poison would have acted in less than an hour from ingesting it. The symptoms generally progress from fairly benign–abdominal pain, nausea, sweating, and confusion–to alarming–muscle twitches and seizures–to life-threatening–cardiac abnormalities."

"In which case, in a somewhat social setting, they would not have realized they had been poisoned until it was too late," Murphy said. "Each of them would have suffered nicely thinking she'd just come down with a slight bug—until she saw one of the other women collapse."

"Why?" Boris asked. "Why not shoot them like—"

"Because it was only one killer," Murphy said while slowly shaking a finger at each one of the three gurneys. "There were three of them." He rushed over to the gurney containing Francine Baxter's body. "Our killer got to Francine's home early. Shot her. And then answered the door when the others arrived."

"Wouldn't they think something was up if someone other than Francine Baxter answered the door, especially if they were conspiring against someone capable of doing this?" Boris asked.

"Could have pretended to be Francine's husband," Dr. Reed said. "My wife is always running out to get ice cream or something or other right before the book club comes over. So there I am answering the door and entertaining the old hens until she gets back."

"Francine Baxter was a widow," Murphy said.

"But according to our information, none of these women knew each other," Boris said. "So the killer could have used any cover to explain his being there. Brother. Friend. Neighbor."

"Could have even claimed to be Francine herself," Murphy said. "Killer could have been a woman. If she was pretending to be the hostess who was a partner in their cause, they would have trusted her enough to drink the punch packed full of poison—"

"They all drank it," Boris said. "They died."

"But Donna Crenshaw was running late," Murphy said. "The killer intercepted her texted message. So he or she had to wait for Donna. When Donna arrived, she saw all the dead bodies and the killer had no option for quietly poisoning her. He or she had to shoot her." His tone filled with sadness. "Leaving Izzy an orphan."

"What's an Izzy?" Dr. Reed asked.

"Donna Crenshaw's daughter," Murphy said.

There was a moment of silence before Dr. Reed asked, "Adopted, right?"

His eyebrows furrowing, Murphy turned to him. "No."

Dr. Reed pointed at the body under the sheet. "This woman suffered from one of the most severe cases of endometriosis that I've ever seen. Untreated. Her ovaries were filled with cysts. She was totally infertile and I saw no evidence during my exam to indicate that her uterus had ever carried a child. This woman never gave birth."

"She has a daughter," Murphy insisted.

"Maybe she does," Dr. Reed said with a shake of his head, "but that daughter didn't come from this woman's womb. I'd stake my medical license on it."

"Maybe Izzy was adopted," Boris suggested during their drive back to the Pentagon from Walter Reed Hospital.

Having taken his SUV, Murphy was at the wheel while Boris admired the leather upholstery and other features of the luxurious vehicle. Behind the wheel of the SUV, Murphy put on his dark driving glasses to block out the bright May afternoon sun.

Shaking his head, Murphy replied, "Why would Donna Crenshaw make up such a horrible lie about being raped and the rapist getting off for it?"

After a long hesitation, Boris said, "Maybe it wasn't Donna Crenshaw who lied."

Murphy cast a glance in his direction.

"Izzy's a child," Boris said. "No family and her single mother had to work hard to make ends meet. She probably got lonely—"

"Lying for attention?" Murphy shook his head. "Her mother was murdered. She's getting plenty of attention. Izzy really believes her birth father was a rapist and that's because Donna Crenshaw told her that."

"Well, according to Dr. Reed, that's not possible because Donna Crenshaw was sterile and had never carried a baby to term."

"We need to talk to Izzy," Murphy said.

"If Izzy is telling the truth as she knows it," Boris said, "then talking to her isn't going to do any good. For one, she's been through enough. She just lost her only family. To tell her in the midst of all this that this woman she thought was her mother wasn't—"

"You're right," Murphy agreed.

"We need to find out who her biological parents are," Boris said. "For all we know, Izzy was stolen as a baby. Donna Crenshaw could be one of those crazy women who wanted to have a baby of her own. She was infertile, and so she stole

Izzy." He allowed himself to grin. "If that's the case, there's probably a couple of parents out there searching for her. It's simple enough to do. Our crime scene investigators collected her DNA this morning to use as an exclusionary sample. We'll simply run it through the system to see if she's in the missing children's database."

"If she is, then something good can come from these murders." Murphy's cell phone rang. The screen on the vehicle console read: "Tristan."

"I have to take this," Murphy told Boris before pressing the hands-free answer button. After connecting the call to his brother-in-law, he asked, "What have you got for me?"

"Her name is Emily Dolan," Tristan said. "She's an assistant manager at Starbucks in Seven Corners, Virginia. That's her day job. Actually, her night job ..." He clarified, "Late day. She works the afternoon and evening shift."

"Which leaves her plenty of time to tail me during the day," Murphy noted.

"Tail?" Boris turned around in his seat to study the cars behind them out the rear window. "Are we being tailed?"

"Who's that?" Tristan asked.

"Who are you and how do you know we're being tailed?" Boris countered.

"Boris," Murphy answered, "this is Tristan Faraday, my brother-in-law. Tristan, this is Boris, the deputy chief of the Naval Criminal investigation staff."

"How does he know we're being tailed and who's tailing us?" Boris asked Murphy.

"*We're* not being tailed," Murphy said. "*I* was being tailed and I had been since yesterday, but I'm not being tailed now. Believe me, if I was, I'd know it. She followed me to work this morning, but she wasn't there when we left."

"That's because she's at work," Tristan said. "We've all got to work for a living. You can find her at Starbucks … at least that's where her cell phone is."

"You're tracking her cell phone?" Boris asked. "Do you have a warrant to do that?"

"Murphy made me!"

"Have you got anything else on Emily Dolan, Tristan?" Murphy interrupted to ask while easing onto the on ramp to cross the Fourteenth Street Bridge into Virginia.

"Plenty," Tristan replied. "She graduated less than two years ago from George Mason University—"

"Did you say George Mason?" Boris tapped Murphy on the arm. "Francine Baxter taught at George Mason University."

"I know," Murphy replied.

"Double degree," Tristan replied. "Bachelors of Science and Arts. Communications and business management. Minor in political science. But, this is where you have trouble, Murph … and probably you, too, Boris. … She's a blogger who has acquired quite a following—a big hard left following—anti-law enforcement and *anti-military*. In other words, she's not your friend."

"What made her target me to follow?" Murphy asked while trying to concentrate on the heavy traffic swarming around him on the bridge. "Does this have anything to do with—"

"Maybe," Tristan interrupted. "I checked out her blog and the last few days she has been talking up quite a buzz about breaking a huge news story about a giant conspiracy and cover-up involving the United States military. Kept telling her followers to stay tuned for her exclusive news-breaking story."

"That must be why she was following me. She saw me at the scene of the murders and thinks I'm involved in the conspiracy and cover-up." Murphy felt his throat tighten. "When is she planning to break the story?"

"Today," Tristan said. "It hasn't posted yet, though. I'm sending the link to her blog to your phone. It's been getting a lot of traffic. She's a pretty popular blogger. Her blog gets a hundred thousand hits a month."

"That's very helpful," Murphy said. "Thanks, Tristan."

"So Monique's staying," Tristan said rather than asked.

"Just keep her locked up." Murphy disconnected the call.

With wide eyes, Boris asked, "Who's Monique and why does she have to stay locked up?"

"She's Tristan's creepy friend."

The two men held up their badges for the guards at the security gates to take them into the parking lot for the Pentagon.

"Emily Dolan," Boris Hamilton repeated the name while typing in the name for the blog on his tablet. "What does she have to do with this case?"

While pulling into an empty parking space, Murphy said, "Francine Baxter taught business courses at the same university where Dolan graduated." He turned off the SUV.

"Should be easy enough to confirm or deny that connection," Boris said. "We just need a warrant to check the class rosters for the courses Baxter taught."

After slipping out of the driver's seat, Murphy put on his navy hat and made a quick check to make sure his uniform was smooth and straight. The last thing he wanted was to be stopped by a superior officer in the Pentagon corridor and dressed down for leaving his fly open. "Considering that all of these women are in some way connected to the army—"

"And this blogger is talking about a conspiracy involving the military." Boris kept in step with Murphy while bringing up the website on his tablet. "Army is military." Finding the site, he stopped walking in the middle of the parking lot and cursed. "She accuses our military of training men and women to be predatory serial killers." He showed the screen of his tablet to Murphy. "Even if the motive of these murders has to do with the military, you certainly can't believe the military had them killed?"

"I'm surprised she hasn't posted that yet," Murphy said. "If she had something, she'd have posted it by now and, if there was any evidence to back it up, it would be all over the news." He resumed the trek across the parking lot to the building.

Shaking his head, Boris continued to explore the blog. "This woman hates police and military. Actually thinks that our country should do away with both of them." After tucking his tablet under his arm, he took his cell phone out of the case on his belt. "Let's bring her in."

Murphy grabbed the deputy chief's phone. "Not before we have something concrete to go on."

"Sounds to me like we already have something concrete to go on," Boris argued. "She's been tailing you and dangling a big conspiracy story before her followers. Our victims were meeting to discuss putting a stop to someone. They were all connected to the military somehow. This Dolan woman has got to be involved in whatever it was they were planning."

"She's anti-military," Murphy said. "That means she's already got a chip on her shoulder. If we drag her in kicking and screaming, she'll *give* us nothing, scream for her lawyer, and post a scathing article on the Internet about how the big, bad, military bullied her." With a grin that broadly displayed his deep dimples, he held up a finger. *"But ...* if we know something, we could bluff her into giving us what she does have. Give me time to get the army's records about our victims and go through them."

"In the meantime, we need to learn everything we can about Dolan and the connection between her and our murder victims," Boris said. "If she was at the meeting, why wasn't she killed?"

"Maybe she did commit the murders or helped the killer escape." Stepping up onto the sidewalk leading to the entrance, Murphy stopped to turn to Boris. "Crenshaw was late due to the accident on the beltway. Maybe Dolan didn't make it there at all for the same reason. She wasn't killed because she couldn't make it to the meeting."

Beyond Boris, parked along the curb, Murphy saw a long, white stretch limousine. A huge man in a black suit and dark glasses waited next to it. Even behind the mirrored glasses, Murphy could see that he was staring straight at him.

"I'll order Perry to get into Dolan's phone records and emails," Boris was saying. "Compare them with Francine Baxter's to see if she was supposed to be there at the meeting."

"If our victims were Dolan's source for this big story that she's planning to break on her blog," Murphy said, "then the killer could be after her. He doesn't seem to be one to take chances. That could make her a potential victim."

"Have you changed your mind about bringing her in?" Boris asked.

"No, I don't want to bring her in yet, but I do want to keep a pair of eyes on her. Maybe we'll get lucky and catch our killer red-handed."

"I'll send a couple of our agents to track her down and keep her under surveillance." Seeing that Murphy was not making any move toward the entrance, Boris paused. "You coming?"

"In a minute," Murphy said. "I need to check in with my CO."

With a quick glance over his shoulder to see who Murphy was looking at, Boris hurried through the security check point.

"Don't let Izzy have any more brownies," Murphy called after him.

Once Boris was out of sight, Murphy sauntered down the sidewalk to where the huge chauffeur slash security guard waited. He stood as still as a statue. Murphy sensed that behind the sunglasses his eyes were bouncing around the parking lot in search of threats to his charge waiting in the back seat of the limousine. He recognized the unmistakable bulge of a weapon under his black jacket.

Even when Murphy walked up to him, he did not move. "Good afternoon, Bernie."

"Afternoon, Lieutenant." Bernie reached over to open the rear door of the limousine.

Taking off his hat, Murphy climbed into the back seat. Bernie closed the door.

Her long slender legs seemed to stretch the length of the rear compartment of the limousine. They appeared even longer in the red stilettos she was wearing. Her hair was pulled up into a twist that was covered by a red fedora, which matched her jacket and pencil skirt. Dark sunglasses concealed her eyes.

"You've been one busy boy, Lieutenant," she said once Murphy was seated next to her. "You've been sending up red flags all over Washington."

"What caused that?" Murphy heard the driver's door shut in the front compartment and felt the limousine engine turn on.

"Your request for copies of files relating to several women attached to the United States Army," she replied.

"They were all murdered," Murphy said.

"They were army," she replied. "You are navy. None of them were active duty army."

"I thought we were all on the same side."

"We're one big family," she replied. "Unfortunately, we're a dysfunctional family. Sibling rivalry is not the least of our issues."

"I'm investigating this case because a murderer waited in Francine Baxter's home for over an hour to put five bullets into Donna Crenshaw, a navy petty officer. That makes her *a*—if not *the*—target."

"I know all about that," she said. "You explained it all on the phone to me yesterday. Your instincts said you needed to investigate this case. It is because I trust your instincts that I authorized you to take it on."

"Do you still trust my instincts?" Murphy asked her.

"They haven't been proven wrong yet," she replied. "Do you think the other four victims were collateral damage with Donna Crenshaw being the intended target?"

"No," Murphy said. "The only common denominator we can identify right now is that all of the victims were women and in one way or another connected to the United States Army."

"Which is why General Graham has requested that the Joint Chiefs order army's CID take the lead in this investigation," she said. "He claims that the navy has no jurisdiction in this case and that you lack the experience to conduct a thorough and complete investigation."

"Is that what the Joint Chiefs are going to do?"

"The case really belongs to the FBI," she said. "I'm surprised they haven't requested it and if they did, then we have no reason not to comply."

In a low voice devoid of emotion, Murphy said, "With all due respect, ma'am, I think it would be best to allow me to stay on the case."

"Why, Lieutenant?"

"Because I'm a Phantom."

With her full body, she turned to him. "What's going on, Lieutenant?"

"I have a feeling about this case ... these murders," Murphy said. "My gut is telling me that there is something very odd behind all this. None of these women knew each other. Did you hear me say that the only thing they had in common was a connection to the army? In some cases, it wasn't even a direct connection."

"Which is why this case belongs with the FBI," she said. "Most likely the motive for the murders has nothing to do with the military."

"With all due respect," Murphy said, "I disagree. Otherwise, why is an anti-military blogger tailing me?"

"What have you gotten yourself into, Lieutenant?"

"This blogger has been creating a lot of buzz about being on the verge of breaking news about a military conspiracy and cover up."

"What kind of conspiracy and cover-up?"

"I don't know," Murphy said. "But if the Joint Chiefs of Staff assign this case to the army to investigate themselves— even if they are not behind the murders—the appearance of a cover-up will still be there. An independent party needs to investigate this case."

"The FBI is an independent party."

"But they're not Phantoms," Murphy argued. "If they uncover a conspiracy inside the military what will they do? Yes, if those behind it are lower ranked, they'll put a stop to it. What if those behind it are higher ups—with enough juice to put pressure on the agents investigating to intimidate them into looking the other way? Isn't that why the Joint Chiefs put the Phantoms together in the first place—to give our country an untouchable team of soldiers willing and able to fight for what is right—no matter who the bad guys are?"

"Do you think this is one of those cases, Lieutenant?"

"My gut is telling me that it is." Murphy nodded his head. "But I will follow the Joint Chiefs' orders."

She sucked in a deep breath. He saw by the firm set of her jaw that she was torn and disgusted which became clear when she asked, "How did you end up with this case in the first place? You're supposed to be the liaison, the connection between the civilian staff of NCIS and the navy. We put you there and told you to keep your eyes and ears open—not work their cases for them. What were you doing at that crime scene in the first place?"

"Staff Chief Hillary Koch sent me."

"She's not your CO," she replied. "I am."

"But she is my direct supervisor," Murphy said.

"Koch is also a moron."

"If you say so, ma'am." He saw the hint of a smile come to her lips. "Ma'am, I have no interest in tarnishing the army's name or reputation. All I want is to solve these murders. All the army has to do is cooperate and turn over those records that I have requested—"

"Where does General George Davis' death fit into all this?" she asked. "The chair of the Joint Chiefs, General Raleigh, was not happy when she got word about that request."

"I'm sorry if my request made her unhappy—"

"CID is claiming that your request for those records proves that you're grasping at straws and possibly on a wild goose chase," she said. "Complaints have been flying up the chain of command. Do you have any evidence or reason to believe that Davis' helicopter crash, which killed six good men, could be connected to the murders of those women?"

"I'm not certain that it does," Murphy replied.

He could feel her eyes boring into the side of his head.

"General Davis is the army connection to Colleen Davis,"

he plunged on. "Every woman in that townhouse was connected to the United States Army. You take General Davis and possibly his death out of the equation, then you lose Colleen Davis' connection. I can't do a complete investigation without at least looking at the case file."

Her voice was steady when she asked, "Do you feel that the United States Army is involved in some sort of conspiracy and cover up, Lieutenant?"

"What I feel or believe about a conspiracy and cover up in the army is irrelevant," Murphy said. "Five women are dead. Five families are grieving their loss. They deserve answers and justice. I promised Donna Crenshaw's daughter that I would do everything in my power to find out who killed her mother and why. I intend to keep that promise, with or without the approval of the Joint Chiefs of Staff. I'm a man of my word. If that doesn't fit in with the Joint Chief's agenda, then I sincerely apologize. But I can't back away from this investigation ... even if they do make the decision to send the case over to the army's investigative unit or the FBI."

There was a long silence while Murphy waited for her response. The limousine pulled up to the curb and came to a halt. Murphy saw through the tinted windows that they were at the same place where they had started. Bernie had simply driven them around the Pentagon's parking lot.

Looking straight ahead, she finally replied, "You will get everything you believe you need to complete your investigation, Lieutenant."

"Thank you, ma'am."

Bernie opened the rear door.

"You're welcome, Lieutenant," she said. "Keep me informed ... about everything."

"Yes, ma'am." When he moved toward the open door, he felt her long slender hand grasp his. He turned to her.

"Take a long thorough look at the Davis file," she whispered.

While her fingernails dug into his wrist, Murphy took a long look at her. Her dark glasses covered up her eyes, concealing the emotion behind her warning. "Thank you, ma'am, I will."

She refused to release her grip on his wrist. "Lieutenant …"

"Yes, ma'am?"

"Be careful," she whispered. "Our country needs you."

CHAPTER THIRTEEN

"So this is the infamous Irving." Jessica peered through the door into the cat carrier resting on the queen sized bed in the loft guest room.

Seemingly unimpressed with the woman studying him, Irving narrowed his eyes into thin emerald slits. He looked like he was about to go to sleep.

"Infamous in Josh's book." Cameron dumped the bag of litter into Irving's box, which she was setting up in the full bath off the guest room. She set the lid on top of the box. "I'm sorry, but I had to bring him." She stepped into the doorway. "Josh threatened to send him to the taxidermist if I left him behind."

"I'm sure he wasn't serious." Jessica was kneeling on the floor in front of the carrier. "Can I let him out now? I'm really curious. I can't believe he looks exactly like a skunk."

"Knock yourself out." Cameron went to the bed to open her suitcase.

Jessica unlatched the door to the carrier. Instead of rushing out, Irving opened his eyes to observe her, as if to determine if she was worthy of him making her acquaintance.

"Okay, big guy," Jessica urged him. "Come on out and strut your stuff."

Irving stared at Jessica who looked back at him.

"Seriously?" she replied to his lack of motion. "You're only going to stare at me?"

"Don't be offended," Cameron said. "I'm afraid Irving is a one-person cat."

Jessica rose to her feet. "Be that way. I'll show you who's boss. I'll introduce you to Spencer, who has yet to meet a cat up close and personal."

With a laugh, Cameron answered her ringing phone. Bringing it to her ear, she stepped out of the bedroom into the sitting room. "Gates here."

"Detective Gates, this is Agent Peter Sanders."

"I remember." In spite of her effort to keep a professional demeanor, she couldn't keep the excitement out of her voice. "I'm here in Washington. I'm ready to roll whenever Bertonelli is available for me to question him."

"I'm sorry to hear that, Detective Gates," the agent replied.

"Why?" Cameron turned around to see that Jessica had managed to extract Irving from the carrier. He actually tolerated her carrying him out into the sitting room. "What's up?"

"Bertonelli is dead," the agent replied. "He was found in his bed late this morning. M.E. says it appears to be a heart attack."

"I don't believe that," Cameron said.

"Neither do we," the agent said. "That's why we're ordering a full autopsy."

"That doesn't help me," she said. "He's the only one who would know why—"

"Last night, when we talked to him about you coming out to see him," Agent Sanders said, "he said that he really couldn't give us or you much information about the Gates hit, except for one thing."

"What one thing?"

"The order for him to make the hit came from Adrian Kalashov."

Cameron repeated the name over and over to commit to memory before saying, "I've heard the name Kalashov—"

"Ivan Kalashov is like the CEO of the Russian mob," Agent Sanders said. "Started out with smuggling. He got on the ground floor when the communist regime fell. Then, he branched into human trafficking. Now, he's into everything from illegal arms, to drugs, to pornography. His son Adrian is rumored to be taking over for him, but that's only rumor. On the surface, he is supposed to be totally legit. American educated, law degree from Yale. As hard as the bureau has tried, we have yet to be able to pin anything on him and make it stick."

"But Sal Bertonelli said Kalashov ordered him to take out Nick," Cameron said.

"And now Bertonelli is dead," Sanders said. "Based on what Bertonelli said, I don't think we can make any connection between your late husband and Kalashov, unless you know of one."

"I don't. Did Bertonelli say anything else?"

"Kalashov did tell him that the hit was for a friend."

"What friend" Cameron asked.

"Bertonelli claims Kalashov didn't elaborate any further."

"And now he's dead."

"Dead men tell no tales," Sanders said.

Blinking the tears out of her eyes, Cameron thanked Agent Sanders for his help and disconnected the call.

"Bad news?" Jessica asked while handing Irving over to her.

"The man who killed my husband is dead." Cameron rubbed her face into Irving's thick fur. The big cat rubbed his face against her jaw.

"That means you can't interrogate him." Jessica reached out to squeeze her arm. "I'm so sorry."

"He did tell the FBI that the hit was a favor for a friend of a big Russian crime boss," Cameron said. "I don't understand. Nick had no connection with organized crime."

"Maybe that he knew of."

"Maybe Jane ..." Carrying Irving in her arms, Cameron rushed back into the bedroom. Dropping Irving onto the bed, she opened her laptop case and reached into the folder section to remove the case file.

"Jane who?" Jessica followed her into the room.

Hurrying out of the room, Irving came to a sudden halt when he came face to face with Spencer who had followed the new scent in her home.

Upon seeing the intruder, the young dog jumped up into the air and landed in the corner of the sitting room with a yelp.

Keeping his eyes on the possible threat with long blue fur, Irving puffed up with every strand of his long fur on point and hissed. Keeping his back arched upward, he bounced on all four feet to the top of the stairs.

Remembering that she was a dog, which put her above the feline in the animal kingdom, Spencer shifted gears to change her yelps to barks and gave chase.

"Spencer, no!" Jessica ran out of the bedroom. She dove for Spencer a moment too late.

The chase was on.

At the bottom of the stairs, Irving turned right and scurried as fast as his paws could carry him through the open doorway into the guest bedroom. In the middle of the room, he leapt to fly up onto the bed. With one bounce, he hit the nightstand, where he zigged around a photograph before returning to the bed. He ended up on the headboard.

To Irving's surprise, Spencer, who was a fraction of Admiral's weight and much younger, had no trouble taking flight. After Irving reached the headboard, he found his options minimalized and the young dog snapping at his tail from directly beneath him.

"Spencer! Bad dog!" Jessica scooped the pup up into her arms and carried her out of the room. "Cameron, I am so sorry." She took the squirming sheltie down the hallway where she locked her inside the master bedroom.

"That's okay," Cameron replied. "I didn't realize Irving would be such a problem." She felt a broken picture frame crumble under her foot when she reached across the bed to retrieve Irving from the headboard. "Oh, man!" She cursed. Irving had broken someone's picture. Kneeling down to the floor, she turned over the picture to observe the two women in army dress uniforms.

"We'll keep Spencer in the bedroom until she settles down," Jessica said upon coming back into the room. She stopped when she saw Cameron staring at the picture in her hand. "Are you okay?"

"This picture frame broke," Cameron said in a low voice. "Who is this?"

"That's Izzy's mother and aunt," Jessica said. "Izzy is the girl whose mother was killed day before yesterday. So sad." She knelt down to the floor to pick up the broken glass.

"Her mother was murdered … the other day?"

"Yes." Jessica stood up to take the broken picture frame from Cameron only to find her holding onto it.

Cameron asked, "Which one was her mother?"

Jessica pointed at the picture of the younger woman, Donna Crenshaw.

"Who is the other one?" Cameron asked. "The one with the curly hair."

"Her aunt," Jessica asked. "Why?"

"What's her name?"

"I don't think I caught it." Jessica corrected herself. "Cecelia. Why?"

Cameron held up the picture for Jessica to see. Pointing at the picture of Cecelia, she said, "This woman is Jane Doe. The woman who died in Nick's arms—the one he was trying to identify when he was murdered."

In his office, Murphy was having trouble concentrating on the words in the forensics reports from the crime scene investigators.

More often than not, Murphy would raise his eyes from the reports to watch Izzy where she was playing with her iPad at his conference table. It took all of his control not to interrogate her about her life with the woman who had raised her—who had lied about being her mother.

Boris was right. It would be simpler to run her DNA through the database to locate her parents or at least a member of her birth family.

Forcing himself to concentrate on the reports before him, Murphy continued reading through the witness statements of Francine Baxter's neighbors.

No one saw or heard anything … or maybe someone had.

Each of the victim's cars had been found parked around the cul-de-sac. Hannah Price's black Porsche was parked in the townhouse driveway. She probably arrived first. Maureen Clark drove a white SUV, which was parked in front. Colleen Davis' blue Mini Cooper was parked behind Maureen's vehicle. Donna Crenshaw drove an eight year old black SUV, which was parked in front of the townhouse next door to the Baxter home.

At various points during the evening, one neighbor or another had seen one or more of the women arrive. One neighbor arriving home from work had even seen Colleen Davis and Maureen Clark arrive at the same time and walk up the steep steps to the front door together.

No one heard anything.

The last witness statement Murphy read caused him to catch his breath.

Eighty year old Eileen Jones, a retired school teacher, lived alone in the townhome directly across the cul-de-sac from Francine Baxter. Eileen had taken her Yorkie for a walk right before her bedtime—at ten-thirty in the evening. As she was leaving her home, she saw a green Volkswagen pull around the cul-de-sac and park along the curb almost directly in front of her house. Eileen and her dog were no more than twenty-feet from the maroon-haired young woman when she got out of her vehicle and practically ran directly across the road to knock on Francine Baxter's door.

Later, when Eileen returned from walking her dog, she heard a door slam and saw the same woman running back to her car. She could see that the maroon-haired woman was sobbing when she got into her car and sped so fast out of the townhouse development that she actually drove her green Volkswagen up onto the curb.

"She was extremely upset," Eileen said in her statement. "No doubt about that. I thought she was one of Dr. Baxter's students and that she had flunked her—never occurred to me that she found all of those women massacred. Why didn't she call the police?"

Good question.

Murphy took note of the time. Ten-thirty. Approximately two hours after Donna Crenshaw's estimated time of death.

Emily Dolan actually went inside Francine Baxter's home. She had to have found the bodies. According to Eileen's statement, it takes her approximately ten minutes to walk her dog, which means Emily Dolan was in the townhouse longer than it took for her to discover the bodies.

What was she doing in the house for ten minutes? She would have instantly found the bodies. Why didn't she call the police? Was it simply because she didn't trust them?

Going to his laptop, Murphy did a search for Starbucks at Seven Corners Shopping Center in Falls Church, Virginia. The café closed at nine o'clock. The overturned tanker had stranded a lot of people that night. Most likely, Emily didn't make the meeting because she had been called into work to cover for employees who couldn't get through the traffic jam.

Not only did she miss the meeting, but she dodged a bullet, too—literally.

"Do you know who killed my mom yet?"

Murphy looked up from the statement to see Izzy's big light brown eyes peering at him from over the top of her iPad.

"Not yet, but we're making progress," he answered. "I'm not doing this alone. Everyone you met today is working hard to find out what happened."

"I know." She returned to her iPad.

Murphy laid down the report in the center of his desk. "Are you bored?"

"Very." Dropping her tablet on top of the table, she sat up, then paused when Perry knocked on the doorframe to Murphy's office.

"Lieutenant, we've got a problem."

In one day, Izzy had learned the drill. While Murphy followed Perry down the hallway to the conference room, she had to gather her things to go to the break room. As a visitor, she was unable to stay alone in his office.

As Murphy approached the conference room, he could hear the voices of those inside growing louder. Two he recognized as Special Agent Susan Archer and Boris Hamilton trying unsuccessfully to be the calm voice of reason.

"That answer is not acceptable!"

Murphy recognized by the booming tone that the center of the problem was either a marine or an army officer—someone who had been trained to lead based on the strength of his voice.

When Perry led him through the doorway, Murphy saw that he was right.

Standing at the head of the conference table, a tall, muscular man in the green uniform of the army—a silver eagle on both his left and right shoulders denoting his rank of colonel—was waving his hand at Boris Hamilton. A pen dangling between his fingers, he demanded, "I want to speak to the lead investigator in this case!"

Assuming an at-ease stance with his hands folded behind his back, Murphy announced, "That would be me, Colonel."

The army officer whirled around on his heels and fired off a glare across the room. With the hand holding the pen, he rubbed his lips while measuring up the navy lieutenant.

"I'm Lieutenant Murphy Thornton, United States Navy, appointed by the Joint Chiefs of Staff to lead in this investigation of the murders at Francine Baxter's home in Reston, Virginia. And you are ..."

"Colonel Lincoln Clark, United States Army. Maureen Clark was my wife." After stepping across the room to Murphy, he brought his face close to his. "I serve on the National Security Council Staff as director for Strategic Capabilities Policy and work very closely with General Sebastian Graham. I assume you know who he is."

"Yes, I do."

"Maureen and I are personal friends of the general," the colonel said. "We are regular visitors to his home. Her murder has been a horrible blow not just to me and our five year old son, but to the Grahams as well."

"I am very sorry for your loss, Colonel," Murphy said, "and—"

"If you're so sorry," Colonel Clark roared, "why are you not out there looking for her killer instead of invading my family's privacy?"

"One of the most effective ways to identify a killer is to understand his victims," Murphy said. "Unfortunately, the best way to do that is to ask probing—even embarrassing—questions."

"I've answered enough of your staffs' questions, now I want some answers of my own!" Colonel Clark yelled while waving the hand dangling a pen.

As volatile and loud as Colonel Clark was, Murphy was calm and soft spoken. "Certainly," he replied, "what questions do you have?"

"How old are you?"

Murphy smirked at the colonel's attempt to intimidate him. "How is my age relevant to your wife's murder?"

"I'm willing to bet I have socks older than you," Colonel Clark said with a sneer. "Have you ever investigated a murder before, boy?"

"Yes, I have." The colonel didn't need to know that Murphy's previous experience had been unofficial.

"What suspects do you have?"

"Unfortunately, I can't answer that." When Colonel Clark scoffed, Murphy asked, "When you were in Iraq, during your three tours before returning state-side, did you publicize the information that your team collected about the enemy?"

"Of course not."

"Why not?" Murphy's face was filled with childlike innocence.

Colonel Clark stuttered before answering, "You know damn well why not. Then the enemy would know what we knew about them and be able to anticipate our next move and how we would proceed."

The corners of Murphy's lips kicked up to reveal a hint of his dimples. "Just like you and your people were doing in Iraq, my team and I are doing here. We're fighting a war against a killer who took out your wife and four other women. The best ammunition we have in this war is every bit of information that we can gather about each one of our victims in order to understand why and how these casualties came about. It's not pleasant, but then, no war is. And some of the questions that we may be asking may not make sense to you, but like your people on the front lines had to trust that you knew what you were doing, I have to ask you to trust my team."

Colonel Clark looked around the room at each agent in the room. Murphy's calmness had its desired effect. If he continued raging, then he would appear to be a hysterical family victim, which was the last thing he would want reported back to his superiors.

"If there's a problem, now would be the time to discuss it," Murphy prompted him.

"My DNA is already in the military database," Colonel Clark said.

With a nod of his head, Murphy acknowledged that he was aware of this. "Every active duty member of the military has his or her DNA listed in the database to help with identification if the worst was to happen."

"But you have no reason to need my son's DNA."

"Actually, we do," Murphy said. "It can help to exclude evidence that might be found at the crime scene."

"He was never at this Baxter woman's home," Colonel Clark said, "so his DNA won't be found there."

"Actually, it's already there." When Colonel Clark opened his mouth, Murphy raised his hand to silence him. "Transference of forensic evidence. Your wife Maureen, after feeding your son macaroni and cheese for dinner, decided to take a couple of minutes to brush your Himalayan cat—getting cat hair on her pants and shirt. Despite her best efforts, she was unable to remove every single strand of that hair. Then, she bathed your son and put him in his pajamas while you sipped your vodka martini. At that point, he transferred epidermal particles from his skin to the front of Maureen's shirt when he splashed bathwater and soap onto her. While you were having your second cocktail to help ease your nerves from giving up smoking, Maureen helped your son to brush his teeth, getting cast off from the brush, barely noticeable, but enough for forensics to pick up the toothpaste. Her clothes had minute odor of the macaroni and cheese he ate for dinner." He leaned in to whisper to the stunned general "Kraft by the way. My favorite too, when I was your son's age. And the scent of the lasagna as well, with minute traces of the parmesan cheese and the sauce also on her sleeves. When you kissed her good-bye, you left your DNA and minute traces of the vodka martini on her lips."

The conference room was filled with stunned silence.

"All of that evidence from your family and home was on Maureen when she went to Francine Baxter's house," Murphy explained. "When she sat down on Francine Baxter's chair, the hair from your cat caught on the chair. As a result, your cat's DNA is in the Baxter home, even though the cat has never been there. Maureen brought it in. That is transference."

Finally, Colonel Clark spoke, "I gave up smoking ... how did—"

"You may have made it through nicotine withdrawal, but the psychological effects are still there," Murphy said. "You've been holding onto that pen and waving it around like a cigarette. When I introduced myself, you almost took a drag on it—until you remembered that it wasn't a cigarette."

Seemingly speechless, Colonel Clark nodded his head.

"We need your son's DNA in order to exclude any evidence found at the scene that Maureen may have brought in from your home," Murphy said.

Colonel Clark stared at Murphy.

"Please, sir," Murphy said.

Colonel Clark swallowed. "No."

Not sure if he heard him right, Murphy said, "Pardon me, sir."

"No, you can't have it." Colonel Clark hurried past Murphy toward the open doorway. Pausing, he turned around. "Maureen is gone. But our son is still here. I know how the military and Department of Defense works. Once his DNA gets into the system, then NSA and our government will be tracking him like a wild animal for the rest of his life. As long as we have some rights left, I'm going to protect our privacy with everything I've got."

Colonel Lincoln Clark hurried out of the conference room, leaving Murphy, Boris Hamilton, Susan Archer, and Perry Latimore in stunned disbelief.

"That … was weird," Susan said. "You would think—"

"How did you know he drank two vodka martinis while Maureen Clark put a leftover lasagna in the oven for him the night she died?" Perry asked Murphy. "We only just got the forensics report. You couldn't have gotten all that. I mean, the martini—"

"I smelled the vodka on his breath," Murphy said.

"From two days ago?" Perry asked.

"From lunch today," Murphy said. "So I made a calculated guess that vodka martini was his drink. I did read about the cat hair on Baxter's chair and Maureen's clothes. That told me that the Clarks have a cat. Knowing the age of their son and seeing what type of man Lincoln Clark was, I speculated about what she would have done before leaving the house to go to Baxter's place that evening."

Boris chuckled. "Based on the look on Clark's face, your surmising was right on target."

Pleased with himself, Murphy shrugged his shoulders with a grin. "What can I say? I've learnt from the best."

"You look like Dad when he'd come home after a long day of getting nowhere," Tristan announced from where he was lounging on the back of the black motorcycle when Murphy climbed out of his SUV after parking it in the garage.

After a quick hello and the bumping of fists with Tristan, Izzy threw open the door to the rec room to find Spencer waiting on the other side. "Hell-o, Blue! Did you have a good day today?"

Spencer answered by jumping into her arms and licking her mouth.

"Let's go see what Newman's watching." Carrying Spencer in her arms, Izzy raced up the stairs.

Sipping a beer, Tristan watched Murphy stop to stretch his arms up over his head and arch his back. After picking up his tablet from the back seat, Murphy moved around the back of the SUV and stepped over to where Tristan was balancing the beer bottle between his crotch and the bike's gas tank while testing out the feel of Murphy's sport motorcycle. "If you like it so much, why don't you buy one? It isn't like you can't afford it. Or maybe you can get really wild and crazy and buy a car."

"I have no need for a car or a motorcycle," Tristan replied. "I'm a city boy. I live downtown and take the metro or walk. It'd be a waste of money to buy a motorcycle only to keep it in storage for an occasional road trip."

Murphy allowed a grin to come to his lips. "Like to Annapolis?"

Tristan sat up straight on the bike. "Who said anything about Annapolis?"

"It's a beautiful drive," Murphy said. "Long stretch of road out before you. When you get out there, the sea air hits you in the face. That's one of my favorite drives." He patted Tristan on the shoulder. "If you want to take her for a ride, just let me know."

Tristan swallowed.

Murphy leaned in to whisper. "I'm talking about the bike."

"I know." Tristan uttered a nervous laugh. "Of course we're talking about the bike."

The two men exchanged knowing grins. With a chuckle, Murphy turned to go inside when Tristan asked, "I don't suppose Jessie's gone for a ride with you yet."

With a frown, Murphy turned back to him. "No, she hasn't. She says, and I quote, 'No way in hell are you getting me on that bike.'"

Tristan sucked in a deep breath. "She worries about you when you take it out."

"I wear a helmet."

Tristan's blue eyes met Murphy's. "So did Felicia," he said in a soft voice.

In silence, Murphy returned his gaze.

"I guess Jessie never told you about Felicia."

"No," Murphy replied. "Who's Felicia?"

"Jessie's best friend," Tristan said. "I didn't think she'd tell you about her. She never talks about her. I guess it's still too painful."

"What happened to her?"

"Jessie and Felicia grew up together," Tristan said. "They'd known each other since kindergarten. When Felicia was in the ninth grade, she started dating this older guy. Mitch." He emphasized with a grin. "*Dad could not stand Mitch.* He was like three years older than Felicia. Had hair down to the middle of his back and tattoos and body piercings. A real rebel, which I think was what attracted Felicia to him." Lost in the memory, he rubbed the gas tank of the motorcycle. "He rode a motorcycle."

"Not everyone who rides a motorcycle is bad," Murphy said. "Look at me. You met my cousin Tad. He's a doctor and he drove nothing but motorcycles up until he got married a few years ago."

"I know," Tristan said. "Everyone swore that Mitch loved Felicia more than anything and that he was really good to her."

"What happened to Felicia, Tristan?"

Tristan sucked in a deep breath. "It was their senior year of high school. Fall. Gorgeous day. Mitch took Felicia out for a drive on his bike after school let out. They went out to Great Falls, where the roads are real windy, up and down—sharp turns. The axle broke on the front wheel and the bike went flying end over end."

"Man," Murphy breathed.

"Felicia was wearing a helmet, but it didn't matter as hard as she hit the pavement," Tristan said. "Broke like an egg shell. They air lifted her out but it didn't do any good. She was brain dead. She was on life support for ten days before her family pulled the plug." He turned to Murphy. "Jessie was there ... holding her hand when she died."

Murphy gazed at the motorcycle he loved. It was his first major purchase after graduating from the naval academy, after becoming one of the elite, covert Phantoms. But now … after learning what bad memories and feelings it brought Jessica …

"I thought you should know why she refuses to ride it with you," Tristan said. "I'm not surprised she didn't tell you."

With a mutter of thanks, Murphy turned away.

"By the way, Cameron's here," Tristan announced. "And so is Irving."

Murphy whirled around from where he was about to pass through the doorway into the rec room. "She brought Irving?"

A sly grin crossed Tristan's face. "She had to. Your dad was threatening to send him to a taxidermist."

"What are we running here? A pet hotel?"

Tristan climbed off the bike. "Want me to call Dad? I'm sure Gnarly would love to come for a sleep over." Chuckling, he took another sip of his beer.

With a growl, which caused Tristan to laugh harder, Murphy trotted inside and up the stairs.

Jessica met him at the top of the stairs. "Cameron's here!" Throwing her arms around him, she covered his mouth with hers to kiss him long and hard. The taste of her mouth melted away his frustration. Wrapping his arms around her, he pulled her in closer for another kiss to make him forget about every roadblock he had run into that day.

"There are other people in the room." Cameron's voice sounded like it was far away in a fog.

"I'm so glad you're home," Jessica whispered into his ear. "We've got lots to tell you."

He had to tear himself away to greet Cameron with a hug and a kiss on the cheek.

"Thank you for letting me stay here," she whispered.

"You're family," Murphy told her while accepting the glass of water poured over mint leaves and ice from Jessica. "We'd be offended if you stayed anywhere else." He tossed his tablet onto the dining room table.

"But now you have a full house." Cameron gestured to the scene that Murphy had failed to notice in the living room.

Izzy was stretched out on her stomach across the living room floor. Batting at her curls, Irving was stretched out along her back. Spencer was pawing and yapping at Izzy's feet, which were bouncing to an inaudible rhythm that seemed to only be in her head. Above her, Newman was enthralled with *My Cat from Hell* on Animal Planet, which both he and Izzy were watching.

"All they need now to make the party complete is Monique," Jessica said.

"I told Izzy that Irving is a one person cat," Cameron said. "Besides me, the only human he goes to is Donny. But she wouldn't listen and Irving took right to her. I've never seen him warm up to another person like that."

Watching the happy group in the living room, Jessica leaned against the wall. "Tristan said the same thing about Monique." She went on to explain, "It is a proven fact that some people have a calming sense with animals. Sort of like Dr. Dolittle. They can relate to animals and animals can relate to them."

"Hey, Newman," Izzy called back over her shoulder, "can we see what's on Investigation Discovery?"

Murphy chuckled. "Like Newman is going to—"

With a slap of the dog's paw on the remote, the channel changed on the television.

"Hit it again, please," Izzy said.

When Newman hit the remote once more, Murphy shook his head and went into the kitchen. "I can't stand it."

They followed him into the kitchen where Cameron had a bottle of root beer that she had started drinking while waiting for Murphy to get home. Jessica took a bottle of white wine from the fridge and poured some into a wine goblet for herself.

"Did the feds give you a time of when we can question the hitman who killed Nick?" Murphy asked Cameron.

"The mob got to him."

Murphy's mouth dropped open. "But he was being protected."

"They made it look like a heart attack, but the feds have their doubts," she said.

"I'm sorry," Murphy said. "But hey, it wasn't a wasted—"

"No, it wasn't." Cameron opened a case file that she had resting on the kitchen counter. "I want you to see something."

Jessica peered around the corner to make sure Izzy was still watching television in the living room.

Murphy moved over to the case file. Cameron had spread two pictures out on the counter. One he instantly recognized as the picture that Izzy had placed on her night stand. The other was a head shot of a woman in a morgue.

"Is it my imagination or is this the same woman in these two pictures?" Cameron asked him.

Murphy placed his hand on the picture of the dead woman. "Who is she?"

"Jane Doe," Cameron answered. "Never identified. Nick found her along the Pennsylvania turnpike less than two weeks before he was killed. It is the only case he was working on. He was trying to identify this woman—had even gone on *America's Most Wanted* asking for information leading to her identity."

"That's Izzy's aunt," Murphy said in a low voice.

"Cecilia." Jessica urged Cameron. "Tell him the rest of it."

"According to the medical examiner's report, this woman gave birth about a week to ten days before her death," Cameron said. "She died thirteen years ago."

"Izzy is thirteen," Jessica said.

Murphy had already brought up Izzy's records on his tablet. "She was born January first—thirteen years ago."

"Then—"

"Cecilia has to be Izzy's mother," Murphy interrupted Cameron. "The medical examiner said that Donna Crenshaw never gave birth. She can't be Izzy's birth mother."

Jessica looked at the picture from Izzy's nightstand. "You can certainly see the resemblance. Cecilia has the curly hair. Izzy said her mother said she was bull-headed just like her."

"Was Cecilia murdered?" Murphy asked Cameron, who nodded her head.

"Then the mob sent a hit man to kill Nick, who was investigating the case," Jessica said. "Then, Izzy's mother—or rather aunt who was raising her—was murdered, too."

"Cecilia's dying words were, 'she's safe,'" Cameron said.

"She could have been talking about either her sister or her daughter," Murphy said.

"Izzy was only a baby when her birth mother was killed," Jessica said. "Do you know anything about her father? Maybe he's behind this. Maybe he killed Cecilia and Donna because he wanted custody of Izzy—"

"Izzy told me that her father was a rapist," Murphy said. "We're running her DNA through the database. If he's been convicted of sexual assault, or has any sort of record, we'll locate him." He shook his head. "These murders are just too well planned."

"I agree," Cameron said. "The mob sent a hit man to kill Nick and make it look like an accident. Whoever is behind this is organized and cunning. He's not your average attack of opportunity rapist that you find in a dark alley."

"When will you know if forensics gets a hit from the database with Izzy's DNA?" Jessica asked.

"Not until tomorrow at the earliest," Murphy said.

The two women groaned.

He said, "We do have one lead we can follow up."

CHAPTER FOURTEEN

"You are aware that if anything happens to you, your father will come tracking me down to kill me," Murphy leaned up to tell Jessica who was sitting in the front seat of Cameron's white SUV. "I'll be forced to kill him in self-defense."

"What makes you so sure that he won't get the jump on you?" Jessica replied over her shoulder.

"Then I'll end up dead and your father will go to jail for murder," Murphy said.

"With all the murder cases he's solved," Jessica laughed. "No one will ever be able to pin your murder on him. They won't even be able to find your body."

"Josh has won murder convictions without bodies," Cameron said from the driver's seat. "If Mac gets the jump on Murphy, then Josh'll be forced to avenge Murphy's murder. The Thorntons are really into this family honor stuff."

"In other words, there's no way things will end well if anything happens to you, Jessie," Murphy said.

"Not that he's putting any pressure on you," Cameron told her.

"For all we know," Murphy said, "whoever killed those women in Reston is on to Dolan. Based on the brutality of those murders, they aren't going to care about collateral damage."

"Jessica'll be with me," Cameron said from the driver's seat. "I'll keep an eye on her."

"Five women, Cameron." With his fingers spread for them to count, Murphy thrust his hand up between the two front seats to show them. "They killed five women that we know about. They may be behind the murder of Izzy's birth mother and your late husband. I'm afraid you may be in over your head this time, Cam." With a sigh, he sat back in his seat. "That's someone else who's going to come after me if anything happens to you."

"Your father isn't going to kill you, Murphy," Jessica said.

"He'll just shoot him in the kneecaps." Cameron shot a smile in Jessica's direction. She glanced up into the rearview mirror to tell him, "Murphy, I am a trained homicide detective and I've been in numerous firefights. Nothing's going to happen to me and I'm not going to let anything happen to Jessica."

"I'm not a total civilian," Jessica told both of them. "I have a gun and took all the gun safety classes. Dad sent me through self-defense classes since I was a kid. Have you forgotten that I'm a licensed private investigator?"

"All I'm going to do is question her," Cameron said. "Emily Dolan was like ten years old when Nick was killed. I wouldn't be surprised if she doesn't know anything about that."

"Then let's turn around and go back home," Murphy said. "You can question her after we pick her up and we know the situation is secure."

"Not on your life," Cameron said. "Nick's and Cecilia's murders are my cases and Emily Dolan is the only possible lead I have. I've only let you come along as a courtesy."

"And I told you where to find her as a courtesy." Muttering, Murphy sat back in his seat and folded his arms across his chest. "When am I going to learn to keep my mouth shut? Dad warned me that you weren't easy to get along with."

"What did you say?" Cameron asked.

"Nothing." Part of Murphy wished that they were living in another time when he could have, as her husband, ordered Jessica to stay home and she would have dutifully obeyed him. But then, he realized, she would not have been the same spunky woman he fell in love with.

They decided to drive Cameron's SUV, which was an unmarked Pennsylvania State police cruiser. Since Emily had been tailing Murphy, it was best to use a vehicle she was unfamiliar with.

The plan called for Cameron and Jessica to go into the coffee shop where Emily worked to question her, while Murphy listened to the interview through covert earpieces that the two women would wear. Knowing the details of the murders at Francine Baxter's home, he could guide the conversation if need be. If he was lucky, Cameron might succeed in getting Dolan to spill information to help him in his case—like why anyone would want to kill five women who didn't know each other.

Cameron's cover story, to get Emily Dolan talking, was to pretend to be a devoted follower of her blog, who was anxiously awaiting her news breaking story about a military cover up.

Late in the evening, less than half an hour from closing time, Emily Dolan's blog had been silent all day, in spite of questions from her many followers about the anticipated news. Some comments left on the site claimed that the promise of a huge breaking story was nothing more than a publicity ploy.

In the back seat of Cameron's cruiser, Murphy took his cell phone from the case and scrolled through his contacts for Special Agent Susan Archer's number. "Are you sure Tristan can take care of Izzy?"

"Izzy's not a baby," Jessica said. "All he has to do is make sure she doesn't set the house on fire."

"She has a dangerous sweet tooth," Murphy said. "I saw her eat four brownies without batting an eye today. She claimed each one counted as a serving of vegetables." He brought the phone to his ear.

"I like her style already," Cameron said.

Susan greeted Murphy from the other end of his phone. "Hey, honey, how's it going?" For the benefit of anyone who may have been watching her and Perry, using the cover of a couple on a date, she pretended to be talking to her child who was at home.

"Are you and Perry having a nice evening?"

"Oh, yes," she replied with an upbeat laugh. "The early show let out a couple of hours ago and we decided to come over to Starbucks to have dessert and coffee. Get to bed. You have school tomorrow. I'll be home by midnight."

Murphy translated her response to mean that she and Perry had taken over the shift from the earlier surveillance team. They were going to follow Dolan to her home after the coffee bar closed. Their replacements would relieve them at midnight. "Any suspicious activity?"

"Oh, we've been having a great time," she said before lowering her voice. "They must be getting ready to close. The assistant manager just sent the clerk behind the counter to the back."

"That's backwards," Murphy said. "I worked one of those places in high school. When it gets close to closing, the manager goes to the office to do the close of business paperwork."

"That's what we thought."

"Well, here's something else for you and Perry to keep an eye on," Murphy said. "Two women on a mission are incoming. ETA five minutes."

"Oh?"

"Jessica and my stepmother," Murphy explained. "My stepmother is a Pennsylvania state homicide detective. There's a slight possibility that Emily Dolan may have information in connection to two murders she's investigating. They're both armed. I'm going to be listening in from Cameron's cruiser in the parking lot."

"Do you really think you should do that, sweetie?" Susan replied.

"I have no leverage to stop them." Murphy felt his heart drop into the pit of his stomach when Jessica directed Cameron on where to turn into the shopping plaza.

"Have you tried handcuffs?" Susan was suggesting when Cameron brought the cruiser to a stop.

Without responding, Murphy disconnected the call.

Cameron swung open the door to her SUV and stepped out. "We need to get in there to order our lattes before the place closes."

Before Jessica could climb out, Murphy grabbed her by the arm to stop her. Still perturbed by his doubt about her going inside, she turned back to him.

"Be careful in there, Buttercup. Seriously ... if anything happened to you ..." He brushed his thumb along her cheek before touching his lips to hers. "I love you, Jessie."

Keeping her eyes closed to take in the full essence of his kiss, she breathed, "Love you more."

"This isn't a lovers' lane." Cameron's voice from outside shattered the mood. "They're going to be closing soon."

They jumped into action. "Have you got your gun?" he asked Jessica.

"In my purse." Jessica grasped her small shoulder bag.

"Loaded and do you have a spare magazine?"

"Of course," she replied while Cameron yanked her out of the passenger seat and closed the door on him.

In the backseat, Murphy adjusted his covert earpiece to make sure he had a clear connection. Through the rear window, he saw Jessica covertly checking her gun while crossing the parking lot. *She should have done that before leaving the house.*

He glanced at the time on his phone. It was twenty minutes until nine o'clock. The shopping center was almost vacant. Judging by the few vehicles scattered around the parking lot, he guessed that the only people left in the few stores that were still open were employees who were going about their closing routines while watching the clock. As soon as the time struck the ninth hour, the manager or assistant manager would turn on the closed sign and lock the doors. With a minimal amount of work left to do, the young employees, mostly teenagers, college students, and working moms, would be out the doors and on their way home soon after that.

Crouched down in the back of the SUV, Murphy surveyed the parking lot. Emily Dolan's Volkswagen was parked under a lamp post. Through the café window, Murphy saw her working behind the service counter.

He had changed out of his white uniform to his black pants, shirt, and a black hoodie jacket, under which he wore his semi-automatic tucked into the back waistband. As always, he had a twenty-two caliber semi-automatic in his ankle-holster. His Walther PPK was as much a part of his regular clothing as his underwear.

Why is Dolan manning the counter right before closing? She's the assistant manager. She should be back in the business office.

Peering through a pair of small binoculars into the coffee shop, Murphy observed two men in military fatigues sitting at a table near the counter. In the Washington metropolitan area, it was not unusual to see soldiers in their fatigues.

Even so, Murphy felt his stomach flip flop. Dolan was anti-military—claiming to have information about a cover up. *What if she had uncovered something?*

Keeping a close eye on the café, he reached into his bag for his fighting knife. Quickly, he took off his belt and threaded it through the weapon's sheath. After putting the belt back on, he tied the lower end of the sheath around his thigh.

The vibration of his phone where he wore it in his belt caused him to jump. *I knew it. Jessica is not ready for this. I should have left her at home handcuffed to the bed.* Without checking the identification, he connected the call and brought it to his ear. "Don't tell me. You forgot the bullets."

"Bullets? For what?"

The familiar whiny male voice made the hair on the back of Murphy's neck stand on end. "Dean?" *Amy's deadbeat husband.*

"Who did you think it was?" Dean asked with a laugh. "What's this about bullets?"

Cursing under his breath, Murphy noticed a full-sized van parked around the corner. He had almost missed it because in the unlit side lot, away from the shopping center's general businesses, the black vehicle blended into the darkness.

"I'm at the shooting range," Murphy lied. "I'm waiting for a friend and thought that maybe he went home because he forgot his bullets. How did you get my number?" Bringing the binoculars to his eyes, Murphy eased toward the rear window of the SUV.

"Amy gave it to me," Dean replied. "Don't they have bullets at the shooting range?"

"He's got a very special weapon." Murphy focused in on the underside of the passenger-side front fender that had a sizable dent in it. With the night vision scope, he was able to focus in on the federal license plate. "Listen, Dean, I have to—"

"Hey, Murph, I've got some Navy SEALS in my book and—I know you're not a SEAL—but I was wondering if you could answer some research questions for me. How about us getting together for lunch?"

"I'm busy," Murphy said.

"I didn't even tell you when."

"I just got handed this huge project that I need to work on. It's going to mean a lot of overtime." With binoculars in hand, Murphy swept the boundaries of the parking lot. Hearing the rattle of doors opening, he swung back around to the van. Two men climbed out of the back. With his binoculars, Murphy zoomed in to see what they were unpacking.

"All I need is an hour of your time," Dean insisted when he received no reply from Murphy. "How about tomorrow for breakfast?"

Moving up close to the window, while trying to stay low, Murphy strained to see what the men were doing. He was able to make out that they were dressed in military fatigues. "What—"

"Tomorrow morning. Breakfast at the Ritz. It's only a stone's throw from the Pentagon."

"Sure, Dean," Murphy said. "Gotta go. My buddy just showed up."

200

He disconnected the call and thumbed Susan Archer's number.

Jessica was beaming on their way through the door.

Spotting her giddy state, Cameron whispered, "Why are you smiling?"

"This is my first undercover operation." Jessica's grin filled her whole face.

"Congratulations." Cameron patted her arm. "Now drop the smile. You look like a fool." With a jerk of her head in the direction of the coffee counter, she urged in a low voice, "You go to the counter and start ordering the drinks. I'll be right behind you. I need to assess the situation before approaching our target."

While Jessica moved up to where Emily Dolan was checking the inventory to restock for the next day, Cameron picked up a magazine from a basket next to a love seat that rested in front of the see-through fireplace. A young couple who appeared to be barely out of their teens cuddled in the loveseat on the other side. When they saw Cameron nearby, they parted, but not without shooting her a chastising look for intruding.

Taking the hint, Cameron turned away.

In one booth against the far wall, a young man wearing earbuds was banging away on his laptop like he was doing a speed test. One of his legs shook while he tapped his foot non-stop.

At the booth nearest the counter, a lone customer was sipping a cup of coffee while scrolling through the screen on his cell phone. A middle-aged man, he donned a suit like the vast majority of men who worked in and around Washington. Unlike most of those men, beneath his suitcoat, he had a bulge on his hip.

Cameron recognized it for what it was. *Is he one of Murphy's agents watching Emily Dolan?*

In the booth directly behind that of the lone customer, another couple was talking to each other in low voices. Older than the kids in the love seat, they seemed to be in their mid-twenties to early thirties. Both were dressed in jeans and button down shirts. The young woman wore her long dark hair in a ponytail gathered low on the back of her neck.

Strolling up to the counter where Jessica was waiting for their coffees, Cameron took note of the woman's shoes. Flat heeled lace ups. Not exactly date wear. Upon seeing the detective checking out her shoes, the woman caught Cameron's eye and gave a slight nod of her head before flicking her eyes toward the counter as if to urge Cameron to move along. *They have to be part of Murphy's team.*

Moving past the lone customer in the suit, Cameron paused. *If they're both part of the same team, why aren't they more spread out? One of them should be on the other side of the café to provide extra coverage.*

The woman agent's cell phone buzzed. Bringing the phone to her ear, she cocked an eyebrow at her date, a slender man with dark hair.

"Cam, our lattes are ready," Jessica called to her from the counter. "Come and get it. You wouldn't believe who this is."

The opening of the door caught Cameron's attention.

Donning dark sun glasses in the evening, two men dressed in worn military desert fatigues, complete with fully loaded utility belts, stepped through the door. Cameron turned to Jessica. Behind her, she noticed two other muscular men dressed likewise at a bistro table next to the window. Looking oversized for the delicate chairs, the muscular men sat with their long legs sticking out into the serving area with their big feet encased in dull, scuffed up combat boots.

Laughing, the two new arrivals strolled up to the counter from which Jessica was stepping away with a latte in each hand.

As she passed them, Jessica noticed that the taller of the two men had thick dark hair and a shock of white hair on the sides, directly above his ears, which reminded her of white stripes. *Sidewalls.* Trying to suppress a giggle, she smiled. She didn't want the tall, muscular soldier to realize she was laughing at him.

The two men at the bistro table stood up. They nodded to the taller of the two men, while his partner faced Emily Dolan behind the counter. She stepped over from where she had just completed her transaction with Jessica to take their orders.

"Murphy," Cameron whispered, "this is going real bad real fast. You need to get in here."

She sensed movement behind her.

The young man who had been typing away had slammed his laptop shut, shoved it into his backpack, and slid out of the booth to trot toward the door to the beat of the music piped in through his earbuds.

At the counter, in a casual motion, almost like that of a man reaching for his wallet in his pocket, all four men in their military fatigues reached for their weapons.

Simultaneously, out of the edge of her peripheral vision, Cameron saw the café door crash open.

The quiet evening at Starbucks erupted into a firefight.

CHAPTER FIFTEEN

In one smooth motion, Sidewall's companion slipped his weapon from of its holster and fired three shots into Emily Dolan's chest.

Behind him, Murphy took a flying leap across the dining room. "Everybody get down!" While firing with one arm at the four assailants, he threw his free arm around Jessica. Together, in a hail of bullets and flying lattes, they dove to the floor between the loveseat and the fireplace.

The assassin who killed Emily Dolan dropped down onto the counter. As he slid to the floor, customers screamed to see that at least one of Murphy's shots had hit its target. He had a gunshot wound to the back of his head.

Screams filled the air while the remaining three gunmen shot at everything that moved in their effort to exterminate any possible witnesses.

"Stay down!" Murphy ordered Jessica while returning fire at the three remaining assassins.

Struggling to get out from where he had her pinned, Jessica extracted her gun from her purse. Her hands were shaking. "How did you—"

"Dull boots!" Pausing to replace the magazine in his gun with a fresh one, Murphy caught sight of a man in a suit running through the swinging door to the back of the café. The men in the military fatigues made no move to stop him.

"Latimore! Where are you?" Murphy yanked his gun from the ankle holster.

"Back here!" Perry yelled from behind the fireplace.

"I told you to cover Dolan!" Murphy jumped up to fire off double-taps with both guns. "Archer, get over here and cover me!"

"I'll cover you, Archer," Cameron volunteered from behind an overturned bistro table.

"Don't leave me!" The young man who was leaving before the chaos erupted begged from where he was clinging to Cameron behind the table.

"Get a grip and stay down!" Jessica heard Cameron order before a barrage of shots flew over her head.

Jessica felt, rather than saw, one of the gunmen fall backwards over a bistro table only a couple of feet from her. By natural instinct, she rose up to see if he was really dead.

With a cocky grin, the downed assassin sat up. He was so close that Jessica could see the Kevlar vest through the bullet holes in his jacket. With a laugh, he stuck out his arm. The barrel of his gun, only inches from her face, looked like a cannon.

She froze like a frightened rabbit looking into the mouth of a wolf drooling over the prospect of a juicy dinner.

Abruptly, she felt a strong hand clamp down on top of her head and shove her to the floor. The two shots that Murphy fired into the assailant's head wiped the smirk off his face. "I told you to stay down!"

Keeping low, Susan scurried up behind them. "What's your plan, Thornton?"

"Keep them busy." Murphy tucked one of his weapons into the waistband of his pants. "I saw a guy in a suit run to the back."

"But—"

"He's with them," Murphy said. "Most likely, he's after Dolan's laptop. I need to get to him before he finds it and wipes it clean."

"On the count of three, go," she told Murphy.

"Count me in." Jessica held up her gun for the agent to see that she was armed and ready.

Susan grinned. "The deb's got guts."

After catching Cameron's attention Susan counted off with her fingers, not unlike a catcher giving signals to a pitcher. On the count of three, Susan, Cameron, and Jessica sprang up and fired off a barrage of shots at the two gunmen who were now pinned behind the counter.

While the gunmen were ducking the hailstorm of bullets, Murphy sprung for the door leading back to the business office and supply room. Bursting through the swinging door, he collided with the man in the suit coming out of the manager's office with a laptop tucked under his arm.

Not only did the collision cause the suited man to drop the laptop to the floor, but it caused Murphy to drop his gun. Both the laptop and gun skidded across the floor in opposite directions.

Spotting the intruder reaching for the gun he was wearing under his suitcoat, Murphy grabbed his wrist and squeezed it while delivering a knee to the man's groin. When he doubled over, Murphy followed up with another knee to his chest.

Instead of collapsing, the intruder quickly recovered to grab Murphy's leg and yanked it out from under him, plunging Murphy flat on his back. Even with the air knocked out of him, Murphy could see his assailant reaching for his gun to finish him off. A swing of his leg sent the gun flying.

Another swipe knocked both of the gunman's legs out from under him.

Spotting his gun a few feet away, Murphy scrambled across the floor for it.

In the instant that he took his eyes off the assassin—less than a foot from his weapon—he heard the click of a gun behind him. He dove for the floor and rolled while feeling the rush of the bullet speeding over his shoulder to pierce the wall in front of him.

Tucking his legs up under him in the roll, Murphy came back up on one knee—knife in hand.

Before the man in the suit saw the knife, it hit its target— the point drove through the front of his neck. The path of the blade severed his spinal cord before coming out the back to pin him to the wall behind him.

The explosions from their guns were almost drowned out by another burst that went off in the middle of the floor— directly in front of the loveseat where Jessica and Susan were seeking cover.

Smoke filled the air. Instantly, tears came to their eyes and smoke filled their lungs.

The shooting stopped.

"Jessica, we need to get out of here!" Susan called out through the smoke. "Head for the door!"

Unable to see through the smoke, Jessica rose up to run in the direction of the door. The smoke cutting off her breathing, she fell to her knees.

"Time to go, Buttercup!" Murphy's arms were around her. She felt her legs shaking when he lifted her to her feet. "Can you stand?"

As if to answer him, her knees crumbled under her. Before she could hit the floor, he lifted her up into his arms and carried her out of the café.

Unable to see through the tears in her burning eyes, she dug her face into his chest while he carried her out into the night air. While she gasped for air, Murphy seemed to only be breathing hard and coughing slightly. As soon as she caught a wisp of the fresh air, she took in a deep breath, only to let go with another round of coughing.

"Take it easy, Buttercup," Murphy soothed her while carrying her across the parking lot. "Don't overdo it. Obviously, you've never experienced a smoke bomb before."

Her vision clearing, she squinted through her tears to see that he was smiling at her. "And you have?"

"As a matter of fact, I have, in training," he said. "Once you know what to expect, then you can handle it better."

"And since I didn't, then you must be having a good laugh," she said.

"No I'm not," Murphy said. "My chief witness is now dead."

"Then why are you grinning?" Sometimes, she hated how the sight of his dimples and that sexy grin got the best of her.

"Because you're not, Buttercup." He pressed his lips to her forehead. "We'll find a way to solve this case," he whispered, "but if anything had happened to you …"

She wrapped her arms around his shoulders and pressed her face into his neck. "I froze."

"I think you can put her down now, Murphy," Cameron said next to them. "I just had to carry a one hundred and fifty pound sci-fi author out of the café—he's still crying like a little girl." She gestured at the front of her shirt.

"Was he hurt?" Jessica asked while Murphy gently put her down next to Cameron's SUV.

"Only emotionally," Cameron said.

Her legs still shaking, Jessica grasped the SUVs door. Murphy wrapped his arm around her waist to steady her. "Are you okay?"

"Considering that my only possible witness is now dead, Jessica's wearing my latte, and that guy left snot all over the front of my shirt, I'm dandy," Cameron answered.

"I was talking to Jessie," Murphy told her.

"Is that any way to talk to your stepmother?" Cameron replied.

"Anybody besides Dolan hurt?" Murphy asked Susan when she approached them. "Are the customers and employees okay?"

"The three employees who were working with Dolan ran out the backdoor as soon as the shooting started and called the police," she reported. "The three customers in the café are shaken up, but okay."

Perry was directing the police and emergency vehicles pouring into the parking lot. Cameron opened up the back of her SUV to extract her utility belt and police detective's badge.

"You and Latimore?" Murphy asked Susan. "Either of you hit?"

Dismissing his question with a wave of her hand, she replied, "This isn't our first rodeo, Thornton. We're fine."

"How many of the shooters are down?" Murphy asked.

"Two of the shooters are down," Susan reported while snapping her badge onto her belt for the police to see. "Emily Dolan is dead too."

"Add to that one accomplice I left in the back room." Murphy reached around behind his back to extract a laptop from where he had tucked it under his coat. "Once the shooting started, he ran back into the manager's office to steal this."

"Are you sure that's Emily Dolan's?" Susan asked.

"The guy was willing to kill me to escape with it." Murphy handed it to Susan. "If it's not hers, he thought it was."

Susan asked, "Do you want me to call Hamilton?"

"I'll call him." Seeing Jessica unsteady in her high heels, Murphy urged her to sit down in the SUV.

"Why aren't any of you ..." Jessica clutched her chest. Her lungs felt like they were going to explode and her heart was beating so hard that she thought it would pop out of her chest. Stars came to her eyes.She heard roaring in her ears.

"We need an EMT here *now!*" she heard Murphy yell as she slipped away into darkness.

The oxygen that the EMTs gave Jessica revived strength to her body. As her breathing improved, so did her mind.

Now that the immediate crisis was over, she was embarrassed. Here she was, touting herself as a licensed private investigator and, when she gets into her first shootout, she froze ... then passed out.

What a newbie! She was no help to Murphy in solving his first official murder case or Cameron in finding out who had arranged Nick's murder. Since Emily Dolan was now dead, so was their best lead to finding out the reason behind all these murders and learning who was behind it all.

Removing the oxygen mask, she reached over to turn off the tank.

"Did they say you could turn that off?" Cameron stepped over from where she had been talking to the deputy chief of Murphy's staff and agents Susan Archer and Perry Latimore. She was carrying a blue t-shirt with POLICE emblazoned on the back. "Here." She handed the shirt to Jessica and stepped into the back of the ambulance. "That coffee should be good and cold by now."

Jessica looked down to notice that the front of her silk blouse was covered with the two lattes that went flying when Murphy charged in.

Cameron's tone softened when she asked her, "Are you feeling better?"

"Are you talking physically or emotionally?" Jessica said with a pout. She took the offered shirt.

"Physically." Cameron eased the rear door of the ambulance shut to allow Jessica privacy to change into the t-shirt. "We're trying to find a killer who is responsible for the murder of eight people—that we know of. I love you, Jessica, but your feelings really aren't at the top of my list. If you need a hug, I'll go get Murphy. If you have a lead, then I'm here for you."

"In other words, get a grip and suck it up." Jessica pulled the blouse off over her head.

"Those are the words."

"Did you know those men in fatigues were phonies?" Jessica said through the fabric of the t-shirt while pulling it on over her head.

"No," Cameron said with a shake of her head. "But the guy in the suit sitting up toward the counter didn't strike me as belonging." She pushed open the rear door of the ambulance and climbed out.

Finger combing her hair, which had been messed during the wardrobe change, Jessica recalled, "Murphy said something about their shoes being dull."

"They didn't shine when they walked under the lamp post," Murphy announced while coming around the side of the door. He held out his hand to help Jessica climb out of the ambulance.

"What does that have to do—"

"You make fun of how hard I work to make my boots and shoes shine," Murphy grinned. "And you laugh when

I say it's regulation. But it's true. When you're in uniform, your shoes and boots, even combat boots, have to shine, unless you're in a combat situation. When those two shooters walked under the lamppost and I saw that their boots were scuffed and dull, I knew."

"I'll never make fun of you shining your shoes again." Jessica held onto him as if she never wanted to let him go. Fighting back tears, she murmured into his ear. "This is the second time you've saved my life. I just wish I could have been more help to you in there."

"We're working on identifying all of the assailants," Boris stepped over to tell them. "Plus, all may not be lost. Since we were here on the scene and Emily Dolan was a material witness in the Baxter case, then we've got the lead in this case. Not only did you save Dolan's laptop, but the accomplice missed her cell phone. The employees confirmed that Dolan was on that laptop all the time. So if she had anything, it will be there. I'll get Latimore to take a look at it."

"Speaking of Latimore," Murphy said, "I told him to cover Dolan." Seeing Perry Latimore coming into view, he turned to him. "You were right there. I called both you and Archer when I saw the shooters going in."

"There were two already in there," Perry said. "How were we supposed to—"

"Men walking into a coffee shop carrying weapons and we know that a possible target is in there," Murphy said. "You should be ready and expect anything. Didn't they teach you that at Quantico?"

"Yes, but maybe they didn't teach it as well as they did at your Naval Academy," Perry replied. "You pinned them as hit men before any of us did. You could have taken out the main shooter before he killed our witness, but instead, you saved your debutant wife and left the rest up to us."

Murphy stepped forward to find Jessica's hand on his chest.

"Stand down, Latimore!" Boris ordered. "That was out of line."

"When did Thornton become our boss?" Perry asked Boris. Seeing no response, he turned to Susan, whose face was void of emotion. "He's the navy liaison. He's the go between for NCIS and the military. Now that he's Patterson's golden boy and has decided he wants to play detective, we have to play along, but when he screws up and people get killed, we take the blame for it."

"Why didn't you cover Dolan?" Susan asked. "You were right there. The shooter had his back to you. You could have taken him down before he fired the shot."

"So could you," Perry said.

"I was following Thornton's orders to cover the civilians."

Stepping into Perry's face, Murphy said, "During the firefight, when I asked where you were and you answered, you were behind me. If you had done as I had ordered, you would have immediately moved up toward the counter, which would have put you in front of all of us—close enough to take out the shooter as soon as he pulled his weapon."

Perry backed away from his gaze. "I don't take orders from you." He turned to walk away, only to find Boris Hamilton's hand on his arm.

"But you do from me," Boris said. "I'll be expecting a full report from you tomorrow."

Perry's lips curled. "You'll get it." He cast a glance back in Murphy's direction. "And so will Chief Koch."

Gritting his teeth, Murphy turned around. With his back to his team, he took a deep cleansing breath. It took all of his restraint to keep from punching the side of the ambulance with his fist.

Jessica grasped his arm in both of her hands. "None of this was your fault," she said in a low voice.

Murphy's eyes met hers. In spite of her words of encouragement, she saw guilt permeating from him.

"Excuse me, Thornton." Susan had stepped away from the group to confide in a low voice, "Sorry about Latimore. He is my partner, but you should know, when the chips are down—it's every man for himself in Latimore's book."

"I think I just found that out," Murphy said.

"But you can count on me to have your back," she said.

Boris clasped his hand on Murphy's shoulder. "And me."

"Thanks," Murphy said.

"Okay, so where do we go from here?" Jessica asked. "Is it just a coincidence that Emily Dolan writes an anti-military blog and that the men who walked into the café to gun her down in front of customers were dressed in military uniforms?"

"The military did not do this," Murphy said.

"I'm not saying that they did," Jessica said, "but to the average customer, witness, who saw this go down, that's what it looks like. Think about it. All over the Internet, Emily Dolan has been promising a big breaking story exposing a military conspiracy on her blog. Her sources were all murdered. And then, before she can reveal her story, four armed soldiers wearing military fatigues walk in and gun her down."

"I have a feeling this is one military conspiracy story that's not going to go away soon," Boris said.

Looking around the edges of the parking lot, they saw that the media was already out in full force. On the other side of the crime scene tape, Murphy spotted the long white limousine. Bernie was strolling toward them. Excusing himself, Murphy broke away from his team to meet the bodyguard where the crime scene tape was stretched across the length of the parking lot.

"Does she want to see me?"

"No, Lieutenant," Bernie said. *"They* want to see you for a debriefing. Nine o'clock tomorrow morning. Seventh floor. She wants a report about what happened here ASAP so that she can brief the Joint Chiefs before your meeting. Wear your service dress whites."

Without another word, Bernie turned around and strode back to the limousine. Murphy watched him climb into the driver's seat, start the car, and pull away.

With no sign or clue from his commanding officer, Murphy could only guess what the Joint Chiefs of Staff had planned for him on the top floor of the Pentagon the next morning.

CHAPTER SIXTEEN

"They certainly don't blame you for what happened," Jessica told Murphy.

He didn't seem to hear her. Saying nothing, he stared up at the ceiling over their bed with his hands folded behind his head.

Any other night, she would have been aroused by the sight of his firm chest and toned stomach. She found it hard to resist stroking his chest with her fingertips, working her way down his stomach.

This night, she was more concerned with how quiet he had been since talking to the mountain of a man after the shooting. The only information she had been able to extract from Murphy was that he was being ordered to the Joint Chiefs of Staff on the seventh floor for a debriefing first thing in the morning.

That was not good. Not good at all.

Murphy had been so distracted that he didn't even notice that Tristan and Izzy had spent the evening pigging out on pizza and chocolate chip cookie dough ice cream while watching a *Scream* marathon with all of the critters, except for Monique, surrounding them. The tarantula preferred making people scream on her own.

As soon as they dragged themselves home, Murphy went straight up to their room and closed the door to write an incident report on the special secured laptop the Joint Chiefs had given him for his Phantom operations. After completing it, he sent it via their secured network to his commanding officer.

After responding to Izzy's questions with vague answers, claiming that it was an open investigation, Jessica hurried upstairs to find Murphy already in bed.

Usually, the newlyweds slept in the nude, but with so many house guests, they had both opted to wear some clothes in case a situation called for them to be needed in a hurry. Murphy had slipped on a pair of sweat pants while Jessica wore panties under an oversized William and Mary t-shirt.

"They can't blame you." Slipping up against him to rest her head on his shoulder, Jessica wrapped her arms around him. "*You* didn't go into the coffee bar and shoot it up."

"They need a scapegoat," Murphy said. "As soon as Emily Dolan's name is released, then conspiracy theorists are going to point to the military. The media is bound to find out that the shooters were dressed in fatigues. Questions will be asked and Latimore will spin things around like he did tonight. I put saving my wife ahead of the lives of others, including an important material witness to a mass murder."

"He's jealous of you. Everyone can see that." She looked up at him. "Why else did he bring up the academy and me?"

Murphy swallowed.

Laying her head down on his chest, she listened to the beating of his heart. "I should have listened to you. I never should have gone in there."

"I should have handcuffed you to the bed," Murphy agreed.

"I don't understand how I froze," she said. "I've taken gun classes and Dad sent me through a battery of self-defense classes when I was in school—"

"None of that prepares you for the real thing," Murphy said. "Civilians and the media have no idea what happens—physically, emotionally—when real bullets start flying and someone is hell bent on killing you. That's why they send me out at night for training—simulating real situations. In the past couple of years, I've been shot at hundreds of times. I've had knifes thrown at me. I've even been snatched off the street when I wasn't expecting it and thrown off a bridge—all by members of my own team."

"Talk about a tough job," Jessica said. "They threw you off a bridge?"

"All to physically—and most importantly mentally—prepare me for when the real thing happens. So that when I do get into those types of situations, my reactions will be second nature."

"Everything happened so fast," Jessica said. "It was impossible for me to process. I kept thinking I should know—"

"But then you stepped up to bat to cover me while I went after their accomplice," Murphy said. "You just needed time to get over the initial shock."

"Then I fainted like a girl."

"You are a girl," he said with a chuckle.

"Cameron didn't."

"Cameron has a lot of experience under her belt," he said.

"I want experience under my belt," she said. "I don't like being a wimp."

"You're not a wimp, Buttercup. Basically, what you need to do is learn how to press your bitch button."

She lifted her head to look up at him. He was grinning down at her. "My bitch button?"

"Everyone has one."

Looking him up and down, she arched an eyebrow. "You have a bitch button?"

"I have a bastard button," Murphy said. "You have a bitch button."

"No—"

"I've seen you when someone pressed it," he said with a grin. "It can be quite effective when activated."

"When have you seen my bitch button activated?"

"In the middle of the night when you beat the daylights out of me," Murphy answered with a chuckle.

"That was an accident," she said with a whine. "I was sound asleep."

"You gave me a black eye on our honeymoon," Murphy said. "So I know for a fact that you know how to throw a punch. You just need to wake up the bitch buried deep inside you ... the one who seems to only come out at night."

Still embarrassed by the recent events of their honeymoon and the discovery that she was a sleep "fighter," Jessica covered her face, which had turned bright pink, with both hands while Murphy continued laughing at her nighttime antics.

More than once since their marriage, Jessica woke up to find bruises on Murphy's arms, legs, or back. Three days into their marriage, Murphy woke up yelling. His nose was bleeding and he had a black eye—both resulted from a single punch swung by his new bride. Two nights after that, he landed on the floor after she had pressed both of her feet to his back and kicked him out of the bed. Some nights he would wake up to her knee making a forceful contact with his groin.

One night, he woke Jessica up while she was twisting his hand so hard that he thought she was going to break his wrist. She had such a grip on his hand that he had to pinch a pressure point on her arm to make her release him.

So far, the only source to which they had been able to trace her violent actions during the night was a recurring nightmare during which she was surrounded by menacing figures wearing black robes and white masks.

"Let's not release my inner bitch." Sparks came to Jessica's violet eyes.

"See?" he laughed. "You just pressed it again. You need to condition yourself to the point that when you get into a life and death situation that you can move beyond the shock, which is what paralyzes most people, to press your bitch button, which puts you on the offense."

"Why not defense?"

"You want to be on the offense when it comes to survival," Murphy said. "When I press my bastard button, all niceties, all manners go out the window. When it comes to life and death, there are no rules. *They* don't play by any rules, so neither do I. You shouldn't either." He wrapped his arms around her. "Then, when it is all over, you can go back to being my sweet Buttercup."

He kissed her. Resting her head on his shoulder, she gazed up at him while brushing her fingertips across his bare chest. "Seeing you in action tonight, I hope I never press your bastard button."

Thinking of his meeting the next morning, she said for a third time, "They can't blame you for them killing Emily Dolan."

"I'm a Phantom, Jessie," Murphy said. "No one is more highly trained than I am. Phantoms receive the most specialized training available—even SEALS and Black Ops. I was best equipped to save Dolan, who was our only lead in this case and the only possible lead that Cameron had in finding out who ordered Nick's murder …" He sucked in a deep breath. "I could have saved her, but chose instead to push that responsibility onto someone else in order to save you myself. That was a mistake. I screwed up."

Together, they stared up at the ceiling in silence.

Jessica could anticipate his reaction before the words came from her mouth, but she was desperate to help him. "Maybe I could call Natalie—"

Murphy sprung up off the pillows. "Admiral Patterson's wife! No!"

"Sure, the whole idea of it not being 'who you know' but 'what you know' is ideal," Jessica argued, "but the fact is, it *is* who you know that matters. Natalie and I have become friends. Why, just yesterday, we spent a few hours here drinking a couple of pitchers of margaritas—"

In his exhausted state, overwhelmed with all the information he had thrown at him during the day, Murphy had to shake his head. "Admiral Patterson's wife? Nata—margaritas? What are you talking about?"

"Her and Paige Graham showed up asking me to go to lunch with them," Jessica said. "They were going to the marina for lunch and Natalie knew I lived right here, so they stopped by. But we ended up not going."

"Why not?" Curious about where this conversation was taking them, Murphy laid back down on his side beside her.

Seeing that she was succeeding in taking his mind off the next morning's meeting, Jessica rolled over onto her side to face him. "After meeting Paige Graham, the last thing I wanted to do was spend an hour or so down at the marina with that snooty bitch. Luckily, she remembered a meeting with some council and left."

"Who is Paige Graham?"

"Sebastian Graham's wife? *General* Graham." she replied. "Don't tell me that with everything going on that you have forgotten about General Sebastian Graham and the

President nominating him to fill General Johnston's slot as Chief of Staff of the United States Army."

Murphy sighed. Conversation with her had relaxed him enough that he allowed himself to stroke her bare thigh with his fingertips. "What did she do that got her on your bad side?"

"It wasn't so much what she did as it was her complete attitude," she said. "Yes, I know she's in charge of the Army Officers' Spouses Club, but she seems to think that makes her queen of everything. The only reason she's their leader is because her husband is General Graham and General Johnston's wife doesn't participate." On a roll, she giggled. "She so reminds me of girls I knew in high school who attached their self-worth directly to their boyfriends' status."

"I thought that went away," Murphy said.

"We would like to think so, but it hasn't totally," Jessica said. "Think about it. Paige Graham is really into this club and being chair on all these charity boards—all because her husband is a big war hero and on the fast track to the Joint Chiefs of Staff. *He* makes her Queen Bee. I bet you she would flip out if the current army's chief of staff, General Johnston's wife, decided to start being active in the club."

"She's too busy doing heart transplants at Johns Hopkins," Murphy said. "Some of these officers' wives take the club very seriously."

"Did your mother?"

Murphy stretched out his hand and shook it in a gesture of somewhat. "It's true that it isn't just the husband, or the wife, who joins the military. It's the whole family. These groups weren't intended to be social clubs with high school hierarchy attached to them."

"It's impossible to get a bunch of women together without that happening," Jessica said.

"I think it depends on the women," Murphy said. "They're meant to offer a support system to each other."

"How involved was your mother in the navy officers' wives club?" Jessica asked. "Did she attach her worth to your father's rank?"

"No, she attached her self-worth to her children's grades," he replied with a laugh. "There were five of us. She would be involved, but really, not as involved as it sounds like Paige Graham is."

"Maybe because the Grahams don't have any kids," Jessica said. "And she doesn't have her own career separate from her husband."

"Don't some women consider their family to be their careers?" Murphy asked. "Mom's whole life revolved around Dad and us kids."

"Did your mom go to Yale on an academic scholarship?"

"My mother's folks owned a roadside diner out toward Kitty Hawk," he said with a laugh. "She waited tables all through high school. She was on her way to a glamourous career of being a short order cook when Dad stopped in for breakfast on his way to the Outer Banks with some friends. He had been at the naval academy only a few weeks." With a grin, he cocked his head at her. "Dad says it was love at first sight. They dated long distance while he attended the academy. The day after he graduated, they got married. J.J. and I were born ten months later."

She brushed her fingers across his bare chest. "Sounds familiar—except for the twins coming along ten months later."

"Guess it runs in the family." He brought her hand to his lips and softly kissed her palm.

Her eyebrows furrowed and she narrowed her violet eyes while peering at him.

"What?" he asked.

"Why would someone like Paige Graham work so hard to get an academic scholarship to Yale University, graduate, and then settle for being an officer's wife?"

"Most military people don't live in the same area very long," Murphy said. "Maybe they've had to move so often because of his career that she isn't settled in any one spot long enough to develop a professional career. So she gave up. We moved four times before I was sixteen. Nowadays, most military wives who want a career do it on the Internet because that's the only way they can."

"I know," she said with a tired sigh. "I have a suspicious mind."

"We both have suspicious minds." He rolled over onto his back. "It helps with what we do. What are you suspicious about?"

He didn't need to say anything else to encourage her. She stretched out onto her stomach next to him. Folding her arms on his chest, she gazed into his face while telling him about how the two officers' wives, both leaders of their respective officer spouse clubs, had arrived unannounced and unexpectedly. After getting the evil eye from Paige Graham for her less than modest attire, Jessica offered them a pitcher of margaritas for a quick cocktail and conversation with the intention of begging off lunch and sending them on their way.

"That was when the conversation got interesting," Jessica said.

"You answer the door dressed like Princess Jasmine to find a four-star general's wife standing on your doorstep, and only then did things get interesting?" Murphy replied with a chuckle.

It felt good to see him smile. "Paige Graham wasted no time bringing up Maureen Clark's murder."

The smile fell from Murphy's face.

"I got the distinct feeling that she was pumping me for information," Jessica said. "She claimed all of the women in the club were upset—"

"Naturally."

"And that I could help them if I could feed them information about the investigation. Of course, I explained that I couldn't."

"Colonel Lincoln Clark was at NCIS yesterday afternoon," Murphy said. "Of course, the army is trying to get the case sent over to CID." He sighed. "After tonight—"

"Paige claimed his wife was disturbed," Jessica said.

"How was she disturbed?"

"Delusional," she explained. "Paige said she had become obsessed with General Graham and imagined a relationship where there wasn't any—"

She stopped when Murphy sat up, forcing her to move off him. He turned to her. "What else did she say about Maureen Clark?"

"That she had withdrawn from many of the club's activities in the last few years," she said. "Social withdrawal is a symptom of emotional illness."

"Colonel Clark came in yesterday to complain because he didn't want our forensics people to take samples of his son's DNA."

"General Graham has quite a reputation for extramarital affairs," Jessica said. "Paige went out of her way to say that these woman claiming to have slept with him were all disturbed and imagining it all."

"Clark said he was trying to protect his son's privacy," Murphy said.

"Sounds to me like he could be trying to protect a family secret."

Cameron's call to Joshua went straight to voice mail. Either he was on the phone or he had left it in airplane mode. He had been known to do that when he was in court. He would turn the phone to airplane mode before going into court and then forget about it. Then he would wonder why she didn't call him.

She was most perturbed. So far, it had not been a good trip.

Sal Bertonelli had been murdered—leaving only one clue behind. The hit was for a friend of Adrian Kalashov. But that could be anyone or even a personal favor for Kalashov himself. For all the federal agents knew, Adrian Kalashov lied to his paid assassin.

Though they were able to identify Jane Doe as Cecilia Crenshaw, the only one who may have been able to explain how she ended up on the Pennsylvania Turnpike that January night was now dead—killed less than two days after Sal Bertonelli had turned government witness.

The only other lead was also dead. Emily Dolan was a long shot, but she was better than nothing, which was what Cameron felt like they were left with.

Only days old when her mother was killed, Izzy Crenshaw had no idea Cecilia was her mother. How could she possibly know what and who was behind all these murders?

Maybe Donna Crenshaw had Cecelia killed so that she could steal Izzy as her own, in which case all of these murders have nothing to do with Izzy at all.

The thought of Izzy made Cameron feel a tug of envy in her heart.

Irving was sleeping with Izzy.

To her shock and dismay, mixed with a pinch of jealousy, when Cameron went up to the loft guest room to go to bed, Irving did not follow. Instead, he followed Izzy into her room. Even when Cameron called to him, he refused to budge from Izzy's bed.

Now I know what it's like.

Sucking in a deep breath, she stared down at the foot of her bed, through the open door out into the sitting room, through which she could make out the city skyline beyond.

In the comfortable bed, exhaustion was setting in. She missed Joshua. She so wanted his arms around her, telling her that everything would be okay. She wanted to feel safe.

Even if I had Irving to press his furry body against me and beg to be petted—that would be something. I wouldn't feel like I was going through this all by myself.

Half asleep and half awake, she could make out the form of a man taking shape where the lights from the waterfront met with the shadows in her room.

No, Cameron, that is not a man. You're tired and frustrated and you're sleeping in a strange bed and city and—

"Cameron, we're not done yet." It was Nick's voice.

The shadowy figure seemed to move towards her.

Breathing in deep breaths, Cameron tried to sit up. *Was it—No, it couldn't—*

"Our girl needs you, babe. She's crying. You need to go to her."

Girl. What girl? We had no children.

"Don't let her be alone. I promised her mother. Now you need to keep that promise for me."

Cameron held her breath. *Okay, I have officially lost my mind. Josh can have me committed when I get home.* Lying there in the quiet of the bedroom, she could barely make out the sound of sobbing down below. The sobs were broken up by choking as if the crier was trying to conceal her sorrow.

She slipped out of the bed and into her bathrobe. Without bothering with slippers, she made her way down the stairs and quietly opened the door to the guest bedroom.

"Izzy?" she whispered.

The child gasped.

"It's me, Cameron."

When she made her way across the room, Cameron found Izzy curled up in the fetal position, hugging Irving against her. Sensing that the girl needed comforting, the cat didn't object.

"Would you like some water?" Cameron offered.

"I want my mom."

"If I could get her for you, I would. I'll get you a drink of water." Taking the glass of water from the night stand, Cameron went into the bathroom. When she came out with the glass of water, Izzy was sitting up in the bed, still hugging Irving, who was licking her chin.

While Izzy drank the water, Cameron sat down on the bed next to her. "I know how you feel."

"How can you?"

"You want answers to a lot of questions about who and why someone took your mom," Cameron said. "Well, we think, we don't know for certain, but we think that whoever took away your mother was the same person behind my first husband's murder. For all these years, I've had questions and no one to answer them. Then, just when I thought I was getting close, someone took that opportunity away from me. I feel like God had given me this big beautiful gift in someone that I truly loved and who truly loved me for who I was, unconditionally, and then the devil stepped in and ripped him out of my life and then stood there laughing at my pain."

Izzy stared at her with wide watery eyes. "That's exactly how I feel." She took another gulp of the water. "How long ago did your husband die?"

"Thirteen years ago." Reminding herself that Izzy was most likely the lost baby Nick was seeking when he was murdered, Cameron gazed into the light brown pools of Izzy's eyes in the small face amongst the mass of unruly curls.

"Do you still cry yourself to sleep at night?" Izzy asked.

"Not every night," Cameron said. "The pain isn't gone. It's always there. But now, it is livable. I have come to love again. That makes the pain easier to deal with."

"Murphy's dad?"

"Yes," Cameron allowed herself to smile. "He hasn't replaced Nick. There will always be a place in my heart that only Nick could fill—just like Josh has a hole in his heart that only Murphy's mother could fill. But the hurts have healed up enough that we were both able to love again and move on with our lives, and that will happen for you, too."

"You're not alone anymore." A fresh pool of tears came to her eyes.

Cameron allowed herself to brush Izzy's curls, moist with tears, from her face. "No, I'm not alone anymore."

"I'm alone," Izzy whispered.

Cameron wrapped her arms around her and kissed her on top of her curly head. "No, you're not, dear." She was surprised when Izzy returned the hug without hesitation. "You'll never be alone. I promise you that."

As if to add his voice in agreement, Irving rose up on his hind legs, to grasp Izzy's arm and pat her tear stained cheek with his paw.

CHAPTER SEVENTEEN

Unable to sleep, Murphy got up at four-thirty and woke up Spencer to go for a morning run. He was through with his yoga and meditation long before the sun rose. With a sense of resignation, he showered and took extra time to pay attention to every detail while putting on his white dress uniform. No need to tick off the Joint Chiefs of Staff with a crooked ribbon or a dog hair on his trousers.

Jessica slept through it all.

Before he left, Murphy looked down at her and wondered how she got any rest the way she tossed and turned all night long. It was only through artful dodging that he had managed to escape any blows to his body.

Marriage does take some getting used to, but the challenge is worth it.

Kneeling down, he brushed a thick lock of dark hair off her cheek and pressed his lips to hers.

With a moan, she opened one violet eye. "You're up."

"Thought I would go have breakfast at Pentagon City before going to the meeting," he said in a whisper.

"What time is it?"

He turned the clock on the nightstand around for her to read. "Six-thirty. You go back to sleep."

She reached out for him. "Everything is going to be fine, Honey Buns."

"I know," he said. "I'm going to call Susan first thing to ask her to interview some of Maureen Clark's friends and relatives. You got me thinking last night. Colonel Clark was adamant about not getting a sample of his son's DNA. We did think it was weird. Suppose Maureen wasn't imagining things about a relationship with General Graham. Suppose it was real and Graham only told his wife that Maureen had imagined it all."

"Clark doesn't want people to find out that his wife was having an affair with General Graham." Now awake, Jessica sat up. "But would that be enough motivation to commit murder? To kill all of those women?"

"Depends on the circumstances. If the killer felt he had too much to lose ...."

In response to a whine from Spencer, who had her head draped across Jessica's stomach, begging for Murphy to acknowledge her, he patted the top of the dog's head. "Take care of Mommy for me, Candi." He bent over to kiss Jessica on the lips. "I gotta go."

"Yeah, you don't want to keep the Joint Chiefs of Staff waiting," she said with sarcasm about the early hour.

"Go back to sleep, Buttercup." He went to the door.

Throwing the comforter aside, Jessica swung her legs around to get up. "Like that's going to happen. Call me after the meeting to let me know what happens."

Seeing a possible means of escape to check out the cat in the guest room down the hall, Spencer flew off the bed and waited with her nose pressed up against the crack of the door, ready to shoot out at the least opportunity.

As soon as Murphy opened the door, Spencer shot out and down the hallway to the guest bedroom.

"Leave Irving alone," Murphy said before starting down the stairs.

"Hey, Murph." Cameron surprised Murphy by coming out of the guest bedroom. In response to his puzzled expression, she explained, "I heard Izzy crying last night, so I slept with her."

Murphy came back up the stairs. "Is she okay now?"

Cameron shrugged her shoulders. "She lost the only family she has."

"I know," he replied. "I wish there was something I could do."

"You're doing it." She reached out to touch his arm. "Don't underestimate the comfort that can come from answers. She and I both need them." She took her cell phone out of her bathrobe pocket. "Have you talked to your father?"

"No." The last person he wanted to talk to after the failure of the night before was his father, the great navy commander who was a legend for successfully prosecuting an admiral for murder.

Cameron explained, "I wasn't able to get ahold of him last night. Finally, a little bit ago, he called to say he got my voice mail but was really short with me." Her forehead wrinkled in a sign of confusion and concern.

"What did he say?"

"That he couldn't talk and he'd see me later." She cocked her head at him. "It sounded to me like something was going on."

"Sounds to me like his court case isn't going well," Murphy said. "When things go bad in court, Dad gets real distracted. He's completely focused on the case and can't think about anything else." Thinking about how he was the night before, a slight grin came to his lips. "It runs in the family." He gave her a quick hug. "Don't worry about it, Cameron. You did talk to him this morning. That's means he's alive and well. He just needs to concentrate on this case. He'll call and tell you all about it after it goes to the jury."

Cameron felt both reassured and foolish. Yes, she had heard from Joshua, which meant he was okay. The resurrection of Nick's murder was bringing back all the old insecurities that had driven her to the bottle years before. She thought she had gotten rid of all that baggage when she made it through her recovery.

It's true. You never completely recover from something like this.

"You're right," she said. "I'm sure he'll call when he's through with this case he's working on."

"You have nothing to worry about." After kissing her on the cheek, Murphy took her into another warm hug. "You're the best thing that's happened to him since Mom, Cameron."

"Does he know that?" she joked into Murphy's chest.

Pulling away, Murphy flashed his wide grin, complete with dimples in both cheeks. "We Thornton men know a good thing when we see her." Placing his hat on his head, he trotted down the stairs.

Kicking herself for worrying about Joshua, Cameron went back into the bedroom to find that Spencer had taken her place in the bed. With Izzy sleeping in the middle, and Irving on the other side, the bed was too full for her.

Guess it's time for me to go to work.

Sometimes, Murphy felt guilty about enjoying a cup of green tea, organic unsweetened orange juice, fruit, and a bowl of steel cut oatmeal at the Ritz-Carlton while catching up on the news on his computer tablet. He was well aware that most of his peers and colleagues were still navigating the morning commute while downing a greasy egg sandwich from a fast food drive-through.

Not only did the Ritz provide a delicious oatmeal and the freshest of fruit, but it also provided Murphy with an active environment to hone his observation skills. He prided himself on being able to figure out each dining patron's story by the time he finished his breakfast. Taking a seat in the corner of the lounge, out of the way, he watched people without being noticed. Over the months, he had come to spot the Ritz's regular breakfast customers. Many were movers and shakers on the political scene. Often, the regular patrons would be holding breakfast meetings with other big fishes in the Washington, D.C., pond.

Often, Murphy would spot one or more members of the Joint Chiefs. Even though each one knew he was one of their hand-picked, elite Phantoms, Murphy would never dare to approach them. To do so would risk blowing his public image of being simply one of thousands upon thousands of the military officers who worked under them.

Rarely, Murphy would notice couples eating together after an illicit rendezvous. Usually, they would breakfast in their rooms and then leave separately. But, occasionally, he would spot a couple who would dine out in the open after pretending to bump into each other.

It was something that took a trained eye to spot. Luckily, Murphy's father had taught him what to look for. The body language was always the giveaway. The familiarity resulting from intimacy would make the couple more inclined to enter each other's space to sneak a touch. The furtive glances—even expressions of guilt for those who had a stronger conscience.

Such couples were always entertaining to watch.

With a flirtatious smile, the server delivered Murphy's oatmeal and another pitcher of hot water for a second green tea when his phone chimed to indicate that a text came in. Half-expecting a romantic greeting from Jessica, he brushed his finger across the screen to see that it was from Cameron.

DNA is a match. Jane Doe is Cecelia Crenshaw.

With a sigh of relief, Murphy brought the hot cup of tea to his lips while surveying the restaurant for any new faces.

There was something in the rhythm of her walk when she entered the lounge that told Murphy that she was not going to be having your average breakfast meeting. Under her blue suit with red silk blouse, the brunette had the figure of a *Sports Illustrated* swimsuit cover, complete with the cleavage. Falling to her mid-thigh, the pencil skirt hugged every curve of her sensuous body.

Carrying a women's briefcase, she followed the host to the table that was only two tables away from where Murphy was sitting. While the host pulled out her chair to seat her, she gave the smart looking navy lieutenant a quick once over before flashing him a grin of approval. While setting down her briefcase next to the table, she bent over to allow him a quick view down the deep neckline of her blouse to see the edges of her red lace bra.

Uncertain if the display was on purpose or not, Murphy offered her a polite smile before returning to his oatmeal. Checking the time on his phone, he saw that he had one full hour left before his meeting on the seventh floor of the Pentagon. Plenty of time to finish reading an article on his tablet about Jeff Bezos' latest endeavors in space travel.

"Dolly, I am so sorry I'm late."

Recognizing the voice, Murphy glanced up from the article with his hand on the hot tea cup to see the uniformed army general hurrying across the restaurant to where the server was delivering two cups of coffee to the brunette.

"No problem at all, General," she said in a business like tone. "I ordered our coffee."

"Thank you, Dolly." He slipped into the empty seat across from her.

Murphy instantly spotted the four stars on his shoulder straps. He didn't need to look for them. While they had never been formally introduced, Murphy had seen the commander of the army's Central Command Center on more than one occasion. He was a regular face around the Pentagon.

General Sebastian Graham was hard to forget. At four inches over six feet tall and with broad shoulders, combined with his military bearing, he was larger than life. With dark hair silvering at the temples, he was an attractive man who knew how to use his charisma to get anything he wanted from anyone.

"I've directed Sandra to reschedule your two o'clock today," Dolly said. "My sources on Capitol Hill think the Senate committee will be wanting to meet with you tomorrow morning and we should spend this afternoon going over what questions they are likely to ask and how best for you to answer them."

"Really, Dolly," General Graham said with a chuckle. "Everyone knows the Senate is simply going to rubber stamp my nomination to Chief of Staff for the army. My record has been and is as clean as a whistle. Far cry from when the FBI tried to reject my security clearance after I got back from the Gulf War—and that was after I saved my people from an ambush. Guess they learned their lesson. My record and career have been impeccable. We have nothing to worry about."

The server delivered a basket of breakfast breads. While the general was placing his order for a country breakfast, Dolly took a roll out of the basket, broke it in half, and buttered both halves. She then placed one half on his plate while proceeding to eat hers.

Murphy's brow furrowed at the act of familiarity.

While taking up his half of the roll, General Graham reached across the table with his other hand to touch hers. "Thank you," he said in a low voice. With a cock of his head, he winked at her.

"No problem." She offered him a smile before withdrawing her hand. "About that problem that came up yesterday ..."

"What about it?"

"NCIS backed down on requesting Tommy's DNA." She took a second roll from the basket and tore it in half before buttering both halves.

Hearing the reference to NCIS, Murphy's ears perked up.

"That's good," Sebastian said. "Very good."

"My source tells me there was an altercation with a blogger at Seven Corner's last night," Dolly set the second half of the roll on his plate. "The blogger was killed."

"That's too bad."

"Not really," she said. "It could be enough of a catalyst for you to ask Johnston to have the case sent over to CID where you can control the investigation. The assassins wore military uniforms. This blogger was claiming to have information about a conspiracy within the—"

"Murphy! There you are."

It was only due to his quick reflexes that Murphy was able to catch the tea cup after knocking his hand into it to keep it from spilling all over the table. While mopping up the tea that did spill onto the white table cloth, Murphy saw a slightly built man in a white shirt with red suspenders and a red bow tie rushing toward him. On top of his head, he wore a brown tweed driving cap reminiscent of the ones worn about Europe during Victorian times.

"You must have gotten my text."

"Text?"

"You hung up last night without us setting a time for our meeting." While Dean pumped Murphy's hand, his handle-bar mustache curled upward to tickle the outer corners of his nostrils. "I took a stab at what time you reported for work and texted you to meet me here at eight o'clock. Sorry, I'm late. I'm not used to driving morning rush hour. How you do this every morning, I don't know." Forming an imaginary gun with his hand, he held his index finger to his temple and pulled the trigger.

"Sorry, Dean, but ... what meeting are you talking about?" Murphy asked while trying to keep an eye on General Graham and Dolly, who was now bent over across the table to wipe something off the edge of the general's mouth with her cloth napkin. He could see that she was giving the general quite a show down the front of her blouse.

Dean gestured at the server. "Can you bring another place setting?" After dropping his hat down in the middle of Murphy's table, he pulled out the chair across from him. "I've got so many questions for you."

"What kind of questions?" Murphy shifted his seat to the side to keep the general and Dolly in his line of vision. With Dean droning on about the plotline of his book, Murphy could forget about hearing what they knew about the shooting the night before and why they wanted to control the investigation.

"—then my protagonist, a SEAL, breaks into the terrorists' warehouse and single-handedly takes out seven terrorists before setting up the bomb on the crate filled with explosives—which he sees by the packing slip had been sent from an American company—and escaping right before the whole place is blown sky-high."

Waiting for his reaction, Dean stared at Murphy, who was noticing that Dolly had slipped her foot out of one of her pumps to brush up the general's pant leg.

What ever happened to being discreet?

"What do you think?" Dean snapped his fingers to snatch his attention from the cheating couple. "Do you like it?"

"Too unbelievable," Murphy muttered while trying to keep some focus on the other table.

When the server arrived with his coffee, Dean placed his order for breakfast. Before she could leave, Dean stopped her. "Hey, Murphy, let me pay for your breakfast. Amy got me a brand new American Express card. You have to help me break it in." When Murphy tried to object, he held up his hand. "I insist."

"Thank you, Dean, you're so generous," Murphy said while checking the time on his tablet. "Damn it! Look at the time." He scrambled out of his seat. "I've got a meeting to go to." Anxious to get away from Dean, he practically broke into a run out into the mall and down to the metro.

Once he was certain he was sure he had made his escape, he dialed Boris' phone number.

"Murphy, where are you?"

"I'm on my way to the Pentagon's seventh floor for a meeting," Murphy explained.

"Well, not to ruin a potentially already bad day," Boris said in a low voice, "but Perry Latimore is in Koch's office giving her a full briefing about last night and our status on the case. I'm anticipating being called in as soon as he leaves and her ordering the case go to CID or the FBI."

Murphy grit his teeth to keep from expressing his full thoughts on the matter. "Hey, Boris, what is the name of Colonel Lincoln Clark's son?"

"Tommy? Why?"

"Can you do me a favor?" Murphy asked.

"Sure, Murphy, what do you need?"

"Ask Archer to make some phone calls to Maureen Clark's friends and or relatives to check on how happy she really was being married to the colonel."

"Do you see him as a suspect?" Boris asked.

"I'm bothered by him not wanting us to take his son's DNA," Murphy said. "It makes me want to take a closer look at it. I feel like I did when Dad told me not to smoke his pipe. Then I was more determined than anything to smoke it. I got sick and threw up all over his recliner, but hey, live and learn."

"Are you saying we should or should not press harder to get Tommy Clark's DNA?"

"There's only one way to find out if Colonel Clark is hiding information important to this case," Murphy said.

"I have a contact at Walter Reed," Boris said. "We might be able to get a look at Tommy Clark's hospital records."

"Thanks, Boris."

"Even as you are about to go down in flames, you're still working this case," Boris laughed.

"They'll have to pry this case out of my cold, dead hands."

CHAPTER EIGHTEEN

Murphy was twenty minutes early for his nine o'clock appointment. Per protocol, he was ordered to sit on a wooden bench in the corridor outside the Joint Chiefs of Staff meeting chambers until they were ready to see him.

Murphy felt the beating of his heart quicken with every minute that ticked by. Mentally, he went over every detail of the case from the moment he stepped into Francine Baxter's home. He even replayed how he ended up there in the first place.

Staff Chief Hillary Koch had sent him.

CO is right. Crotch is a moron. I'm the staff military liaison. I wasn't supposed to be there. I should have refused to go and went to the Four Seasons to have lunch with Jessica. Why didn't I? With a groan, Murphy shifted in his seat on the hard bench. *Because I wanted to go, that's why. I wanted to be out in the field instead of behind that desk. Now another woman is dead and the military will be blamed for it.*

His thoughts turned to Jessica and how she was trembling in his arms when he carried her out of the coffee shop. *She never should have been there. Neither should have Cameron.*

How could I have been so stupid allowing civilians in on my investigation?

He checked the time on his cell phone. It was ten minutes to nine. His father was most likely on his way to court. He was probably in his office across from the court house. Usually court did not start until ten o'clock.

With a brush of his thumb across the screen, he brought up the speed dial number that was ID'd "Dad." Another touch on the screen sent the call through. Murphy listened to the call go straight to voice mail. When the beep indicated that he could leave a message, Murphy silently held the phone to his ear while trying to think of what to say. *I screwed up, Dad. I know your worst nightmare was that you'd raise a loser. Never in my wildest dreams did I think it would be me.*

The clatter of dress shoes on the hardwood floor in the corridor warned Murphy of the approach of a group of six officers in the United States Marines. Brushing his thumb across the "end" button, he hung up without leaving a message.

Once again, he shifted his position on the wooden bench and wished they were cushioned. He surmised they were uncomfortable on purpose. It was the military version of the hot seat. Directly outside the Joint Chiefs' chambers, it was a given that anyone sitting on the bench was waiting to be called to the carpet by the highest ranking officials of the United States military.

Talking among themselves, the marines filed into the offices down from the formal chamber. Their quick glances in his direction reminded him of how school children would behave upon spotting a classmate sitting outside the principal's office.

Curiosity. Amusement. Pity. They may have been grown up and working in the distinguished halls of the Pentagon, but the attitudes remained the same.

The more things change, the more they remain the same. Naval Academy graduate. Officer. Phantom. And I'm still getting time outs.

Alone, Murphy made one last check of his uniform to make sure everything was in order. No wrinkles. The crease in his pants was straight. No dog hair on his legs or sleeves. His white shoes were shiny. No scuff marks.

The elevator doors at the end of the hall opened again. Admiral Clarence Patterson and the Chief of Naval Operations stepped off. Jumping up off the bench, Murphy stood at attention and raised his right hand in a salute.

Without slowing down, the same admiral who had only two days before pinned the Bronze Star to Murphy's chest and called Jessica charming, barely slowed down to return Murphy's salute, as did the admiral who served as Chief of Naval Operations.

"Good morning, sirs," Murphy said after bringing his right arm back down to his side.

They did not even offer a polite nod to acknowledge Murphy's presence before going into the chamber.

With a quick glance at the time on his cell phone, Murphy noted that it was seven minutes before nine o'clock.

I'm so screwed. Time to say good-bye to the Phantoms.

The Phantoms were hand-picked. It was not a position on a team that anyone knew about—therefore it was not something that a military cadet could strive for like the SEALS.

Comprised of the best of the best from every branch of the military, defense, and law enforcement agency in the government, the Phantoms worked with the top equipment and received the best training. Their sole mission was to protect the United States and its citizens without the influence and intimidation of politicians and deal makers with their own personal and political agendas.

Being the best physically and intellectually was a given to be a candidate for the Phantom team—but that was second to integrity and character. Each chief of staff in the military had seen too many lives lost due to appointed or elected leaders in the government whose lack of character and integrity directly resulted in their making poor decisions for the sole purpose of covering up their own moral flaws.

The Phantoms worked completely off the grid. They only knew and met each other during operations or training. The unit was so covert that he had a special untraceable phone that he received and made calls on which went directly to his commanding officer, whose name he did not know.

When circumstances required her to provide a name as Murphy or another Phantom's commanding officer, she would introduce herself as "Captain Diana King." It was an official covert alias, complete with a fictionalized background.

Murphy simply referred to her as "CO." Because she hid her hair under hats or scarves and her eyes behind sun glasses, he was uncertain what she looked like. All he ever saw of her was her fabulous legs. Her sultry voice was unmistakable.

Being personally recruited by Admiral Clarence Patterson to become a Phantom was a huge honor. It was also a risk. Murphy understood going in that if he was ever caught overseas or domestically while working under the radar for the Joint Chiefs of Staff, it would compromise the whole unit. The Joint Chiefs would deny any connection to him. Most likely, he would end up being arrested ... or executed.

But it was a risk Murphy was willing to take to protect his country.

Now, not only was his position of Phantom at stake, but so was his whole military career.

The edge of the wooden bench was digging across the back of his thighs. Shifting again, Murphy checked the time on his phone. It was eighteen minutes after nine o'clock.

"Lieutenant Thornton. They're ready to see you now."

Murphy jumped in his seat. He had not noticed the door to the chamber open. A female lieutenant in the dress white uniform was holding one of the double doors open for him. He stood up and made one last check of his uniform. His hat in his hand, he marched into the Joint Chiefs of Staff chamber. Once he was inside, the lieutenant closed the door, with herself out in the hallway.

The meeting chamber was dimly lit. The tall windows at one end of the room provided a view of the Washington Monument on the other side of the Potomac River. Murphy's footsteps clapped the hardwood floor when he made his way to a single straight-backed chair resting in the middle of the vacant floor—waiting for him.

The chair was facing the long curved table on a raised stage at the other side of the chamber where each chief of staff for every branch of the American military waited for him—all seven members. There were desk lamps in front of each of them.

A second row of tables with chairs at which the chiefs' assistants would sit, ready to look up information or run to and fro if needed, was empty. The assistants were excluded from this meeting because they would be discussing Phantom business. Even the Joint Chiefs' assistants had no knowledge about the covert unit.

Off to one side, Murphy's commanding officer sat next to a table, one long leg crossed over the other. Even still, she concealed her eyes behind dark sun glasses. Bernie stood against the wall directly behind her.

The only ones included in the meeting was the Joint Chiefs of Staff, the Phantoms' commanding officer, Bernie, and Murphy himself.

Stepping over to stand in front of the chair, Murphy stood at attention and raised his hand in a salute. "Lieutenant Murphy Thornton, United States Navy, reporting as ordered, sirs and ma'am."

Sitting near middle of the half-circle, Admiral Clarence Patterson returned the salute. "At ease, Lieutenant."

Murphy stood at parade rest with his hands folded behind his back. The only sound in the chamber was the rustle of papers and the murmur of low voices while the chiefs seemed to compare notes.

Staring straight ahead, he waited while each of the chiefs put on his or her reading glasses and referred to reports in front of them. Murphy assumed it was the statement that he had written up and emailed to his commanding officer in the middle of the night.

In her early sixties, the chair of the Joint Chiefs of Staff, General Maxine Raleigh, USAF, Max to her friends, had an attractive face and long white hair that she wore in a French twist. Murphy was aware of her peering at him with her eyes narrowed while Admiral Patterson whispered to her. He was unsure if she was squinting at him with disgust or because she could not see him clearly beyond the glare from the light of the desk lamps.

While the silence stretched on, Murphy was grateful for the years that he had been practicing yoga, which entailed him remaining in one position for long periods of time. While the seven chiefs were conferring, he was standing up straight with his feet at shoulder width with his hands clasped behind his back. Most men would have started to get leg cramps by the time the air force general cleared her throat and checked around the table. Wordlessly, she asked if they were ready to begin.

"Lieutenant Murphy Thornton, thank you for coming," she said.

"Pleasure to be here, ma'am," Murphy replied.

General Raleigh responded with silence. She put on her reading glasses and referred to the report before saying, "We have read the statement that you sent to your commanding officer last night about the incident at Starbucks, located at the Seven Corners Shopping Center in Falls Church, Virginia. Would you care to summarize what happened for us now in your own words, Lieutenant?"

"Yes, ma'am," Murphy replied. "During the course of a murder investigation that I was leading for the Naval Criminal Investigation Staff, we discovered a potential witness, Ms. Emily Dolan, who had entered and left the crime scene of the murders of five women in Reston, Virginia, shortly after the murders had occurred. Two members of my team were keeping Dolan under surveillance because we believed that she had information important to our investigation. We also feared that, if her identity was known to the perpetrator, her life could be in danger."

General Raleigh interrupted, "If you thought Dolan's life could be in danger, why did you not bring her in?"

"Because Dolan was a civilian, ma'am. As an investigator with the military, my authority is limited," Murphy said. "She wrote an anti-military and anti-law enforcement blog. It was clear that she had a lack of trust and heavy dislike for both the military and law enforcement. It was a calculated decision on my part to wait until we could get more evidence to use as leverage to get her to willingly cooperate with us. In the meantime, I assigned agents to keep her under protective surveillance. "

"Obviously you failed, Lieutenant," General Raleigh said in a blunt tone. "Ms. Dolan is dead. Care to explain to our staff how that happened if you were watching her?"

"Certainly, ma'am and sirs." Murphy swallowed. "During the course of our investigation it came to our attention that one of the victims in the Reston murders had a sister who had been killed on the Pennsylvania Turnpike several years ago."

Adjusting his reading glasses, Admiral Patterson referred to his copy of Murphy's statement. "That's not in your report."

"The identity of the sister was only confirmed this morning, sir," Murphy said. "Yesterday, we received an unofficial identification from the homicide detective investigating that case. This morning, the detective texted me that DNA comparison has identified the Jane Doe as Army Specialist Cecelia Crenshaw, sister to Petty Officer Crenshaw. Last evening, the detective requested my assistance in questioning Dolan to determine if the two murders could be connected. I agreed to go with her."

"Are these two cases connected, Lieutenant?" General Raleigh asked.

"I am sorry to say we can't be sure of that at this time," Murphy replied. "A hit squad entered the establishment and killed Dolan before the homicide detective had a chance to question her."

General Raleigh put on her reading glasses and referred to her report. "Where were you when the hit squad entered Starbucks, Lieutenant?"

"I was in the parking lot, ma'am," Murphy answered. "It had come to my attention that Ms. Dolan had been tailing me during her hours off work. Therefore, she knew me. So, I stayed out of sight in the parking lot while monitoring the situation via audio communications. When I saw the hit squad approaching, I called the two NCIS team members stationed inside to warn them and ordered that they protect Dolan and the civilians on the scene."

"You order them to protect Dolan, who hates the military?" General Raleigh replied with doubt.

"Her feelings toward the military were irrelevant to me, ma'am," Murphy said. "She was an American citizen and I took an oath to protect my country and her citizens. Nowhere in that oath does it make reference to protecting only those citizens with my same worldview."

"But she is now dead," General Raleigh said.

"Yes, ma'am."

"If it is your job to protect our country and its citizens, Lieutenant," General Raleigh's voice rose, "how it is that Dolan, the only lead you had in this murder case, ended up dead? You said you were in the parking lot. Where were you while this hit squad was gunning down your only witness?"

"I came in directly behind the hit squad, ma'am."

"But you failed to save Dolan and two members of that hit squad escaped."

"That is correct, ma'am," Murphy said. "Two members of the hit squad escaped and I failed to save Emily Dolan."

General Raleigh smirked at the other members of the Joint Chiefs of Staff. They each looked at each other. The Joint Chief of Staff's chair shook her head. "And you call yourself a Phantom, Lieutenant."

"We did—"

"You are a disgrace to the Phantoms, Lieutenant," General Raleigh said in a loud voice.

"I'm sorry, ma'am."

"Not only are you a disgrace to the Phantoms, Lieutenant," the chair roared, "but you are a disgrace to that uniform, the United States Navy, and the United States military and the United States of America. You knew that an American citizen was in danger, but you didn't warn her."

"She—"

The chair waved her reading glasses in Murphy's direction. "And you know why you didn't warn her?"

"Be-because—" Murphy found that he was stuttering.

"Because that woman—that woman who hated the military and the police—scared you!"

"No," Murphy objected in a quiet voice.

"You are a coward, Lieutenant! This garbage about you not having the authority to question her and to bring her in is nothing but a bunch of crap. You are a Phantom! You were selected to be a Phantom because you're supposed to be smart enough and cunning enough and have the integrity and courage to go up against anyone, no matter what their beliefs or agendas to get what needs to be done done—and yet, the first time you run up against a girl who doesn't like you—you run and hide even though you know that she is in danger of being killed. Well, guess what, Lieutenant— your fear of this little girl—this American citizen—got her assassinated!"

Rising out of her seat, General Raleigh pointed her finger directly at Murphy. "You, Lieutenant Murphy Thornton, are a coward! Because of your cowardice, Ms. Dolan, an America citizen you swore to protect is now dead! You are a disgrace to the Phantoms, your uniform, and your country!"

Adverting his eyes from the raging general, Murphy swallowed. Bile from his breakfast was threatening to come up. During the tirade, his commanding officer was checking what appeared to be a chipped fingernail. He sucked in a deep breath and swallowed again.

"The Joint Chiefs of Staff will go over your statement and the evidence that you have collected on this case," General Raleigh said. "But we can tell you right now that you are not worthy of being a Phantom. After our review of this case, we will determine if you are even worthy of being an officer in the United States Navy. In the meantime, I want you out of my sight! You are dismissed, Lieutenant Thornton."

Dropping back into her seat, General Raleigh tossed her reading glasses down onto the table and glowered at Murphy.

Silence dropped over the chamber. All eyes were on Murphy, waiting for the young lieutenant to slink out of the chamber with his tail between his legs.

Dropping his hands to his side, Murphy turned toward the door. Then, standing up straight, he turned back to the row of distinguished officers lined up before him. *What have I got to lose? Nothing more, really.* "Permission to speak, ma'am, sirs?"

"Do you have something to say, Lieutenant?" Admiral Patterson asked.

"Yes, sirs, ma'am."

"Then say it."

"With all due respect, ma'am, I disagree with your assessment, Madam Chair," Murphy said.

A gasp went throughout the room. General Raleigh sat up straight in her seat. "Really, Lieutenant Thornton?"

"Really, ma'am," Murphy replied. "Yes, things did go badly last night. A hit squad came in. I saw them coming. Out of everyone else that was there, including my two team members inside, I was the only one who spotted them for what they were. I had only seconds to warn my team and to get inside that coffee shop to help save everyone that we could and we did it. Things would have gone much worse— most of those civilians and possibly my own team would have perished if I had not acted with what little time I had to do so. Yes, one civilian, our witness did die, but every-one else—witnesses that the hit squad clearly intended to eliminate—survived. Plus, we took out two presumably professional assassins and an accomplice attempting to steal possible evidence that Dolan possessed. Through those three men, we hope to be able to find out who had hired them and who is behind these murders. Saving the lives of innocent bystanders and taking out three assailants sounds like a win to me and if you disagree with that assessment, then I suggest you talk to those civilians we did save last night and their families."

Stunned, the Joint Chiefs turned to the chair, who asked in a tone devoid of emotion. "Do you have anything else to say, Lieutenant?"

"Yes, I've made mistakes," Murphy said. "Everyone makes mistakes. But when I make a mistake, I'm man enough to step up to the plate and take responsibility for it. Maybe I should have brought in that witness sooner. But it wasn't cowardice that kept me from doing it. It was a calculated risk based on her attitude toward the military—the type of decisions that officers have to make every day. I'm a good navy officer. As a matter of fact, I'm an exceptional naval officer. All the way through my career as a cadet and active member of the military, I have made the best decisions that I know how to make and if that isn't good enough for you or the Phantoms, then so be it.

"But I will tell you this," Murphy said, "I was chosen to be a Phantom because of my character and my integrity. You told me when you recruited me that it was a quality that you were looking for in the Phantoms. Kick me out of the Phantoms and you will find those assets to be a curse as well, because I can tell you right now that there is nothing you can do in heaven and earth that will get me off of this case. I made a promise to a young girl to find out who killed her mother, and I intend to keep that promise either as a navy officer or a Phantom or just as an American citizen whose character won't let him walk away from finding out what's going on in our United States Army that brought about the deaths of seven women and one police officer."

"Seven?" the marine commandant asked.

Murphy counted off. "The five women in Reston, Emily Dolan in Starbucks, and Army Specialist Cecelia Crenshaw in Pennsylvania thirteen years ago, plus Pennsylvania State Trooper Nicholas Gates."

"Is that all you have to say, Lieutenant?" Admiral Patterson asked.

Murphy swallowed. "Yes, sirs and ma'am. That is all." Assuming an at ease position, he waited to be shot—even if only verbally.

A silence fell over the chamber once again.

The six men and one woman looked around the table at each other.

Finally, General Maxine Raleigh cleared her throat again. "You are quite impressive, Lieutenant Thornton. You are an eloquent speaker, too. You have passion."

"Thank you, ma'am."

"While I expected you to defend yourself, I must admit I underestimated you. I didn't expect you to stand up for yourself the way you did. Usually, in a setting like this, the vast majority of young officers would have slinked out of here with their tails between their legs. You didn't."

Murphy detected a slight curl to the corner of the chair's lips. "Congratulations, Lieutenant. You passed."

A collective sigh of relief filled the chamber.

Looking across the line of the distinguished officers sitting at the table, Murphy saw that each of the chiefs was grinning. He didn't know whether to be relieved or angry. "This was a test?"

"Smile, Lieutenant," Admiral Patterson uttered a hearty laugh. "You just made me six hundred dollars."

With effort, Murphy forced a good natured grin onto his face.

The chair turned serious. "I apologize for being so harsh, Lieutenant, but we needed to make sure you were immune to intimidation no matter what its source. From what we've seen, there's no telling where this case is going to lead you."

Murphy asked, "I'm still on this case?"

"Of course," General Raleigh said. "You are an excellent investigator and an exceptional officer. You do the military ... and the Phantoms ... proud."

Murphy fought the grin working its way to his lips.

"Unfortunately, we feel that the scope of this investigation is beyond your rank," Admiral Patterson said. "While you have the guts to pursue the case wherever the evidence may take you, we feel that the team leading it needs someone with the authority and experience to carry it to completion." He nodded his head in Bernie's direction.

Standing up from where he was leaning against the wall, Bernie crossed the chamber, going behind Murphy, and across the room to the double doors through which Murphy had entered earlier.

The queasiness in Murphy's stomach that had disappeared moments before returned. Until this time, he had basically been a lone wolf. As a Phantom, he had worked virtually every operation alone. While working as the liaison for NCIS, he worked freely without direct supervision, though he had to keep Hillary Koch happy.

He liked it that way. He liked either depending completely on himself or leading the team. Now, he was going to be working directly under someone new.

The clap of the footsteps on the hardwood floor approaching him from behind made the hair on the back of Murphy's neck stand on end.

Suck it up, Murphy. Dad always accused you of not playing well with others.

The footsteps stopped when the navy officer halted to stand shoulder to shoulder with Murphy. Out of the corner of his eye, Murphy saw the flash of captain's stripes on his shoulder board when his new leader raised his arm up to salute the Joint Chiefs.

"Captain Joshua Thornton, United States Navy, reporting for duty, ma'am and sirs."

CHAPTER NINETEEN

It took all of Murphy's restraint to keep from turning to look directly at his father. He thought he was over five hours away in West Virginia prosecuting a major murder case. Instead, he was standing next to him on the seventh floor of the Pentagon before the Joint Chiefs of Staff.

"Lieutenant Thornton," Admiral Patterson said, "I believe you are familiar with Captain Thornton."

"Very much, sir," Murphy replied.

"Captain Thornton," Admiral Patterson said, "the Joint Chiefs appreciate you coming here on such short notice."

"I was told that it was imperative that I make myself available for this assignment, sir."

"We have come to believe that it is," the admiral said.

The men on the panel turned their attention to the chair, who regarded the two navy officers standing before them.

Once again, there was a long silence before the general uttered a deep sigh. "Lieutenant Thornton, yesterday, you requested a copy of the case file pertaining to the death of Lieutenant General George Davis."

Murphy felt his father's eyes flick, only for an instant, in his direction before he returned to staring straight ahead.

"Please explain to the staff and the captain here why you made that request," the general ordered.

"Because," Murphy began slowly, trying to recall the details of his own reasoning for requesting the case file. "Because his daughter, Colleen Davis, was one of the women poisoned at the Baxter home in Reston. You see, in this case, according to friends and relatives, none of these women knew each other before that evening. There was no reason for them to be socializing with each other. But they had to have one thing in common to bring them all together. All that we could find was either a direct or indirect connection to the army. In Colleen Davis' case, that connection was her father, who was killed in a helicopter crash. I can't say for certain that it was what brought her to the Baxter home, because I have not seen the file."

"Lieutenant General George Davis was a personal friend of mine, Lieutenant," General Johnston, Chief of Staff of the United States Army said.

"I'm sorry, sir," Murphy said in a soft voice.

"I have seen that file, Lieutenant." General Johnston's expression was stern. "The helicopter crash that killed him and five other good men was no accident. There was a bomb on board the chopper. The Department of Defense kept that information from the media because they were concerned that the public would panic if they knew terrorists were striking military targets here on our soil."

"Permission to speak, sir?" Joshua spoke up.

"Yes, Captain."

Joshua cleared his throat. "Do you believe these murders and the attack at the coffee shop last night were terrorist attacks?"

"No," the army's chief of staff said, "but we do believe it is a conspiracy of some sort. Witnesses of the helicopter crash swore that it exploded in the air. CID uncovered evidence of the bomb. Their best agent was assigned to the case. He found something—something so important that he called me at home. By then, I had been appointed to chief of staff of the army. The agent made an appointment to speak to me about what he had uncovered the next morning. That night, his home burnt down with him, his wife, and two children inside."

Murphy could feel his father's body stiffen where he stood next to him.

"If I may ask, ma'am and sirs," Joshua replied after a long silence, "why us? I would recommend that this case be sent to the FBI."

"Because we don't know who is behind it," General Raleigh said. "Whoever it is has deep pockets and resources."

"Lieutenant Thornton just informed us that whoever is behind this also had a Pennsylvania state trooper killed," Admiral Patterson said.

Joshua turned his head to look directly at Murphy's profile. "Nick?" he whispered.

Noticing that Joshua had shaved his beard and cut his long hair, Murphy paused. After recovering from the shock, he offered a slight nod of his head.

"This conspiracy is running deep and wide and apparently stretches back many years," General Raleigh said. "There's no telling what level of authority the perpetrator may have reached. But we can almost be certain that he or she is connected to the army."

"But doesn't appear to be connected to the navy," Admiral Patterson said. "Granted, Lieutenant Thornton, you seem to have caught this case completely by accident. We are going to keep this investigation in house here in the military—under the Phantoms. Captain Thornton will lead the investigation with Lieutenant Thornton taking second in command."

"You are right, Captain," General Raleigh said. "The FBI does need to be involved in this. However, we want this investigation to stay with the Phantoms until we can get a handle on who is behind it. Luckily, we have a Phantom within the FBI. She will be contacting you, Captain. The rest of your team, we are free to hand pick."

"Thank you, ma'am, sirs," Joshua said. "May I ask where this investigation is going to be taking place?"

Admiral Patterson chuckled. "Well, since NCIS Chief Hillary Koch got Lieutenant Thornton into this mess ..."

It was all Murphy could do to keep from hugging his father after the Joint Chiefs had dismissed them and they left the chambers on the seventh floor. They may not have been in front of the chiefs, but they were still in the Pentagon with uniformed colleagues all about. Such public displays were not encouraged.

However, Murphy did allow himself to reach out his hand to squeeze his father's shoulder while admiring his captain stripes. "Captain? When did that happen?"

"Middle of the night. Early this morning." Joshua reached out to press the elevator call button to take them down to the fifth floor where the Pentagon's NCIS offices were located. "CO called me after reading your report. I reminded her that I was retired and I'm in the middle of a court case." He glanced over at Murphy. "She said nothing about your case being connected to Nick's murder. Then, Admiral Patterson called a half hour later and asked what it would take to get me to drop everything and come out to Washington. Just off the top of my head I said a promotion to captain. Five minutes later, he called back and said I got it. They had a private military transport waiting for me at Pittsburgh airport at six o'clock this morning."

The elevator doors opened. Before Murphy could reach out to hold the doors open for his father, General Sebastian Graham and the woman Murphy had seen him having breakfast with stepped out. General Graham's and Joshua's eyes met.

"Thornton?" The general extended his hand out to Joshua. "Get out of here. It really *is* you. I heard you retired." He looked from one shoulder pad to the other.

"I was reactivated." Joshua gestured to Murphy who was waiting behind the general. "This is my son, Lieutenant Murphy Thornton."

"A chip off the old block, huh?" Startling Murphy, General Graham stuck out his hand to break a stare down that Murphy was having with Dolly, whose expression revealed that she recognized him as the same young lieutenant sitting nearby at the Ritz-Carlton. "Nice to meet you, Lieutenant. Where are you assigned?"

Aware of the general and his companion's earlier conversation, Murphy replied, "A special naval task force. The subject is classified."

"Aren't they all?" the general said with a chuckle before gesturing at the brunette. "I'd like you to meet Dolly Scanlon, my personal assistant." His expression was not unlike that of an adolescent boy proud of having the hottest date for the prom.

"Nice to meet you, Ms. Scanlon," Joshua said while shaking her hand. "I take it you're not in the military."

While she shook her head, General Graham explained, "She's my personal assistant. I'm afraid they have me so busy nowadays, plus my personal endeavors, that I had no choice but to hire my own assistant." He puffed up with pride. "I'm sure you heard about my nomination to the Joint Chiefs— army's chief of staff."

"Yes, I did," Joshua said. "Congratulations. You've earned it."

When the elevator doors opened again, Murphy reached out his hand to hold them open. "Sir, we need to go now."

Seeing that Murphy was in a rush, Joshua stepped onto the car. "What was that about?" he asked once the doors were closed while admiring the Bronze Star on Murphy's chest. A proud grin crossed his face.

"General Graham is having an affair with that woman," Murphy said. "I saw them at the Ritz-Carlton this morning."

"I have no doubt about that," Joshua said with a laugh. "I've known Sebastian Graham for over twenty years. He would not hire a woman who wouldn't sleep with him."

"There's more. I believe he had an affair with one of our murder victims." The elevator doors opened and Murphy stepped forward. He held the door open for Joshua to step off.

Joshua turned serious. "Are you sure about that?"

"I heard him and his assistant during breakfast," Murphy said. "They had no idea who I was. The husband of one of our victims, Colonel Lincoln Clark, refused to allow us to take his son's DNA for exclusionary purposes. Graham and Dolly were talking about how fortunate it was that we backed off. Then, they were talking about using last night to put pressure on the Joint Chiefs to order this investigation sent to CID so that Graham could control the outcome of the investigation."

"Sounds like you overheard quite a bit," Joshua said. "Why does Graham want to control the outcome of the investigation?"

"Either to cover up that he fathered Colonel Clark's son, or worse, that he was behind the murders," Murphy said with a sigh. "I got interrupted and didn't hear the rest of the conversation."

"But you heard enough." Joshua patted him on the shoulder. "Go get the conference room ready for the case files. I'm going to go to security to make arrangements for a temporary clearance for Cameron."

"Sure, Dad."

Murphy turned on his heel only to have Joshua grip his arm and spin him back to face him.

"Don't call me that." The stern look in Joshua's blue eyes struck the same fear that it did when he was a child.

"What?" Murphy breathed.

"Dad," Joshua said. "When we're in uniform and we pass that security gate, I'm Captain Thornton and you're Lieutenant Thornton. We're in a very unique situation, son. Everyone on our team is going to be aware that we are father and son. If I cut you any breaks, show you any leniency, then any career benefits you get from this case will be viewed as the result of nepotism. Do you understand?"

"Yes."

Joshua narrowed his eyes at him.

Murphy stood up straighter. "Sir, yes, sir."

"I have two goals, Lieutenant." Joshua held up two fingers. "One is to make you hate me by the time we catch this killer. Two is to solve this case so that Cameron can have peace of mind and closure over Nick's murder, and to get back to Chester in time to walk Tracy down the aisle."

"That's three," Murphy said.

"Are you correcting me, Lieutenant?" Joshua replied in a firm voice that made Murphy start.

"Sir, no, sir."

Joshua stepped up to glare into Murphy's eyes. "How many goals do I have, Lieutenant?"

"Two, sir. One is to make me hate you, sir. Two is to solve this case to get closure for Cameron and to get back home in time to walk Tracy down the aisle. That's two goals, sir."

"Very good, Lieutenant." Joshua stepped back. "Now go prepare the conference room and brew a pot of coffee. I need it. I was up all night. The judge declared a mistrial on my case and I had to cut my hair and shave my beard. In other words, I'm in a very foul mood."

"You're covering it up very well, sir," Murphy said. "On the up side, sir, you did get a promotion to captain."

"If I had known I was in a bargaining position, I would have insisted they let me keep my beard."

"What do I say to Staff Chief Hillary Crotch—I mean Koch, sir. Her name is *Koch*. Hillary Koch."

To Murphy's surprise, Joshua chuckled. "Crotch? I like that."

"What do I say to her, sir?" Murphy couldn't wait to ruin Hillary Koch's day. He could sense her waiting to pounce on him when he came through the door, especially after being called on the carpet on the seventh floor.

A wicked grin came to Joshua's lips. "Say nothing. Leave Crotch to me."

"Well, I see they didn't have security escort you out." Boris Hamilton leaned back against the empty desk next to the coffeemaker while Murphy prepared the pot for brewing.

"No, they didn't," Murphy said.

"What happened?"

Hearing Murphy's voice, Special Agent Susan Archer came rushing out of her office. "Are we still on the case?"

Over his shoulder Murphy saw that Wendy and Perry, who was hanging out at the administrative assistant's desk, were listening in. "Yes."

"Since when do you drink coffee?" Wendy called over to ask.

"I don't," Murphy replied.

"Thornton!" Hillary Koch had stepped into the doorway of her office. "I want a word with you."

"I'm sure you do, Koch." Murphy hit the switch to turn on the coffeemaker.

When he turned around to go to her office, he found that she had sauntered across the office to stand before him with her hands on her hips. A smug grin filled her face. "I understand you got a witness killed last night."

Murphy shot a glance beyond Hillary to where Perry avoided looking at him. In avoiding Murphy, Perry's eyes met Susan's glare. In an attempt to evade her, he turned in the other direction to meet Boris's penetrating gaze.

"No," Murphy said. "I did not get a witness killed. Yes, a witness was killed. Since I was the leader of the team who had her under surveillance, then I will take responsibility for failing to keep her alive. But, if you expect me to take responsibility for her murder—no I won't take that, because I didn't pull the trigger. The person behind that hit squad is responsible for her death and we intend to find whoever that is and make them pay for it."

Hands on her hips, Hillary wagged her head. "*We*. Is this the royal we?"

"No, my team and I," Murphy said. "Don't worry. That won't include you ... or Latimore."

"Nor anyone else on *my* staff."

Behind her, Joshua Thornton came through the door. Spotting Murphy and the coffeemaker, he made his way toward him while Hillary shook her finger in Murphy's face. "You have to be on drugs, Thornton. You had and have no authority to come into my office and hijack my staff to conduct your own crazy murder investigation, which you didn't even have the authority to take the lead on in the first place!"

With a crooked grin, Murphy shook his head. "With all due respect, I disagree. You sent me there—"

"To get into a phony pissing contest that you were ordered to lose! The last thing this office needs is a multiple homicide case."

"Oh, I'm sorry," Murphy said, "I thought the name of this office was Naval *Criminal* Investigative Service. I thought its purpose was to conduct *criminal investigations* of crimes perpetrated against or by navy or marine personnel. A petty officer was murdered. She was targeted. That makes it our case—or rather yours but you didn't want it, so I took it because someone needs to investigate it."

"That someone isn't going to be you," Koch said. "I called your CO and she said you aren't leading this investigation. They're sending someone else to lead it." She sneered. "I guess they forgot to tell you that upstairs. If I were you, I'd go clean out your office and move into the break room down the hall."

"Actually," Joshua said from behind her, "You can move into the break room, Koch, because I will be taking over *your* office while leading this team."

While Murphy watched the color drain from Hillary Koch's face, Joshua stepped around her to pour the freshly brewed coffee into a disposable cup.

"Doesn't sound to me like it should be much of a problem," Joshua leaned in to whisper to her, "since you don't bog yourself down by taking on any criminal investigations."

Casually, he strolled past her, across the reception area. At her office door, he stopped and turned around. "Lieutenant Thornton, while I'm reviewing the case file, prepare the conference room and brief our team. I want you in my office in twenty minutes for a total debriefing." Before Murphy had time to respond, he stepped into the office and closed the door.

Her mouth hanging open, Hillary Koch's face turned from a sickly white to a furious red. Her eyes bulged.

"Who's that?" Susan asked.

"Captain Joshua Thornton," Murphy said. "Our new team leader."

"Thornton?" Boris asked. "Is he the one Dr. Reed called 'brilliant?'"

"Yep, that's my dad."

CHAPTER TWENTY

"I learned something about myself last night," Jessica told Cameron. "I don't like getting shot at."

"Who would?" Izzy said from the back seat of Cameron's SUV.

Since Jessica was taking responsibility for Izzy that day, they had to take Cameron's Pennsylvania police cruiser, which had a back seat. While Jessica's Ferrari was long on looks, it was rather short on passenger space.

They were following the GPS to the home of Maureen Clark, the army colonel's wife who had been poisoned in Francine Baxter's home two nights before. In her role as a military officer's wife, Jessica was dressed up in a demure black dress and was armed with a baked ham that they had purchased from a caterer to get in the door.

Ever since learning of Colonel Clark and General Graham's desire to keep Tommy's DNA away from NCIS, Murphy had been determined to get hold of it. It took only a couple of phone calls for Jessica to learn through the navy wives—many with siblings or family belonging to other branches of the military—that the Clark family was accepting visitors at their home the afternoon before the official wake at the funeral home.

They hoped to be able to slip into the Clark home under the guise of offering condolences to collect some of Tommy's DNA. Of course, unless the DNA was in the trash out on the curb, it would not be admissible in court, but possibly it would provide a necessary piece to the puzzle to lead them in the right direction.

"Good," Cameron said when they noticed that the driveway and street in front of the large French Country home were packed with cars. A steady flow of people entered and left the house. "This should be easy enough. We may be able to get in without anyone noticing that we've been there."

"We don't know what this kid looks like," Jessica said.

"He's a five year old boy," Cameron said. "They'll have family pictures inside. We take a look at the pictures and find our target among the crowd. Hopefully, he'll be eating or drinking something, we swipe it, and then we get out."

"What do you want me to do?" Izzy asked from where she was sitting in the back.

"You be the lookout," Cameron said.

"I can feel us getting into trouble," Izzy said.

The door was open for them to freely walk into the luxurious home filled with family and friends. In spite of the dozens of visitors, the house was quiet. Everyone spoke in low tones out of respect for the young army wife and mother.

Carrying the heavy platter of baked ham, Jessica was searching for which direction to go. As soon as she crossed the foyer a woman in a black dress hurried in from the rear of the house. "Oh, you didn't have to do that." She took a sniff. "Ham! We were just about to run out. You are a life saver! Do you know where the kitchen is?"

Jessica could only shake her head before the woman acting as host led the way across the living room and through the formal dining room into the country kitchen. Izzy and Cameron were already studying the faces in the family portraits that had been put out on display for the mourners.

The host chatted away. "We weren't expecting so many of Maureen's friends to come this afternoon. We thought they would go to the wake tonight. The coroner won't release the body until tomorrow. But Lincoln wanted to get it over with as soon as possible."

Upon entering the kitchen, Jessica saw two distinguished men part like fighting dogs shot with a water hose. Both were in full army dress uniforms. The older man was in the uniform of a colonel. The other's rank was captain. She recognized the colonel's face from the family picture.

The host's introductions confirmed Jessica's conclusion. "This is Lincoln, Maureen's husband," she rattled on while taking the cover off the ham. "And this is my husband, Duke. He's Maureen's brother." With a gasp, she realized she had not introduced herself. "I'm Denise, by the way."

Jessica was shaking both men's hands when the colonel said, "I didn't catch your name."

"Jessica," she replied. "I'm so sorry for your loss. I didn't know Maureen well—I knew her through the officers' wives, but what I did know, she was a wonderful, lovely person and a devoted wife and mother."

"Yes, she was," Denise said while Duke glared at Lincoln.

Saying that he needed air, Duke stomped his feet while crossing the kitchen and went out the back door.

"This has been very hard on all of us," Denise apologized. "It was so sudden."

"I understand." Excusing herself, Jessica went in search of the Clark's son, Tommy.

In the dining room, Jessica found Cameron watching the guests from one side of the alcove leading into the living room. From her focal point, she was able to see everyone. After ladling a drink for herself from the punch bowl, Jessica made her way through the guests to her. "Did you find him?"

With a nod of her head and a jerk of her chin, Cameron gestured to a corner on the far side of the living room where a group of children were huddled around a computer tablet. "Izzy brought her iPad and has some hot new game on it. Between that and being a teenager, she instantly became a star. You should have seen the total adoration on Tommy's face when she blew his nose for him. I think he's in love."

Comparing the little boy in the family picture to the faces of the half dozen small children gathered around her, Jessica found that Tommy was kneeling next to Izzy. He had his head pressed against her arm. With a sly grin in their direction, Izzy handed her iPad to the little boy while taking the paper cup that contained his drink from him. Then, excusing herself while the children continued playing, she rose from the group and made her way across the room.

"Time for the switch." Cameron rushed to the punch bowl to fill an identical paper cup.

"Jessica, I'm surprised to see you here."

Jessica felt her heart jump into her mouth. Forcing a smile on her face, she turned around to see that Paige Graham, General Sebastian Graham's wife, was standing before her.

"I didn't know you knew Maureen," Paige said in a voice that was a bit louder than necessary.

"Not personally, no. But I couldn't get the family out of my mind after hearing of the murders. It was so senseless and tragic," Jessica said. "As a new officer's wife, I felt it was proper for me to offer my condolences."

Behind Paige, Jessica watched Cameron pour what was left in Tommy's paper cup into a new one while turning her back to the guests to slip the cup into her oversized handbag. Izzy rushed back to the children to rejoin them.

"Is something wrong, Paige?" Lincoln Clark demanded to know.

"Maybe," Paige said. "This is Lieutenant Murphy Thornton's wife. The same navy lieutenant investigating Maureen's murder."

"Don't you people have any respect?" Lincoln asked loudly.

Jessica felt her cheeks turn red with embarrassment as every mourner in the house turned around to look directly at her.

"First, your husband accuses me of killing not only my wife, but these total strangers who I had no reason to harm, and now he has the gall to send his wife here to invade our privacy," the colonel raged.

"First," Jessica shot back, "asking questions is not an invasion of privacy. The only way to get to the bottom of things is to ask questions and when it comes to murder, sometimes those questions are damn personal because diving into the nitty gritty stuff is the only way to uncover the truth. Second, your wife was *murdered*. My husband did not do that. Someone else did. But for some bizarre reason, you're making him out to be the bad guy, which in and of itself looks extremely suspicious to me. My dad was and is a homicide detective and you know what he says? 'When someone starts putting up roadblocks in a murder investigation, then you *know* you're doing something right.' So, we can do this the easy way. You cooperate and we find out who murdered your wife. Or we can do it the hard way, by opening up all of the closets in your life and shaking out the skeletons until *they* tell us who killed your wife. It's your choice."

Stepping up to the colonel, she said in a low voice, "Lastly, my husband did not send me here. I volunteered because in spite of your lack of desire to find out who killed the wife you claim to be mourning, I care about finding out who killed your son's mother."

"I think you should leave," Paige said, "and take your friends with you."

Jessica took one last glance around the home. She saw Denise scurry back into the kitchen. Squaring her shoulders, she made her way through the guests regarding her and Cameron with disdain to the front door. Izzy grabbed up her iPad and gave Tommy a hug and kiss on top of his head before trotting over to join them.

"Wait a minute!" Colonel Clark called out before they were able to make their exit. "I want that cup that your friend put in her purse."

Slumping her shoulders, Cameron took the cup out of her hand bag and handed it to the colonel who made a show of balling it up and tossing it to the floor. "Tell your husband that I'll be reporting this to General Graham, who will be having a word with his CO."

Without another word, Jessica, Izzy, and Cameron walked out the door. In silence, they climbed into the cruiser. After a collective sigh, Jessica said, "I should have known Paige Graham would have been there."

"If you ask me, I think Clark already knows who killed his wife," Cameron said while glaring out the window at the large home. "Question is, was he in on it?"

"Can you get DNA from snot?"

Jumping in their seats, Jessica and Cameron turned to where Izzy was holding out her hand over the center console. Resting in her open palm was a balled up tissue.

"I could kiss you." Jessica bumped fists with Izzy while Cameron yanked an evidence bag from her purse.

"I prefer a banana split."

"You got it!" While slipping the used tissue into the bag, Cameron looked over Jessica's shoulder and out the passenger window. "We have company."

Maureen's brother Duke had his hand raised to knock on the window when Jessica opened the door. "You ladies look like you could use a drink," he said.

"Actually," Izzy said from the back seat, "we could use a round of banana splits."

Duke laughed. "I could handle that. There's a Friendly's one exit down." He pointed at a big black pick-up truck that had pulled up next to them in the street. Denise was in the driver's seat. "Follow us and I'll make it worth your while."

Cameron tapped Jessica on the shoulder. "Who—"

"He's Maureen's brother," Jessica said in a low voice.

With a nod of her head, Cameron stuffed the evidence bag into her purse and turned on the engine. "You lead the way."

Before he could step away, Jessica reached out for his hand. "Thank you."

There were tears in his eyes when he met her gaze. "No, thank *you*."

"Lieutenant Thornton!"

The boom of Joshua's voice throughout the staff office sent shockwaves that made every agent and clerk jump in their seat.

In his office next door, Murphy leapt to his feet and ran to the doorway where he almost collided with Joshua. Upon seeing the fury in his father's blue eyes, Murphy stood at attention. "Yes, sir."

Joshua pointed to the office he had commandeered from Hillary Koch. "My office. Now!"

Murphy scurried into the office with Joshua directly behind him. Once inside, Joshua slammed the door shut.

"Sit down, Lieutenant."

While lowering himself into the chair across from the desk, Murphy saw that Joshua had been reading the incident report he had sent to his commanding officer. Feeling his heartbeat kick up a notch, he swallowed.

Behind the desk, Joshua picked up the report. He had the same expression on his face that he did the night Murphy had snuck his classic Corvette out for a date, landed in a ditch, and broke the rear axle. It took Murphy nine months of mowing lawns, trimming trees, cleaning gutters, and every other type of dirty work for practically every home in their neighborhood to pay for the damage.

Through clenched teeth, Joshua bit out each word in his question. "What was Jessica doing at Starbucks?"

"Buying lattes," Murphy said with a weak grin.

Joshua's eyes narrowed to blue slits. Placing both hands on the desktop, he leaned toward Murphy. "You knew there was a possibility that the perpetrator of this mass murder would be after Emily Dolan. He or she took out five women—that you knew of. Then, it comes to your attention that he or she may be behind Nick's murder and this Jane Doe. That's seven people—"

"I know."

"And you let your *wife* walk into that!"

"There's no *letting* with Jessie, Dad!" Murphy replied.

Joshua rose to his height.

"Captain!" Murphy corrected himself. "Both of our wives knew the score. I told them the score. I begged them not to go—but they insisted. The only option I had was to go along, survey the situation, make my team aware of it, and do the best I could to keep everyone safe. If I had the power to keep them both home, I would have done that.

But they're their own individuals. Short of duct taping them to the kitchen chair, there was no way I could keep them from going to Starbucks to question Dolan about Cecilia Crenshaw's and Nick's murders."

Joshua placed his hands on his hips.

A long silence stretched between them.

"Then, when bullets started flying, your first priority was Jessica ... not Dolan," Joshua said.

"That was a mistake, sir," Murphy said. "I wish I could tell you that it won't happen again, but that would be a lie. There's no way I could not put Jessie first."

"I would have done the same thing if I was there and it was Cameron in danger," Joshua said. "That's why it is best to keep your family out of these type of situations—so your loyalties are not divided." His voice softened. "Can you even imagine if anything had happened to Jessie?"

"I've been imagining," Murphy said, "ever since last night it's all I can think about."

Deep in thought, they wordlessly stared at each other.

"What are you going to do, sir?" Murphy asked.

"I'd like to send you to your room without supper," Joshua replied, "but that stopped being effective when you turned ten." With a heavy sigh, he pointed to the door. "Go to your office and think about what you did."

Slowly, Murphy got up from the chair and moved to the office door. He stopped with his hand on the doorknob. "What was I supposed to do?" He turned back to where Joshua had sat down behind the desk. "If it was you, how would you have stopped the two of them?"

"Slipped them a mickey."

"What?" Murphy replied.

"A mickey. A tranquilizer. Sleeping pill," Joshua said. "By the time they woke up, hopefully the case would have been solved, or at the very least, the danger would have passed."

"Is that what you do when Cameron wants to go off and do something dangerous?"

"Hell, no," Joshua replied with a loud laugh. "If I did that, as soon as she'd realized what I've done, Cameron would kill me in my sleep."

CHAPTER TWENTY-ONE

In the padded chair behind the staff chief's desk, Joshua enjoyed the sweet sound of Hillary Koch cursing in the break room down the hall. How she had managed to get on board with the Naval Criminal Investigative Service he did not know. *Correction*, he thought with a deep sigh. *I know exactly how she got with NCIS. Last time I'll make a deal like that.*

He refocused on the pile of medical examiner reports he had organized into four piles in front of him. Three were for the victims of the murders at Francine Baxter's home. One for the host, Francine. Shot twice. Once in the back. Second to the head. The second stack held three reports for the women who had been poisoned. The third stack was for Petty Officer Donna Crenshaw. Shot five times. A fourth pile was for Emily Dolan, the anti-military blogger who had been gunned down the night before.

Remembering the reason for Cameron's visit to Washington in the first place, Joshua told himself that he needed a fifth and sixth pile. One for Army Specialist Cecilia Crenshaw, who had been abducted and seemed to have jumped out of a moving vehicle on the Pennsylvania

Turnpike. And the last pile for Pennsylvania State Trooper Nicholas Gates, who was run down while trying to identify her.

Sitting back in his seat, Joshua pressed the fingertips of both hands together while staring at the piles of reports.

Is it really possible that all of these murders are connected to one person? Someone paid a hitman to run Nick down. That hit man was connected to the Russian mob. Could the United States Army really be connected to the Russian mob? Illegal arms deals maybe?

"Dad?"

Joshua looked up to see that Murphy was standing in front of his desk. He held a laptop in his hand. Joshua silently reminded him of their earlier conversation with the arch of his eyebrow. Murphy jumped to stand at attention and brought his right hand up in a salute.

After returning the salute, Joshua said, "As you were, Lieutenant."

"I apologize for interrupting you, sir," Murphy said, "but we got the results from Izzy's DNA profile. There are enough markers to confirm that Izzy is Cecilia Crenshaw's biological daughter. Petty Officer Donna Crenshaw was Cecilia's sister—Izzy's aunt."

"Cecilia's autopsy shows that she gave birth less than two weeks before she disappeared," Joshua said. "Her dying words were, 'She's safe.' She must have been talking about Izzy."

"Izzy's birthdate works out with the timeline," Murphy said. "To protect Izzy, Petty Officer Crenshaw raised her as her own daughter—never telling her about Cecilia being her mother and her disappearance."

"And never coming forward to identify her sister in order to protect Izzy," Joshua said. "Safe from what? Or who? The murders of Donna and those other women have to be connected in some way to Cecilia's abduction."

"If I may, sir." Murphy held up the laptop. "We've downloaded the mirror image of Francine Baxter's laptop onto this one." He went over to the conference desk and set the laptop down. "We got her emails and files—everything. One folder was password-protected, but the IT department was able to crack it. You're going to want to see this."

Joshua took the seat Murphy offered in front of the laptop. After taking out his reading glasses and adjusting them, he pressed the enter button on the laptop to open up a folder that was titled: MONSTER

The folder contained over a dozen folders inside which were labeled. Among the names were Price, Clark, Davis, and Crenshaw.

"Aren't those the names of the murder victims at Baxter's house?" Joshua asked.

With a nod of his head, Murphy reached over Joshua's shoulder to move the cursor to the folder labeled Crenshaw. Upon opening it, they saw that the folder contained numerous pdf files.

"Francine Baxter had been a human resource officer in the army. Some of the paperwork is dated after she'd left. She must have convinced someone to slip these documents from the army's files."

"She was putting together a case against someone she considered a monster," Joshua said, "whoever that is."

"She stated in a text to Crenshaw that they needed her in order to stop *him*. It's definitely a man." Murphy pulled a chair over to sit next to Joshua. "This folder she put together for Specialist Cecilia Crenshaw is particularly damning. Baxter was Crenshaw's human resource officer. After she came back from a tour in Iraq, Crenshaw was sent to work at Foggy Bottom. She was getting rave reviews from her CO and recommended for awards from the commandant. Everything looked great until around March when she showed up in Baxter's office first thing one Monday morning with a fat lip."

Murphy hit the button to open a file that was filled with digital pictures of Cecilia Crenshaw with a fat lip and other bruises on her body. The images also included a torn skirt and panties.

"Who did that to her?" Joshua asked.

"The then commandant at Foggy Bottom," Murphy zoomed in on a name in the report.

Joshua sucked in a deep breath.

"Crenshaw went on maternity leave right before Christmas," Murphy said. "Izzy was born in Walter Reed Hospital on New Year's Day. Cecilia's sister reported her missing on January seventh."

"Nick found her January sixth," Joshua recalled from the case report Cameron had shown him.

Murphy went on. "Cecilia Crenshaw had four months maternity leave. She was to return to duty on April twentieth. She was reported AWOL on April twenty-first. Francine Baxter resigned from the army before the end of that year." He concluded, "She must have known what happened to Cecilia and who was behind it. That's why she put together this monster file and insisted that Petty Officer Crenshaw be at their meeting."

Joshua dreaded the answer to his next question. "What's in the other folders?"

"It gets worse."

"I like the way you think, Izzy." Cameron and Izzy bumped fists before digging into their respective banana splits.

Across the table at the ice cream restaurant, Denise and Duke grinned wistfully.

"Maureen loved ice cream when she was your age," Duke said. "Then she became health conscious. She used to run marathons … until she stopped a couple of years ago."

Denise said, "I was meeting her for breakfast on that day … the day she stopped."

Jessica paused in sipping her root beer float to ask, "What made her stop?"

"I used to babysit Tommy in the morning while Maureen would run," Denise said. "We'd meet someplace for breakfast at the end of a running path and she would pick up Tommy. That morning, she had come in and went to the restroom. When she came out, I saw a man bump into her and he said something to her. Her face got white—like she'd seen a ghost. I asked her what he'd said and she said that he told her she shouldn't go running alone because he'd hate to see something happen to her pretty legs."

"What did that mean?" Jessica asked.

"It was a threat," Cameron said. "Did you find out who it was?"

"Tommy's father," Duke said.

"Colonel Clark?" Izzy asked.

Reminded of the girl's presence, Duke and Denise paused.

"You can talk in front of me," Izzy said. "I know where babies come from."

"We're discussing a murder case," Cameron said.

"Yeah, my mom's," Izzy said. "Whoever killed Tommy's mom killed mine, too." She turned to the couple. "So spill it. Did Tommy's dad kill my mom because he was ticked-off at his wife?"

"Lincoln is not Tommy's biological father," Denise said. "She was raped … It happened during Lincoln's last tour. She said nothing to anyone … until she ended up pregnant …"

"Why didn't she report it?" Jessica asked.

"Because she knew who it was," Duke said forcibly. "She refused to tell us," he shook a finger at them, "but Lincoln knows."

"Then why doesn't he—"

"Whoever it is has enough power to do whatever he wants," Denise interrupted Jessica to say. "Lincoln was furious when he found out Denise was pregnant. Everyone knew Tommy wasn't his. He couldn't be. Lincoln was in Afghanistan for a full year. They had home leave in Europe but by the time that came about, Maureen was already eight weeks pregnant. Most of our friends think she had an affair and that any problems Lincoln and she had was because she cheated. Only the immediate family knows the truth."

Duke said, "Whoever did it has some juice because right after Tommy was born, Lincoln's career took off. I know Maureen told him who'd raped her and Lincoln took advantage of it." He grumbled, "But she wouldn't tell us."

"Because she knew you'd kill him," Denise told him. "Then where would you be?"

"Do you think Lincoln is blackmailing the rapist?" Cameron asked.

"I know he is," Duke said. "He flat out told me that if I knew what was good for my career that I'd just go along and forget trying to find out who raped my sister."

"That proves whoever did it was military," Jessica said.

"Could Maureen have been lying about the rape?" Cameron asked as gently as she could. "Her husband was gone for a year. Maybe she did have a fling."

"No," Denise shook her head. "She told me how it happened. Not who it was but what had happened. He came to the house to check on her because he knew Lincoln was away and she was home alone. She invited him in for a drink, and then he forced himself on her. She said she kept saying no, and then when she started to scream, he pinned her down and bit her lip. She took pictures of the bruises on her arms where he held her down. I saw them."

"If she invited him in," Jessica said, "then she had to know him."

"But then you said this guy threatened her a couple of years ago," Cameron said. "Had he been threatening her all along? Why would he suddenly be threatening her years later if the rapist had an agreement with Lincoln?"

"Because Maureen started resenting Lincoln using the rape and Tommy to advance his career," Denise said. "By the time she was murdered, she hated the army. She used to be active in the officers' wives club, but Paige Graham practically ran her out."

"Why?" Cameron asked.

"Because Maureen was making waves," Denise said. "She hated the general. His wife, Paige is delusional—add to that vindictive. Every wife knows that General Graham is a skirt-chasing hound. But if Paige hears any of the wives even suggesting that it's true … well, let's just say things would not turn out well in the club if you so much as breathed the ugly truth." With a shake of her head, she added, "I heard someone say he had a different mistress for every day of the week—including Sunday."

"But Maureen was not one of them," Duke insisted.

"No, she wasn't" Denise agreed. "She hated the air he breathed."

"Paige Graham was at the Clark home today," Jessica pointed out.

"I still belong to the club," Denise said, "but I'll be leaving after Duke gets out."

"This whole thing has soured me on the army, too," Duke said. "I got an offer from a private contractor and I snapped at it."

"Paige Graham had said something about Maureen making some accusations against General Graham," Jessica said. "Is that why she ran Maureen out?"

"But that had nothing to do with the rape," Denise said with a shake of her head. "It was shortly after Tommy was born. After the rape and ... Maureen was very sensitive. The Grahams were having a party and Maureen slapped the general. She accused him of groping her breast. He denied it. Maureen went off on him." She sighed with disgust. "Paige ordered Maureen to apologize to him in front of everyone and admit that she had overreacted, that it didn't happen—that it was her imagination—"

"She had to or Paige would have ostracized her from the officers' wives," Duke said, "and General Graham did have the power to ruin Lincoln's career."

"If he had the power to ruin Lincoln's career," Cameron asked, "wouldn't he also have the power to make it?"

Duke and Denise exchanged stunned looks.

"Maybe he did grope her breast and she overreacted because he'd raped her and she was scared he was going to do it again," Jessica said.

"I flat-out asked her afterwards if it was General Graham," Duke insisted. "She swore it wasn't."

"Look," Denise said, "the general is a cheat, but he's no *rapist*. He doesn't have to be. Women are always throwing themselves at him."

"Or so he thinks," Cameron said.

"Rape is not about sex," Jessica said. "It's about power, control, and domination. It has nothing to do with sex. They are two different things. If he was the one who raped Maureen, she very well could have lied to protect you or your career because she knew you'd go after him and there was no way you could come out with your career intact afterwards."

"You said she was threatened," Cameron said. "Rape is traumatic enough, even without being threatened. That's why so often it is not reported—even today."

"Especially when the man is as powerful as General Graham," Jessica agreed. "Just now, Denise, you said General Graham was not a rapist because he doesn't have to be. He can have any woman he wants. After a lifetime of yes-men and women telling him that, he's probably come to believe it himself—not just that he can have any woman he wants, but that he's *entitled* to any woman he wants."

Ashamed, Denise looked down at the table top. After a long silence around the table, she said, "Maureen was leaving Lincoln."

Cameron asked, "Do you know that for a fact?"

"Definitely," Denise said. "If she hadn't been killed, she would have been gone by now. She was planning to take off while Lincoln was at work the other day. She was killed about twelve hours before she was going to leave."

"That's suspicious timing," Cameron said.

"My thought exactly," Duke said.

Denise said, "We had arranged for her to stay with a friend of ours in upstate New York until she got a permanent place to live."

"Did Lincoln know about her plans to leave?" Cameron asked.

"She didn't tell him," Denise said, "but he could have found out. Maureen was scared to death that he would. He was always nosing around. She wasn't just leaving. I think she was planning to file criminal charges against this rapist."

"And Lincoln's golden goose would have flown away with his career when the slimy cretin went to jail," Duke said with a wave of his hand.

"Not only that, but it would not look good for Lincoln at all if word got out that he used a sexual attack on his wife to advance his military career," Jessica said.

"But if his wife died before she could charge her attacker with rape," Cameron said, "then all would be good."

"Exactly," Duke said. "If General Graham did rape my sister, from what we've seen, he has some powerful friends who will do anything to keep his dirty habit under wraps."

CHAPTER TWENTY-TWO

"Makes me sick," Cameron muttered while trying to follow the directions on her GPS at the same time that she was watching the steadily increasing traffic. During late afternoon rush hour traffic, failure to make it into the correct merging lane on the Capital Beltway can easily suck a vehicle into traffic heading in the wrong direction—trapping it in a fast-moving vehicular river with no escape for miles.

"We have a general who's possibly a rapist, a rape victim who doesn't report it, and a husband who takes advantage of the sexual assault to advance his career," Jessica said.

"But can we prove it?" Cameron asked. "Even if the DNA from Tommy's snot comes back proving that General Graham is his biological father, we'll still have no proof that it was rape. He'll claim it was consensual and without a report of rape, who's to say he's lying."

"My mom was raped," Izzy said from the back seat.

Startled, Jessica turned around to look over her shoulder at Izzy. "I didn't know that."

"I told Murphy," Izzy said.

Aware that Izzy did not know that Donna Crenshaw was not her birth mother, Jessica and Cameron exchanged glances, before Jessica asked, "Did she report it ... to the police I mean?"

"I think she did," Izzy said. "She said the guy got off for it. I kind of thought that meant she called the police."

"Maybe it's the same guy, and that's who these women were ganging together to stop," Cameron said.

"Ninety-eight percent of rapists don't spend a day in jail," Jessica said. "Sixty-eight percent of rape victims don't report it. But there's strength in numbers. Suppose these women found out about each other. Here, the news is making a big deal of General Graham being on the brink of becoming the army's chief of staff and they decide to band together and go public to expose him for the sexual perpetrator that he is."

"That would mean General Graham is my father," Izzy said from the back seat. "Damn!"

"And you and Tommy are brother and sister," Jessica said. "If we're talking about the same perpetrator."

A smile came to Izzy's lips. "I like Tommy."

"Don't get me wrong," Cameron waved her hand at Jessica. "I'm just a dumb detective."

"You're not dumb, Cameron," Jessica said.

"You mentioned back there that these big powerful successful men, who are surrounded by yes-men, start to think that they are entitled to any woman they want," Cameron said. "But don't tell me that they don't know that it is wrong to pin a woman down by the shoulders and bite her lip to make her stop screaming while they rip her clothes off."

"I never met General Graham," Jessica said. "But some cases that I researched in school point to the sense of control in dominating the woman, intimidating her, humiliating her, that makes them do it. People look at these men who are huge achievers in sports, military, politics, business, and they don't realize that along with the money and power, they are also under a lot of stress. A lot of people depend on them." She laughed. "That's why Murphy is obsessive compulsive about his exercise and diet routine."

"Is there no such thing as being a simple run of a mill health nut anymore?" Cameron asked. "Why do you have to slap criminals with tags labeling them as sick? General Graham isn't *sick*. He doesn't deserve the sympathy of someone with an illness. Give sympathy to the ones who deserve it—his victims. He's a sexual predator and a rapist. Plain and simple. His butt belongs in jail."

Jessica held up her hand to silence her. "I am not making excuses for what he did. I am only explaining the psychology behind it. I'm not condoning serial rapists who earn in the top one percent any more than I would a serial killer lurking in dark alleys."

In her rearview mirror, Cameron noticed a black van that had been following directly behind her on Route 190 leading to Interstate 495. Granted, it was approaching rush hour and the flow of traffic was increasing, and everyone seemed to be heading toward the beltway, but Cameron had noticed the van pull out of the shopping center directly behind them and it had a few opportunities to pass them. Instead, it was riding right on the cruiser's tail.

"What drives them is this need to feel like they're in control," Jessica continued with her dissertation. "How better to do that than to target a woman in a subordinate position and harass, force himself, or even rape her. Makes him feel like a man."

"There's nothing that a man loves more than feeling like he's in control," Cameron said while eying the van that now made its move up along the driver's side of her cruiser.

"It's not just a man thing."

Cameron's grip on the steering wheel tightened. Her eyes flicked around to every mirror and window within the cruiser. As soon as the van had moved over, a truck had pulled up behind her.

"Cameron, what's wrong?" Jessica craned her neck to observe the van moving up alongside them.

There was a long line of vehicles racing onto the beltway's onramp in hopes of getting safely home before the height of rush hour.

The side door to the van slid open as it moved alongside them.

Cameron saw the flash of an assault rifle's muzzle. "Everybody down!" She swung the steering wheel. The only place she had to go was off to the side of the road.

"Izzy, hit the floor!" Jessica reached back to grab Izzy by the top of the head and they both dropped down in their seats.

In the same instant, the spray of bullets shattered the side and windows of the cruiser.

The front tire exploded, sending the cruiser into a spin back out into traffic. With Izzy screaming, Cameron fought the wheel of the SUV while it bounced off cars and trucks like a ping pong ball spinning back and forth across both lanes of traffic all the way onto the beltway. The airbags deployed—blocking Cameron's view in trying to maneuver the cruiser away from the heavy fast moving traffic.

Up ahead, she saw that the frontage road along the freeway ended at a bridge crossing over a two-lane road filled with rush hour traffic. She continued to pump the brake pedal to slow down the vehicle spinning out of control.

"Cameron! Please!" she heard Izzy beg before the rear of the cruiser slammed into the bridge embankment, spun, and then toppled like a toy over the top. Finally, the SUV came to rest—caught by the rear wheel axles with the front half of the vehicle facing downwards at the commuters on the road below.

"Don't anybody move!" Cameron reached over to Jessica, who was holding her breath for fear that to exhale would shift the weight of the cruiser enough to make it topple straight down to their deaths.

Sobbing, Izzy sat up in her seat and finger combed her thick curls out of her face. Seeing the cement stretched several feet below them, she screamed.

"Izzy, no!" Jessica whirled around in her seat.

The shift of the weight caused the cruiser to rock. Jessica turned back around, which made it shift again.

"Everyone freeze!" Cameron bellowed like they were suspects caught in the midst of committing a crime.

Both Izzy and Jessica froze in fear of the detective's wrath as much as the death looming several feet below.

"I don't want to die," Izzy sobbed from where she clung to her seat in the back.

"We're not going to die." As gently as she could, without turning around, Cameron reached her arm back and grasped Izzy's knobby knee with her hand. "Listen, Izzy. Can you hear them?"

The sirens of emergency vehicles could be heard in the distance.

"They're going to get us out." Jessica clung to the dashboard with both hands as if she could hold back the force of the impact if the cruiser were to plummet nose-first down to the pavement below.

"We just need to stay perfectly still and pray," Cameron said. "Can you do that, Izzy?"

Izzy sobbed. "I don't know how."

"That's okay," Cameron said. "It's not hard. Jessica and I will teach you."

"Really?" Izzy sniffed. "You'll teach me how to pray to God?"

"Sure, Izzy," Jessica said with bated breath. "We're not doing anything else right now."

CHAPTER TWENTY-THREE

Time was running out.

A cunning killer was in the process of covering his tracks. If they weren't able to gather enough evidence to stop him, he was going to get away with it.

While Joshua Thornton made a conference call to the chair and vice chair of the Joint Chiefs of Staff, Murphy gathered their team into the conference room to go over their evidence and the files they had found on Francine Baxter's hard drive. He connected his laptop, as well as the one containing the mirror image of Francine's laptop, to the smart board so that they could all see it.

"You know what his attorneys are going to claim," Susan told Murphy after seeing the documentation, "one, this is all a frame up committed by a disgruntled ex-army officer—that being Francine Baxter. Two, that most of these files were illegally obtained—making them inadmissible in court."

"Does any of that documentation prove a connection between your suspect and the Russian mob?" Boris asked in a doubtful tone.

Not expecting this question, Murphy paused before answering, "No, I didn't see any type of connection like that."

The door to the conference room flew open.

"Hello, lady and gentlemen." Joshua stepped over to the head of the conference table and tossed his notepad down. "The Joint Chiefs of Staff have given us until sunrise tomorrow to solve this case and put together direct evidence connecting our suspect to these murders. Tell me where we are right now."

"I'll start," Boris said. "FBI says those three hitmen taken out last night are tightly connected to the Russian mob. Very professional—very well planned. That license plate number Murphy took off their van—the plate was stolen from a federal vehicle that was parked in a government motor pool."

"It was a planned hit," Susan said. "No doubt about that."

"Do the FBI's records have these guys connected to any group in particular?" Joshua asked.

Boris nodded his head. "Specifically, these guys have done a lot of work for Ivan Kalashov, or rather his son Adrian. Ivan is virtually retired. The RICO division has been trying to nail Adrian for years but they say he's like Teflon. Law degree from Yale. He knows the law inside and out—most especially the loop holes."

"Kalashov?" Joshua asked. "Are you sure about that, Hamilton?"

Boris glanced down at his report. "Positive."

"Bertonelli, the hitman contracted to kill Cameron's first husband, committed hits for Kalashov," Joshua said.

"That's a twist I didn't see coming," Susan said.

"Cameron's first husband was a Pennsylvania state trooper. Nicholas Gates," Murphy said. "He was run down thirteen years ago on the Pennsylvania Turnpike—hit and run. Everyone assumed it was a drunk driver. This week, the feds told us that a hit man turned federal witness told them that it was a paid hit for Kalashov—as a favor for a friend."

"Was Gates connected to the army?" Boris asked.

"No," Joshua said.

"But he was investigating the death of a Jane Doe he had found on the Pennsylvania turnpike," Murphy said. "That Jane Doe turned out to be Army Specialist Cecilia Crenshaw, Donna Crenshaw's sister. That gives him an indirect connection to the army."

"That means this relationship between the army and organized crime stretches back at least thirteen years," Boris said. "That must have been what Dolan's news breaking story was about. Our United States Army is in bed with the Russian mob."

"Did we uncover anything concrete from the anti-military blogger's laptop?" Joshua asked. "What's her relationship to the murders at Baxter's place?"

"Emily Dolan took three business administration courses with Francine Baxter," Susan said. "While there's no emails to Dolan from Baxter's email account, we did find emails sent to her from Baxter's IP address through a Hotmail account that she had set up on the same day that the first email was sent. We only found a few emails—all referencing that Baxter had information for Dolan's blog that would make for a huge news breaking story about a conspiracy and cover up in the army."

"But she didn't say what it was," Murphy said.

"Had to be about the army's connection to the Russian mob," Boris said.

"Baxter was too smart to put it in an email," Susan said. "She told Emily Dolan to call her. The cell phone number she gave was not her regular number."

"Probably a burner phone," Murphy said. "Was one found at the Baxter home?"

"No," Susan said. "However, we found Emily Dolan's cell phone in her purse and the log shows texts back and forth between Dolan and Baxter up until a half hour before Dolan's murder."

Joshua said, "The killer found Baxter's burner phone and continued communicating with Dolan after the murders in Reston."

"But we have a witness who saw Emily Dolan go into Baxter's home hours after the murders," Murphy said. "There's no way she couldn't know Baxter was already dead."

Susan explained, "According to the texts going back and forth between them, the killer identified her or himself to Dolan as being a witness who had managed to escape the murders in Reston. She said that the military killed Baxter and the others and was using the police to cover it up."

Susan pointed at Murphy. "Dolan texted about seeing a navy officer coming out of the Baxter home. The killer, we assume it is the killer, texted back not to trust him because they all work together and that if she went to him, she would end up dead."

Joshua sucked in a deep breath and let it out slowly. "And since she already didn't trust us, she played right into the killer's hands."

With a pound of his fist on the table top, Boris shook his head. "Why didn't she go to the police? They could have used that communication to track down the killer and Dolan would still be alive."

"Because Dolan considered the police and military the enemy," Murphy said.

"What were the texts saying?" Joshua asked Susan.

Susan handed each of them a report transcribing the texts. "Basically, the killer took advantage of Dolan being in the dark. We found evidence on her laptop that indicates she knew no specific details about this conspiracy."

Boris said, "Dolan's fingerprints are a match for prints found on Baxter's laptop and all around her study. From what it looks like, Baxter and all of Dolan's sources were murdered before they could give her the story."

"The witness said Dolan was inside the Baxter home for at least ten minutes," Murphy said. "She must have been searching for clues to the cover-up and conspiracy that got those women murdered."

Susan agreed. "It appears to us that Francine Baxter either wanted to protect her—the less she knew the safer she would be—or that she wanted the shock value of springing the whole story on her at the meeting.

"The last texts were arranging for Dolan and this witness to get together so that the witness could give her the story," Susan said. "That night. Dolan told the killer when she was working. How to recognize her. Everything. That's how the hitmen knew who to hit."

"I assume the phone sending the texts to Dolan is now off," Joshua said.

"Ever since Dolan's murder."

"Since the hit squad was wearing military fatigues. . . " Boris said. "As soon as the media finds out that Dolan was an anti-military blogger who was creating a buzz about having inside info about a military conspiracy. . ."

"Wait a minute," Murphy interrupted him.

"What'd I say?" Boris asked.

"The media doesn't know about Dolan being an anti-military blogger?"

"We haven't released her name or about her being a blogger," Boris said. "We've been keeping everything tight to our vest, but it's only a matter of time before—"

His mouth hanging open, Murphy turned to Joshua.

"What is it, Lieutenant?" Joshua prompted him. "Out with it."

With effort, Murphy tried to recall who he had overheard and what she had said. "This morning at breakfast, I overheard General Graham's assistant telling him about the hit on Starbucks last night. She knew that the target was an anti-military blogger. If none of that was released to the media, how did she know about Dolan being a blogger who was biased against the military? How did she know the hit on Starbucks was even connected to our case?"

"Good questions," Joshua said. "And this was General Graham's assistant?"

"Dolly Scanlon."

"I think we need to have a talk with Dolly Scanlon," Joshua said.

"As well as General Graham," Murphy said.

"All of our victims had some connection to General Sebastian Graham," Boris said. "He was the commandant at Foggy Bottom where Cecilia Crenshaw worked when she reported being raped. The military police did a cursory investigation—claimed they found nothing conclusive. She dropped the charges."

"Why did she drop the charges?" Murphy asked.

"Most likely she was threatened," Susan said. "I cast the net wider and talked to friends of all the victims. Back when she was nineteen years old, Colleen Davis, the kindergarten teacher, took a bottle of sleeping pills. I got in touch with her old college roommate and she told me that a few months before that suicide attempt Colleen had gone to a popular lounge in Florida with some friends. This club was frequented by the military and Sebastian Graham was there. He was a friend of Colleen's father—"

"Lieutenant General George Davis," Joshua confirmed.

"Exactly," Susan said. "Well, Graham bought Colleen a drink—a soda—since she was only eighteen years old at that time. Not long after that, she started feeling ill. The evening was still young and her friends didn't want to go, so they all thought Graham was being a nice guy when he offered to drive her home and let them continue with the party. Colleen told her roommate that she passed out and then came to in a hotel room to find Graham getting dressed. She threatened to tell her father and he said that would not be a good idea."

"Keep in mind that Lieutenant General George Davis outranked Graham," Boris said.

"And Colleen was his daughter." Joshua's teeth were clenched.

"Colleen also had a boyfriend who had just graduated from West Point and was stationed overseas," Boris said.

Susan picked up the story. "Graham told her that if she breathed a word about the rape to anyone that he would see to it that her boyfriend would end up in a hot zone and have a horrible accident."

Boris said, "Cecilia's sister Donna was in the army. Graham probably used the same threat against her."

"Well, his threats worked on Colleen," Susan said. "She told no one, but all of her friends and her father noticed that something was wrong. A few months later, she tried to kill herself. That was when her roommate dragged it out of her, but only after she swore her to secrecy."

"Maybe if she hadn't, Colleen would still be alive today," Joshua said.

"That's what she said. She's willing to testify to what Colleen told her."

"Unfortunately, her testimony will be considered hearsay," Joshua said. "Odds of getting it admitted into court would be slim to none, especially against the lawyers Graham will have defending him."

"Colleen's roommate said that General Davis kept asking questions and digging," Susan said. "He did find out about General Graham being at the bar that night and kept pressing him with questions about if he had seen anything that would explain Colleen's depression. Not long after that, the helicopter crashed, General Davis was dead, and Graham's problem went away. Oh, by the way, you wouldn't believe who drove General Davis to the base the morning of the helicopter crash?"

"General Sebastian Graham?" Joshua asked.

Susan said, "He was still on the base when the helicopter exploded and crashed minutes after take-off."

"CID did find bomb parts in the wreckage," Murphy said. "The agent conducting the investigation believed he was on the right path to identifying the killer. He called the army's chief of staff to tell him that he had something. That night, the investigator and his family died in an arson fire in their home. Days after that, two airmen who had worked on the base the morning of the helicopter accident were killed in a horrible vehicle accident."

"Our killer is very good at covering his tracks," Joshua said.

"Francine Baxter's husband was killed in a car accident," Murphy said, "one month after Cecilia disappeared. According to the copy of the police statement we found on her computer, the investigators found paint transfer on the car. Her husband's car was in the shop. He was driving her car on the day of the crash."

Narrowing his eyes, Joshua sat up in his seat.

"General Sebastian Graham is a sexual predator, Dad."

Joshua cleared his throat.

Murphy corrected himself. "I mean, Captain." He hit a button on his laptop. "He's had women filing sexual assault charges against him going all the way back to West Point. While he was an army cadet, two different women filed charges against him for rape. Both charges were reduced down to misdemeanors. Graham paid a fine and didn't spend a day in jail. He's *never* spent a day in jail."

In silence, Joshua rubbed his face with both hands.

"During the Gulf War, a female fellow officer charged him with rape," Murphy said. "Then, Graham saved his team in that firefight and the rape charge got buried under all the hoopla of him being a hero." He grumbled. "The list goes on and on but never once was General Graham ever held accountable. He's not a war hero, he's a common run of the mill serial rapist."

"He's not run of the mill," Joshua said. "He's a distinguished war hero who has a lot of people protecting—and enabling—his behavior."

"Which gave him a license to move up from serial rapist to serial killer." Murphy advanced the screen on his laptop to display a long list, complete with pictures, on the smart board for them all to see.

"General Sebastian Graham is the same age you are, Captain," Murphy announced. "Not counting deaths in combat, how many supervisors, colleagues, and acquaintances who are associated with you professionally suffered sudden or violent deaths due to accidents, suicide, or murder?"

Counting in his head, Joshua finally answered, "Maybe five at the most."

"In General Sebastian Graham's case," Murphy said, "close to three dozen."

Stunned, Boris and Susan stared up at the extensive list.

"Francine Baxter had put together a hit list," Murphy said, "of everyone who has ever gotten in the way of Sebastian's military career who suddenly died—eliminating the road block. Less than five years after his return from Kuwait, he was up for the position of commandant of the Army War College. The position was given to Major General Wilbur Frost who outranked him. Within weeks, less than a month after assuming the position, Frost went home for lunch and blew his brains out with his own service weapon. To this day, everyone swears he displayed no suicidal tendencies. After this very convenient suicide, Sebastian Graham got the position."

"Argument could be made by Graham's attorneys that this is just a coincidence," Joshua said.

"I've heard you explain to juries that circumstantial evidence is just as important as direct evidence," Murphy said. "Circumstances prove the reasoning behind the suspect's actions and behavior. Sebastian Graham is a sociopath who believes that he can have any woman he wants, even if she says no. So he takes her. Then, when she threatens the continuance of his behavior or the advancement of his military career, he threatens her or buys her off or, if those tactics don't work, he uses murder to clean up his mess."

Standing up, he went to the smart board to point to the image of a young woman with dark hair. "Sixteen years ago, Hannah Price filed a police report saying that she had been raped. She had attended a cocktail reception on the top floor of the Executive Office Building. She woke up in a hotel room with no memory of how she ended up there. Blood tests revealed that she had been slipped a roofie. General Sebastian Graham was in attendance at that very party. Days later, his executive officer, First Lieutenant Julie Wagner requested a transfer from her position even though it was actually considered to be quite a prestigious assignment. She wouldn't tell her personnel officer why. Two days after making that request, she died after falling off her bicycle and hitting her head. The medical examiner said she had *two* blows to the head." He added, "She was at that party in the Executive Office Building. The last call she made before her accident was to Hannah Price."

"Not long after that, Hannah Price and her husband set up an engineering company and have been getting lucrative military contracts ever since," Susan said.

Murphy pointed to another picture on the list of another army officer. "Less than two years after Graham came back from Kuwait a hero, his CO was killed in a car accident. It was ruled a homicide because police found his brake lines cut. Colleagues told CID that the CO and Graham did not get along and he was recommending against promotion. The CO's replacement was a longtime mentor of Graham who did recommend him for promotion."

"But no charges were brought against Graham," Joshua said.

"Because there—"

"Was no evidence to prove he was behind it," Joshua finished.

"How about a second lieutenant who charged him with sexual harassment sixteen years ago?" Murphy said. "She ended up going AWOL. All credit card activity stopped. Her family and friends have never heard from her. Her body was never found and the military police presume she's dead."

"The sheer volume in this list proves that General Graham is a psychopath," Boris said, "or at the very least has a psychopathic guardian angel."

"My vote is on *him* being the psychopath," Murphy said while scrolling down the list on the computer. "Dad—I mean Captain, how many personal assistants have you had?"

"You know the answer to that," Joshua said. "None, unless you want to count biological offspring."

Murphy stopped scrolling at a screen that showed four pictures of young beautiful women. A listing was next to each one. "Graham has had four personal assistants in a little over a dozen years. Dolly Scanlon is the fifth." He stepped up to the board and pointed at the photograph of a pretty blonde at the top of the screen. "His first assistant was with him for twenty-six months—until she went missing. Her body was found over a year later in a heavily wooded area of a park."

He pointed at the second picture of an attractive brunette. "Assistant number two worked for Graham for three and a half years. She committed suicide by jumping out the window of her fifth floor condo."

Eying his father, Murphy pointed to a third picture of a young woman with big eyes. "Number three worked for Graham for three years. She drowned in her hot tub." He pressed his fingertips on the fourth picture of a woman with long dark hair. "Assistant number four quit via overdose of booze mixed with sleeping pills. She lasted two years."

"The office morale must be toxic when you work for General Sebastian Graham," Boris said.

"Why hasn't he ever been investigated?" Susan asked. "Why did the President nominate him for the army's chief of staff?"

The team turned to Joshua Thornton. At the head of the table, he pressed his fingertips together while studying the hit list Murphy had displayed on the smart board.

"Because … " After a long pause, Joshua turned to the staff's deputy chief. "Boris, what was the first thing you learned when you started out in the military?"

"Two things," Boris answered. "Watch your back and cover your butt."

"How about 'don't upset the apple cart?'" Joshua asked with a sigh. "I can see exactly how this happened. I've seen it before in the military, government, politics, and even in the private sector. If anything, in the last twenty years, the problem has only gotten worse."

Joshua gestured up at the smart board on which displayed an extensive list of General Sebastian Graham's victims. "In the beginning, West Point didn't want their reputation tarnished by having one of their cadets convicted of being a rapist. I have no doubt Graham's father, a four-star general, played a big part in convincing them that it would be in their interest to bury the whole thing. Sebastian Graham was third generation West Point. With no thought to what the future held for the military—they caved into pressure from Graham's father."

With a shake of his head, Boris said, "I can't tell you how many times I've seen that happen."

Joshua said, "So West Point and Graham's powerful family convinced, or maybe a better word is bullied, the local prosecutor to reduce the charges and the Grahams paid off the victims for their silence."

"And those first rape charges turn into misdemeanors," Susan said. "Because of Graham's war record and charisma, he gets away with explaining the initial charges as a simple misunderstanding." Disgusted, her eyes narrowed to slits. She shook her head.

"Sebastian Graham graduates and becomes the army's problem," Joshua said. "In Kuwait, he rapes a female colleague. The army probably would have acted on her charges, but fate intervened. Suddenly, Sebastian Graham was a hero and the media made him a celebrity. The Gulf War was one of the first military engagements in which women were sent into hot zones. If the rape had been made public, with a military hero being the perpetrator—"

"It would have negatively affected the feminist cause for equal opportunity in the military," Susan said.

"Undoubtedly," Murphy said, "since Graham was then getting headlines as a hero, the rape charge would have received a lot of negative publicity, which would have threatened women's chances of going into combat."

"The victim was probably told that dropping the charges and keeping quiet about what had to have been an isolated incident was for the greater good," Joshua said.

"With no thought to Graham's future victims," Boris said.

"And since his earlier sexual assaults were buried," Murphy said, "then Graham's victim in Kuwait had no idea about the role she played in allowing this predator to continue using the United States Army for a hunting ground."

"It's a safe bet that in every step of the line," Joshua explained, "the person who had the opportunity and power to stop him hoped that the next man or woman whose problem Graham would become could put a stop to him."

Getting out of his chair, Joshua went up to the list on the smart board. "Unfortunately, every step of the way, Graham's previous attacks and incidents would be buried, which concealed his pattern to his current COs and any investigators who would be brought in."

Joshua shook his head. "The police investigating Specialist Cecelia Crenshaw's rape charge against Graham were unaware of the rapes at West Point, in Kuwait, or the sexual harassment charge. So, I can clearly see why, after she cried rape, they dismissed it. At that point, Graham was in his thirties and as far as what they saw on the surface, he had a sparkling clear record and friends in all the right places."

"They dismissed Specialist Crenshaw as a troublemaking fruit loop," Susan said.

"Only Francine Baxter believed her and decided to dig beneath the cover-ups to reveal General Sebastian Graham's pattern of behavior," Joshua said.

"Those cover-ups by people too cowardly to go up against a war hero with powerful friends proved to be tragic for a lot of people," Murphy said. "Based on the list Baxter put together, every time someone has tried to stop Graham, they've ended up dead."

"No doubt, this has gone way too far," Joshua said while studying the list displayed on the smart board. "At first, it was to protect the army's reputation. Then, as Graham advanced in his career, with all the power he accumulated, looking the other way became a matter of self-preservation." He glanced around the room. "Who here in this room besides me has the balls to go up against a four-star general and accuse him of being a serial rapist and killer?"

"I do," Murphy said without hesitation.

"I know you do," Joshua said. "Who else?" He looked directly at Susan. "Are you naive enough to believe you'll have a career next week?"

"Based on that hit list," Boris said, "I'd be more concerned about making sure my life insurance is paid up. It's not just your career you have to worry about."

"So we just let him get away with this?" Murphy asked. "We're simply going to turn our backs and pretend this isn't happening like every other wuss who did nothing?"

"Son, I agree with you," Joshua said with a sigh, "but we need to be smart about how we proceed." Seeing the fire in Murphy's eyes, he cleared his throat. *"Lieutenant,* I agree with you, but we can't go up against a general who is on the very short list for Chief of Staff of the United States Army with nothing more than what could be construed as a hit list made up by some women scorned, which is what the general's attorneys are going to argue."

"He's going before the Senate tomorrow," Murphy said. "We need to get the President to withdraw his nomination."

"Like that's going to happen." Joshua was still studying the list on the smart board when his cell phone rang. His gaze focused on the extensive list, he brought the phone to his ear. "Captain Joshua Thornton here."

"Joshua Thornton," the voice said in an official tone. "Are you married to Detective Cameron Gates with the Pennsylvania State Police?"

His heart going up into his throat, Joshua turned away from the hit list. "Yes."

"I'm sorry to say, sir, that there has been an accident."

CHAPTER TWENTY-FOUR

It pays to have friends in high places. One phone call to their CO got Joshua and Murphy a navy helicopter on the Pentagon's helipad to fly them out to the Capital Beltway. Otherwise, they wouldn't have been able to get within five miles of the accident.

The beltway was shut down in both directions due to the Pennsylvania State police cruiser hanging by its rear wheels and axle from the overpass, as well as the two lane road over which it was dangling. Within minutes of the assault on Cameron's cruiser, Washington metropolitan traffic had come to a grinding halt. With the major freeway, used by the majority of commuters to get from one part of the Nation's Capital to another, shut down, vehicles were scrambling to find alternate routes, most of which were smaller, two-lane roads—creating gridlock.

A fleet of emergency vehicles, including ambulances and fire trucks, were parked both on the overpass and the road down below. In the helicopter high above, Joshua and Murphy observed a path of wrecked vehicles, broken glass and auto parts, and emergency vehicles leading up to the trapped cruiser.

"What happened?" Unable to believe that his wife was in the midst of the chaos, Murphy lowered his sunglasses for a closer take on the scene.

"Looks like a bad day on the beltway," the pilot said. "Glad I'm flying."

Murphy felt the blood drain from his face and extremities with the realization that Jessica was in the vehicle hanging precariously from the overpass. "Jessie ..."

The touch of Joshua's hand squeezing his arm drew his attention from the wreck. Joshua removed his sunglasses so that he could read the message in his eyes. *They're going to be okay.*

The helicopter had to land on the beltway heading north toward Baltimore. After disembarking, Murphy hurdled the road divider and ducked under the crime scene tape to get pushed back by two Maryland state troopers.

"My wife is in that car!" Murphy tried to force his way through the human barricade until he spotted a firetruck spraying chemicals on gasoline leaking from underneath the cruiser.

The sight made him ill.

"The gas tank is leaking! You have to get them out of there!" Once again, he tried to break through the line of troopers trying to hold him back. "She's my wife! You have to let me save her!" He threw back his fist ready to punch anyone who got in his way.

"Murphy! Stand down!"

The roar of Joshua's voice blasted through Murphy's fright to make him drop his fist.

Joshua wedged himself between the navy officer and the troopers. In spite of the calm in Joshua's tone, Murphy could hear the familiar edge that dared him to cross the line. "This is no time to play Captain America. These are the good guys. They will do everything they can. Lord knows it's not easy but this time, we need to stand down and let them do their jobs."

Joshua turned around to tell the troopers. "Is there someone we can speak to regarding what happened?"

"FBI just got here," one of the troopers pointed to a blue SUV parked inside the crime scene tape on the side of the beltway where the helicopter had landed.

Tearing his eyes from the sight of the cruiser where Jessica was trapped, Murphy spotted a slender, dark haired young woman, who didn't appear to be much older than he was, speaking to the senior ranking state trooper. He also saw her FBI gold shield clipped to her utility belt next to her service weapon.

Grabbing Murphy by the elbow, Joshua led him toward the road divider.

Casting one more look at the cruiser, Murphy saw that two rescuers were attaching a cable and hook to the rear axle in order to pull it back off the embankment. "They have to get them out." He tried to remember a time when he felt so helpless. He came up with none.

"They're going to be okay," Joshua said. "I don't like it any more than you do, but this is one time when you and I are not calling the shots. Cameron and Jessica are in good hands."

"Izzy's in there, too," Murphy said. "I promised that I wouldn't let anything bad happen to her."

"Cameron and Jessica will take care of her," Joshua said. "In the meantime, we need to find out how this happened." Releasing his grip on Murphy's elbow, Joshua crossed over the center divide between the southbound and northbound lanes.

Wanting to be as close to Jessica as possible, Murphy remained on the fringes of the rescuers, watching them work diligently to save the vehicle's passengers. It took all of his restraint to not jump in to hurry them along.

Finally, the urge to do something useful won out. If he could not work hands on to save Jessica, Cameron, and Izzy, he could very well find out who was behind this accident. With a new sense of resolve, Murphy climbed over the divider and followed Joshua over to where the FBI agent was being briefed by the trooper in charge.

"Excuse me," was all Joshua got out before the agent turned to face him.

"Captain Thornton." She offered him her hand. "Special Agent Ripley Vaccaro." Seeing Murphy, she took his hand in a firm shake. "Lieutenant Murphy Thornton. I've heard a lot about you."

"From—"

"We have mutual acquaintances," she cut Murphy off before turning back to Joshua. "I was going to call you but then I was interrupted by this." She shot them a naughty smile partnered with an arched eyebrow. "Since I *happened* to be in the neighborhood, my supervisors gave me this case."

Joshua glanced in Murphy's direction. The curl in the corner of his father's lips told him that Agent Ripley Vaccaro had just given them a coded message. Unfortunately, Murphy was more focused on wanting to hold Jessica in his arms again than deciphering coded messages.

Up close, Murphy saw that the federal agent was actually older than he was—possibly by as much as a decade. It was her slender, athletic build and long dark hair, which was misleading.

"Can you tell us what happened, Agent Vaccaro?" Joshua asked her.

"Witnesses said Detective Gates' cruiser was shot at with a machine gun by someone in a dark van," Ripley said. "All we know is that it was a dark color, nothing more specific. They pulled up alongside the cruiser, opened their side door, and opened fire."

"Was anyone hurt or killed?" Joshua asked.

"A couple of people had to be taken away by ambulance," she reported, "but they aren't life threatening injuries."

The sound of the crane tore Murphy's attention from the conversation. "Dad, they're pulling them up!" Without waiting for Joshua to join him, he raced over to where the cruiser was being dragged up from over the ledge while the fire department hosed down the spilt gasoline.

"Five women killed at a Cozy Cook party," Ripley counted off. "A potential witness gunned down at Starbucks in a major shopping center last night. And now the wives of two Phantoms attacked on the Beltway at the start of rush hour. Sounds like we're going up against some mighty badass dudes who really don't care who gets between them and their target."

"The assassins taken out last night had ties to the Russian mob," Joshua said. "Where does the mob figure into all this besides them being the muscle?"

"Our friend told me the direction you're going on your end," she said, "I'll start digging through FBI records to see if I can find anything on my end."

"They may be badass," Joshua said while watching Murphy elbow his way through the rescuers to get to Jessica, "but they just made a very bad mistake."

"What's that?"

"They've made it personal."

Murphy waded through the rescuers to reach the passenger side of the cruiser. Peering through the men between him and the car, he could see Jessica pushing against the crushed door from the inside to free herself, while the workers on the outside were prying it open on their side.

She's alive!

For the first time since he had landed on the freeway, Murphy felt as if he could breathe.

The door opened with a loud creak of dented metal against metal. Jessica scurried out like she was afraid the cruiser would go back over the edge with her in it.

A rescuer was reaching for her hand when Murphy pushed him aside to take her into his arms.

Never had she felt so good. She belonged there.

"Oh, Murphy," she gasped into his chest, "you're here! I was afraid—" She clung to him with both arms.

"Sshhh." Murphy kissed her on the forehead before wrapping his arms around her and holding her as tightly as he could. "I just want to hold you."

Joshua made it to the driver's side of the cruiser in time for the rescuers to pry open the door and Cameron to climb out. Taking her into his arms, he could feel her body trembling. "You had me worried," he whispered into her hair.

"You think I wasn't?" She tightened her grip around him. "Hold me," she said into his neck while an EMT draped a blanket over her to prevent shock.

"I may never let you go." He tightened his grip only to have her push him away when they heard sobbing from the back seat of the car.

"Izzy. I need to be there. I promised—" She turned around in time to gather the girl crawling out of the crumbled cruiser into her arms and hold her tight while she sobbed into Cameron's shoulder. Jessica and Murphy ran around from the other side of the car to take the girl into a group hug which included emergency workers trying to examine the victims for injuries. With the group huddled around the girl, Joshua couldn't get a clear look at her, other than to see that her hair was a mass of tight ash-blonde curls.

"I-I was so sc-scared," the girl wept while holding on tightly to Cameron. "Why. . .what. . .they were trying to kill—" Shoving Cameron away with both hands, she dropped down onto her knees and threw up—expelling half-digested banana split onto Joshua Thornton's shiny white shoes.

"Oh, man," Murphy groaned into Jessica's ear. "This is not good. Not good at all."

The participants of the group hug jumped back, while an EMT draped the blanket he had been trying to cover Izzy with down across her shoulders. "We need to take her to the hospital to check her out." With a jerk of his chin at Jessica, who had returned to Murphy's embrace, and Cameron, he said, "We need to take all three of you into the hospital."

Cameron dropped down to the ground where Izzy was clutching her stomach. "We'll go with you, honey. Josh and I aren't going to leave you. We'll stay with you to make sure nothing else happens to you."

Izzy turned to look over at Cameron, who was hugging her shoulders. "Who's Josh?"

"My husband." Cameron helped her up to her feet. "He's right here."

Izzy raised her eyes up from the discharged ice cream treat covering the white shoes, up the stark white slacks to the uniform covered with ribbons and medals to the face of the man studying her behind dark sunglasses.

"This is my husband Joshua Thornton," Cameron said. "Josh, this is Izzy."

Dropping her eyes to his soiled shoes, Izzy said, "Sorry 'bout barfing on your feet."

"That's okay," he said. "They're only shoes." Grasping her shoulder in a loving grip, he smiled. "Let's get you ladies checked out and then catch these bad guys."

"That poor girl has had such a tough week," Murphy whispered to Joshua while they stared into their drinks in the hospital waiting room. "First she loses her mother, who ends up not being her mother—which we still haven't told her about yet. Then she's put in a group home where a teenaged Al Capone tries to take her iPad in exchange for protection. Then she gets shot at, run off the road, and almost killed." He took a long drink from the bottled water he had gotten from the vending machine.

"Cameron's week isn't much better." Joshua fingered the loose label of his soft drink bottle. "Thank God they're all right. Shaken up, but all right. They didn't end up on Graham's hit list."

"So you admit—"

"We're missing something." Letting out a breath, Joshua sat up in his seat.

"What?" The frustration in Murphy's tone was unmistakable.

"The connection between Graham and the Russian mob," Joshua said.

"He's made a deal with them," Murphy said. "He supplies them with illegal arms or information for them to sell to Iran or terrorists or the drug cartels—take your pick—in exchange for the syndicate providing clean-up service after his messes."

"I looked at Francine Baxter's files, son," Joshua said. "Nowhere do I see any evidence, circumstantial or otherwise of him supplying information or arms to the Russian mob—not even a hint of it."

"Then he's using someone else as a go-between," Murphy said. "Someone close to him." A broad grin crossed his face. "Dolly Scanlon." He snapped his fingers. "She was briefing him about the hit at Starbucks. She gave him the information about the anti-military blogger."

"But why come after us?" Cameron came into the waiting room and slipped her arm across Joshua's shoulders. "I got a blue ribbon for good health. A few bruises here and there, but otherwise clean." Easing down onto the seat next to him, she kissed Joshua on the lips before continuing, "As for our bad guy, I never talked to General Graham. He had no way of knowing Jessica and I were a threat."

"He wanted to get to me," Murphy said. "What better way to get me out of the way than to go after my wife, who was in your car?"

"No offense, Murphy," Joshua said, "but you're not really a threat. General Graham's nomination has not been threatened—yet. As far as he knows, he's not a suspect. He didn't get where he is being stupid. You're simply a lieutenant. As far as Graham knows, he can squash you and your investigation like a bug with one phone call to the army's chief of staff." He shook his head. "Something else happened to trigger this."

Murphy wasn't paying attention. Upon seeing Jessica coming out of the examination room, he was trotting down the hall to take her into his arms.

"Colonel Lincoln Clark could have called him," Cameron told Joshua. "Paige Graham outed Jessica at the Clark place. He threw us out."

"Paige Graham?" Joshua looked up at where Jessica and Murphy joined them.

"General Graham's wife," Jessica said. "She leads the army officers' wives club with an iron fist."

"Which means her husband's reputation is very important to her," Joshua said.

"She saw us nosing around at Clark's place," Cameron said. "She called her husband, who called out the hitmen."

"That's all speculation," Joshua said.

Cameron groaned. "You're going into lawyer mode again."

"The President will not withdraw his nomination without real evidence of any wrongdoing on the part of General Sebastian Graham," Joshua said. "We can speculate from here to doomsday but without any hard irrefutable proof of anything, General Sebastian Graham is on his way to becoming chief of staff of the army."

"Excuse me," a nurse stepped into the waiting room to break the glaring contest between Joshua and the rest of the group. "Are any of you family members for Isadora Crenshaw?"

"She has no family," Murphy said forcibly in Joshua's direction. "Someone murdered them."

Joshua fired back his own glare.

"I'm sorry to hear that," the nurse replied.

Seeing that the nurse was embarrassed to have walked into the middle of their emotional debate, Jessica laid her hand on her elbow. "We're legally responsible for Izzy."

"The doctor has finished examining her," the nurse said. "She's a little banged up. Some scrapes and bruises, mainly. She's been shaken up pretty bad."

"She threw up," Cameron said.

"That was due to the emotional trauma," the nurse said. "The doctor gave her a very mild sedative. It's already making her drowsy. You can take her home with you. She'll probably sleep through the night."

After the nurse escorted Cameron down the hallway to the examination room to help Izzy out of her robe and dress to go home, Jessica touched Murphy's arm to break the glaring contest he was engaging in with his father. "I'll go hail a cab to take us home." With the point of her finger, she ordered them, "You two play nice while I'm gone."

Too angry to stay with his father, Murphy turned to follow after her only to find Joshua's hand on his arm—holding him back.

"I do intend to make sure Graham is held accountable for what he's done," Joshua said in a low voice. "But we have to go about it the right way."

"How's that?" Murphy asked.

"When we get home, I want to hear word for word what you overheard at the Ritz this morning. Maybe we'll get lucky and you heard more than you thought."

As soon as the taxi pulled up in front of the Faraday-Thornton brownstone, Tristan threw open the front door and hurried down the steps to meet them. "Are you sure everyone's okay?" he asked. "Dad's called twice and Archie three times. He's threatening to fly out here."

When he saw Joshua Thornton in his naval uniform climb out of the front passenger seat, he jumped to stand at attention even though he had never been in the military. "Mr. Thornton!"

"You called me Josh at the wedding," he replied while holding the rear door open for Murphy, whose arms were full with a sleeping Izzy, to climb out. Cameron ran up the steps to go inside to prepare Izzy's bed.

"Why are you standing at attention?" Jessica asked Tristan in a low voice after climbing out behind Murphy.

"Just something about him compels me to." The cab was pulling away when Tristan turned to her to demand, "Why didn't you tell me that *he* was here?" He yanked his cell phone from his pocket. His fingers flew across the screen.

"Because between closing down the Capital Beltway during rush hour and hanging out in the ER, I've been a little busy." She tried to read the name of the contact he was urgently texting. "Who are you texting? Dad?"

"No, Sarah." He was breathing heavily while pacing up and down the sidewalk. "Abort. Abort. Oh, God, I hope she hasn't left yet."

CHAPTER TWENTY-FIVE

While Jessica and Cameron were putting Izzy to bed, Murphy started running a bath for Jessica in the master bathroom. He knew from experience that the shock from the accident would make her sore the next day. Nothing like a hot whirlpool bath and deep massage to ease the soreness.

Holding the soiled pair of white navy shoes, Joshua was admiring the view from the window seat in the sitting room when Murphy came out of the bathroom. "I have to tell you, this is nothing like the apartment your mother and I started out in when we got married."

"What is it Mom used to tell us every time we had to move?" Murphy went to his closet on the other side of the bedroom. "It isn't how many bedrooms or bathrooms or windows that make a house a home. It's the occupants." He knelt down to pick up a pair of white navy shoes from the shoe rack. Holding them up, he said, "I think you and I have the same size feet."

"So you did listen to me about making sure you had a spare uniform." Joshua took the shoes and checked the label inside for the size. "Thank God you're not Donny. His feet are two sizes bigger than mine."

"Donny has gorilla feet."

Tucking the fresh shoes under his arm, Joshua said, "Now let's see what else you have that fits me. My suitcase is still at the Pentagon and I'd really like to get out of these whites."

Stepping aside, Murphy gestured to the interior of the closet. "The store is open. Take whatever you need."

While searching through Murphy's drawers for slacks and a shirt, Joshua said, "I see Cameron has really taken to Izzy."

"So has Irving," Murphy said. "And the dogs. Even Tristan's spider likes her."

Joshua paused in his search. "Monique? She's met Monique?"

"Tristan's townhouse got flooded," Murphy said. "He's staying with us while repairs are being made and, apparently, kennels don't take tarantulas."

With a chuckle, Joshua resumed his search. "I half expect Mac Faraday to show up at your door with Gnarly to join the party."

"I like Gnarly," Murphy said. "I don't like Monique."

Having selected his change of clothes, Joshua stepped out of the closet. "The truth is, when you get married, like it or not, you become part of a whole 'nother family. And you know what they say. You can chose your friends but not your family—even when you marry into it."

"I really love the Faradays," Murphy said. "Mac scares the daylights out of me, but I can get used to that."

"Do you think Tristan can get used to me scaring him?" Joshua said with a grin.

"Him, I'm not so sure."

"How long has he been seeing Sarah?"

"Since the wedding," Murphy said. "But not in the traditional sense. They have not actually gone out on a real date."

"It's tough to date long distance, especially when you're attending a military academy," Joshua said.

"I think they have a hook up planned for real soon," Murphy said in a low voice. "But pretend you don't know about it. It makes things more exciting."

"You can be so cruel sometimes," Joshua replied in a whisper.

"It's in my genes."

Downstairs, Jessica walked into the kitchen to find Tristan hissing into the phone. "I don't know what he's doing here. I didn't ask … No, *Murphy* didn't blow our cover. He doesn't know." Seeing his sister, he said, "Just a minute." Hitting the mute button, he said, "Sarah is halfway here from Annapolis and everything is at a dead halt because the beltway is still closed due to fuel clean up from *your* accident."

"*My* accident?" Jessica put a hand on her hip. "Oh, yeah, I asked those hitmen to shoot at Cameron's cruiser."

"Help me out, sis," Tristan said with a plea in his voice. "Sarah and I had a totally romantic hook-up planned."

With wide eyes, Jessica's usually calm tone took on a hysterical tone. Clutching her breast, she cried out, "Not here!"

"Of course not," Tristan said.

Letting out a sigh of relief, Jessica said, "Thank you, God. I had visions of Murphy coming downstairs in the middle of the night to find you and his sister in your birthday suits making margaritas."

Envisioning Murphy's stunningly sensuous sister naked, Tristan said in a breathy voice, "That would be totally awesome."

"You do know Murphy can kill you with his pinky?" Jessica replied.

"But it would be totally awesome until he did," Tristan said. "No problem, sis. I booked us a room at the Embassy Suites. One of the top floors with a view of D.C. that's to die for. I got champagne, flowers, and even booked a couple's massage."

"Did you listen to a word I said to you the other day about the risk you two would be taking?" Jessica said. "About how awkward things will be for our two families if things don't work out since Murphy and I are married?"

"I heard every word you said," Tristan said, "and I talked to Sarah about it."

"And?"

"We decided you have no room to talk."

"But—"

Tristan pressed his finger to her lips. "You and Murphy got married thirty-six hours after meeting each other, sis. Now you were the one who introduced us. Therefore, you need to help us out. Sarah was going to swing by here to pick me up, but between all traffic in the city coming to a screeching halt and the commander lying in wait upstairs—"

"Captain," Jessica corrected him.

"What?"

"Josh was promoted to captain."

"So now I'll get killed by a navy captain instead of a commander," Tristan said. "Is that supposed to make me feel important?"

"Just have Sarah meet you at the hotel," Jessica said. "No one will know she was ever in the city."

"Did you hear me?" Tristan asked. "Sarah can't get into the city."

"Where is she?" Jessica snatched the phone from his hand. "Sarah, where are you?"

When she didn't receive an answer, Tristan told her, "It's on mute."

Jessica hit the button to unmute the call. "Sarah, where are you?"

"I'm in Bowie with a bunch of ticked off motorists," Sarah said. "It's pretty ugly." Jessica heard a rustle of the phone followed by Sarah cursing loudly in the background. "Who taught you how to drive, buddy? A pre-schooler? Yeah? You wanna come over here and say that?"

Sarah returned to the phone to discover that Jessica had handed it back to Tristan to open up the tablet she had resting on the kitchen counter. "There's a Marriott Suites that's out of the way in Bowie. It's clean, nice, quiet, and can be romantic."

"What's going on?" Sarah asked Tristan.

Jessica ordered, "Tell her to get off onto Route 301."

"Can you get off onto Route 301?" Tristan asked.

"I'm right there," Sarah said with excitement in her tone.

"Tell her to go down Route 301 to Mitchellville Road," Jessica instructed while typing away on the tablet. "Find the Travel Suites, it's a Marriott." With a flourish of her hand, she grinned. "I made reservations for a suite for you two kids under the name Faraday."

"I'm on my way," Sarah yelled out of the phone's speaker. "You're a sweetheart, Jessie."

"I know," she said.

"Oh, and Tristan," Sarah said with a husky tone, "I got that gift you sent to me. I can't wait for us to break it in."

"Neither can I. See you later." Disconnecting the call, he shook his head at Jessica. "You know I don't have a car."

"What present did you send to her?" Jessica took her keys off a key hook on the wall and tossed them to him.

He caught the keys in mid-air. "Nothing."

Observing a pink tone in his cheeks, she cocked her head at him. "Are you sure?"

"Positive. Thanks, sis." He kissed her cheek before galloping down the stairs leading to the garage.

"Be gentle with her," she called after him.

"Oh, I'm sure Sarah can take care of herself."

"I was talking about the Ferrari," she replied.

Jessica didn't realize how tense she was until she slipped into the hot, whirling water of the sunken tub. With a moan of pleasure, she sank back to rest her head against Murphy's shoulder. Taking her into his arms, he massaged her thighs. The warm touch of his hands made her melt against him.

"That feels great." She turned her head to nuzzle his neck.

"You will be sore tomorrow," he said in a low voice. "A good massage to relax your muscles before the soreness sets in will do you a world of good." He rubbed her hips and thighs.

"You take such good care of me." She ran her fingertips along his chin.

He smiled back at her.

She slid up to press her back against him.

Taking in a deep breath, he turned her head to plant a long, lingering kiss on her cheek. "I love you," he whispered into her ear.

Rubbing his thighs on either side of her, she grinned at him. He wrapped his arms around her to hold her close while kissing her deeply.

Pressing his chin against her forehead, he said, "I'm selling my bike."

She pulled away so fast that the water slapped up against the sides of the tub to splash onto the floor. Whirling around, she asked, "What?"

The moment ruined, he repeated in a stronger voice. "I'm going to sell my bike."

"That's what I thought you said," she replied. "Where did that come from?" A hint of anger crept into her tone. "You love that bike."

"I love you more."

"Have I told you to sell it?"

"No, but—"

"Then why in heaven's name would you even consider selling it?" Her voice went up a full octave.

"Because seeing you in that cruiser dangling twenty feet above that road made me realize what you must go through every time I take that bike out," Murphy said. "I was only watching for five to ten minutes, but those were the longest minutes of my life. I didn't know if I was ever going to have this with you again—" he gestured at the two of them naked in the tub. "I thought I was going to lose you. And if I put you through that every time I go out riding, then I don't want it."

She gazed at him for several beats before her expression softened. Once again, she moved in to wrap her arms around his shoulders. "You were talking to Tristan. He told you about Felicia."

"Why didn't you?"

He saw the answer to his question when she swallowed. Tears seeped into her violet eyes. She licked her lips and rested her head on his shoulder. He held her close.

"I don't want you to sell the bike," she finally said. "I know you love it. You'll be destined to resent me for it. One day, in the middle of a fight, you'll bring it up and I'll feel horrible."

"I can't enjoy riding it if I know you're worried sick when I'm out on it," Murphy said.

She lifted her head from his shoulder. Her eyes met his. "I'm worried sick every time you leave this house. I'm not naïve. When you go on a mission, odds of you not coming back are worse than when you go out riding. You think I don't know the score? If you get captured on one of those missions, there will be no arrest—they'll just kill you and probably in some horrendous matter. The federal government will deny that you ever existed. There'll be no chaplain coming to the door to give me his condolences, because your missions are off the grid. There'll be no funeral because no one will know where your body is. You'll just kiss me good-bye one day and leave this house and I'll never see you again. The only way that I'll know for certain that you're gone for good will be a coded message from your CO directing me to open that dreaded death box of yours and to follow the instructions inside."

"You can consider yourself lucky," Murphy said. "In the black ops, families and spouses are left totally in the dark. You're lucky that the Joint Chiefs chose to let spouses know."

Pressing her forehead against his, she said in a low voice, "Sometimes, when you're gone on a mission, I feel like it would be easier for me if I was in the dark."

He held her tight. "I am so sorry you have to go through all this."

Lifting her head, she met his gaze. "Tell me, Lieutenant Thornton, are you going to leave the Phantoms?"

Slowly, Murphy shook his head.

"I wouldn't ask you to," she said. "I knew what I was getting into when we got married."

Glaring at him with piercing violet eyes, she lifted up out of the water to straddle him. "If you sell that bike, I'm going to have to hurt you." She brought her mouth close to his. "Do you understand what I am saying, my love?"

He brought his lips to hers. "Yes, ma'am."

CHAPTER TWENTY-SIX

On the rooftop terrace, Joshua was startled out of his admiration of the multi-colored lights of the Capital Wheel, as close as a football field away, by the touch of cold glass on the back of his arm. He turned around to find Murphy offering him beer in a frosted mug. Like father, the son had changed into black jeans and a black pullover. Instead of shoes, he went barefoot.

"Brewsky?" Murphy asked.

Upon seeing what appeared to be beer in his son's other hand, Joshua said, "I thought you didn't drink."

Murphy held up the mug for him to see. "It's Clausthaler Amber. Non-alcoholic and totally organic. Tastes just like the real thing without any of the toxins. Want a taste?"

Intrigued, Joshua gave Murphy his drink in favor of having a taste of the German beer. He was surprised to find that it did indeed taste like the real stuff. "Interesting." He traded back before turning back to admire the Ferris wheel.

"I have six cooling in the fridge and a whole case down in the pantry if you want to switch after you finish that." Murphy stepped up to stand next to him. "I suppose you want to get to work."

"Nah, I would prefer to just take in your view while our killer moves closer to a slot on the Joint Chiefs of Staff," Joshua said in in a sarcastic tone. Murphy was about to reply when a voice sounded from directly behind them.

Startled, Joshua whirled around. Jessica's voice was coming out of a built-in intercom on the wall. "I'm going to pour a glass of wine for myself. Cameron, Murphy has a case of non-alcoholic beer. It's organic. Would you like one?"

Throwing open the bedroom door on the other side of the sitting room, Cameron announced that she preferred a root beer instead. Looking around confused, she asked, "Wait, where's Jessica?"

With a laugh, Murphy stepped into the sitting room to show them the intercom before pressing the button to order a root beer for Cameron.

"Roger, that," Jessica replied. "Be up in a few."

While Murphy was placing her drink order, Cameron went out onto the terrace and stopped short when she saw Joshua reach out to grasp her hand before kissing her on the cheek. "What happened to your beard?"

Her outburst was so sudden that he had to laugh. "You just now noticed that?" He gestured at the bedroom she had just left. "You didn't even notice it when we were in the shower together?"

"Don't tell me that you shaved it off a month ago," she said with a hint of warning in her voice while brushing her hand across his jaw and chin. His five o'clock stubble scratched her palm.

Joshua slipped his arms around her waist. "No, I had to shave it off early this morning before appearing before the Joint Chiefs of Staff. If I had known I had so much leverage, I would have requested a waiver to keep it."

"And your long hair." Cameron ran her fingers through his non-existent locks. His hair, that had only the day before fallen to the top of his collar in silver waves, was now cut into a proper military style—not touching his ears or collar. With a deep sigh, she said, "My darling silver fox, you did this to help us catch Nick's killer."

Joshua took her hand and kissed her fingertips before caressing her hand against his chest. "It's only hair. It will grow back."

Carrying a serving tray, Jessica stepped onto the terrace. She handed a glass of ice and a bottle of root beer to Cameron before taking her own glass of white wine, which she held up. "May I make a toast to my newest relatives in our first home together?"

"Of course," Joshua said.

"You probably know, but Murphy may not," Jessica began, "my dad was adopted as a baby—"

"I knew that," Murphy said with a grin.

She held up her hand to stop him. "But this you may not know. My adopted grandmother was a robust Italian from a huge family, and my grandfather was an Irish Catholic, who loved nothing more than to tell an Irish yarn and had a toast for every occasion. This toast was a favorite one of his and it seems very appropriate for this week."

"Now you have me worried," Murphy said.

"Here it is." She held up her glass. "May your home always be too small to hold all your friends."

"And pets," Murphy added with a laugh while they clinked their glasses and took sips. "Especially Monique. Tristan did take Monique with him, didn't he?"

"I'll take care of Monique," Jessica assured him. "You won't even know she's here."

Joshua pulled a chair out from the table on the terrace and sat down. "Well, I hate to spoil our fun, but we have a lot of work to do. While we were waiting in the ER, I called Ripley Vacarro, the FBI agent assigned to investigate the shooting on the beltway, to dig out every record they have on Graham. Maybe there's something buried—"

"What about Dolly Scanlon?" Murphy asked.

"As his personal assistant, she has to have a security clearance since her job is to follow him around," Joshua said. "The FBI did participate in the background checks on both of them. I'm hoping that maybe something turned up in their background investigations."

Murphy sat forward in his seat. "How far back did you ask Ripley to look?"

"I told her to get me everything," Joshua said. "But we don't have a lot of time. Graham will be going to Capitol Hill tomorrow to be interviewed by the Senate."

"At one point, the FBI did find something that threatened Graham's security clearance." In an effort to knock the memory loose, Murphy tapped his forehead with his fingertips. "Graham was laughing about it this morning in talking about how clean his record is and how smooth his career has gone."

"The FBI had to have uncovered the rapes," Cameron said.

"But since Graham pleaded to misdemeanors," Joshua said, "then it would not really threaten his clearance, especially with his father paving the way."

"It was after he came back from the Gulf War," Murphy recalled.

"It might be nothing, or it may be the key to this whole thing." Joshua searched through the contacts on his cell phone for Ripley Vaccaro before bringing the phone to his ear. "There's only one way to find out." He thrust the phone into Murphy's hand. "Here, ask her yourself."

Covering his other ear to hear the agent more clearly, Murphy stepped away from the table.

Cameron said, "There has to be someone who knows what is going on and, under the right circumstances, will testify against General Graham. Maybe if we confront Paige Graham with such undeniable proof of his affairs, she'll be so furious that she'll give us everything we need." She grinned. "From what I've seen, she's all about appearances. Humiliate her by making her husband's affairs public—in such a way that there's no denying it—and she'll bury him with everything she's got."

"Maureen's sister-in-law did say Paige Graham was very vindictive," Jessica agreed.

"We don't have enough time for that," Joshua got up from the table. "There's too much at stake and too little time. I'm not just worried about getting General Sebastian Graham locked up." Stepping up to the wall lining the terrace, he observed the brightly lit Washington Monument. "There's a more critical issue at stake here. It's the Phantoms."

"What about the Phantoms?" Jessica asked.

"The Phantoms were created by the Joint Chiefs of Staff to operate off the grid—at their bidding," Joshua said. "They answer to no one else. The only ones who know about them are the members of the Joint Chiefs of Staff."

Murphy hung up the phone. "Not even their assistants know about us."

"If a serial rapist and killer gets into a position where he has an elite team like the Phantoms at his disposal," swallowing, Joshua shook his head, "the whole reason behind the operation would be at risk."

"We were established to protect our country and its citizens from people exactly like Graham who are already in leadership positions." Murphy gazed out at the Capital Wheel. "We have to do something to keep that from happening."

"You said Dolly Scanlon was reporting to Graham about the hit at Starbucks," Joshua said.

"And she knew the victim was an anti-military blogger," Murphy said, "which hadn't been released to the media. She mentioned having a source."

"She either knew that information before the hit because she and Graham were behind it," Joshua said, "or they have an informant inside the investigation who told her."

"Perry Latimore?" Murphy asked. "Or Crotch?"

"Why would they do that?" Joshua asked. "My money is on her knowing it first-hand."

"Because *she* hired the hit men?" Cameron said.

"Arranged the contract for Graham," Joshua said. "She is Graham's personal assistant. He's been using the Russian mob to clean up his messes. Well, as big as he is, he can't be caught calling the mob himself to order them to clean up this mess."

"So he has his assistant do it for him," Murphy said.

"But as careful as Francine Baxter was—I mean using burner phones and password-protecting her documents—how did Graham find out about it?" Joshua asked.

"Lincoln Clark told him," Jessica said. "Maureen's brother and sister-in-law told us that she was leaving him and was scared to death that he would sense something was up."

"He must have started snooping around and found out about the meeting," Cameron said. "He definitely knows who's behind his wife's murder."

"Now we're getting someplace." Joshua picked up his cell phone. "If we can get Clark to admit he told Graham about Maureen's plan to expose him as a rapist, we can threaten Clark with multiple counts of conspiracy to commit homicide. It might be enough to make him turn on the general."

"If he lives long enough to testify against him," Murphy said.

"Clark will lawyer up if you go anywhere near him," Jessica warned.

"No problem," Joshua said. "This investigation is now off the grid and no lawyers are invited."

CHAPTER TWENTY-SEVEN

Colonel Lincoln Clark's Home - Night

After a long day of having condolences heaped upon him both at home and at the wake, as well as making numerous calls to his lawyer and insurance company handling Maureen's life insurance policy, Colonel Lincoln Clark was exhausted.

So was Tommy. A child handles exhaustion differently from a middle-aged man and, in his inconsolable grief, Tommy could not understand that his mother was never going to return home. After hours of trying to soothe the five year old enough for him to fall asleep, Lincoln's patience was to the breaking point.

There's a reason I secretly had a vasectomy before marrying Maureen, Lincoln cursed while pouring himself a good stiff drink. *So I wouldn't have to deal with squalling kids.* Reminding himself that he was going to have to have another talk with Sebastian Graham about this turn of events, and the need for a nanny—preferably one who was young and eager to please— he downed his scotch in one gulp and poured another before going upstairs to bed.

Lincoln was on the verge of sleep when he heard the security alarm go off. Grabbing his gun out of the nightstand, he crept down the stairs, dressed only in his boxer shorts, in search of the intruder. In the foyer, he went to the control panel to check the screen. It flashed an error code that indicated that the system had been tripped by a power surge.

"Damn it!" Lincoln cursed before resetting the alarm. While scurrying across the foyer in his bare feet to go back up the stairs, he saw a shadow move in the living room. "Who's there?"

Pointing his weapon at the floor, he eased his way into the living room. Breathing heavily, he scanned every corner of the room in search of the interloper. He was about to let out a sigh of relief when he saw a movement in the dining room.

"I see you in there!" Lincoln yelled. "I have a gun and I'm not afraid to use it."

His threat was met with silence.

Gingerly making his way across the cold hardwood floor, Lincoln stepped into the dining room—gun first. Before he could pass the threshold into the room, an arm came crashing down on both wrists holding his weapon. Before he had time to realize what was happening, the intruder had him face down on the floor and was pressing the muzzle of his own gun to the base of his neck.

"You're making a big mistake!" Lincoln yelled. "I have friends—" His threats were cut short with a knee pressed against his shoulder blade while his hands were being zip-tied behind his back.

Effortlessly, he was pulled up from the floor and shoved into the chair at the head of the dining room table. This was the first chance he had to see his attacker.

In the darkness of the room, late at night, all Lincoln could see was a tall, slender, and powerfully-built man dressed in black, right down to the black hoodie, with the hood pulled up. He had a utility belt strapped low on his hips. Even in the dark, Lincoln could make out the forms of semi-automatic pistols in holsters on both sides of his hip and a knife in a sheath strapped to one thigh. He wore black leather gloves.

Between the hoodie and the darkness, the colonel was unable to see his face.

"The police are going to crucify you when they get here!" Lincoln yelled. "You tripped the alarm. They're on their way."

Without a word, the dark figure moved down the length of the long dining room table.

"If you know what's good for you, you'll just take what you want and get out of here."

Instead of going about robbing the home, the figure turned around the chair at the other end of the table and straddled the back. All Lincoln could see was the silhouette of a man sitting still and silent across from him. While he couldn't see his eyes, he could feel him staring at him.

"What do you want?"

Without a word, the figure pointed a finger at the colonel.

"Me? Who sent you?" A gasp came from his lips. "*She* sent you … Why would she have sent you after me?"

The figure did not move or make a sound.

"I did all that I was told," Lincoln said. "If it wasn't for me calling Dolly when I found those texts Francine Baxter had sent to Maureen, telling her about their plans to expose Graham, his nomination to Chiefs of Staff would have been history. I did that! I saved him! Would I have done that if I was a threat?"

The lack of response from the figure only frightened Lincoln Clark more. He would have preferred it if the intruder provided some clue that he was listening—either by nodding his head in agreement or shaking it in argument. Anything would have been better than his silence.

"All these years, I've kept quiet about Graham raping Maureen after sending me off to the Middle East," Lincoln said. "Never once did I ask for money to raise Tommy. All I ever asked of Graham was that he remember my loyalty when it came to my career. I could have threatened him. I could have done a lot of things, but I didn't. Damn it! I let him rape and then kill my wife—damn it!"

The silence pushing him over the edge, Lincoln raged, "Say something, you son of a bitch!"

In silence, the figure stood up from the chair and went into the kitchen.

Assuming the assassin was going for a butcher knife to finish his assignment, Lincoln took deep breaths while fighting the angry tears coming to his eyes. He waited in silence, until he heard the sound of police sirens approaching from the distance.

A block away, Murphy Thornton ducked into the bushes where he had his motorcycle concealed. "Dad, did you get that?" He opened the carrier department under the seat and pulled the hoodie off over his head. "Clark called Dolly Scanlon when he discovered Maureen's plans for exposing Graham." He folded up the hoodie and placed it in the carrier department. He then took out a light leather riding jacket and helmet.

"Got it," Joshua responded. "The techs recorded everything and are forwarding it to the chiefs now. Good work."

"I did just like you told me. I didn't say a word." Chuckling, Murphy shrugged into the jacket and straddled his motorcycle. "I can't believe how he spilled everything."

"Basic human principle, son. The imagination can be so much scarier than reality." With a laugh, Joshua said, "Think about every time you've confessed to me about things you did growing up. The vast majority of the time, it wasn't because of the questions I asked, it was because I didn't say anything. I just gave you the evil eye and let your imagination do the job."

"Damn!"

Constitution Avenue, Washington, D.C.

The existence and location of General Sebastian Graham's love nest for his extramarital activities was common knowledge to the higher ranking officers around the Pentagon. It took only one phone call to General Johnston to get the address and apartment number.

Joshua Thornton was uncertain if the condo's proximity to the Capitol Building, only two blocks away, was meant to be ironic or merely convenient.

Sitting in the front seat of Murphy's SUV, watching some of the most famous and powerful of Capitol Hill going into the apartment building with companions who Joshua could tell were not their spouses, he concluded that it was simply convenience.

After receiving confirmation from Murphy that Lincoln Clark had sold his wife out to Dolly Scanlon, Joshua slipped out of the driver's seat, checked the equipment on his utility belt, including his service weapon, and trotted across the street. Bypassing the front entrance, which was guarded by a doorman who had a build not unlike that of a professional football linebacker, he turned the corner and went around to the service entrance.

In the alley, he examined the lock on the rear door. As he expected, the thirty-year-old building did not have up-to-date locks or security. Surveillance cameras would threaten revealing the secret lifestyles of those who lived—or, rather, frequently visited—the apartment building. Robbery, injury, or even death would be preferable to public exposure risked by a leaked security video.

In less than one minute, Joshua picked the lock on the rear door. On his way inside, he slipped a magnetic plate over the latch. The door would shut without latching.

"I'm in," he whispered for the benefit of Murphy listening in through his earpiece. "Service entrance door is unlocked. Come on up when you get here."

"Copy that," Murphy replied. "I'm on my way." Joshua could hear the roar of the motorcycle in the background.

Down the hallway, Joshua heard a washer and dryer running to the groaning and moaning of a woman. Slipping past the doorway, he peeked inside to see a red-haired woman in her late fifties, if not early sixties, on top of a washer that seemed to be in the spin cycle.

Jewels hung from her wrinkled neck, dripped from her ears, and adorned her bony fingers. Wearing red stiletto heels, her legs were wrapped around a young man, who was naked from the waist down.

His face filled with determination, the young man was pumping his hips while she snapped orders at him like a queen to a servant.

Joshua recognized the woman as an influential congresswoman—married to a powerful CEO who was much older and bore no resemblance to the man servicing her.

I have a feeling, Josh, we're not in Chester anymore.

Closing the door, Joshua hurried down the hallway to the stairwell and climbed up to the fifth floor. Making his way to a two-bedroom corner unit, he used his lockpick to effortlessly unlock the door and enter the apartment.

Once inside, he could hear the sounds of sex coming from the master bedroom on the other side of the apartment.

What kind of place is this?

He was creeping toward the bedroom when Murphy's voice inside his ear made him jump. "Dad, are you okay?"

"Will you stop doing that?" Joshua hissed as quietly as possible.

"Doing what?"

"Sneaking up on me."

"I'm not even there," Murphy replied. "I'm eight minutes out."

Grumbling, Joshua pressed himself up against the wall and eased the bedroom door open to peer inside.

Naked, Dolly Scanlon straddled Sebastian Graham's midsection. Panting, moaning, groaning, and uttering dirty platitudes of ecstasy, they were so enthralled with their sexual exercise that a three ring circus complete with elephants could have entered the room and marched around the bed without either of them noticing.

"Get your butt out here, Murphy. I'm going in." Joshua placed his hand on the grip of the gun he had in the holster. With a wide grin, he threw open the door and stepped into the bedroom. "Good evening, General, is this a bad time?" He flipped on the switch for the overhead light.

Shrieking and running ensued.

"Holy—" General Graham fell out of the bed in his scramble for clothes.

Cursing loudly, Dolly whirled around to where Joshua stood at the foot of the bed with a wicked grin on his face. "What the hell is this? Who do you think you are?"

"I'm the good guy on the trail of a cold-blooded killer," Joshua said, "and that trail has led me to this apartment."

"Is this some sort of sick joke?" General Graham jabbed his thumb at his chest. "I'm only one step away from the army's chief of staff. Now you may be navy, Thornton, but once the senate votes, all I have to do is say a word or two to the admiral and you'll find yourself out and that son of yours in a hell hole someplace."

"Yeah, so I've heard." Joshua plopped down on the edge of the bed.

"Heard what?" General Graham placed his feet into his boxers and pulled them up.

Joshua turned his head to avoid looking at his hips and thighs and privates covered in body fluid. On the other side of the bed, Dolly was lighting a cigarette with a jeweled lighter.

"I've been hearing that is a favorite threat of yours," Joshua said. "Throughout your career, it has been very effective in keeping your victims quiet." He chuckled at him. "I thought you knew me better than that, Sebastian. Those type of threats don't work with me."

"What are you talking about?"

"He's crazy." Dolly blew a stream of smoke out of the side of her mouth. "Call General Johnston."

"Yeah, let's do that." Joshua dug the cell phone out of the case on his utility belt. "We'll make a party of it. We can add Admiral Patterson for fun. How about General Raleigh, too. We'll all have drinks and discuss the thing that Hannah Price, Maureen Clark, Colleen Davis, and Donna Crenshaw all have in common—besides them all being murdered, I mean."

General Graham eyed Joshua who waved his thumb over the contact number on his cell phone.

"Going once," Joshua taunted him. "Going twice. I guess we're going to have a party."

Before his thumb could make contact with the phone, General Graham snatched it out of his hand. "I did not engage in inappropriate behavior with any of those women. I've never even met Donna Crenshaw."

"But you did meet her sister. Cecelia Crenshaw." He leaned in to whisper, "I have the pictures."

His eyes growing wide, General Graham sucked in his bottom lip.

"So you admit it." Joshua snatched the phone back and placed it in the case on his belt.

"Yes, I had sex with Price, Clark, and Davis," General Graham said. "I also had sex with Cecelia Crenshaw. And yes, I'm married. But Paige and I have an agreement. She knows all about this apartment and my companions. You see, I have a very active libido, and Paige has no interest in sex. It is actually a relief to her for me to pursue my hobby here—with other women. So if you think you can blackmail me—"

"We're not talking about your infidelity," Joshua said. "I couldn't care less about any weird arrangements you have with your wife and your mistresses." He gestured at Dolly, who was still propped up on the pillows, smoking her cigarette. She had covered herself with a thin sheet. "What I do care about is rape and murder."

"I am not a rapist," General Graham said forcibly.

"You're not just a rapist, but a serial rapist and a murderer," Joshua said. "You raped three of the five women who were murdered in Reston the other day. The fourth woman was the sister of another rape victim who had your baby. Cecilia Crenshaw was found dead on the Pennsylvania Turnpike days after giving birth to someone we believe to be *your* baby. The fifth woman, the owner of the townhouse was Francine Baxter, who worked in human resources in the army. Cecilia went to her the morning after you raped her." He leaned forward to whisper to the General. "Baxter was a very good record keeper. She had uncovered copies of all the complaints of sexual assault that have been filed against you throughout your career—going all the way back to West Point."

"It was consensual sex with every one of those women." General Graham's face turned red. "It's a frame up—a conspiracy by my enemies who have their own protégés they want to see get on the Joint Chiefs of Staff."

Joshua's phone vibrated on his hip. Since only his CO, Murphy, and those connected to the Phantoms had the number for this special cell, he had to answer it. "And you expect me to believe that your enemies would be so bent on discrediting you that they would murder these women when they got together to plan how to stop you?" he replied while reading the caller ID. It read "Ripley."

"I didn't even know they were getting together," General Graham insisted.

Holding up his finger, Joshua rose from the bed and went over toward the doorway leading into the rest of the apartment. "Thornton here."

"Have you caught up with General Graham and Dolly Scanlon?" Ripley asked in a hurried tone.

"Yes." He looked across the room at where General Graham was pacing. His jaw was clenched and he was breathing heavily. The man was about ready to burst with outrage.

"Dolly Scanlon there, too?"

"Yes."

Eying Joshua, Dolly Scanlon put out her cigarette.

"You've got a problem with her," Ripley said. ""I checked through her records like Murphy asked. Everything looked clean until I realized her passport photo from seven years ago doesn't match the photo in her Office of Personnel Management folder. I checked NSA and several other agencies. None of them match her passport photo. We ran facial recognition programs and while the images are similar, they do not match. According to our background check, Dolly

Scanlon has no family. Raised in a Catholic orphanage. Went to Princeton. Totally clean. Somewhere along the line, in the last seven years, someone stole her identity."

Trying to appear casual, Joshua shrugged his shoulder. "I'll take care of that. No problem." Disconnecting the call, he shoved the phone into its case.

"Copy that, Dad," Murphy said in his ear, "I'm two blocks away."

"Now, where were we?" Scratching his neck with his left hand, he turned to the side to conceal his reach for the gun holstered on his right side. Slipping the gun from its holster he turned around to face the muzzle of a gun aimed right between his eyes.

Chapter Twenty-Eight

"Dolly, what are you doing?" General Sebastian Graham raged behind the naked woman pointing a silver-plated .45 caliber Colt semi-automatic at Joshua.

"She's not Dolly," Joshua told the general. "She stole Dolly Scanlon's identity and, if we're not mistaken, her security clearance to get close to you." He locked eyes with the woman holding the gun. "Most likely, the real Dolly Scanlon is dead."

The corners of her lips curled upwards.

"That has to be a mistake," General Graham said.

"Sebastian," Joshua said, "she's standing here aiming a gun at my face. I think we can safely assume in some way, shape, or form that she's a bad person."

With a moan, General Graham put his hands on his head and shook it. He collapsed onto the bed. "I need to call my lawyers." He gathered up his pants and began digging through the pockets.

"Drop that phone!" she ordered while keeping her gun aimed at Joshua.

"I pay my lawyers a lot of money to keep me out of bad situations," General Graham said. "I'm sure with the proper spin, that they should be able to get you and me out of this while making Josh out to be the bad guy. He broke into my apartment and started making deranged accusations. You feared for your safety, so you pulled a gun on him to protect yourself ... Yeah, that will work. I'm sure you understand, Josh. It's nothing personal."

"Drop that phone now!" she shouted.

The force of her demand caused the general to drop the phone to the floor and clasped his hands to his face.

"You," she ordered Joshua, "Toss your gun to the floor and kick it to me."

Without moving, Joshua said, "You don't want to do this."

She stepped toward him. "Do you think I would hesitate to kill you?" She laughed. "Don't tell me that you haven't figured it out. I killed five women the other day. Shot that old woman twice. Lincoln Clark had cloned his wife's phone so that he could read her texts. He told me that none of them knew each other. So it was easy for me to get into the old woman's place."

"You probably said you were one of the other women and got there early to help her set up," Joshua said.

"And I did set up," Dolly said with a grin.

"You put poison in the punch to kill them," Joshua said. "That made for four murders. Then, Donna Crenshaw arrived."

She took in a deep breath. "She knew Francine Baxter by sight. She thought I was one of the other ladies until we got up into the dining room and I said something that gave it away." With a shake of her head, she concluded. "That last one refused to go down as easily as the others. I had to put five bullets in her before she would die."

"Then you arranged for the murder of Emily Dolan," Joshua said.

"Well, I can't do everything," she said with a laugh. "Enough talk. Throw your gun to the floor."

Instead of following her order, Joshua told the general, "See what you've done, Sebastian?"

"I did not authorize those murders!" General Graham replied.

"I would not have had to kill any of them if they had just kept their mouths shut like they all agreed to do," she said. "We knew Maureen Clark was the weak link. She had a very bad attitude. It was only a matter of time before she would go public with Tommy being Sebastian's son. We weren't one bit surprised when Clark called to say that she was meeting with Sebastian's other victims."

"Victims is such an inflammatory word," General Graham said.

"We did get Tommy's DNA." Slipping his weapon back into its holster, Joshua eased forward. "It's at the lab now. That will prove that you're his birth father and you raped his mother."

"Be quiet!" With both hands on the gun, Dolly moved in closer to where Joshua was glaring at the general.

"Clark was going nowhere until I got behind him," General Graham said.

"After climbing on top of his unwilling wife." Joshua took a step toward him. "The only difference between you and those predators lurking in dark alleys is that you have a nicer uniform."

"Shut up!" she yelled.

General Graham climbed up onto his feet. "That's the way it's done in the real world, Josh! People do each other favors. You give me what I want, and I'll make your dreams come true. Clark wants to be a general. I introduced him and whispered the right things to the right people. If his wife had kept her mouth shut, then it was only a matter of time before it happened."

"Where was she when you two signed this agreement between men?" Joshua asked. "Did anyone ask her if she wanted to be a high-priced whore?"

"Any problem she had with the agreement was between her and her husband," General Graham said.

"I'm the one with the gun!" She shoved the gun into Joshua's chest.

With one hand, Joshua grabbed the top of the gun while shoving it around with the other. Stepping to the side, he thrust his foot at the side of her knee to buckle her leg out from under her.

By the time she hit the floor, Joshua was aiming her gun down at her. "Now who has the gun?"

The bedroom door burst in and Murphy raced in with two guns ready to fire. Finding a naked woman at his feet, he tried to look away. "Everything here taken care of, Captain?"

"What took you so long?" Joshua demanded to know.

"Traffic was a little backed up in Georgetown," Murphy holstered one of his weapons.

"You came through Georgetown? You took Clara Barton Parkway?"

Murphy nodded his head. "How did you think I got here?"

"George Washington Parkway," Joshua said.

"It's four miles longer."

"But the traffic moves faster."

"Maybe during rush hour, but it's not rush hour and Clara Barton is a more direct route."

"Hey," she said, "if we're done here—"

"Shut up," Joshua ordered.

"Your son is right." The general picked up his phone from the floor. "Clara Barton Parkway is faster during non-rush hour."

Murphy grinned broadly at Joshua.

Tucking the gun he had taken from her into the waist of his pants, Joshua told him, "Cuff her while I take care of one last thing."

Taking in her unclothed state, Murphy swallowed. "You want *me* to cuff *her*."

"Son, if you've never touched a naked woman before, you need to have a long talk with Jessica." Joshua went over to where General Sebastian Graham had already hit the speed dial for his lawyer.

"Good work, Joshua." General Graham put the phone to his ear. "I knew I could count on you to take care of things."

Joshua ripped the phone from his ear and hurled it across the room, where it shattered a mirror hanging on the wall. General Graham's mouth dropped open at the same time Joshua's fist punched him across the jaw. The general fell back onto the bed and slid unconscious to the floor.

"To answer your earlier question, Sebastian, I do understand but I still take it personally."

CHAPTER TWENTY-NINE

Since the Phantom investigation into the murders of the women was being conducted under the cover of NCIS, General Sebastian Graham and the unknown woman who had taken over Dolly Scanlon's identity were dressed and transported to the NCIS headquarters at Quantico to be interviewed.

The Phantom operation had too much to lose if General Sebastian Graham discovered their existence. Therefore, as far as the general and his mistress knew, the investigation of the murders at Francine Baxter's home, and the subsequent discoveries, was all done under NCIS, by a navy captain and lieutenant.

Upon the creation of the Phantom Team, the Chief of Staff for the United States Marines had arranged for a private headquarters for use when needed. An older building at the end of an out-of-the-way road at Quantico served the purpose perfectly. As far as everyone except the Phantoms knew, it was a retreat site for the Joint Chiefs of Staff to get away to work on classified projects in secrecy. The building had several offices, up to date computer technology, interrogation and observation rooms, and even four cells in which to temporarily hold prisoners.

The first order of business was to separate the general and his personal assistant so that they could not compare notes. Assuming that the murders and cover-ups were a conspiracy, they had obviously had more than enough time already to come up with their cover stories. Even if this was the case, Joshua and Murphy hoped that with things falling apart, self-preservation may move one or both of them to make deals in exchange for the truth.

After putting them each in a separate interrogation room, Murphy met Joshua in the observation room where he was watching General Sebastian Graham pace. Since seeing him at the Pentagon twelve hours earlier, the four-star general had transformed from a celebrated war hero on his way to the highest post in the United States Army, to a pathetic older man angrily clinging to what was left of his reputation. His face was pale and drawn. His dark hair with silver at the temples was disheveled from repeatedly rubbing his scalp in frustration.

He stopped and turned to the two-way mirror. "Thornton, I want to talk to General Johnston—now! You have no right to hold me here!"

"How pathetic," Murphy said.

"He's a four-star general," Joshua said. "I met him in Kuwait during the Gulf War. Back then, he was a good soldier."

"Who raped a fellow soldier and got away with it," Murphy said. "He's a serial rapist and killer."

"I agree."

"Who's never spent a day in jail and never will," Murphy said, "because the army doesn't want to tarnish its image by having one of their most celebrated and highest ranking officers exposed as a rapist and murderer who killed his way to the top."

Joshua cocked his head at him. "When did you get so cynical?"

"When I saw the list of victims whose lives this man has ruined over the last thirty years." Murphy jabbed his finger in the direction of the interrogation room. "How many times during this man's criminal career did the opportunity present itself to stop him? How many people turned their heads and looked the other way? All because doing the right thing would make them or their organization look bad, or because they didn't have the guts to go up against Graham and his friends in high places, or because it was more beneficial personally to cover it up. You know what? Every one of them—from the commandant at West Point to Colonel Clark—had a hand in creating Graham into the monster that he is today. They own a part in every rape and murder he's committed."

"And you think I'm going to be one of those people who will let him walk out of here?" Joshua asked.

"Not directly," Murphy said. "But he's claiming he did nothing wrong. I learned enough from you to know that in spite of the lists and reports Francine Baxter has, those women who did report the assaults ended up withdrawing their complaints after a few days. With their deaths, without them to testify, no way can we get him in court for rape."

"So you think we're beat?" A grin crossed Joshua's face. "You don't know me very well."

Feeling the vibration on his hip, Murphy took the cell phone out of its case to read the text from Ripley Vacarro. "FBI got a match on our phony Dolly Scanlon's fingerprints. She's Maya Fedorov. She immigrated here to the United States as a child with her family. Her father and brother are both in tight with the Russian crime family."

"Kalashov."

Gesturing with his cell phone, Murphy said, "You were looking for the connection between General Graham and the Russian mob. There you have it. It was his assistant and mistress."

Joshua was checking a text message on his phone. "Send a Phantom team to Fedorov's place to search for evidence proving her connection to the mob and what arrangements they have with Graham. Did you get that gun we took off her over to evidence?"

Murphy nodded his head. "The bullets were hollow, exactly like the type used on Baxter and Crenshaw. And forty-five caliber, too, which makes them the same size. The only problem is that the bullets they took out of our victims were too broken up for comparison."

"Won't need it," Joshua said. "We've recorded her confessing to the murders in Graham's apartment. Now we need to find a way to prove the general was involved in the conspiracy to take them out."

Murphy pressed the phone's speed dial number to connect with their commanding officer. "Are you going in to interrogate him?"

"Not quite yet," Joshua said with a sly grin.

While Murphy was on the phone to request the search, he noticed Joshua staring through the glass at the increasingly nervous general. He disconnected the call at the same time there was a knock on the door of the observation room.

Dressed completely in black, and wearing an armed utility belt, Major Seth Monroe stepped in. His eyes met Murphy's. "*Captain* Thornton?"

Murphy gestured at Joshua who turned from the window. "That would be me."

With a chuckle, the major said, "I should have known." He jerked his head in the direction of the hallway. "He's here.

We have him in the back of the van. What do you want us to do?"

"I want to play show and tell," Joshua replied with a grin.

"I had no knowledge of what that woman had done!" General Sebastian Graham raged when Joshua, carrying a thick folder under his arm, and Murphy stepped through the door. While Joshua approached the table, Murphy perched himself by the door.

"I am as much—more—" he emphasized with the pounding of his fist on the table top "—of a victim here than anyone else. No one wants to see you get to the truth more than I do!"

"Then why did you put Colonel Clark on the fast track as a reward for his silence in the rape of his wife?" Joshua asked in a steady tone.

"It was not rape!" the general yelled. "I am not a rapist! These women throw themselves at me! They seduce me! Okay, I have a weakness when it comes to the ladies. Then after it's over, they go bonkers and start screaming rape."

Without a word, Joshua sat down at the table and opened the folder only enough to reach inside and take out a photograph. He slid the photo to the other side of the table for the general to see.

Perplexed, the general pulled out the chair and sat down. His salt and pepper eyebrows met in the middle of his forehead as he picked up the picture and studied the image of a woman's face with a welt on her cheek and a bruised and swollen lip.

"What's this?"

"That's one of many pictures Francine Baxter took of Cecilia Crenshaw the morning after you raped her. Crenshaw showed up at Baxter's office to report you," Joshua said.

"Now, I don't know about you, but I have had my fair share of sexual activity in my day and never did I leave a woman's face in that condition after consensual sex."

"My women like it rough." The general slid the picture back across to Joshua.

"Or rather, you like to rough up women." Joshua slid another picture across the table of Maureen Clark holding up her wrists to display the bruises.

"I am not a common, low-life rapist." The general bit off each word.

"No, you are not a common, low-life rapist." Joshua leaned in to tell him in a low voice. "You're a common, *high-powered monster.*"

Abruptly, the door flew open. Murphy whirled around to close it again, but not before Major Monroe and Tawkeel Said led Colonel Lincoln Clark, his hands cuffed behind his back, inside.

"This room is taken," Murphy said while pushing them back out the door.

The general's and colonel's eyes met.

"Sorry," Major Monroe said. "We thought you had said interrogation room one."

"No!" Joshua stood up from the table. "Are you deaf? I said three! Interrogation room *three.* Can't you see I'm in the middle of taking this man's statement? Get out of here!"

While Major Monroe backed Colonel Clark out of the room, Tawkeel Said stared at Joshua with his mouth hanging open.

"Tawk," Monroe whispered. "Let's go."

Tawkeel's dark face turned pale.

Murphy gently ushered the Phantom who had been smuggled out of Iraq decades before out of the room. "You need to go."

Quickly nodding his head, Tawkeel backed out of the room—his eyes never leaving Joshua's face.

After Murphy shut the door and turned around, General Sebastian Graham swallowed. His eyes were wide. "You picked up Clark? On what?"

"Conspiracy to commit murder," Joshua said. "You heard your personal assistant. He called her to give you the heads-up about your victims banding together to go public. She killed them. . . to protect you. My only question is, are we going to nail you for conspiracy as well or will it be accessory before or after the fact." He leaned across the table. "You can forget about becoming Chief of Staff. What we're looking at now is Leavenworth."

"Where's my lawyer?"

Joshua called to Murphy over his shoulder. "The general wants his lawyer."

Murphy shrugged his shoulders in a sign of dismissal. "He's coming."

Joshua stood up. "And while we're waiting, I'll go take Colonel Clark's statement." He stopped and turned back to the general. "You do know that I'm a lawyer?"

"Yeah, I heard about when you were moving up in JAG."

"So, I have a little bit of experience in these things," Joshua said. "Someone sent a hit squad after my wife and daughter-in-law today after they left Colonel Clark's home, where there was an altercation between him and them about our investigation." He gestured with a wave of his hands. "Which was a huge mistake because now this case is totally personal to us." He pressed his finger on the table top. "Now, a simple check of the phone records will show us who Clark called after they left. If we find in those logs that he called your assistant, well—basically, you're toast, Sebastian."

"Clark's career will be toast if he turns on me," General Graham said.

"It's already toast," Joshua said. "We got Tommy Clark's DNA. Yours is in the system because you served overseas. I'm sure you remember giving it up for identification purposes. Once we compare—"

"We had an affair!"

"Keep saying that and you might convince yourself." Joshua scoffed. "Actually, I think you've already convinced yourself of that. Clark knows his career is over because he knows you're going down. It's just a matter of if he wants to stay on your sinking ship or not." He chuckled. "Do you want to make a bet about which ship he'll choose?" He lowered his voice. "Considering that he traded in his wife for career advancement—I wouldn't count on his loyalty if I were you."

Joshua slid out of the seat. "I still have some pull with the legal community. If you voluntarily withdraw your name from consideration for the nomination to the Joint Chiefs of Staff and make a full confession about the rapes and murders—"

"I had nothing to do with any murders!" The general slammed both fists down on the table.

"Seriously?" Murphy replied. "Every one of your personal assistants was either murdered or committed suicide. Lieutenant General Davis was blown up in a helicopter that you drove him to—all because he was asking too many questions about his daughter's depression. You knew that as soon as he found out about you raping her that your career would be over."

With a growl, Murphy added, "And that's just scratching the surface. You're nothing more than a parasite murdering your entire way to the top of the food chain from day one!"

"Stand down, Lieutenant!" Joshua yelled.

To Joshua's surprise, the general's jowls were trembling. His voice was soft when he replied to Murphy's accusation, "No, that's not true."

"Oh, you just have rotten luck with personal assistants?" Murphy shot back.

"That's what I thought," General Graham said in a low voice. "They'd get disgruntled or all moralistic after catching me cheating on them. Two got mad because they realized I wouldn't leave Paige. Three threatened to go public about my long list of mistresses—like I really cared."

"And then they would suddenly be dead and your problems would be solved," Murphy said. "That's been the case throughout your whole career."

General Sebastian Graham raised his eyes to Murphy's.

Joshua saw disbelief in the war hero's eyes.

Seeing red with rage, Murphy slammed his fist down on the table top. "You're not a man to take any chances. You even had a Pennsylvania State trooper killed for refusing to give up trying to identify a rape victim you had abducted when she became a threat after having your baby."

"What the hell are you talking about?" General Graham yelled.

"Officer Nicholas Gates," Murphy said. "He had only been married four months. Cecelia Crenshaw died in his arms. He made it his mission to find her family—that's all he wanted to do. He even went on national television to identify her so that he could let her family—her daughter—your daughter—know what happened to her. But you saw him on television, didn't you?"

General Graham's mouth hung open.

"And you could not take a chance on anyone finding out what you did," Murphy continued. "So you sent out your Russian clean up team to run him down—all because he wanted to let Cecelia Crenshaw's family know the truth about what had happened to her."

"N-no." General Graham's voice shook.

"That's enough, Lieutenant!" Joshua yanked Murphy back and pushed him toward the door. "We need to go take Colonel Clark's statement now." He turned back to General Graham. "We'll let you know when your lawyer gets here."

Joshua watched the general while Murphy left the room. His face was frozen in an expression of shock. An inkling of concern for the general crept into his gut. Stepping forward, he slammed his hand flat down on the table top to snap him back into the moment. "Sebastian, we'll call your lawyer and tell him to meet you here."

"Thank you, Joshua," he said in a low voice.

Joshua turned to leave. When he opened the door, General Sebastian Graham called his name again.

"Yes, Sebastian?"

The general seemed to have aged ten years in a matter of minutes. "I never wanted to be a monster."

"None of us do," Joshua replied. "It's been my experience, from what I have seen in criminal court cases, it happens when you're not looking—while entertaining your inner demons."

Joshua found Murphy talking to Tawkeel Said in the corridor outside Colonel Clark's interrogation room.

After a polite nod of his head to Tawkeel, Joshua asked Murphy, "Who's watching Tommy Clark?"

"One of our agents called Maureen Clark's brother using the NCIS cover," Murphy said. "They told them that Clark was being brought in for questioning. The agent stayed at the Clark home until he got there to take both Tommy and the Clark's cat home with him."

Joshua nodded his approval before turning to Tawkeel. "Did Clark say anything when you and Major Monroe picked him up?"

Tawkeel stood up straight, almost to attention. "He says Graham is tying up loose ends and sent a hit man to kill him tonight. He'd be dead if the police had not chased the assassin away."

Joshua fought the grin working its way to his lips. "Sounds like he's ready." He reached for the door knob to enter the interrogation room.

"Billy?" Tawkeel asked.

Joshua stopped. Slowly, he turned his head to look at the young man from the Middle East.

"They called you Billy," Tawkeel said.

Stunned, Joshua looked him up and down.

"Dad ..." Murphy asked. "What's wrong?"

"When did you come over from Iraq?" Joshua whispered.

"Nineteen-ninety-five," Tawkeel said. "Me, my father—"

"Your mother's family poisoned her," Joshua said. "We found you and your family hiding in the desert. You'd been hiding in a cave for days. We got you out one step ahead of a death squad."

Tears in Tawkeel's eyes, he nodded while digging into his pants pocket. He extracted a gold pocket watch on a chain with an eagle on the lid. "I still have it. I carry it always to remind me that I am truly an American—just like you and the soldiers who saved me and my family."

Seeing the watch, Murphy felt his heart jump up into his throat. Joshua laid his fingers on the watch. As if struck with a thought, he jerked to look at Murphy from over his shoulder. With a proud grin, Murphy nodded his head at him.

"And now you're a Phantom, Tawkeel," Joshua said.

"Ask not what your country can do for you," Tawkeel quoted the late President John F. Kennedy, "but what you can do for your country."

Joshua patted the young man on the cheek. "It was an honor bringing you and your family to America."

Down the hallway, Major Monroe turned the corner at a run. "Captain, we have a problem!"

Seeing that the major's hands were bloody, Murphy ran down the corridor and followed him into the interrogation room where General Sebastian Graham was waiting for his lawyer.

The army general was stretched out on the floor in a growing pool of blood. An ink pen stuck out of his neck. His teeth chattered while he convulsed from blood-loss.

"Sebastian!" Joshua rushed to him and tried to plug with his hand the blood flowing from around the pen that the general had plunged deep into his throat—striking the jugular vein. "Who gave him the pen?" he yelled over his shoulder at the major who had been keeping an eye on him.

"He asked for a pen and paper because he wanted to write out a confession," the major said. "I was watching from the observation room. He was writing. Then out of the blue, he took that pen and stabbed himself in the throat. He did it so fast."

"Sebastian, why?" Joshua asked him.

"We're the good guys." He choked on blood spilling out of his mouth. "We send out young people ... over there ... to destroy the monsters. Here ... I was one and ... never knew it."

Murphy picked up the yellow notepad on which General Graham had written out his confession.

Dear God,

Please forgive me for what I have become and grant me the courage to be a hero just one last time.

General Sebastian Graham, USA

CHAPTER THIRTY

It was three in the morning by the time Joshua and Murphy had finished taking down Colonel Lincoln Clark's statement. Clark confirmed contacting General Sebastian Graham's personal assistant after discovering that his wife was meeting with other victims of Graham's sexual assaults at Francine Baxter's home.

"But I never thought for a minute that they would kill all of them," the colonel claimed.

"What did you think they were going to do?" Joshua asked.

"Threaten them," Colonel Clark said. "Intimidate them all into silence." He threw up his hands. "Bribe them."

"Like he paid you off?" Joshua said. "What kind of man allows another man to do to his wife what Sebastian Graham did to yours and does nothing?"

"Like if we had reported it he would have spent one day in jail," Colonel Clark said. "It would have been a losing battle anyway. With all the friends and connections General Graham has, he would have gotten off and my career would have been over. I would have been drummed out of the army after spending two or three more tours in some hell hole. The best choice was to play ball with him."

"Which got your wife killed," Joshua said. "Did you tell General Graham that Maureen was leaving you because of this arrangement you two made without her consent?"

"No," Colonel Clark said. "Graham's not stupid. We communicated through Dolly, his assistant."

"He told you that if there were any problem to call Dolly?" Joshua said.

"Yeah," the colonel replied before changing his mind. "No, as a matter of fact, it wasn't the general but his wife who told me to call Dolly or her if there were any problems with Maureen. It was after Maureen blew-up at a party at the general's house. He grabbed her breast and she slapped him. Paige ordered Maureen to apologize, which she finally did but, afterwards, she threatened to report the rape to the police. I warned Sebastian. A few days later, a man threatened Maureen after she'd gone running. Said something bad was going to happen to her pretty legs. That settled her down real fast. The next day, Paige called me and said that if there were ever any other problems with Maureen to call Dolly."

The colonel looked across the table at Joshua, who sat back in his seat, crossed his arms, and stared back at him.

"You know," the colonel broke his silence, "there's no way you can come out ahead in bringing this case against Graham."

"Actually, we already have," Joshua said. "He offed himself a couple of hours ago."

Colonel Lincoln Clark's jaw dropped open. "He's dead?"

Joshua nodded his head.

"Why am I still here?"

"Because you arranged the murder of your wife and four other women." Joshua stood up out of his chair. "Make yourself comfortable. You're going to be here for a while."

Murphy was waiting for Joshua in the hallway. "You're not going to believe this." He referred to the notes in his tablet.

"Tell me about Paige Graham," Joshua ordered.

"That's what you're not going to believe," Murphy said. "Ripley called. She was the issue that threatened Sebastian Graham's security clearance when he came back from the Gulf War. He married her. During their background check on her, the FBI discovered that not only was her father tight with the Russian mob—the Kalashov family to be exact, but Paige had lived with Adrian Kalashov for over two years while they both attended Yale."

"That's our Russian connection," Joshua said. "Any proof that they're still connected?"

"According to the RICO division," Murphy said, "their inside guy tells them that Adrian Kalashov has a woman friend whom he infrequently meets at out of the way places—bed and breakfasts, resorts—very low key. They're sort of friends with benefits. No one knew her name until Ripley sent them Paige's picture. They identified Paige as that woman." He tapped Joshua on the arm. "Here's the kicker. Ripley says RICO told her that Adrian Kalashov is in the city now. He came down last night with some of his heavy hitters. Something is going down."

"Anything to prove that he came down because of General Graham?"

"He's obviously got a vested interest in Graham's future," Murphy said. "Guess who provided Maya Fedorov with a character reference on her last security update."

"Paige Graham," Joshua said.

"Paige claimed to have known Dolly Scanlon, aka Maya Fedorov, for over twenty years and she recommended her for the job as her husband's personal assistant. They met through charitable work in New York. The organization she claimed she had met Federov through has ties to one of Kalashov's shell companies."

"Everything now fits," Joshua said. "Paige Graham was at the Clark home when Cameron tried to collect Tommy's DNA. She knew that would expose her husband."

"So she called in her mob connections to stop Cameron and Jessica," Murphy said. "Makes sense, because we found no phone calls from Clark to Dolly or Graham."

Joshua shook his head, "I didn't think you would. Sebastian was completely caught off guard when you confronted him with all the murders that have cleared the way for him."

"You mean you don't think he knew anything about them? Even if he wasn't behind them, you'd think he'd question why so many of his enemies were dying suddenly at such convenient times."

"Denial can be a powerful thing," Joshua said. "But when you confronted him with the facts, he couldn't deny it anymore. He was too much of a coward to face that his wife had been using her own personal mob connections to clear his way to the Joint Chiefs of Staff and probably beyond."

"That's why the mob positioned one of their own people close to General Graham," Murphy said. "They saw how he was moving up and decided to take advantage. They wanted to be ready to cash in when he got into a position where it would benefit them."

"And that never would have happened if Francine Baxter and those women had gone public about Sebastian Graham being a sexual predator."

"We need to pick up Paige Graham before she puts a hit out on anyone else," Murphy said.

"What makes you think she hasn't?"

In the early morning hours, Joshua drove Murphy's SUV to the Graham estate, a sprawling mansion with plenty of acreage and security in a northern Virginia suburb. Murphy followed on his motorcycle. They arrived to find that their commanding officer had already send a team of Phantoms to infiltrate and secure the property. After being directed to park off a side road, the leader of the Phantom team, Major Marshall Ford, a bald headed marine, stepped up to the driver's side of the SUV.

"The place was a fortress armed with former military types," Major Ford reported. "We managed to take them all down without firing a shot and got inside. Paige Graham isn't there. Their head of security says that shortly after she got a call from the army's chief of staff that her husband had committed suicide, she made one phone call. Less than an hour later, a limousine showed up. Two men went inside. One had dark hair with white at the temples. The other wore a suit that costs more than this SUV. About a half hour later, she left in the limo with the two of them. That was about an hour ago."

Overhearing this, Murphy said, "The guy with the black and white hair sounds like one of the shooters that escaped from Starbucks. Maybe Paige Graham's making a run for it. The Russian mob is helping her escape."

Joshua was shaking his head. "Did the guards ever see these two men before?" he asked the major who replied that they hadn't.

"She was raised in the mob, Murphy," Joshua said. "She's invested many years to her husband and clearing the way for him to get to the top. Now that we've taken away her prize stud when he was on the brink of greatness—she's going to demand payback."

"Jessica and Cameron!" Murphy ran back to his motorcycle. He threw open the travel compartment and extracted his utility belt, which contained two service weapons and his knife.

"Does she know where you live?" Major Ford asked.

Murphy was already back on his motorcycle. "Admiral Patterson's wife showed her." He turned on the bike and spun out on his way out onto the dark country road to take him home.

CHAPTER THIRTY-ONE

"I can't believe we're tearing this house apart in the middle of the night to find a spider." With a sigh of exhaustion, Cameron sat up from where she was shining a flashlight under the sofa. "What were you doing feeding her in the middle of the night anyway?"

"I forgot to before I went to bed," Jessica said from where she was laying on her back under the dining room table searching its underside. Having not bothered to put on her bathrobe before rushing off to feed Monique, she was dressed only in an oversized navy t-shirt and blue lace panties. "I woke up at three o'clock and remembered and was afraid I'd forget this morning. When I went downstairs, I found that some *animal* must have knocked the lid off her tank—" she cast a glare in Spencer's direction "and she got out."

On the sofa, Spencer laid back her ears and buried her snout under her paws.

"She'll turn up," Cameron assured her. "We're all tired and keyed up. Let's go to bed."

Jessica rolled over and crawled out from under the table. "Being a detective, don't you resent not going with Joshua and Murphy?"

"I'm not a Phantom," she said. "No visitors allowed. Besides, we still don't know who or what was behind that hit on us this afternoon. They could have been going after Izzy since she is most likely General Graham's daughter." She patted the gun she had tucked in the pocket of her bathrobe. "So I'm not exactly stuck here making soup and sandwiches while waiting for our men."

Gesturing for Jessica to follow her, Cameron went over to the stairs leading to the floors above. "Let's go to bed."

Groaning about not finding Monique, Jessica went over to the front door to check the lock and the security panel. "Oh, no."

"What oh no?" Cameron stepped back down from the stairs.

"The security system is off," Jessica said.

"You mean you forgot to activate it when Murphy and Josh left?"

"No, I activated it," Jessica said, an edge of panic to her voice. "That was the last thing Murphy told me when he left. I mean it is off as in powered off. Like the system has been completely shut down."

Pushing Jessica up against the wall, Cameron pulled her gun from her pocket. "Where's your gun?"

Keeping low, Jessica hurried to the end table next to Newman's chair and took a nine-millimeter Beretta from the top drawer. She checked the magazine. It was fully loaded.

"Good." Cameron picked up Jessica's cell phone from where she had left it on the dining room table and tossed it to her. "Call the police. I'll go upstairs and get Izzy. You stay here by the door and don't open it until the police arrive. Don't go outside until they get here. These people are professionals. They could be waiting outside to shoot you when we step out into the open."

Watching Cameron race up the stairs, Jessica sank to the floor to dial the police. Sensing her fear, Spencer trotted over to press up against her.

"Murphy will be here soon," Jessica said while giving the dog a hug. Glancing over to the living room, she saw that Newman was eying her with question in his eyes. "I don't suppose you'd be any good against an assassin."

As if to answer her, Newman hit the power button on his remote to start the television.

The emergency operator had just picked up the phone when the doorbell sounded. With a shriek, Jessica dropped the phone and inched up to peer out the door.

Two men in police uniforms were waiting on the other side.

"Nine-one-one," the emergency operator said, "what's your emergency?"

"Mrs. Thornton," one of the officers said, "it's the police. Sorry to wake you up. Your security company called to report that your security system has shut down. They asked that we come to check on you."

Sounds reasonable.

"Jessica!" Cameron hissed from up the stairs. "Ask for them to hold their badges up for you to see, and then ask the emergency operator to confirm."

"Hello?" the police operator was still calling to her from the phone.

"I know what to do," Jessica told Cameron before bringing the phone to her ear. "Can you hold on just a minute? I need for you to check a couple of badges for me." Clutching her gun in both hands, she called through the door, "Press your badges up to the door so that I can read the numbers."

There was a long silence.

On the stairs, Cameron craned her neck to peer through the cut glass in the front door. She saw that one of the officers

stayed on the stoop while the other stepped away. "Jessica ..."
Two more figures appeared on either side of the door.

"It's taking them an awfully long time to get their badges," Jessica said.

Cameron saw two of the figures swinging their arms in unison. "Duck!"

The door exploded inward from the force of a metal battering ram. What had seconds before served as a barricade between the women and the assassins was now nothing more than shards of glass, wood, and metal.

Jessica and Spencer scrambled toward the dining room to take refuge behind the wall.

Cameron took down the first assassin through the door with three shots. The first one to his thigh brought him down to the floor. She finished him off with two shots to his head. Without stopping, she drove the assailant's partners back out the door with a continuous stream of gunfire.

Dropping back to replace her magazine, she yelled down the stairs, "Make 'em head shots, Jessie! They're wearing vests!"

Newman responded to the violence by slapping the remote with a paw to up the volume on the television.

"Cameron!" Izzy screamed from upstairs. "What's happening?"

"Hide, Izzy!" Cameron yelled.

Head shots. They're wearing vests. Need to make it head shots. Taking deep breaths, Jessica pressed up against the wall. She clutched her gun in both hands. *No rules, Jessie. Time to stomp on your bitch button!*

Determined to make her shots at the intruders count, she sucked in a deep breath and whirled around to take aim at the doorway. Before she could pull the trigger, she felt a powerful hand grasp the back of her head and ram it into the wall.

As she slid down to the floor, she heard a rough voice chuckle. "What a lovely piece of ass you are. We're gonna have some fun with you before we finish this job."

Fighting to remain conscious long enough to see her attacker, Jessica could make out his dark hair with white temples. *Sidewalls.*

On the stairs, Cameron waited for more assailants to attempt coming through the door. There were none.

The silence was more frightening than the gunshots.

Spencer's barks broke through the silence. The blue sheltie shot out of the dining room and ran out the shattered front door.

Where's Jessica?

Her heart racing, Cameron raced down the stairs and to the doorway. Pausing at the door, she peered outside to see a uniformed police officer opening the side door of a van while another, carrying an unconscious Jessica over his shoulder like a sack of potatoes. They had used the downstairs entrance to snatch her.

"Halt!" Cameron screamed.

The hitman holding the door open turned to shoot, but Cameron was ready for him. She put a bullet through his knee before finishing him off as he fell with a shot to the neck and head.

Without pausing, the man carrying Jessica threw her into the van and jumped in himself while it sped off.

The roar of Murphy's motorcycle came to Cameron's ears. In her bare feet, she ran down the steps to meet him when he pulled up. Gesturing at the van, she screamed for him to hear her over the motorcycle's engine. "After them! They took Jessica in a black van!"

Murphy gave chase.

Chapter Thirty-Two

Cameron only paused long enough to give the fallen assailant a quick check to ensure he was dead before replacing the magazine in her gun with the last one she had in her pocket and running back inside to check on Izzy.

Neighbors were waking up to the gunshots. Some called the police to report it. Others were outside with their cell phones recording everything they could to post on the Internet.

When Joshua rounded the corner in Murphy's SUV with a van filled with Phantoms behind him, he cursed. This was more public than he needed. Hitting the button on his cell phone, he called back to Major Ford. "They were already here. Civilians are out and about."

"No problem, Captain," Ford responded. "We've got it covered. No one will ever know this was us."

Upstairs, Izzy was cowering under the bed. Holding her breath for fear the shooters could hear her, she clutched Irving to her chest. She felt her heartbeat pounding against the cat's large furry body.

A stream of light fell across the floor next to the bed. Peering out from under the edge of the comforter, she saw a pair of women's feet make their way across the room to the bed.

Izzy sensed that the feet did not belong to Cameron or Jessica. Sucking in her breath, she curled up as tightly as she could to make herself as small as possible. Irving wriggled out of her grasp.

No, stay, Irving. It's dangerous.

She saw the legs lower down for the knees to meet the floor. While the intruder prepared to peer under the bed, Izzy caught sight of the shiny blade of a butcher knife. Tears of fear welled up in her eyes.

The intruder grasped the bottom of the bed's skirt and lifted—releasing twenty-five pounds of furry wrath.

With a screech, Irving shot out from under the bed with all claws extended. Most of them found their mark.

Grabbing her face with both hands, Paige Graham leapt to her feet. Screaming, she whirled around while trying to capture the enraged animal that continued to claw and scratch her with every ounce of rage he had inside him, before bouncing off the top of her head to the dresser, and then scurrying out the door.

Letting off a string of curses, she wiped the blood from her face. Seeing her own blood in the palm of her hand only infuriated her more.

She didn't remember being this angry with anyone since Sebastian's parents threatened to go to the army's criminal investigation division with evidence that she had arranged the murder of that idiot commanding officer who threatened to ruin her husband's career.

Snatching the butcher knife from the floor, Paige admired the shiny blade. A grin came to her lips while recalling the shocked looks on her in-laws' faces when they realized their foolishness in thinking that she was not worthy, or worse, clever enough to be the wife of a distinguished military leader.

"It's over, Paige."

Paige Graham looked up from where she was staring at the knife to face Cameron who was aiming not one but two guns at her.

"Drop the knife."

"My husband was General Sebastian Graham," Paige said. "He was going to be the Chief of Staff for our United States Army. In no time, he would have been chairman of the Joint Chiefs. After that, it would have only been a short jog to President of the United States. You have no idea how brilliant Sebastian was. He was going to do great things for this country—all thanks to me."

"Thanks to you for enabling his predatory behavior against women."

"Nobody's perfect," Paige said. "Every great man has had a weakness. Sebastian's was women. So he's raped some. But when you take into consideration those lives he saved in the Middle East, and the fabulous plans he had for our country when he got to the White House—the price these women paid is really quite insignificant."

Cameron squinted her eyes. She couldn't stop the laughter that worked its way up her throat. "You're looney." She scoffed. "You really believe that these women your husband forced himself on should have felt *honored* that he selected them to rape?"

"Why would they not?"

Steadying her aim on Paige, Cameron ordered, "Drop the knife or I will shoot."

With a shrug of her shoulders, Paige tossed the knife to the bed.

"Now put your hands on top of your head and turn around."

Paige did as she was directed.

After tucking Jessica's Beretta into her robe's pocket and her smaller semi-automatic into the waistband of her pajamas, Cameron removed the belt from her bathrobe and stepped forward to grab Paige's wrist. She had just gotten in reach of her when Paige whirled around and slapped Cameron against the side of her head with her fist. She followed up the blow with a kick to the knee that dropped Cameron down onto the bed. She felt her gun break loose to drop down into her pajamas pants.

By the time Cameron sat up, Paige was pointing the Beretta she had snatched from Cameron's pocket at her.

"You all make the same mistake," she said. "You all underestimate the power of the woman behind the man."

Paige held out the gun to aim her shot between Cameron's eyes. Her arm tingled with the feel of something itchy working its way up her forearm. In the dim light of the room, she could only make out something several inches in diameter and made up of black fur scurrying up to her elbow. Her jaw dropped open upon realizing that the enormous furry thing was not only the size of a luncheon plate, but had eight legs.

With a scream, Paige dropped the gun and swiped at Monique, who hopped up her arm until the spider landed on her shoulder.

Hysterical, Paige twisted, whirled and jumped while slapping and hitting herself in an attempt to kill the oversized bug. Panting with madness, she ended her dance at the top of the stairs where she collapsed over the bannister.

"Paige Graham, you're under arrest!"

When her presence of mind returned, Paige found herself staring down at the muzzle of Joshua Thornton's gun.

Looking down at her hand by her side, she saw that she was still clutching Cameron's weapon.

Regaining consciousness, Jessica was aware of the van speeding down the road. Staring out the back window, Sidewalls was sitting next to her with a gun pressed against her side.

"You haven't lost him yet?" Sidewalls growled up at the driver.

"He's been sticking to us like glue. The guy's on a motorcycle and he knows how to weave his way around traffic."

No rules.

Keeping her eyes shut, Jessica pretended to be unconscious while waiting for her opportunity.

"Run the red lights," Sidewalls ordered. "Let's see him weave around a semi without getting squashed like a bug."

Can't lose sight of them.

The capital's rush hour traffic started with the sun rise. As the sun crested the horizon, vehicles took to the streets. Murphy had managed to catch up to the speeding van when it hit the four lane road heading away from Washington on Oxen Hill Road. Luckily, most of the heavy traffic was heading in the opposite direction—toward the city.

Weaving around vehicles driven by sleepy commuters, Murphy tried to form a plan for attack once he caught the van. It was unlikely that he could force it off the road with only his motorcycle—unless he shot the driver. But with Jessica inside, he considered the risk too great.

The best bet was to run them down to the ground and take them all out when they stopped.

Keeping on the van's tail, Murphy revved the bike's engine to race through a red light of a busy intersection. The long blast of a loud horn announced that a semi-truck and trailer with the right of way was coming through.

Going too fast to stop and not wanting to risk losing sight of the van, Murphy leaned to the side and plowed right on through the intersection—clearing the space underneath the moving trailer.

Without missing a beat, on the other side, he righted the bike and revved the engine to catch up with the van racing away with his wife.

In the van, Sidewalls cursed when he saw that Murphy was still on their tail. "I don't believe it!" Leaning up toward the back of the driver's seat, he said, "We'll make it a two-fer. Lead him someplace nice and secluded. We'll let him watch us play fun and games with his wife before killing her in front of him. Then, we'll kill him nice and slow for being so much trouble."

The driver's laughter was cut off by the blast of Sidewall's gun through the back of his seat.

Focused on trying to shake Murphy, Sidewalls had forgotten about Jessica—until she jumped up to grab the gun he was clutching while talking to the driver, pointed it to the back of the seat, and pulled the trigger.

Jessica's sense of success was cut short when the driver collapsed over the steering wheel and his foot hit the gas pedal.

CHAPTER THIRTY-THREE

The television was blaring.

"Give it up, Paige!" Joshua yelled over *The Power Rangers* opening song. At the bottom of the stairs, he was braced against the wall with his weapon aimed at her. "My people have the place surrounded. There is no way you can get out of here alive unless you give yourself up."

Paige Graham slowly raised the hand clutching the gun and eased it up over the banister. "You have no idea who you're dealing with."

"I do." Cameron pressed the muzzle of her gun against the base of Paige's neck. With her other hand, she snatched her gun from Paige's hand. "It's over, Ms. Fruit Loop."

Standing up tall, Paige said, "It's over when I say it's over." She whirled around and grabbed the gun Cameron had pressed against the back of her neck. Afraid Paige would once more get her gun, Cameron backed up.

In a surprise move, instead of wresting the gun out of Cameron's hand, Paige shoved her body against the muzzle, up under her ribs, and, with Cameron's hand still on the weapon, pulled the trigger.

By the time Joshua reached the top of the stairs, Paige was down on the floor.

"She grabbed my gun ... and pulled the trigger," Cameron sputtered out. Gasping, she realized, "She said it was over when she said it was over."

Joshua was checking Paige's pulse.

Her eyes glassy, Paige's usually tough expression softened. With blood filling her mouth, she murmured, "My darling Sebastian, we almost made it. ... Top ... of the ... world."

The general's wife died.

"How's that for commitment?" Joshua said. "He was a rapist and she still loved him."

"Nobody's perfect," Cameron quoted Paige with sarcasm.

Joshua rose to his feet. "Where's Izzy?"

"Hiding under the bed."

"We need to get out of here." Tucking his gun into its holster, Joshua ran into bedroom. "Now!" Racing into the bedroom, he dropped down to the floor. "Izzy, it's me, Josh. Come on, sweetie, we need to get out of here. We'll take you someplace safe."

"We can't forget Monique."

Carefully holding the huge black spider, Izzy thrust out both hands. Upon seeing the fur covered, eight legged creature, Joshua uttered a gasp and fell back to land on his rump.

"Grow some guts." Cameron scooped up Monique and deposited her in a makeshift well in the front of her nightshirt. "That giant bug saved my life."

"I'll remember this next time you find a spider in the bath tub." As soon as Izzy was out from under the bed, Joshua lifted her up into his arms. She wrapped her legs around his waist and her arms around his shoulders.

"What about Irving?" Izzy asked.

"We'll get Irving and all the critters," Joshua assured her.

With Cameron leading the way, they ran down the stairs to find the broken out front door blocked by a man dressed in a tailored suit and tie. He wielded an M249 machine gun in his hands.

Cameron stepped in front of Joshua and Izzy.

"You can't crush a man's investment without paying a certain price," the newest intruder said in a well-cultured voice.

Unable to hear his threat over the battle the Power Rangers were fighting on the television, Cameron could only conclude that this well-dressed man was not happy about the death of Paige Graham and or her assassins.

"Adrian Kalashov I presume," Joshua yelled to be heard over the television that Newman had jacked up to maximum volume to hear over the gun fights.

"My company has invested a lot of time and money in making General—" Gritting his teeth with anger over his grand moment being drowned out by a children's television show, the Russian mobster turned to the dog in the living room. "Turn that thing down!"

Newman sat up in his seat and growled at the mobster.

"No mutt growls at me."

While Cameron and Izzy screamed, Adrian leveled his machine gun at the dog.

They felt the whizz of the blade through the air before it made contact with Adrian Kalashov's back. The force of the throw and size of the knife made the blade go through the mobster's back to slice through the center of his heart.

Adrian Kalashov was dead before he hit the floor.

Feeling Izzy tremble in his arms, Joshua turned around so that she could not see the dead man.

"Is he on our side?" Izzy asked.

Turning his head to see who she was pointing at, Joshua saw Tawkeel Said step out of the dining room. He wore a ballistics vest with "FBI" emblazoned across the front and back.

"Yes, he is. He is a very good man."

"We must go, Billy," Tawkeel said. "We have a van outside to take everyone to a safe house."

"We can't forget Irving, Newman, and Blue," Izzy said.

"We leave no American left behind, even the fur covered ones." Tawkeel ushered them toward the door.

"Where's Murphy?" Joshua asked.

"We don't know, sir."

CHAPTER THIRTY-FOUR

Murphy was horrified when he saw the van careen over to the side of the road and sideswipe an SUV, which swerved onto the shoulder trying to escape. *Jessica must have found her bitch button.* Lurching forward on the bike, Murphy gave the bike all the gas he could.

Inside the van, the force of the van swerving to hit the SUV knocked Sidewalls to the floor. The gun fell out of his hand and slid under the front passenger seat.

Seeing another opening, Jessica sprang over on top of him and rammed her knee into his groin. When he sat up to clutch his privates, she spotted the front seatbelt hanging nearby. Grabbing it, she wrapped it around his neck and pulled down on it with all her weight.

Sidewalls was gasping and groaning. Jessica allowed herself to grin at her success—until the van swerved to the other side of the road, knocking her onto her back.

Recovering enough to go on the offensive, Sidewalls tore at the seatbelt around his neck. "You little bitch! I should have killed you when I had the chance." He grabbed her ankle and pulled her to him. The rough floor of the van tore through her t-shirt to scratch her back.

Keeping his legs together to protect his privates as best he could in the vehicle that was swerving back and forth across the road, he tried to grab her other foot. "No way, Bucko!" she yelled before kicking him in the kneecap.

Uttering a curse, Sidewalls dropped forward to grasp his wounded knee.

With everything she had, Jessica turned her foot to the side to kick him right in the throat.

When the van swerved to the other side, she went with the flow to grab him by the shoulders and deliver a head butt between the eyes.

Sidewalls collapsed onto the seat.

Damn that hurts! She grasped her forehead. *Why don't head butts hurt in the movies?* Fighting the stars dancing before her eyes, Jessica crawled over Sidewalls to throw open the side door.

With the wind whipping around her, blowing up her oversized navy t-shirt to expose her blue silk panties, she paused to take in the road rushing by her. There was no mistaking the black motorcycle and its rider weaving in unison with the out of control van.

Murphy held out his hand to her.

The joy at seeing the possible escape on the bike turned to fear. Clutching the door, Jessica took in her bare feet and legs and the pavement rushing beneath them.

Is this how it looked to Felicia right before she hit the pavement?

The van was easing off the road. Eventually, Murphy would run out of pavement and be on gravel, which would give way to a grassy side embankment.

No rules!

Bracing herself, Jessica reached for Murphy's hand only to find it suddenly gone. To her horror, he snatched his gun out of the holster, aimed it at the van, and fired.

Oh, no! It's not Murphy! I imagined—

The shot whizzed past her. Sidewalls fell against her back. Clinging to the door, she scrambled back inside. Collapsing, Sidewalls and the gun he had aimed at her back tumbled out of the moving van and dropped onto the gravel racing by them.

With a sigh of relief, she saw that Murphy had re-holstered his gun and eased the bike closer to the open door. Holding out his hand, he screamed, "Jump, Buttercup! Now!"

Seeing that they were quickly running out of road, Jessica grabbed his arm and leapt toward the speeding motorcycle. Grabbing his shoulders, she dropped down onto the seat behind him and encased his chest with both arms.

"Hold on!" she heard him yell before screeching the bike to a halt, throwing gravel everywhere to prick her bare legs.

Murphy turned the handlebars and gunned the engine to go around to the other side of the van, which sped across the gravel and into the embankment. Hitting the grassy patch at top speed, the van rolled nose over end, then side over side before it came to a halt. The gasoline from the punctured gas tank quickly caught fire.

Weaving through the traffic, the bike was speeding up the road when they heard the explosion.

Murphy pulled over into a gas station further up the road. Even after he turned off the engine, Jessica didn't want to let go of her hold on him. After taking off his helmet, he gently freed himself from her grip to turn around to kiss her. "Are you okay?"

All she could do was nod her head while clinging to him.

"Did they hurt you?" He examined the bruise forming on her forehead from the head butt she had delivered to Sidewalls. Grateful that it was her only injury, he pressed his lips against it.

Upon hearing police sirens, they both looked up to see two police cars, lights and sirens blaring, race by them in response to calls about a van on fire.

"Remind me never to push your bitch button," he said.

With a laugh, she replied, "Copy that, Thornton."

CHAPTER THIRTY-FIVE

While Murphy was able to offer Jessica his leather jacket for the ride home, there was nothing he could do for her bare feet and legs. They would just have to deal with her being his sexy riding partner for the ride back to their brownstone, which they found surrounded by police, federal agents, and a black moving truck.

"What's going on?" Jessica asked Murphy about the moving truck with the open back. Men in black overalls were wheeling a trolley down the loading ramp.

Spotting Major Ford gingerly making his way down the front steps with Monique's tank, Murphy jumped off the bike and went over to where Joshua was talking to Cameron, who was seated in the front seat of Murphy's SUV. She held Irving in her lap. Spencer and Newman were loaded in the back seat.

Izzy opened up the back of the SUV to help Major Ford load the tarantula inside. "Don't forget her food," she said.

"Food?" the major asked.

"Crickets," Izzy said. "I'll get them."

Cameron reached through the open window to grab Jessica's hand. "We were so worried. Are you okay?"

Aware of her scantily clad state in front of the many male agents and neighbors watching from their yards, Jessica hugged Murphy's jacket closer. "I'm fine. Murphy saved me. … of course."

"She's being modest," Murphy said. "Dad, what's with the moving van?"

"We have to talk." Taking Murphy by the arm, Joshua led him away from the SUV and listening ears.

"What's—"

"You're moving," Joshua said.

"No!" Murphy shook his head.

"Your home has been compromised," Joshua said. "Paige Graham brought the leader of the Russian mob here. A band of hitmen know where you live. There's no telling who in the organization still has that information and is willing to sell it to anyone who wants it. In your line of work, if you get on anyone's radar like you did with this case, not only will you be at risk, but so will Jessica."

"This is our home," Murphy said angrily.

"You'll find a new one," Joshua said. "Right now, we're going to a safe house where you and Jessica can stay until you find a new home. You can stay there as long as you want— rent free. You're too valuable to the Joint Chiefs to take any chances with your safety."

Joshua's firm expression communicated that there was no more conversation about the matter. As a Phantom, Murphy had no choice … and neither did Jessica.

"I'm sorry," Joshua said. "It has to be done."

Murphy grit his teeth. "Remember your first goal in this case?"

"To make you hate me?" Joshua said.

"You've obtained it."

"I'd rather you be safe and hate me," Joshua said with a slight grin, "than dead."

As soon as Joshua stepped away, Jessica was by Murphy's side. Her eyes were pools of violet. "What's going on?"

"We have to move." Murphy hugged her while whispering into her ear, "Now. Today,"

"But—"

"Our home has been compromised. Because I'm a Phantom, it's too risky for us to stay here." Pulling away, he held both of her hands in his. "I am so sorry, Buttercup. I know how much you love this house. It was our first home together and now because of me. . ."

"My home is where you are." She brushed her hand across his cheek.

He kissed the inside of her palm before pulling her in to kiss her tenderly on the lips. Together, they turned to where the movers were hauling yet to be unpacked moving boxes from the rec room.

"Look on the bright side, Buttercup," Murphy said. "Since we still haven't finished unpacking from our last move, we don't have much packing to do."

By noon, the Phantoms had enough evidence to nail Dolly Scanlon, aka Maya Fedorov, for Donna Crenshaw's and Francine Baxter's murders.

While ballistics was unable to match the bullets from her gun with the shattered bullets taken from the victim's bodies, an elementary school security camera had photographed not only Maya Fedorov's car parked in the school parking lot, but Maya Fedorov herself leaving the parking lot on foot—heading in the direction of Francine Baxter's home, two blocks away, shortly before her murder. The camera also caught her returning to her car that evening—after Donna Crenshaw's murder.

Between the security video and Fedorov's confession in Sebastian Graham's apartment, the Attorney General had all he needed for a multiple murder conviction.

With Adrian Kalashov dead, his brother was stepping up to take the reins of the Russian crime family, which sent the FBI knocking on Maya Fedorov's cell door in hopes of her becoming a witness against the Kalashov family. The FBI had big hopes that Maya Fedorov, who had grown up in the crime organization, could provide the break needed to shut it down—in exchange for a sweet deal.

The safe house Murphy and Jessica had been sent to was nicer than most people's homes. The four bedroom ranch-style home even had an in-ground swimming pool, in which Izzy and Spencer had fun splashing.

Still, it was not their brownstone—the newlywed's first home together.

Murphy's CO sent word to Tristan about their new location for after his weekend getaway.

It wasn't until the end of the day, while the sun was setting, and the shock of what everyone had been through was gradually wearing off, that exhaustion set in.

Over a dinner of Oriental take-out at the dining room table that looked out on the pool where Izzy was playing with Spencer, who was now answering to the name Blue, Jessica expressed surprise upon learning of General Sebastian Graham's suicide and that Paige Graham was, in fact, behind the murders that helped him climb up the ladder to the top.

"I've never met him," she said, "but from what you told me about the rapes, I thought these attacks were about control. He was a narcissist. Those types don't usually commit suicide."

"The man I met in Kuwait all those years ago was a great soldier," Joshua said. "There's no denying that there was something in him that made him save his men in that ambush."

"But he was also a rapist," Cameron said. "He was a rapist before he went over to the Middle East and saved his team—after raping a female colleague."

"Don't you believe that it's possible for a bad person to have good qualities?" Joshua asked the two women sitting at the dining room table with him.

"The man actually managed to convince himself that every one of his victims seduced him," Murphy said with sarcasm from where he was keeping a vigil on Izzy in the swimming pool. He didn't like the idea of her being alone in the pool.

"He believed his own press releases," Jessica said. "Felt entitled to those women. When one would say no, then that pressed a button inside him—enraged him even. Then, afterwards, since he truly believed he was entitled because he was a great man, then he would convince himself that it wasn't rape."

"But I think Murphy struck a cord inside him." Joshua pushed his paper plate away. "When he confronted Graham with many of the irrefutable facts—including the pattern of sudden deaths of his assistants—he couldn't remain in denial any longer."

"Like an intervention," Jessica got up from the table to gather the used paper plates and plastic utensils for the trash.

"But Sebastian didn't arrange those murders," Murphy said. "His wife had."

"And I believe deep down, Graham knew it all along," Joshua said. "He had to. There were so many. He had to have at least suspected it. When you laid out the facts, Murphy, he could no longer deny what was happening and who was behind it."

After mouthing a thank you to Jessica who took his plate, Joshua continued, "Graham realized that the woman behind the man, Paige, was covering up his messes and killing his way to the top. She turned him into a monster. Faced with the facts of what he had become, the great man I once knew came to the surface and he knew what he had to do for the sake of his country."

"Kill the monster before he did any more damage," Murphy said in a quiet voice. "With his death, he would not be able to prey on any more women and Paige and her mobster friends would no longer have to kill to cover up his messes."

Folding her hands, Cameron turned to Jessica, who had returned to take her seat at the table. "Now this is what I don't understand. How can a woman, a supposedly smart woman, like Paige Graham, rationalize that her husband was a great man entitled to raping women? She couldn't have honestly believed, with all these accusations that crept up throughout the years and the cover ups she had engineered, that he was not a sexual predator." When Jessica opened her mouth to respond, Cameron interjected, "Don't tell me it was denial."

"Why do women who marry pedophiles stay with them, even when they're violating their own children?" Jessica asked. "They rationalize that he's a good husband, a great provider, and that they would be worse off without him."

"Paige Graham said that General Graham was a brilliant man who could do great things for our country," Cameron recalled with a nod of her head. "She was planning to get him to the White House."

"There you have it," Jessica said. "Using that rationalization, one could argue that if Charles Manson was a gifted and charismatic politician that our country should elect him president." With a roll of her eyes, she shrugged her shoulders. "So he's a mass murderer? Hey, nobody's perfect. As long as unemployment is down and the economy is up ..."

After enjoying a hearty chuckle at Jessica's sarcasm, Murphy pointed out, "Don't laugh. If this case hadn't landed in my lap, it could have happened."

"No wonder Kalashov was so angry when Graham ended up dead," Joshua said. "With all the murders the mob had committed on his behalf, with all they had on Graham, if he had made it to the White House ..." He shook his head. "Think of all the potential political favors that went down the tube when Graham plunged that pen into his neck."

"Still ..." Cameron shook her head with a sigh, "Paige not only simply stayed with that animal, she actually went to the trouble of having people killed to protect him. That's not normal."

"What's normal to you?" Jessica shot back.

In thought, Cameron narrowed her eyes and cocked her head.

"Based on Paige's background," Jessica said, "her father was a dock worker who had ties to the mob. That means she grew up in and around that environment."

"Complete with their ethics or lack thereof," Joshua said.

"She lived with Adrian Kalashov for a while," Jessica said, "who was being groomed to take over the Kalashov operation—whose businesses included prostitution and pornography."

"So she was surrounded by people who believed women were property to be used for profit," Murphy said. "Then she took up with Graham, who viewed them as prey."

"Funny how that happens," Jessica said.

"What happens?" Murphy asked.

"That people like that," Jessica said, "a serial predator like Graham and a psychopath like Paige find each other. That actually happens a lot. I don't know if it's a signal they send out to each other or what, but somehow …" With a shake of her head, she shrugged her shoulders. "People are weird."

"Well," Joshua said, "we were able to put a stop to both of them."

"Score one for the good guys," Murphy said while opening the door to allow Izzy and Spencer, both draped in wet towels to run inside.

"Do we have ice cream?" Izzy asked. "Blue and I are starving!" Without waiting for a response, they ran down the hallway to the bedroom she had claimed for her own.

"What about dinner?" Murphy called after her.

"If we have room after dessert, then we'll eat dinner," she replied before slamming the bedroom door.

With a chuckle, Joshua told Murphy, "Reminds me of you when you were that age."

Murphy and Jessica were the first to turn in. Judging by their tired expressions, Joshua doubted if they were going to be participating in any newlywed activities after closing the door to their master suite.

Izzy crashed next, her head dropping onto the table in the middle of a poker game with Joshua and Cameron. Gingerly, Joshua lifted her from the kitchen chair and carried her down the hallway to her room.

One step ahead of them, Irving led the way down the hallway and into the bedroom. Inside, he jumped up onto the bed and went up to the pillows. Turning to Joshua, he seemed to order, "Put her here. I'll watch over her."

At Izzy's insistence, Monique's tank had been set up on the dresser so that she could care for the spider until Tristan's return.

Cameron pulled back the covers for Joshua to place the girl between the sheets. When Cameron started to pull up the covers, Joshua stopped her so that he could remove her shoes. Irving curled up next to her while Spencer took the foot of the bed.

"Should she be sleeping with all these animals?" Cameron asked.

"I don't think Izzy or they would have it any other way." Joshua ushered her out the door and turned off the light. Taking her by the hand, he led her into the next bedroom and closed the door. "Let's go to bed." Taking her in his arms, he kissed her passionately while backing up to the bed until they tumbled down onto it.

"I missed you." Joshua rolled over on top of her. He breathed into her ear. "You have no idea how much you mean to me." He reached his hands up under her shirt.

"I suspect I do," she said while he kissed her on the neck. "After this week, the way you came flying out here—blowing your case—shaving your beard and cutting your hair to help me and Murphy—I have no doubt that you would do anything for me."

He kissed her deeply on the lips. "I love you, Cam."

She caressed his face in both of her hands. The seriousness of her expression made his heart sink.

"Joshua, we have to talk," she said.

Seventh Floor Pentagon - Twelve Hours Later

Murphy was back in his whites and sitting on that same hard wooden bench outside the Joint Chiefs of Staff chamber. This time, it was Captain Joshua Thornton inside. Together, the two of them had debriefed the Joint Chiefs about the case, which had unveiled a long, ongoing conspiracy and cover-up to protect a war hero.

Immediately, General Johnston, Chief of Staff of the United States Army, announced that he was delaying his retirement until there was a full investigation. How, he wanted to know, was a serial rapist able to rise through the ranks without someone in the beginning having the guts to put a stop to him—like when he committed his first known assaults at West Point or the military police who had investigated the rape that took place in Kuwait—before that rapist returned to the states as a hero?

First on his agenda, after withdrawing his request to retire, was to make an example of Colonel Lincoln Clark by taking action to have him court-martialed for behavior unbefitting an officer by not reporting General Sebastian Graham's actions against his wife. In addition, Clark was being brought up on multiple charges of conspiracy and accessory to commit murder.

Even if Colonel Lincoln Clark managed to escape jail time, his military career was over.

Upon hearing about the Russian mob participating in the cover-ups with hopes of using General Sebastian Graham's power to their advantage, the chair of the Joint Chiefs of Staff said, "This is precisely why good character is not something to be dismissed as a nice-to-have quality. It is essential for people in positions of power because good character is the root of making wise choices. Bad character is what makes one vulnerable to be exploited by our enemies—both on our shores and abroad."

Soon after that, Murphy was dismissed while the Joint Chiefs of Staff continued onto the next matter on their agenda.

Considering that the Joint Chiefs had not called in their assistants, Murphy had a sick feeling in his stomach that the topic of this discussion was the fate of the Phantoms. Joshua had warned that General Sebastian Graham had gotten too close. If he had succeeded with his goal of getting on the Joint Chiefs of Staff, then not only would he have had access to the Phantoms, but the Russian crime organization could have, through General Graham, used the team for their own benefit—all under the guise of a covert military operation.

Unable to sit any longer, Murphy got up and paced down the hallway to peer out a window. Down below, he could see the National 9-11 memorial dedicated to the tragic events that occurred on Sept. 11, 2001. All 184 lives lost in the attack on the Pentagon were represented by "Memorial Units." Each unit had a victim's age and location at the time of the attack inscribed on it.

How could so many people here in Washington forget about what happened on that day and the evil behind it—the evil that is still striving to kill us because we don't believe the way they do?

"Murphy?"

The tone of his father's voice was enough to tell Murphy the decision made in the meeting was not going to go well for him. Turning around, he made his way back to the bench, where Joshua gestured with his hand for him to sit down. With a sigh, Murphy lowered himself onto the bench and braced himself.

Joshua looked at the wall directly across from them. "Son, the Joint Chiefs of Staff have made the decision to disband the Phantoms. I'm sorry."

"Because we're too dangerous."

"In the wrong hands, yes."

"What about—"

"They assured me that they will take good care of you." Joshua allowed himself to grasp Murphy's wrist. "Patterson will give you free choice of where you want to go. The SEALS want you. All you have to do is say the word and you'll be out from behind that desk—away from Koch—and out in the field."

Murphy looked at him out of the corner of his eyes. "Was I imagining that you had met Crotch before?"

"I'm sorry about that," Joshua said.

"What did you do?"

"I should have buried Hillary Koch when she was working for me," Joshua said. "She used to be in JAG. I was her CO. To make a long story short, she screwed up big. I caught her doing things to win cases that, while they were legal, were unethical. I found out when the wife of a marine called me personally to beg for help. Her husband spent over a year in jail for a crime he didn't commit because Koch was too lazy to check out a statement from a witness and used a jailhouse source who had a long history of lying. After that, I dug deeper and found a whole history of unethical, crooked, and improper actions that she was taking to win cases."

"She's a lawyer?" Murphy asked.

Joshua shook his head. "Not anymore. While she was as crooked at they come, I couldn't find enough evidence to have her disbarred. But I did find enough circumstantial evidence of her fraternizing with an enlisted man. That was enough to drum her out of JAG and force her to resign from the navy or face a dishonorable discharge. She became an assistant county prosecutor. A couple of years later, her license was yanked. I don't know the particulars of that." He sucked in a deep breath. "I should have pushed for a dishonorable discharge. If I had, then NCIS would never have hired her."

"Jessie was right then," Murphy said.

"Jessie?"

"After meeting her for only a few minutes," Murphy said, "Jessie analyzed Crotch and said that she was prejudiced against the military and white males because she was drummed out of the military by a white male." He uttered a low laugh. "I guess that was you. No wonder she hates me."

"Jessie can be very perceptive." Joshua grinned. "If you join the SEALS, you'll never have to deal with *Crotch* again."

"I'll go to SEALS then," Murphy said in a low voice. "It's where I was going to go until Admiral Patterson recruited me for the Phantoms."

"You'll be on home leave for six weeks to find a new house," Joshua said. "Until you move, you will remain in the safe house. When you return to active duty, you'll go on to your next assignment with a SEAL team."

"Wherever that is."

"Sarah will be so jealous," Joshua said. "Her dream is to be the first female SEAL."

"Well, that's one good thing that's come from this."

The two men folded their arms across their chests and stared at the wall across from them. After a long silence filled with reflection on the last several days and their respective situations, Joshua broke the silence. "Cameron and I are going to adopt Izzy."

The announcement made Murphy uncross his arms and sit up in his seat. He turned to Joshua. "Seriously? I thought Cameron wasn't the maternal type."

"She is when it comes to Izzy," Joshua said. "Those two have made a connection of some sort. Jessica would say that it is because Nick was looking for Izzy when he was murdered ... or because Izzy's mother died in Nick's arms." He shrugged. "I don't know but I saw it when Cameron went rushing back to the cruiser to help Izzy out."

"Do you want to adopt her?" Murphy asked. "That'll make six kids."

"Yes, I do," Joshua said with conviction in his tone. "Your mother always said there are never too many children for a parent to love." With a shrug of his shoulders, he added, "Besides, there's no telling what Irving will do if we go home without her."

With a chuckle, Murphy sat back in his seat and folded his arms again. "Then I have a new sister."

"Do you object?"

"No," Murphy replied with a firm shake of his head. "I've been worried about what would become of her since she has no family ... except Tommy Clark who turns out to be her half-brother."

"Izzy was talking last night about wanting to visit Tommy regularly since she's his big sister," Joshua said. "Maureen's brother is already suing for full custody of Tommy. Since Colonel Clark is not his biological father, and played a role in Maureen's murder, then they stand a good chance of winning."

"Did you talk to Izzy about the adoption?"

"I'm making phone calls to find out how to go about it," Joshua said. "Once I know what all is involved, then Cameron and I will sit down to talk to her about it tonight."

"What about Donny?"

"I called him first thing this morning," Joshua said. "You know him."

"Mr. Laidback himself," Murphy said. "As long as he gets to keep his bedroom, he'll be fine."

"That's pretty much what he said verbatim."

The two men resumed staring at the wall, lost in their thoughts about the changes that were coming in both of their lives.

"Murphy," Joshua said with a sigh, "about the watch."

"What watch?" Murphy's eyebrows were furrowed in confusion.

"The one I gave Tawkeel ... I saw that you recognized it. You gave it to me as a gift and—"

"You told me you lost it," Murphy said.

"I lied," Joshua confessed. "You were like five years old and I didn't know how to tell you I gave it to another boy."

"Who needed it more," Murphy said. "Dad, I get it. Here was a child who was being ripped from his home—his mother was murdered by her own family—he was coming to a strange land and that watch—with the American Eagle on it—served as a symbol of all the promises that our country offered to him. And to be given it by the big white knight named Billy—" He grinned. "You represent everything I want to be."

Joshua let out a big sigh of relief. "I'm glad you understand."

"Only one thing I don't understand," Murphy said. "Why did they call you Billy?"

"Short for *hillbilly*," Joshua said. "No one ever let me forget I came from West Virginia." He stood up. "Guess it's time for us to go. I need to make phone calls and get Cameron and Izzy on their way back home before Donny turns the house into the county's party center."

"Everyone made out in this case except me," Murphy said miserably. "We lost our house. Now they're taking the Phantoms away from me."

Joshua shrugged. "But you still have Jessica."

A smile came to Murphy's lips. "I guess I have everything I need then, huh?"

EPILOGUE

Thornton Family Home—Chester, West Virginia—One Month Later

That would never happen. Some crime writers. Don't they even know how to use Google? With a snarl on her lips, Cameron forwarded the police procedural on her e-reader to the next page when she heard the front door open downstairs. Multiple voices filled the lower levels of the house.

Picking out Izzy's voice among them, Irving jumped up from where he was lounging against Cameron's leg and raced out of the master bedroom. As he went out, Izzy ran in and threw herself onto the bed next to Cameron. Seeing the object of his affection, Irving whirled around, jumped back up onto the bed, and climbed up to rub against her chin.

After greeting Cameron with a hug and a kiss, Izzy said, "Oh, Cam, you should have come to the rehearsal and dinner afterwards!" Sitting up, she stroked Irving from the top of his head all the way down to the tip of his tail. "They had chicken and prime rib and this really delicious sauce for the prime rib—and the dessert!" She rolled her eyes.

"Chocolate fudge tuxedo cheesecake. Tracy made it from scratch! Murphy let me have his piece, so I ate two!" She held up her fingers.

Tossing the e-reader aside, Cameron told her, "I'm glad you had a good time, Izzy."

The girl cocked her head at her. "Tracy says you're not going to come to the wedding. Why not? This is the first time that I've been a real bridesmaid and I want everyone to be there to see me."

"Josh and everyone else will be there," Cameron said.

"But I want you to see me in my strapless dress and high heels," Izzy said. "I look like I'm seventeen. Donny is going to introduce me to the brother of one of his friends. He says he's cute. Maybe he'll dance with me. Wouldn't that be cool?"

"I don't do well at weddings," Cameron said.

"Because you and Nick had a big wedding and then he died four months later?"

"Something like that."

Izzy laid down next to her and rested her head on her shoulder. "But this is different."

"Not really," Cameron said.

"Yes, it is," Izzy argued. "When Nick died, you were left alone. All you had were your memories of him and that was all you could think about. But you're not alone anymore. You have Dad and this big wonderful family—not the least of whom now includes *me.*"

She sprang up and smiled so broadly that Cameron couldn't help but laugh.

"And Irving!" Izzy picked up the cat and gave him a big hug. "And Admiral." She reached down to stroke the huge Irish Wolfhound-Great Dane mix who seemed bigger than the petite teenaged girl. "This wedding will be totally different because everywhere you look, you won't see memories of things that are lost, but everything that you now have. Dad said at his toast tonight that without family, you have nothing. With family, you have everything. Man, is he right!"

With a smile, Cameron noted that Izzy had taken to being a member of the Thornton family like hot fudge to ice cream. She and Donny had formed an instant camaraderie that reminded Cameron of Mutt and Jeff. At six-feet-four, Donny towered over Izzy who was barely five feet tall and one hundred pounds.

By the time they had crossed the West Virginia state line with Izzy in the back seat, she was calling Joshua "Dad." Since she never had a father, Izzy took great joy in now having one.

She had asked Cameron's permission to call her "Cam" instead of "Mom" out of respect for her aunt whom she called "Mom," as well as her birth mother who had been murdered on the Pennsylvania Turnpike.

Cameron and Joshua had feared that Izzy would feel betrayed by her aunt, Donna, when she found out that she was not really her mother. But, upon learning the full story, the teenaged girl saw it as a confirmation of her aunt's love for her—by going to such lengths to protect her. Not only that, but Izzy recalled numerous stories that Donna had often told about her sister Cecelia. Looking back, Izzy realized that it was because she wanted to keep her mother alive in her mind.

Now, Cameron and Joshua were taking up the torch to do the same thing. In packing up Izzy's belongings at the Crenshaw home, they had found a treasure trove of mementoes of Cecelia and Donna Crenshaw going all the way back to their childhood, which Izzy now kept in a chest in her room in her new home in Chester, West Virginia.

After Cameron had located Cecelia Crenshaw's remains, they had her body exhumed to be buried with full military honors next to her sister in a cemetery near the Thornton home. Every member of Izzy's new family and friends in Chester turned out for the memorial service at the Thornton church for her mother and aunt.

Behind the scenes, the Joint Chiefs of Staff put pressure on the Veteran's Administration to ensure that Izzy received every penny due to her in death benefits from the military for Cecelia and Donna Crenshaw. As a result, Izzy was accumulating quite a college fund, which was a relief for Joshua. She had already announced that she intended to go to veterinary school to become a veterinarian. No surprise there.

As expected, the President had released an emotional statement about the suicides of General Sebastian Graham, who was still touted as a war hero, and his wife, a leader in charitable good works. In spite of all the evidence proving that General Graham was a serial rapist and his wife a serial killer, the decision was made by those in command not to dirty an otherwise great man's reputation.

So far, the media showed little interest in digging very deep to uncover why a war hero on the brink of making Chief of Staff of the United States Army would take his own life. A handful of investigative journalists had uncovered a long pattern, stretching back many years, of incidents that pointed to Paige Graham being emotionally unstable. Therefore, when it was discovered that she committed suicide by cop after breaking into a private home and attacking a female police officer, they concluded that she was emotionally ill and had driven her husband to suicide.

Within days, General Sebastian Graham was being portrayed in the media as a patient and suffering martyr.

Only those close to the case, all of whom were unable to publicly speak about it, knew about the monster behind the war hero's mask.

As far as the Thorntons were concerned, the only good thing General Sebastian Graham had done since returning from Kuwait was fathering Izzy Crenshaw and Tommy Clark—though the circumstances of those occurrences left more than a lot to be desired.

In spite of their origins, Izzy and Tommy were forming a sister-brother bond. Izzy delighted in having a little brother as much as Tommy was proud of having a big sister who was a teenager. Izzy and Tommy contacted each other on Skype on a regular basis.

When faced with the threat of his inaction toward his wife's rapist being made public in a custody battle, Colonel Lincoln Clark relinquished custody of Tommy to his aunt and uncle, who agreed to allow Izzy to visit her half-brother whenever possible.

Since the three shooters killed at Starbucks were traced back to the Russian mob, the media speculated that Emily Dolan had ruffled the wrong feathers on her blog. None of the media connected the Starbucks shooting to the mass murder in Reston.

By the time Joshua, Cameron, and Izzy had left Washington, the news media had released news from a confidential source inside NCIS about the murder of five women in a townhome in Reston. According to the confidential source, the murders had been committed by an assassin hired by Colonel Lincoln Clark. The primary target was his wife Maureen, who he had discovered was planning to leave him.

The charges brought against him by the military court only strengthened the media's case against him.

In no way was Izzy alone anymore. She found herself in the midst of a huge loving family.

Rocking the cat in her arms, Izzy said, "You should get a grip, Cam, and come to the wedding to celebrate our family."

With Irving in her arms and Admiral by her side, she practically skipped out of the bedroom to go join in the festivities in the kitchen.

Joshua Thornton was manning his famous ice cream bar, which he had set up along the kitchen counter. Waving his ice cream scooper like a flag, he called out, "Okay, who wants what?"

In response, Donny yelled up the stairs at the top of his voice, "Izzy! Get down here! You're missing Dad's ice cream sundae bar!"

With Admiral and Irving racing down the stairs with her, Izzy resembled a leaf being bounced down a river rapid. "Dibs on Murphy's share!"

"You had two slices of cheesecake," Murphy objected from where he was sitting at the table with Jessica in his lap.

"That was close to two hours ago."

Looking around the kitchen, Joshua marveled at the full house he now had. In a flash, he recalled when he had first moved back home with his five motherless children. He thought the three story stone house was full then.

Back then, J.J and Murphy were about to enter their junior year in high school. Now, Murphy was a distinguished navy officer and married to a stunning and clever young woman. J.J. was only a year away from graduating law school. They weren't exactly identical anymore. J.J. had let his hair grow out to long waves that stopped at his shoulders. Next to him was his live-in girlfriend—a quiet, plain young college student named Destiny.

On the other side of the table, Jessica's brother Tristan appeared to have made himself at home with Joshua's younger daughter, Sarah. The young man had invested in a car—a Jaguar—which he let Sarah drive to Chester for the wedding. From what Joshua had learned, Murphy and Jessica's new home—a six bedroom house tucked behind a security gate, located on four acres in Great Falls, Virginia—had a guest cottage, which Tristan had offered to rent from them. The only downside was that the mansion in the quiet wooded neighborhood did not have metro.

Tristan claimed that was why he was forced to invest in a car. Murphy suspected it was so that he could make regular trips to Annapolis to visit Sarah.

Tracy's fiancé, Hunter, and Donny were showing the newest Thornton family member how to play yet another new game on Donny's cell phone. So far, Donny embraced the idea of having a younger sister. Joshua was proud of how he had gone out of his way to make her feel welcome. Even Tracy, a month before the wedding, added another bridesmaid and groomsman to the wedding party in order to include Izzy.

Then, there was Joshua's little girl, Tracy, who was warming up the hot fudge at the stove. In her apron, with her blonde hair, she reminded him so much of his late wife in her caring and compassion.

"She's not coming, is she?" Tracy jarred Joshua out of his thoughts by whispering into his ear.

"Who's not coming?" Joshua replied.

At the kitchen table, Murphy looked over his shoulder at the two of them.

"Cameron," Tracy hissed. "She wasn't at the rehearsal dinner. She's not here now. She's not coming to the wedding, is she?"

Keeping his voice low, Joshua replied, "She's—we've both been through a lot this last month. Cut her a break."

"I've been cutting her a break." She set the dish of hot fudge on the counter. "I think it's time she cuts me a break." She took off her apron and hung it on the coatrack near the door.

"Tracy …"

After kissing him on the cheek, she murmured, "I'm going to go check the weather for tomorrow."

Seeing his sister going down the hall, Murphy eased Jessica off his lap. Whispering in her ear that he'd be back, he followed Tracy into the study.

"What do we do?" Izzy asked.

"You call out what you want on your sundae and Dad will build it for you," Donny ordered.

"I want everything," Izzy shouted to him.

"I like her," Sarah said.

"Tristan, what do you want?" Joshua asked in a sharp tone.

Tristan dropped the lock of Sarah's hair which he had been sniffing. It smelled like the ocean. "Whatever you want me to have, sir," he replied.

Donny, Hunter, and J.J. covered their mouths to conceal their smirks at Tristan's nervous response.

"Do you like hot fudge, Tristan?" Joshua asked.

"Do you want me to like hot fudge?" Tristan replied.

Narrowing his eyes at Sarah's young man, Joshua wondered if Mac Faraday had ever requested a paternity test for his son.

In the study, Murphy found Tracy on the family computer set up behind their father's desk. After closing the door, he went over to see that she was checking on the weather for the next day—her wedding day.

"It's supposed to be clear tomorrow," he said.

Startled to realize she was not alone, Tracy jumped in her seat and turned around. "Why can't you make noise when you sneak up on a person?"

"If I made noise when I sneaked up on people, then I wouldn't be sneaking up on them."

With a growl in her throat, she turned back to the computer.

"Nervous?" Murphy slipped up onto the corner of the desk.

"Of course," she said. "But I love Hunter. I've been in love with him for years. It's just—I want tomorrow to be perfect."

"Sometimes, less than perfect, if you go into it with the right attitude, can be more fun," Murphy said. "Look at Jessie's and my wedding. I know you heard about it."

"You mean the wedding you and Jessica hijacked?" she said with a laugh.

"Yeah, that one," Murphy said. "Still, five months later, people who were there are saying our wedding was the most fun they ever had. Because we knew that since we were throwing things together things would go wrong. So what? Jessie was there and that was all I cared about. And all she cared about was that I was there. Hell! She didn't even wear a real wedding dress."

"So I heard," Tracy said.

Murphy sucked in a deep breath before saying in a soft voice. "I almost lost Jessie last month."

"I know. Cameron was in that cruiser, too. So was Izzy."

Murphy swallowed. "And all I could do was pray and watch those rescuers work to save them. If Jessie had gone off that overpass in that cruiser and been killed—do you know what?"

"What?"

"We would have been married only four months at that point—like Cameron and Nick had been when he was killed."

Tracy lifted her eyes to gaze up at him.

"If that had happened," Murphy said, "I doubt if I would have been able to be here for your wedding. It would have just been too painful."

"This is about Cameron," Tracy said.

"Until you walk a mile in her shoes, cut her a break." Murphy bent over to kiss her on the forehead before whispering, "Take some advice from your old married brother—forget about all the details and just have fun tomorrow."

He stood up and left Tracy alone with her thoughts.

The ice cream sundae party was in full swing when Cameron came down the stairs. Upon seeing her, the brood of grown children and their friends and mates cheered and clapped their hands.

"Oh, Cameron, sorry to tell you this, but Izzy ate your sundae." With an exaggerated shrug, Donny said, "You snooze, you lose."

"He's lying," Izzy said with a loud laugh.

Cameron turned back to the kitchen counter to find Joshua in the process of making their own special sundae—made for two—in their personal oversized bowl. She went up behind him, wrapped her arms around his waist, and kissed his shoulder. "I heard I missed a great rehearsal and dinner," she said in a low voice.

Dipping his finger in the fudge, Joshua shrugged. "Everyone understands why you weren't there." He turned around to allow her to lick off the gooey treat.

Murphy came in and pulled up a chair to squeeze in at the table next to Jessica. When Tracy came in, many heads turned in her direction. Was there going to be a showdown between the bride and mother of the bride over her not appearing at the rehearsal dinner? Was Tracy going to demand a commitment from her stepmother about the wedding?

Tracy walked up to her. "Hi, Cameron."

"Hello, Tracy." Cameron took in the soft blue dress that Tracy had worn for the rehearsal dinner. "You look lovely."

"Thank you," Tracy said in a brisk tone. "I wanted to talk to you about tomorrow."

There was a collective gasp throughout the kitchen.

Joshua moved in closer. "Tracy …"

"No, Dad," Tracy said. "I need to say this. I've been selfish. I've been thinking of this whole wedding thing as my day, when really, it is meant to be a celebration for our whole family—both of our families—to celebrate love and everyone coming together to become one family. And part of being a family is to consider the feelings of those you love."

She glanced over at Murphy who had his arm draped across Jessica's shoulders. "It was learning about what happened last month—almost losing you and Jessie and Izzy, too, that made me realize how stupid and selfish I've been." She turned back to Cameron. "So, if you can't come to the wedding tomorrow, I understand completely." She leaned in to kiss Cameron on the cheek. "I love you and I'm glad you're part of our family."

There was a stunned silence in the kitchen while everyone waited for Cameron's response to the olive branch that Tracy had extended to her.

"So let me get this straight," Cameron said, "you've been nagging me for months to come to this wedding and now you're *disinviting* me? Seriously?"

"No," Tracy sputtered. "I mean, if you *want* to come—" She stopped when she saw corners of Cameron's lips curl. "You're bad."

"Of course, I am." Taking in the mob that filled her kitchen, she announced, "I'll be there tomorrow." Turning back to Tracy, she added, "But I'm not wearing teal."

With a laugh, Tracy hugged her. "You can wear whatever you want, Cameron!" Hunter got up from his seat at the table to join in the hug. When the hug was over, Tracy let out a squeal of delight. "She's coming!"

Grasping Cameron by the shoulders, Joshua asked her, "Really? Are you sure you want to do this?"

"This time will be different," she said while hugging him. "I won't be going alone. I'll be with my family." Over his shoulder, she shot Izzy a thumbs up sign, which the girl returned.

The family responded with a cheer that seemed to vibrate the windows in the old house.

Resting her head on Joshua's shoulder, Cameron took note of the brood. "May your home always be too small for all your friends—and family."

Twenty-Nine Hours Later

The ring of the phone brought Murphy straight up out of the bed. Next to him, Jessica was snoring softly. She always snored after drinking too much champagne, which flowed freely at the wedding. They had dropped right into bed in their guest room at the Thornton home only a couple of hours before the phone's ring woke Murphy up from a sound sleep.

The phone rang a second time before Murphy realized it wasn't a dream. It was the secure cell phone that the CO of his SEAL team had given to him.

Seriously? But I haven't reported for duty with them yet.

He remembered that he had used his go-to bag to pack his electronics for the trip. The cell phone had to be in the pocket. He was tearing through the bag when the phone rang a third and fourth time.

Cursing, Murphy turned over the bag and emptied everything to the floor. Still ringing, the phone clattered out of the bag and bounced off a book to slide across the hardwood floor. Like a skater chasing a puck on ice, Murphy grappled for the phone to answer it before whoever it was hung up.

"Hello …" he asked with a gasp.

"Lieutenant Thornton," came the sultry voice of his CO—the leader of the Phantoms.

"Yes."

"You are to report to the seventh floor of the Pentagon in eight hours for a mission. A plane will be waiting at Pittsburgh airport to fly you into Washington. You are to be there by six o'clock."

"But the Phantoms have been disbanded," Murphy objected.

"Not anymore."

The End

About the Author

Lauren Carr

Lauren Carr is the international best-selling author of the Mac Faraday and Lovers in Crime Mysteries. Lauren introduced the key detectives in the Thorny Rose Mysteries in *Three Days to Forever*, which was released in January 2015.

The owner of Acorn Book Services, Lauren is also a publishing manager, consultant, editor, cover and layout designer, and marketing agent for independent authors. Visit Acorn Book Services website for more information.

Lauren is a popular speaker who has made appearances at schools, youth groups, and on author panels at conventions. She also passes on what she has learnt in her years of writing and publishing by conducting workshops and teaching in community education classes.

She lives with her husband, son, and three dogs on a mountain in Harpers Ferry, WV.

Visit Lauren Carr's website at www.mysterylady.net to learn more about Lauren and her upcoming mysteries.

CHECK OUT
LAUREN CARR'S MYSTERIES!

All of Lauren Carr's books are stand alone. However for those readers wanting to start at the beginning, here is the list of Lauren Carr's mysteries. The number next to the book title is the actual order in which the book was released.

Joshua Thornton Mysteries:

Fans of the *Lovers in Crime Mysteries* may wish to read these two books which feature Joshua Thornton before meeting Cameron Gates. In these mysteries, readers will meet Joshua Thornton's five children before they have flown the nest.

1) A Small Case of Murder
2) A Reunion to Die For

Mac Faraday Mysteries

3) It's Murder, My Son
4) Old Loves Die Hard
5) Shades of Murder (introduces the Lovers in Crime: Joshua Thornton & Cameron Gates)
7) Blast from the Past
8) The Murders at Astaire Castle
9) The Lady Who Cried Murder (The Lovers in Crime make a guest appearance in this Mac Faraday Mystery)
10) Twelve to Murder
12) A Wedding and a Killing
13) Three Days to Forever
14) Open Season for Murder
16) Cancelled Vows (Winter 2015)

Lovers in Crime Mysteries

6) Dead on Ice
11) Real Murder

Thorny Rose Mystery

15) Kill and Run (Featuring the Lovers in Crime in Lauren Carr's latest series)

Cancelled Vows

A Mac Faraday Mystery

Police Chief David O'Callaghan and Chelsea Adams' wedding day is fast approaching. Unfortunately, at the last minute, David discovers that there is one small problem that he has to take care of before he can walk down the aisle—divorce his first wife!

Lauren Carr takes fans of the Mac Faraday mysteries to the Big Apple in this nail biting adventure. In *Cancelled Vows,* David, Mac, and Gnarly, too, rush to New York City to dissolve David's marriage to an old girlfriend—and he's got less than a week to get it done. When his wife ends up murdered, it is up to David's best man, Mac Faraday, and Gnarly, K9-in-waiting, to sort through the clues to get David to the church in time!

Coming Winter 2015!

Printed in Great Britain
by Amazon

12406787R10240